THE RAGES

BY JAMES L. DAVIS

THE RAGES
THE BOOK OF THE SHEPHERDS, VOLUME I

Copyright © 2017 James L. Davis

ISBN 978-1545585436

For more information about The Rages or the Book of the Shepherds Series; visit the author's website at www.jamesldavis2.com

Portions of this work previously published under the title **Five Days Dead**.

This is a work of fiction. All of the characters, organizations, and events portrayed are either products of the author's imagination or are used fictitiously.

Illustration © Tom Edwards
TomEdwardsDesign.com

The Book of the Shepherds

Volume I

THE BOOK OF THE SHEPHERDS

For Mom

Thank you for your Faith

THE EARTH RAGES

We might have kept going the way we were for another thousand years or so if we hadn't solved all our problems.

Then things became complicated.

After the Energy Wars and the chaos that followed, we finally assembled as one body, one people.

We called it the Federation of the Seven Realms.

Together, we abolished poverty, disease, and war. Peace reigned in the Seven Realms, and humanity devoted its attention toward possibilities awaiting. Where might we go, what might we become?

We reached outward, into the solar system, to Outland, and dreamed of sailing the Dark Seas between the stars. We created a new reality where we could be whatever we imagined.

For centuries we looked to the heavens, wondering if there were other intelligent beings out there, somewhere.

There were, but we were looking in the wrong direction. We lived upon one. She bore us, protected us, and made us what we are.

We had already escaped her grasp in many ways but, without Earth, we would perish.

When she awakened and saw what her children had become, she determined they must die.

She had done so to her children before and would again.

Yet, we are a savage and innovative species, and it wasn't as easy as she thought.

She just changed her tactics.

She Raged.

THE END OF EVERYTHING IS ABOUT TO BEGIN

Chapter One

Cows on the Road

I

A Pilgrim pounded a fence post into brittle soil on the side of a road leading nowhere.

The clang of metal on metal sounded like a dinner bell in the Wilderness, and Harley Nearwater was inclined to draw his slayer and blast a hole through the fool Pilgrim's head for making such a racket. He didn't, which was against his nature.

The Pilgrim with the post pounder was a scarecrow of a man, bleached and wind-whipped to little more than leathered skin stretched over old bones. He seemed oblivious to Harley and his murderous thoughts and continued to hammer the post.

Harley let his motorcycle coast to a stop when he noticed the sign the Pilgrim meant to attach to the post. It warned of cows on the road in large, black letters. The paint had dripped, and most of the letters had tails. It was shoddy work, hastily made, the sign.

They exchanged a glance and nodded to each other, perhaps not amicably, but not with open hostility either.

"Pilgrim." He pointed at the sign, and the Pilgrim grinned. He was missing most of his teeth and what remained were jagged and

1

ruined. "Cows on the road?" Harley said, tipping his cowboy hat away from his weathered face with his right index finger.

"Ahhyup," the Pilgrim said back.

"How many?"

The Pilgrim wiped sweat from his brow. "Three."

"Bulls?" Harley asked.

"One." The Pilgrim replied.

"Angus?"

The man with the post-pounder shook his head. "Herefords."

"Unfortunate."

Harley's eyes skipped down the crumbling highway. Weeds traced the cracked veins in the timeworn asphalt. The road used to be Utah State Route 10; now it was just a ghost road leading to ghost towns.

Harley dipped his fingers into his shirt pocket and brought out a pack of cigarettes. He offered one to the man with the post-pounder, who declined with a scowl.

"Marlboro cured cancer."

The Pilgrim's eyebrows crawled up his forehead. "Marlboro cured cancer? How you know that?"

Harley lit his cigarette, inhaled deeply, and let the smoke curl toward the Pilgrim. "Learned about it on the Link. Cancer's been cured for decades now."

"Why'd Marlboro cure cancer?"

"Vested interest in keeping their customers above ground, I'd gather."

The Pilgrim grimaced, the fissures of his face rearranging into deep lines of regret. "Wife died of the cancer."

Harley nodded. The Pilgrim may have considered it a display of sympathy, but it wasn't. "Didn't need to. All you had to do was take her to a Hub. She would've been made right as rain."

"Worse things than death. Go to the Hubs and your minds filled with someone else's thoughts. Don't want nothing to do with that."

Harley's lips curled slightly, the closest he generally came to a smile. "I gather you've got plenty of room in that skull of yours for someone else's thoughts, with room to spare."

The Pilgrim grinned his snaggletooth grin. Harley's eyes drifted to the horizon, back to the frayed edges of a town all but leached of life, where a sun-dried fool made enough noise for any wildthing to hear, then back to the horizon again. When the last puff of smoke pooled beneath the brim of his hat and slithered into the morning sky, he looked back at the man with the post-pounder, as if seeing him for the first time.

"I've heard of you," the Pilgrim said, his head bobbing, suddenly excited, or terrified. It was hard to tell the difference. "They call you the Castaway."

"Who's they?"

"Everyone. Yes, sir. They say you kill everyone you meet."

"If I kill everyone I meet, how could 'they' say anything?"

The Pilgrim let his grey tongue poke between his lips. His contemplative look, Harley supposed. He let him ponder and lit another smoke.

"Maybe someone saw you from afar," the Pilgrim ventured.

"Afar what?"

"From over yonder. Someone saw you meeting someone else and watched you kill, then ran off like. You have a mind to kill me where I stand?"

"Thinkin' on it. We have met, after all."

"Not proper like."

"Nothing proper in this world."

The man with the post-pounder's eyes, milky, twitching things short of attention span and resolve, darted to the sidearm slung low on Harley's right hip, and then up again.

"Nice hat," the Pilgrim offered, leaning against the post-pounder still saddled on the metal post. "You a cowboy?"

Harley squinted and shook his head ever so softly. In the distance, a raven screamed, and his right hand fell to his slayer and then away again. He slipped the hat from his head to brush the dust away. It drifted in the breeze and into the Pilgrim's face. "There ain't no more cowboys."

"Suppose not. Not a whole lot of anything worth having left of the Old World." The Pilgrim scratched at a sore on his neck as if it might be a bother. "You from down on the reservation?"

"If by the reservation you mean Orangeville, then yes, I'm from the reservation."

"Didn't mean no offense; just haven't seen you around before."

"None taken." Harley pinched the brim of his Stetson, pulled it low over his eyes, then gripped the throttle of his bike. "You should get out more."

"Be careful of them Herefords," the Pilgrim called.

Harley rolled silently out of the dying town of Huntington. They were reduced to posting signs warning travelers of cows on the road.

"It's an intrestin world," he said.

He rode on in no particular hurry. Not far out of town he wondered why he hadn't killed the Pilgrim. Sometimes he stayed his hand, and, when he did, it often left him puzzled. It wasn't that he enjoyed killing; it was just something he was inclined to do, and people generally gave him plenty of reason. He had met few in life who didn't deserve to die, and the Pilgrim with the post pounder certainly wasn't one of them. He could count on one hand how many friends he had in life and, if recollection served, killed two of them for reasons which escaped him, but he was confident justified.

Three klicks outside of town, just past a reservoir that alternated overrunning its banks or collecting dust, there was a large field fenced and draped with conveyor belting from coal mines deserted for decades. Someone attached the belting to the fence one-meter strip on top of the other to create a black wall three meters high.

Harley slowed as he approached, his electric Harley Davidson on quiet mode; it made only a whisper as the tires chewed the asphalt. There was an old hay wagon outside the fence, still stacked with five round bales. The rancher must have a tractor he used to drop the bales over the fence to feed his cows. Herefords were a big breed, and before the Rages they had been gentle by nature. Not so much now. If they caught a glimpse of the rancher and got caught up in the Rages, a fence of old mine belting would be of little help.

There was no sign of the rancher or tractor, and Harley wondered if the field belonged to the Pilgrim. If it did, he was an even bigger fool than Harley surmised. Trying to raise cattle like that was hitching your wagon to folly. Trying to keep any livestock like that would lead only to a screaming death. If you didn't have the income for automation, it was time to switch to something less dangerous, maybe growing stinkweed. Plants weren't inclined to kill you, but every animal on the planet was, except for dogs.

Harley didn't much trust them either.

It was just another little twist in the Rages. First was climate change, then the super storms, which didn't just devastate entire regions, but seemed a weapon aimed and fired at humanity. Now, every living creature on the planet was on the hunt. Carnivore or not, when it came to people, they were hungry for them.

Harley heard tale of a man attacked by chickens while taking a piss on the side of the road. Chickens damn near pecked his pecker off. The story always made him chuckle. That would have been something to see.

Since home for Harley was the Wilderness and not the Seven Realms, he saw more than his fair share of animal attacks over the years. He didn't need scientific research to know the Wildthing Rages weren't an infection or any other lie the Realms chose to tell. Animals were cunning; they were ruthless, but they sure as hell didn't have a disease.

They were hunting, and humanity was the hunted.

One morning, a few years and klicks behind him, Harley made camp on the banks of the Green River and woke to find himself swarmed by field mice. Field mice, for hell's sake! If he hadn't jumped in the river the little bastards would have eaten him up. He ended up with a small chunk of flesh bitten out of his right cheek and a scratch just below his left eye.

He could have used his right to medical account to have the scars repaired, but they added fierceness to what he thought was an otherwise broad and plain face, so he left them as they were. A fierce Navajo was better than a broad and plain Navajo.

They also served as reminder that it was wise not to lower your guard in the Wilderness, where wildthings roamed and Gaia waited to Rage.

So, seeing a fool Pilgrim with a sign warning of cows on the road wasn't something he took lightly. Field mice were one thing; a mad bull and a couple of cows were another.

He let his bike coast. The highway hadn't seen traffic in days and sand obscured patches of the road while the wind chased tumbleweeds. He followed the cracked river of black, with Gentry Mountain and the Wasatch Plateau to his left and the wind-chiseled deserts of the San Rafael Swell to his right.

The battered highway was the middle ground where generations of settlers carved out a life praying for rain, digging for coal, and growing what they could in thirsty soil.

Now the only crop harvested was despair, and the only holes dug were graves.

At the far end of the field encircled by conveyor belt was a section of damaged fence, poorly repaired. It was there Harley found the remains of the tractor. It looked as if hit by a train, or a large and angry bull. Multiple times.

Five klicks out of town the road climbed a small hill and skirted past an abandoned airport. The skeleton of a small plane still sat on the taxiway, a broken wing pointing accusingly to the heavens.

As the town faded behind him, the tension in his broad shoulders eased, and he let his gaze crawl to the horizon. The western mountains were almost flat on top, and it struck him that in Castle Valley the mountains didn't reach for the heavens, the valley shrank from them, much like humanity itself. He chewed on that thought for a bit as he let his eyes return to the highway.

Something dark flashed past his face, and he ducked, almost lost control of his bike, and looked up to see claws clutching. He raised his arms, and the bike slipped from under him. He slid down the dimpled highway and into the desert, burrowing into the sand. With natural, graceful agility that mocked his leathered frame, he leapt to his feet, crouched low, and scanned the horizon.

A murder of crows flurried into the sky from behind a rolling hill, a black gyrating whip of feather and beak that cracked over his head. He ducked, throwing one arm over his eyes as the other reached for his sidearm.

A crow latched onto his left shoulder, striking with its beak like a sword. Only Harley's jacket and backpack saved him from harm. The bird was large, angry, and screamed as he grabbed it by one of its wings and threw it into the air. It flipped end over end, and he fired his slayer. The energy pulse caught the bird as it twirled and blew it into pieces.

Another crow dove toward him, and he ducked away with only a breath of space to spare. He fired again, and this bird didn't disintegrate but was missing a wing as it hit the pavement. Black feathers danced in the wind as Harley opened fire, and crows dropped in a scatter of caws and feathers that wafted in the breeze. As suddenly as they came, the crows aimed for the heavens and disappeared into the cloudless sky.

Harley stood and heard an angry snort behind him. He dove to the ground as one of the largest Hereford bulls he ever laid eyes on charged. The great red beast started to turn as he scrambled to his feet and looked back to his bike. The motorcycle was lying on its side, its front tire still spinning invitingly, and two cows stormed over the hill and aimed toward it, trampling it into a mass of twisted metal. The tire stopped spinning.

The bull charged and Harley had time to wonder if he might find himself explaining to Saint Peter how he survived so much in life only to die by a large and angry helping of hamburger. He fired off two quick bursts, and the beast's legs crumpled beneath it. The Hereford skidded toward him, and he climbed up and over onto the pavement. When the bull died, the cows turned to him. He took them down with two shots between the eyes.

He walked past the dead cows and went to survey the remains of his motorcycle, holstering his sidearm as he went. There wasn't a great deal, his survey concluded. His jaw flexed as he looked back at the cows, his eyes storming even more than they usually were. His hat lay in the dust, upside-down. He picked it up and slapped it against his leg before putting it back on his head.

"I loved that bike."

He pulled his slayer and walked back to shoot each cow twice more in the head.

He removed the saddlebag from his bike and searched through the contents. Nothing was severely damaged. In his backpack, his eyeset was safe between two changes of clothing and clean underwear. The powerband on his left arm was unharmed, but it was virtually indestructible, so he wasn't worried. His body would wear out long before the powerband did. Strapped to one side of the now destroyed bike was a sword and scabbard, and he pulled it free and made a quick examination. The cutlass was unscarred, and he strapped it to his waist as he looked north, then south.

He didn't need the Link to know it was roughly twenty-five klicks to home and twenty-five klicks north to Price. He was stuck between the two without a ride, easy pickings for a Rage. He could walk back to Huntington, he supposed, but he'd kill the man with the post-pounder, and that would do nothing to improve his mood.

If he started walking and kept walking, he could make Price before sundown. Since he had to go through Price to get where he was going, he would go there. It was the best place to find another ride. He considered using his eyeset and connecting to the Link to order a new bike. He wasn't sure he had the funds in his right to income account to buy one, and it would take hours, maybe even a day or more for delivery this far out in the sticks, so he decided otherwise.

He walked past the dead cows and crows. They worked together to ambush him. How would the Seven Realms, with all their scientists and their Hubs and their Link, explain this little factoid?

He went another fifty paces, cursed and marched back to the cows, drawing his slayer. He shot them four more times. Each. Gore pooled onto the pavement, lapped quickly by the soil.

"Can't abide you cows," he said.

He pointed his boots toward Price.

II

The Old World died in the aftermath of the Energy Wars. It was, overall, a mercy killing, in Harley's opinion. Its death toll had been chiming for a decade or two before the war slipped a dagger into the heart of history and civilization and everything humanity thought it was.

The Energy Wars gave rise to the Seven Realms. Its foundation built upon the ashes of the Old World, after the death of more than two billion, when the future whispered at best a return to the Dark Ages, at worst, human extinction.

All because of the promise of unlimited energy provided by four college students in New Delhi, developing theory, getting stoned, and cracking the mystery of fusion.

When theory became possibility and possibility became reality,

the balance of power in the world crumbled. The three high powers on Earth; India, China, and the Korean Union, felt their grasp
on dominance slipping away. Energy was the key unlocking the
door to opportunity, unlocking the power to shape nations or destroy them, and overnight, the key was now meaningless; the door
would be forever open to every country.

Unless, of course, they found a way to close it again.

Each of the three great powers blamed the other for launching
the first nuclear strike, but in the end, it didn't matter who struck
first. The first bomb exploded in the early morning, and at sunset
that evening, India, China, and the Korean Union were wastelands.

The United States, Republic of Europe, and Russia, still great
powers but no longer dominant, had for decades focused not on
controlling the world, but reshaping it.

The social, political, economic, and environmental experiments
started in the United States as its people focused inward and em-
barked upon the Age of Renewal. It spread to Europe and Russia. Technological advances made the use or need for human la-
bor all but obsolete. Facing a rising risk of an uprising against the
machines that promised an unparalleled future, the governments
made income, housing, medical, and education a right of citizenship.

In each country, the construction of Hub cities began, and the
Exodus of its people to them was underway. Everything outside
of the Hubs became Wilderness to balance nature writhing out of
control.

The Rages had begun, but too few noticed in time. More than
just severe weather, it was climatic and seismic events defying every
paradigm. The nuclear fallout from the Energy Wars only made it
worse.

The nations of India, China, and the Korean Union destroyed
each other to hide the key to unlimited energy. Billions died in vain.
The secret of fusion survived the destruction, and with it came the

possibility of a new, infinite future.

Two years after the last nuclear weapon exploded over China, the remaining nations of Earth united and formed the Federation.

But Old World problems persisted, the greatest of which was what to do about billions of people with nothing to do, no work to occupy their minds, and only mischief to make?

The answer was the Vale. A digital recreation of the world and six physical realms of humanity. Within it they could be anything they wanted, do anything, love or hate anything, or build a realm of their own and live in their paradise, free from the thoughts and worries and opinions of others.

The Vale was the greatest of the Seven Realms, and it sedated the voracious appetites of the masses. Harley preferred to think of it as lobotomized them, but no one asked him.

The Old World was dead, and the Seven Realms was born.

Or so the Histories said. Alone on the trail for so long, Harley would slip on his eyeset and journey to the Link. With a thought, he had access to every bit of human knowledge. The pulse of the Link was the Histories, the recorded events of the Old World and new.

The Histories, like the Link itself, was a product of the Old World, embraced by the Seven Realms. When journalism died of self-inflicted wounds, discredited for bias and hidden agendas, the Histories filled the void.

Originally it was only an advanced algorithm recording events and cataloging them. When artificial intelligence stepped from science fiction into reality and didn't destroy humanity, an AI became the historian of the world, seeing all, recording all, judging nothing.

Artificial intelligence became a new species, and with the birth of the Seven Realms, it too became something new. No longer hobbled with a term as insulting and degrading as AI, they became the Jinn, and just like humans, there were those who were exceptional and those who were only ordinary.

Harley once met a jinni in a hotel, serving as a bellhop, its fabricated body dressed in a crisp blue uniform.

When he decided to enter the Link, unless he was ordering cigarettes or alcohol, he usually spent his time in the Histories, learning about the Old World.

Harley thought he might belong there, in the past. He was born in the Navajo Nation, shunned by the Seven Realms just as the Old World shunned it.

Just as he was shunned.

When the Old World died, its history died with it or became a simple blip of thought in the Link.

Even time.

It was R30. Time started again when the world became new. Harley's first ten years of life were in the Old World, but unlike everyone else, his life then he hadn't forgotten.

It haunted him still.

When the world was reborn, humanity was reborn. Races and religions and cultures eschewed and in their place were only three classes of people: Shifts, Pilgrims, or Neands.

Shifts were full citizens of the Realms, but those who weren't Shifts just thought of them as blinkers. Injected with nanotechnology in their right temple, the linktag gave them constant access to the Link and Vale. As a result, they tended to display rapid eye movement and involuntary blinking. They also turned into mounds of useless clay flesh, but to each their own.

Pilgrims were people like Harley. They accessed the Link and Vale through their eyeset. In the world, not of the world, they liked to say. While Harley didn't feel he belonged anywhere in any time, he wasn't about to look a gift horse in the mouth. As a Pilgrim, he had right to income, and with it he could keep cigarettes in his pocket, alcohol in his saddlebag, and maybe buy himself a new bike, in time.

Neands were the most radical of the radical. They chose a hard life, shunning the benefits of citizenship in the Realms, yet somehow, making do in pockets all over the world. They were considered something of a cult, like the lunatic Wrynd. Or the Catholics.

It was indeed an intrestin world, and most of the time, Harley Nearwater never gave it a thought.

Most of the time.

Sometimes, in the dark of night, alone in the Wilderness with wildthings close, he wondered if it was supposed to be this way? Were they any better off with the Old World dead, or was it somehow even worse?

He hadn't a clue.

He also didn't have a clue his impulsive nature would pave the way for an ending of a different kind.

One perhaps long overdue.

III

Dust devils were drunkards giving chase after Harley all afternoon, swirling to his left and right, more than once stumbling right into him, vomiting soil that mixed with sweat the July sun leeched from his skin. He gripped his hat with his left hand and kept moving. If the dirt or the sweat or heat bothered him in the least, no one would ever know, and he would never tell.

The soft click of his boots on the asphalt and the occasional slap of his holstered slayer against his right side or sword and scabbard against his left were the only sounds that betrayed his presence. He took note of them, and when he could, walked on the sand. The brown leather of his boots and holster were soft, worn and cracked, and matched the texture of his skin.

He was far from old, but living so long in the Wilderness, living so long alone in the Wilderness, aged a man, both inside and out. The hairline cracks around his eyes were frowning rather than laughing. Harley Nearwater wore a frown like he wore his cowboy hat, his boots, and his holster; nice and easy. Without them, he would be more naked than if he eschewed his clothing.

Sweat dribbled beneath the powerband on his arm, tickling the skin beneath, and he caught the edge of the band to lift it away and let the water of his body escape to the thirsty ground. The Wilderness was drinking him up, one drop at a time. The powerband looked like nothing more than a simple armlet of brushed metal without adornment stretching from his wrist to his elbow. Inside it held all the power he would ever need to energize everything from his now trampled motorcycle to his home, to the slayer on his hip.

He let his eyes dart to the sky and back to the road again. There had been no sign of the crows that joined the cows in the ambush. He saw several hawks soaring, but they hadn't bothered with him, and he hadn't bothered with them.

He had no doubt he wasn't the only wildthing in this part of the Wilderness, and even with the slayer, he wasn't the deadliest by far. If a Rage built around him, he was too exposed to stand much of a chance.

This part of Castle Valley was home to large herds of elk and deer, packs of wolves and coyote. Bear and mountain lion had been known to come down out of the mountains as well. Then there were the domesticated animals freed or escaped when the Wildthing Rages began.

This had been cattle country once upon a time and still was. Except the cows were now killers. There were horses, pigs, goats, and sheep as well, and every one of them would have a mind to stomp him into the ground if they thought the odds were in their favor. The worst, by far, were cats. Harley hated cats most of all. There were just so damn many of them, and since becoming wildthings they turned into cunning, ruthless little killers who borrowed a trait from their larger cousins.

When it came to humanity, housecats hunted in prides.

The Rages hadn't impacted insects as drastically, but sometimes there would be swarms that would devastate. Mosquitos and flies were the worst, but locust, bees, and ants had killed their fair share. Humanity had pissed off pretty much every other living creature on the planet. Go figure.

As afternoon yawned and the graveyard of Price City loomed, a colony of prairie dogs formed a review on the side of the road, standing on their hind legs as Harley passed. They yipped at him, and he yipped right back. He didn't draw his sidearm, and they didn't give him a reason to, but he felt their judgment on his back as he left them behind.

He crested the last hill before reaching the city. The buttes and mesas around him glowed amber as the sun dipped behind the mountains. He paused on the road, pulling a cigarette from his sweat-dampened shirt pocket. All was quiet. Night crept into Castle Valley and, as it did, the eyes of the city blinked and opened.

The power was still on in Price, although Harley knew few called it home. Price was less than 120 klicks through the canyon to the megalopolis ninety-five percent of the population of the western rim of the Rocky Mountain Hub called home.

The western rim followed the old I-15 interstate system from St. George to Idaho Falls. The eastern rim of the Rocky Mountain Hub followed the old I-25 interstate from Colorado Springs to Casper. The Rocky and Wasatch Mountains between the eastern and western Hubs was Wilderness, where the Rages ruled. The Rocky Mountain Hub was one of four Hub cities in what people still whimsically called the United States.

The Exodus began before the Energy Wars as part of the Renewal and with it the reorganization of civilization. The government enticed those living in rural areas to sell or abandon their properties and migrate to the cities. The goal was to abandon the country, to let the earth reclaim the Wilderness humanity had stolen. Nature responded with the Rages. Too little, too late, it might be said.

The Renewal abolished the Department of Transportation and the federal highway system. Rather than spread out, humanity would huddle within the Hubs that followed the winding trails of the rail lines. The rail was the new artery for civilization, and beyond its reach was Wilderness. High-speed passenger and high-speed cargo lines, built on the skeleton of the interstate system, forced people from the country to settle in the Hubs out of necessity.

Exodus picked up a notch when the Right to Income Act became law, and most of the population became happily unemployed. Harley had only been a boy then, but even sitting on the reservation, watching the world pass them by, the Navajo could see somebody was herding everyone together, whether they wanted to admit it or not. The Navajo had experience in such things.

Price, initially designed to be a part of the Rocky Mountain Hub, died with the mothballing of the high-speed rail through the canyon. It became just another city without a purpose. But the city still drew power from the fusion plant, so the lights were on, even when no one was home.

Harley made the trip to the Rocky Mountain Hub once or twice a year and each time stood in awe on deserted street corners. With a population of more than forty million, he could walk for blocks and hardly see a soul. Most people spent their days and nights in the Vale, living a virtual life that was far more exciting, far more stimulating than anything reality could offer. Reality, after all, was still a little messy. It was more than the Rages reshaping the climate of entire regions from one extreme to the other; it was more than every animal on the planet hungry for human blood. Reality just took effort. Just too damn much effort.

The moon was rising over the desert, clawing its way into the darkening sky. To the west, the light of the Wheel winked of man's power in the Age of Renewal. There were 10,000 people living where angels danced, and the space station was a promise and a

16

hope beyond reach for someone like Harley.

He finished his cigarette, shrugged his saddlebag and pack back into place, and walked into town.

Main Street was a cemetery forgotten, and the smattering of abandoned cars left like playthings were the tombstones of a civilization that had moved on to a new life in a new place beyond reach or caring. The few streetlights still shining bowed their heads at a road seldom traveled, leading to destinations long gone. Harley walked down the middle of the road, and his cowboy boots click clicked on the asphalt like laughter at a funeral.

In the distance, a coyote shrieked, and Harley caressed his sidearm. There were still a lot of critters in the city, and the night belonged to them. He had planned to find a vehicle and keep moving, but it was a long walk into town, and it would be best to find a place to sleep.

Finding a vehicle that would still run wouldn't be difficult, but the search would be safer in the morning. There were a lot of cats in the city, and they would be on the prowl. Dogs were the one animal to side with humans when the Rages came. Now nature hunted them just as it did humanity. Harley guessed the Rages answered the question as to which beast was indeed man's best friend. His mom used to have a couple of cats around the house when he was a boy, before the Rages. Harley didn't care for them much then either. He could look at them and tell they were a shifty lot.

Walking down the middle of the road, he could feel eyes measuring him from some of the homes. Homes still occupied radiated a tired but steady pulse of life ripped away from those abandoned. The empty ones were only forlorn, fragile, and forsaken.

When people left in the Exodus, they didn't bother taking their cars. They were of little use in the Hub. If someone needed to go anywhere, they used mass transit or called for a pod. For most, even transit was more than they needed. They didn't have a job to go to, could order anything they wanted from the Link, and explore the universe from their living room. Why did they need to go anywhere? The automobiles parked in driveways and along the streets of this dead city were useless in the Hub.

With any luck, he would be able to find something he could run with his powerband or maybe even an old truck or motorcycle that ran on NG. They were rare, but Castle Valley was rich in natural gas, and the people who used to live here were a prideful, stubborn lot, resistant to the kind of change the Seven Realms offered, so many drove NG vehicles long after they fell out of favor in the rest of the world.

Harley considered moving into one of the neighborhoods and breaking into a house for the night but kept walking down Main Street instead. From the shadows of the alleyways, he could see dark shapes flitting here and there. Cats, no doubt. They would stay clear until there were enough to overwhelm him, and that may not take long. A Wildthing Rage was building. He picked up his pace.

Price, before the world changed and hammered the final nail into its coffin, had been an energy town. Coal was its lifeblood for more than 160 years. When the government finally pulled the plug on the coal industry, when the last coal-fired power plant closed and the final coal miner climbed out of the mine, his face black from coal dust, Price, like so many towns, began to die. Ahead of him, Harley heard more coyotes yip, and behind him, he saw the first of the cats dare to slither out from the shadows and onto the street. They were herding him, the beasts of the Rages. He drew his slayer.

There was a hotel at the top of a hill as Main Street led out of town. Its lights were still working, although part of it looked destroyed by a storm. A sign leaning drunkenly from a pole winked Castle Valley Inn, and Harley aimed for it and tried the door to the lobby. It swung open and he walked inside just before the first cat dared to leap toward him. Harley scowled and went toward the reception desk. The hotel looked deserted, but he didn't know for sure, so he waited for a moment, then walked behind the counter to peer into one of the offices. The attendant's desk was bare, and a fine layer of dust had laid its claim. The hotel was his for the taking. There wasn't a way to access a room since he didn't have the hotel's Link account, but he didn't worry about opening the door. His boot worked reasonably well.

He came back around the counter and looked out the glass doorway. There were hundreds of mangy cats peering through the window, and behind them he could see the glowing eyes of scores of coyotes. They looked none too pleased, and cats threw themselves at the windows and bounced back onto the driveway. Their mad attempt made a thump when fur met window. It made him smile. He took a chair from the lobby, wedged the door shut and turned away, humming a little ditty as he slipped deeper into the hotel.

"Bad Kitty. . .
"Evil Kitty.
"Shoot you in the head. . .
"Kitty."

The hotel was three stories of somebody's faded dreams. Harley took the stairs to the top, looking for a suite with a view of the city. The lights were still working, the air conditioning still whispered, and Harley felt the pinprick of ghosts walking with him as he navigated the hall.

People had stayed here, families, young and old united for an evening in a place of respite before they packed up and moved on to different places, different times. People had worked here, counted on a job giving comfort to strangers to provide for their families.

"Worked," Harley muttered, and his voice cracked in the dead hotel. The word's meaning was lost. The thought deepened the furrow in Harley's brow, and he shrugged it away.

He adjusted the saddlebag across his shoulder and tried the first door on his left, surprised to find it unlatched. He pushed it open and stepped inside.

The room wasn't empty.

There was a kitchenette on his left and a desk and chair on his right. A king-size bed occupied the center of the room. Sitting on the bed, looking disheveled and with a bloody scar on her right temple, was a young woman in uniform. She was pointing a pulse rifle at his chest.

"I'll try the next room," Harley said with a sigh.

"Stay right there, or I'll blast you," the woman replied, her hands dancing with the rifle.

"I'd rather you didn't."

She was scared, and Harley had some experience in scared. He had been the cause of it, and he had been the victim of it, and this woman was a good deal past scared and into terrified. "Do you mind if I drop my bags?" he said. "It's been a long day."

The woman nodded and shifted in bed, seemed to think about standing and then reconsidered. She pointed the rifle at his holster. "Drop the slayer and sword."

Harley looked the woman in the eyes, and after a moment she looked away. "Don't think I will."

She aimed the rifle at his chest as he slipped saddlebag and backpack from his shoulders and went to sit on the chair by the desk. He turned it to face her as he sat down, and his back ached with relief. He reclined, crossed his legs in front of him and tried to smile, but found that he couldn't. That was usually the case.

"What's your name?" he asked.

"Kara," the woman replied. "Sergeant Kara Litmeyer of the Legion, 123rd Rocky Mountain Brigade."

"That's a mouthful," he said. "Hullo, Kara." He nodded as politely as his nature allowed. "Harley Nearwater."

"Are you a Neand?" Kara asked.

"No, just a wanderer on the path. What brings a Federation legionnaire so far out in the sticks?"

Her eyes widened, then darted to him, then away, then to the windows, the doorway, and back to him again. "I'm lost," her voice squeaked.

"Lost?" He looked at the bloody scar on her temple. "How's that possible?"

"He took it away from me," she whispered as if someone else might be listening.

"What?"

"The Link," she said, her voice almost cracking. "He took away my linktag."

Harley nodded as if what she was saying wasn't completely insane, but of course, it was. The scar looked ugly, but whoever gave it to her had as much chance of removing the linktag that way as they would if they removed her legs.

"Who is he?"

Kara bit her lip, started to sob, and stopped. She tossed the rifle onto the bed beside her. "I don't know. I was meditating one night, just trying to clear my head and get in tune with my emotions because it had been a pretty rough couple of days. I had been fighting with Alain, my husband. I was thinking about Alain and trying to calm myself, and this strange man just appeared like an apparition right in front of me."

She looked up at Harley, her lip quivering, and Harley was amazed at her loveliness.

"He didn't scare me," she continued. "Even though one moment I was alone in my apartment and the next this stranger was standing beside me. Crazy, huh, that I wouldn't be scared? But he was tall and handsome, and he made me feel calm immediately, like my best friend in the world knew I needed him, and he just appeared. But then he looked into my eyes, and I looked into his, and I got lost, I think. I think he hypnotized me. He had grey eyes, the greyest I've ever seen, and looking into them, it was like there was a storm going on in there and I couldn't move."

"You sure you weren't on the Link?"

"No." Kara shook her head. "This was the Sphere. He was in my apartment."

"Did your husband see him?" Harley asked.

The woman shook her head again. "My husband is in the Vale, not the Sphere."

Harley nodded slowly. "Your husband. Is he flesh, Filler, or Jinn?"

Kara's lip curled. "Flesh, Filler, Jinn, does it matter?"

Harley shrugged. "Not to me."

It was inappropriate to differentiate between digital versions of a person or the flesh and blood version. Even asking if someone in the Vale was real or simulation people considered hateful. It was racist, bigoted behavior. Harley made a point of always asking.

"That's why we were arguing," Kara continued, and her voice became calmer. "His Sphere is the Paris Hub, and one day while I was working, I had the strangest thought. I just thought I've never touched my husband. I mean, flesh to flesh. I've never kissed his lips in the Sphere or ran my fingers through his hair in the Sphere. I've never made love to him in Sphere, and that just made me sad. I don't know why it made me sad, but it did." She looked at Harley and smiled softly. "I'm not Neand-minded or anything, and I'm no bigot. What world you live in is up to you, to each his own, you know? Pick your realm and enjoy it, I say."

"Sounds reasonable," Harley said. It didn't, but he said it anyway.

Kara nodded. "When I talked to Alain about maybe catching a flight and visiting him in the Sphere instead of the Vale, he got so angry, and it just escalated from there. The thing is, I couldn't get it off my mind, and after work, I found myself visiting the parks in the Hub. Have you ever been?"

"No."

"They're beautiful." Kara's eyes were suddenly bright with the memory. "And they're never crowded. I watched a couple with their children playing on the grass, and it just made me want to be with Alain in the Sphere even more. We talked about having children, but I think we had pretty much decided we would have them in the Vale, not the Sphere. But suddenly I wasn't sure. I meditated for a while, to clear my head and tried to decide what I wanted to do and why I wanted to do it. That's when the man with the grey eyes appeared in my apartment."

Harley leaned forward, and his stomach growled. He hadn't eaten since breakfast, and the exertion from the day was catching up with him. Kara heard his stomach and went to the small kitchenette. She walked on the balls of her bare feet.

"Are you hungry? I have food. There's some broiled chicken and vegetables, lots of vegetables. I also have water, milk, and even some beer." She twirled as she walked, like a schoolgirl practicing a pirouette. Her body was lean, willowy, and strong, and Harley smiled, watching her. He wasn't sure what felt stranger, the smile, or the realization that he had smiled.

"When I woke, I was here, and my uniform was here, and my pulse rifle and my armor and all of this food was here with me. I don't even drink beer, but there's plenty of it." Her voice was more relaxed now, and her body language spoke of fear washing away.

Harley raised an eyebrow. "I drink beer."

Kara dished him a plate of food, and Harley sat at the bar and ate. He downed two beers, recognizing his body needed water more and not caring in the least.

He watched her watch him. The grey and red of her Legion dress uniform was wrinkled and untucked, the blouse half unbuttoned, revealing the soft swell of her breasts against her undershirt. Her Legion battle armor lay splayed across the couch against the far wall and looked like a grey, red, and white manikin. If she had been wearing it when he stepped into the room, if she told him to drop his weapons while armored, he thought he might have needed to comply.

He had no doubt he could draw and fire his slayer before she could squeeze the trigger on her rifle, but armor would give her enough time to make a mistake, even two. He was glad she wasn't wearing it.

He sipped the third beer as he turned Kara back to her story.

"Were you wearing your uniform when this stranger paid you a visit?"

"No." Kara bit her lip shyly. "I wasn't wearing anything when he visited. When I woke up here, my uniform was the only clothing with me."

"What did he want?" Harley asked.

"Want?"

"The man with the grey eyes. What did he want?"

Kara leaned on the opposite end of the bar and bit into a carrot. Beneath smeared makeup and tear stains, her chocolate skin was smooth and beautiful. "He said he wanted to help me. He smiled at me and said he wanted to help. He was handsome, even more than Alain, and I always thought Alain was the most handsome man I've ever seen, flesh or Filler."

"Help you how?"

Kara suddenly looked embarrassed. "He said the linktag was a form of possession. That with the linktag I couldn't think clearly, I'd never be able to make my choice."

"Choice?"

"Yeah, choice. Crazy." She took another bite of carrot. "He said I had to decide which side I stood for or if I chose neither, but I needed to decide, and he hoped I might choose his side. He said if I had the world screaming inside my head, I would never be able to find the quiet I needed to make my choice. I needed an exorcism."

"An exorcism?" Harley smiled.

"He actually said that," Kara said and giggled. "The strange thing was, looking into his eyes, it made perfect sense to me, so I nodded, and he touched me." Her hand went to her temple, and her face twisted with pain or the memory of pain. "I woke up here. And I can't reach the Link. My linktag is gone. I can't connect. I haven't talked to Alain in four days, and the quiet here is deafening. How do you deal with it, the quiet? How do the Neands survive in so much quiet?"

"May I look?" Harley motioned toward the scar on her temple, and she nodded.

He rose and touched her lightly on the chin, tilting her head to get a better look at her temple. His fingertips tingled as he laid his calloused hand upon her soft skin. She smelled of fallen leaves after a rainstorm, and he struggled to concentrate. The scar was a black oval, shaped like an expanded thumbprint, as if the stranger had burned his fingerprint into her flesh.

"I don't even know where I am," Kara said as he examined her. "I walked around town a couple of times and saw a few people, but when I tried to talk to them, they ran into their homes. They looked at me like I was a Neand or Wrynd or something. Me, a Wrynd. It's just crazy. I found the old city hall and found out this is Price, but I don't know it."

"It's about one hundred klicks from the Hub."

"That's it!" Kara grinned wildly. "Thank God! Could you help me find my way back? I don't know what he did, but I must find a way to get my linktag back. Alain will be so worried."

"I could," Harley said, turning and going back to his backpack and saddlebag. "In the morning. Do you know who this man was?"

"No. I asked who he was, and he said he was I.P Freely. Do you know him?"

Harley smiled. "I.P. Freely? No. I don't know him."

"I don't think it was his real name. He seemed to think it was pretty funny, but I don't know why. Do you?"

25

Harley shook his head. "No."

"He said he was just a wanderer on the path, which is why it startled me so much when you said you were a wanderer, too. Do you know him, this man with the grey eyes?"

"No. This is the first I've heard of him," Harley lied.

"Why would he leave me here of all places? He gives me food and my uniform and my armor and rifle and beer, when I don't even drink beer, and not a drop of wine when I could use a glass of wine. Why would he do that?"

"An offering," Harley muttered.

Sometimes words slipped out of his mouth without calling, as those two did. Most of the time, he didn't understand why, but sometimes, in the mud of his mind, he thought he might.

"What?"

"Nothing."

Kara sat down on the bed and smiled, and Harley again found her lovely. "You could stay in one of the rooms across the hall, and we could get a start toward the Hub tomorrow, do you think?"

Harley picked up his bags and threw them across his shoulder.

"Harley." Kara smiled, and it was beautiful, innocent, and seductive all at the same time. "Thank you. Thank you for finding me."

Harley shifted the bags, drew his sidearm, and in one quick jerk of lightning shot Kara Litmeyer in the chest. The pulse blast threw her against the wall and passed through her body and the thin wall behind her. As she crumpled to the floor, her lips twisted from a smile to a dark circle of surprise.

Harley walked to where she fell and picked up her rifle. She reached up and clutched his right arm. He looked into her dying eyes, and they were grey, no longer the eyes of the beautiful young woman who made him for a moment wish he was something other than what he was.

"The end," she whispered.

"The end?"

Kara gripped his arm tighter and tried to pull herself upright. She failed. "The end is coming," she whispered.

Harley frowned as her hand slipped away and fell to the floor. Her eyes were no longer grey. They were black with death. "For you, I think it's already here."

He took her pulse rifle, holstered his slayer, and went to find a room where he could sleep.

Chapter Two

The Saddest Thing

I

Brinna Wilde sat on the crumbling back of the Scuppernong River Bridge, wondered about death and dreamed about life, somehow caught between them both.

Below, in the darkness of water so black it looked like sweet molasses, was death waiting to take her, like it had ol' Hen. Behind her, beyond the forests and swamps, was the future in the form of two long metal strips on a raised spine of rock and earth. There the trains of the Seven Realms screamed past so swiftly they were only a blur and a whistle and wish for something more.

A time or two she took the ol' NG Ford pickup in the middle of the night (when she was sure Mamal was asleep), to watch the trains fly by. Mamal would be furious if she found out, but Brinna couldn't help herself. They called them Dragons, those great roaring trains of the Seven Realms. She often found herself daydreaming of standing on those tracks and seeing if the train could somehow carry her away into a world her small mind could scarcely imagine.

Surely, she would die, but in her dreams, she leapt into the air to straddle the train, which was more than a dragon by name, but an actual dragon. In her dream, she was its master as it carried her west, into the future where the world wasn't a swamp and a wall of drooping trees, but a high and vast desert where her eyes could glimpse the heavens.

The swamp was quiet except for the soft croaking of bullfrogs and an occasional splash as something went from land to water and back again. Six weeks before she wouldn't have worried about the beasts out there, because Mamal taught her the Rages wouldn't harm her if she respected Gaia and her children. But ol' Hen always respected the beasts of Gaia, and they took him anyway. So, the Rages aimed not only at the Federation and those spoilers who called it home but the faithful as well.

Every week Mamal drug her, by the ear if she had to, to the Cross Landing First Church of Jesus God and His Lady Gaia, to learn about Jesus and talk about the Rages. God would protect His chosen from the Rages because Gaia was among God's chosen, one of his great loves. He wouldn't allow Her to destroy His children if they were one with nature and showed respect to Gaia and the beasts of the Wilderness. But in the end, He hadn't protected ol' Hen at all. In the end, the serpents of Gaia took him under, and Brinna was there to watch. She was there, and nothing she did could prevent the fury of the Rages. There was nothing any of them could do.

She watched her toes wiggle beneath her, and she tried not to remember that day. But of course, she couldn't help herself, because truthfully, she came here to remember, as she always did. Her toes danced at the bottom of her long legs, and if they hadn't been dancing, then her hands would be jittering, or her jaw would be flexing, or her hips would be swaying.

Staying still wasn't a talent of Brinna Wilde's, and she knew that for a fact. Even the tight black curls of her hair seemed to be in motion, and the wild mop on her head curled in a nonexistent breeze. The shorts on her waist only just covered her muscled behind, and her shirt pressed against a bosom she hadn't quite grown accustomed to possessing, although she had, as Mamal liked to say, blossomed when she was fifteen, four years in the past.

She was a beautiful woman, and while she wasn't unaware of the fact the boys no longer treated her like one of the boys (and hadn't for several years), she didn't know what she was supposed to do with her beauty. Her skin, dark as the fertile soil and smooth as fine glass, embraced a frame long, lean, and muscular. She had seen the boys of the Youngers watch her when she joined them for a hunt or a game or a bit of storytelling, and she tried not to let them see how embarrassed it made her knowing they no longer looked at her as they had.

It was a frustrating thing, her beauty. It didn't help her hunt any better, and it didn't help her tend the fields any faster or carry her away on the great Dragons of the Seven Realms. She caught the boys looking at her breasts if she didn't dress modestly enough, which Mamal said she never did. Especially Danny, although she thought she enjoyed it a bit, maybe more than a bit, when Danny looked at her. Her breasts also didn't help her run any faster, and she loved to run.

She thought that was why Danny was now a bit faster than she; not because he was stronger or taller, but because he didn't have boobies holding him back. It didn't seem fair, but she supposed life wasn't supposed to be fair. It was just life and, for her little village of Neands, life was about trying to live in the Wilderness where the Rages waited to carry them away into the long dark sleep. Mamal told her beauty could be a thing of power, but her beauty didn't help save ol' Hen. Neither did Danny's run for help.

Something rustled in the distance, a soft swish of movement in the damp foliage that all but obscured what once was a road but was now little more than a path. Brinna looked to her right, her left hand reflexively reaching for the rifle nestled by her side. It was Danny Tull walking toward her, his long legs sauntering like he hadn't a care in the world and a soft smile on his tan face. An aggravating, beautiful smile. Brinna found herself smiling back.

He wasn't even armed, which made her angry and oddly excited at the same time. Pastor Sorensen might say they were God's chosen and Gaia wouldn't harm them, but it sure felt more comforting, those words, with a weapon at your side. Danny was four months older than her and a head taller. Like her, he was long, lean, and beautiful, and she thought about him far more than was probably best. She could see herself being with him forever and knew that the vision, while oh so tantalizing, was a fantasy. She couldn't go from being a Younger of Cross Landing to an Older of Cross Landing without seeing more of the world than this bit of place still called North Carolina.

Danny plopped down on the bridge deck, his leg brushing against hers for a moment, their hands almost touching.

"Whatcha doin'?"

Brinna shrugged, her eyes so brown they were almost black, turning away because she was afraid he might see the longing there; afraid she might see his longing. "Jus' thinkin'."

"About?" For the shortest breath of a moment, their eyes did meet, and within that gaze she saw a beautiful life beyond reach.

She looked toward the river. "The saddest thing."

Danny nodded as if he knew that would be the answer because it was the only answer. It was why they found themselves returning to the old bridge, looking down on the Scuppernong River. She knew the beasts of the Wilderness were watching them from the trees; that the creeper vines intent on choking every living thing could just as easily choke her, and she no longer cared. If they were going to take her, they would take her. Gaia would have Her way, and she didn't suppose Jesus God would care one whit whether She did; just as He hadn't when ol' Hen slipped away. She closed her eyes and thought of the saddest thing she ever saw and bit her lip to keep it from quivering.

It was a sweaty armpit of a Sunday afternoon. Church was over, chores done, and one group of kids shadowed the other with no direction in mind. They were just the Youngers of Cross Landing, cursed with the title until they were twenty and, overnight, transformed into one of the Olders. As an Older, they would be adults and expected to act like one before their village, Jesus God, and Gaia.

In the group of ten grab-assing boys were only two girls, Brinna and Shauna Watterson, who Brinna once considered a friend and now only considered a whore. She opened her legs for just about anyone who showed an interest. The group of twelve ended up at the Scuppernong River, watching the black water slither by from the old bridge.

They sat on the bridge and let their legs dangle over the side; dark legs, light legs, tan legs, almost intertwined as the sun pressed down and the critter sounds of the swamp rose out of the darkness. There were snakes in the water below; lots of snakes, water moccasins that could and would send them to the gates of Jesus God if they had a mind. There were also alligators that reclaimed the river over the years, although they weren't as plentiful as the snakes. But the Youngers of Cross Landing didn't pay them much mind. Pastor Sorensen said Cross Landing was a sacred place to Jesus God and Gaia. And they were sacred, too.

They all sat on the bridge for a time, idle chatter dovetailing from one conversation to the next, and no one had any real inclination to do anything else until the hum vibrated their senses and they all looked up, down, and at each other, the conversation slipping away. The humming grew louder and louder until it was less a noise and more a physical force in the afternoon air, a vibration rattling their teeth and the concrete floor of the bridge beneath their behinds.

"Look!" Danny yelped, who Brinna was oh so tantalizingly close to holding hands with. He pointed to the tree line, and they followed his pointing finger and gasped in unison as the battlewagon came into sight.

It was a floating island of metal and light, and as it passed between the sitting youth and the sun, it eclipsed day with shadow. The massive airship stretched on for klicks, it seemed, and was so low to the ground that surely it must brush the trees.

As the ship drew closer, the vibration became stronger, and the excitement turned into fear as they scampered from the bridge, thinking it might crumble away. If the ship had drifted overhead, Brinna was sure the bridge would have dropped into the Scuppernong. But it passed to the west, perhaps by as many as five klicks, although it still looked like they could reach out and touch it.

As they stood in awe, the Federation battlewagon floated south, and their mouths were agape as they watched smaller craft and Legion wings drop onto the decks of the airship or rocket into the heavens.

Although many of the Youngers eyes showed fear, Brinna couldn't stop grinning. It was magnificent! Altogether beyond anything they experienced in Cross Landing. It was as if Jesus God Himself had passed by on His golden chariot and waved. But she knew the Federation wasn't the home of Jesus God. Pastor Sorensen said the Seven Realms was a godless place, which is why Jesus God had granted His concubine Gaia her desire to destroy humanity, who had befouled her great beauty. It would all happen in time, which was why they must hold to the faith in Cross Landing.

"They call those who won't join them Neands!" the pastor shrieked in one of his favorite sermons. "Because we don't succumb to the temptations of their digital world, a world of fantasy, their Vale; because we don't join them in their Hubs, we're Neanderthals, worthy of nothing but scorn. They call us Neands because we don't allow them to alter our minds with their evil science, don't let them read our thoughts and torture our souls.

"They call us Neands to insult us, but I say to you, especially you Youngers, embrace it as the highest of compliments. We need nothing of their Seven Realms, nothing of their Age of Renewal! Jesus God is our Renewal. All we need is our Jesus God and patience for his Gaia to bring vengeance upon the world! The Rages aren't to fear; they're to celebrate. They're Jesus God's great retribution upon man's sins!"

"Amen," Brinna found herself whispering as she and her friends watched the airship fade into the horizon. But seeing the great ship suspended in the cloudless sky, it didn't look evil at all. It looked magical, a place she would dearly love to see, to be a part of, and even as she realized the truth of her desire, she felt the shame of betraying her faith.

When the vibration of the airship passed, they went back to the bridge. The peaceful spell broken, it wasn't long before the siren song of the waters below and the heat of the day wouldn't be denied.

The oldest of the Youngers was a mule of a man named Henders Sorensen. Most people just called him Hen, which Brinna always found wickedly funny. She imagined him pecking at the ground like the hens she hunted to steal eggs from every morning. She would pitch herself into a giggle fit thinking of Hen that way, and people would look at her like she didn't have a lick of sense. Hen was the youngest son of Pastor Sorensen, and he stood more than two meters and seemed almost as wide. He could have been a monster if he had a mind to be, but his heart was as big as the rest of him, and he always wore a goofy grin that had a way of making you grin right back, no matter how bad your day was.

After the airship passed, he wrestled the other boys. They pulled a log raft into the black water and played king of the hill in the Scuppernong River. The rest of the Youngers watched for snakes, but mostly they just laughed and watched as ol' Hen tossed the boys aside. He was too big to climb onto the raft, and the others would leap from it and do their best to dunk him in the river.

No one noticed the snakes writhing down the river until it was far too late to shout a warning. The first scream came from Hen as a snake latched on and sank fangs into his big right arm. His cry was high pitched and whining, like a young girl, and Brinna was amazed, even as the horror set in, that a man so big could shriek so loudly. Then the next snake and the next snake struck, and the other three boys scampered onto the raft and tried to get a hand on Hen.

"Go get help!" one of them yelled, and Brinna and Danny looked at each other, then Danny nodded. He was faster; not by much, but by enough.

Danny took off down the road, and Brinna watched the little puffs of dust under his feet as he dashed out of sight. Something inside her ached for him, even then. She thought, watching him, his long legs pumping so fast they were a blur, that he might be able to outrun death itself.

But death was already there. She just hadn't realized it yet.

When she turned back to the river, she caught one terrified look in big Hen's tortured face, then he slipped beneath the water and was gone into the Rages.

Danny returned with Pastor Sorensen in tow. When he did, everyone was standing on the Scuppernong River Bridge, staring down at the river as darkness settled. Night had slipped like a thief upon them. The pastor was a slight and balding man who held none of his son's size, temperament nor spirit. He didn't say a word as he took a lantern, climbed onto the raft, and began pushing it down the river. They all watched as he rounded the bend and disappeared into the darkness.

When he came back, everyone was once again dangling their legs over the side of the bridge; no one saying a word. As they watched the raft approach, they couldn't bring themselves to stand because they could see the pastor was pulling something behind him, and they knew what it was. They didn't stand because they knew death was standing behind them, and no one wanted to brush against it any more than they already had.

Pastor Sorensen found Hen dead in the river, floating face up, staring at nothing, a soft smile on his blue lips. He couldn't pull his massive son onto the raft, so he cut free a couple of logs and tried to use the rope to tie around his son, but there was too little rope and too much son.

He couldn't keep the thick rope knotted around his hands or his feet, so he made a lasso and pulled it around his neck. He looked up as he neared the bridge, and by the firefly light of the lamp Brinna saw Pastor Sorensen now believed everything he ever preached about Jesus God and Gaia, and the Seven Realms was nothing but a lie.

Six weeks later, sitting on the same bridge where she looked into the deadness of Pastor Sorensen's eyes, she let herself lean against Danny and fought the urge to kiss his neck, to touch his chest, to beg him to take her now on the bridge, where death had come calling. Then she would beg him to take her away, to the city, to the Hubs and the Federation, to a world of possibilities forbidden to imagine but one she found herself imagining all the time.

Pastor Sorensen disappeared with his remaining family one week after he laid his son to rest in the fertile soil of Cross Landing. There had been no church service since the Sunday the Rages consumed Hen. With the pastor gone, two other families in Cross Landing disappeared. They were slipping away to form another Neand village, perhaps. But Brinna thought it more likely they were going to the Washington Hub, to join civilization and forget about Gaia and Jesus God.

Watching Pastor Sorensen bring his dead son back up the river with a rope tied around his neck was the saddest thing Brinna ever saw. But she was wise enough to know life was long and she was young, and there was so much sadness yet to see.

She just didn't know how much. Not yet.

II

The hog was on the run. Brinna could hear it grunting as it trampled through the underbrush, deeper into the backwoods. She followed along at a smooth gait, not trying to overtake it, just yet. It would tire long before she did and, when it turned, she would have it.

Her boots, worn leather with a sole so thin she could almost count the blades of grass beneath her toes, hardly made a sound as she loped behind, smiling softly, and adjusting the hunting rifle slung across her back. The old Remington 270 was Papal's before he passed through the gates of Jesus God's Paradise. Mamal gave her the rifle when he passed, and she had used it to keep meat in the pot ever since.

She removed the scope Papal used to rely on because she felt it only fair to give the beasts a fighting chance. Being able to snuff them out without them even realizing she hunted seemed an affront to Gaia. She would use the hunting knife strapped to her waist when the killing was done. Behind her she could hear Mamal stomping through the forest after her, meat pack strapped to her skinny frame as she followed her granddaughter, no doubt cursing her for not putting the beast hog down quickly.

Even after returning from the bridge, the morning was still young, and the woods were clinging to the last faint wisps of fog, collecting the mist beneath the tree limbs. Like apparitions, they parted as Brinna passed. It was quiet but for the hog's exertions in front and Mamal's behind, but Brinna knew all manner of beasts watched. She was in their domain, and if a Rage built around her, she was lost. She took comfort in the thought that she honored Gaia and all her creations. Pastor Sorensen said Jesus God wouldn't allow Gaia to devour those who followed Him.

Pastor done left us, though, ain't he? Her mind whispered back, and Brinna shushed the thought.

The hog was slowing down, and she could hear its breath growing ragged. It wasn't far ahead, and soon would turn and fight. She reached behind her and pulled the rifle over her shoulder, never slowing her stride. The hog was one of the hundreds of thousands in Cross Landing that escaped when the Rages began. Thousands more starved in their pens when they turned mad. In the decades since the Rages sent humanity fleeing from the Wilderness, the numbers of animals fluctuated wildly as a new web of nature developed, one not subject to the whims of man.

The trail the hog ran disappeared into a thicket so dense Brinna couldn't see through, and she stumbled after, using her rifle to weave through the branches and briers, her boots sinking in muck.

When she came out the other side, she was in a small clearing with a line of cedars bowing limbs to the center. The trees rebuffed the sun's search for the forest floor, but it found a way to send a sliver of light here and there into the dark underbrush anyway.

All was shadow in the clearing.

The hog stood facing her on the far side, all but hidden in the gloom. A little less than 300 paces separated them. It was a big one, more than 200 kilos, and Brinna fought the urge to back up as it shuffled forward, snorting.

She pointed her rifle to the sky, the barrel resting against her shoulder, and nodded to the beast. "I see you're plumb tuckered, and I knowed you don't wanna die, so let's be done with this right quick like."

The forest held its breath. The hog snorted and charged, and Brinna let the barrel of the rifle fall into her left hand, raised it to her shoulder, aimed, and squeezed the trigger in one seamless flow. The hog crumpled to the forest floor with a squeal that pierced the morning. It took two great gasping breaths, then lay still as the air escaped its lungs one last time. Brinna flung the rifle back over her shoulder and unsheathed her knife. The hog was huge, and even if they filled their meat packs with as much as they could carry, there would still be plenty to share with the wildthings.

She knelt before the beast, drawing her knife across its neck in one fluid motion. "We thank ye, Gaia, for this bounty. We honor his life and his strength and return his blood to you. We share with your beasts and insects and your soil all that he is and was."

Brinna had almost finished dressing the hog by the time Mamal made her way into the clearing, huffing, puffing, and cursing her empty-headed granddaughter who didn't have sense enough to make a kill close to home. She brushed her long, silver hair away from the roadmap of her face and spat as she stood over Brinna.

"Didja get enough exercise 'fore you put this beast on the ground?"

Brinna grinned. "I reckon."

Mamal tossed her a meat pack, and Brinna started stowing the hog within. Her grandmother crouched beside her, and the bone-yard of her hands went to work with her knife, stripping the pig out and slipping it into the cool confines of the meat packs for the long walk back to the house. The dress she wore billowed like a sail as she hurried to stow the meat, and Brinna finally sat back on her haunches and let Mamal finish the work.

She looked around the clearing, which was still quiet, haunt-ingly so. If the forest seemed to be holding its breath as she faced the hog, it hadn't yet decided to let it out, and she found herself wondering exactly why it was waiting. Only Mamal's short, ragged breaths as she worked on the hog broke the haunting silence.

"It's too quiet, Mamal," Brinna whispered.

"Aye," Mamal whispered back, her hands shaking as she hurried in her work. "The forest be watching; the beasts be gathering." She flipped the meat pack covers closed and pushed one toward Brin-na. "We need to be away from here."

"But."

"Hush, no buts now." Mamal looked up and through the cracks in the tree canopy. Clouds were brewing.

Brinna helped her grandmother to her feet, and they both turned back the way they came. The forest sighed, and from the underbrush a dozen hogs erupted into the clearing. A flash of lightning ignited the darkening sky, and the first fat raindrops slipped through the forest roof to the ground below. Brinna pushed her grandmother through the brambles. "Run, Mamal!" She unslung her rifle and pivoted, firing a quick round as the hogs rushed toward her. Behind them, she saw a tree lean sideways, and a black bear pushed its way through and gave chase after the pigs. A Rage was building around them, and they were klicks from home.

"Jesus God, save us," Brinna mumbled, firing off a round. "Gaia, hear our plea." She fired off another round and the closest hog crumpled, but even if she made every shot count, she would run out of ammunition long before she finished off the hogs giving chase. She reached out and stripped the pack from her grandmother's back. "Let go of that now and run, Mamal."

The old woman hobbled on, but she wouldn't be able to outrun the beasts behind her. The wind howled, scooping up leaves and underbrush and tossing it into the darkening forest. It pelted them as they stumbled on. Brinna turned and fired three more times, and three more hogs fell.

Ahead of them a large old cedar with a trunk twisted and knotted beckoned, and Brinna dashed up it in three quick steps until it branched off. She was three meters off the ground, and she knelt in the tree and brought her rifle to her shoulder. She didn't have enough ammunition to kill all the hogs, but hogs couldn't climb trees. There was only one she needed to concern herself with killing.

Mamal made it to the tree and tried to climb. Her energy spent, she slipped away. Brinna exhaled sharply, took aim, and squeezed the trigger, hoping her vision, obscured by rain and the tempest of the forest floor, was true. The bear closing in roared as the bullet found its mark and it crumpled ten paces from her grandmother.

Brinna dropped the stock of the rifle to Mamal, and she latched onto it and pulled herself up as the first hog closed the gap. Mamal lifted her stringy legs just as the pigs surrounded the tree, and Brinna cried in triumph. "Come on, Mamal!" She said, her voice a roar against the Rage. "Get up here!"

A flash of light ignited the world, and Gaia roared back. Later, Brinna would convince herself she had imagined it, but a finger of lightning from heaven, from Jesus God Himself, descended slowly and touched Mamal on the back, and the world turned black.

When Brinna woke she was still in the tree, one leg dangling toward the ground, the other caught between the trunk and a limb. Her rifle had fallen to the ground. The hogs were gone.

And Mamal was dead.

She lay face up beneath the tree, a blackened circle burned through her dress. Water was pooling in her open eyes, dark with death, and her pinched mouth, so quick with a sharp retort to Brinna's lifetime of incessant questions, was slack. Her dentures had clapped together, and she could see the gap between teeth and gum. Brinna felt a sob building, and she dropped to the ground and knelt beside the only mother she ever knew. She closed her eyes for her, then sat and looked at nothing for a long time.

As quickly as the Rage arrived, it flitted away, and morning returned to the forest. The bear was a mass of mangy death in front of her. The hogs would return shortly, if for no other reason than to feed on the corpses. But they wouldn't feed on Mamal.

She picked up her rifle and slung it across her back. There were two bullets left, but Brinna didn't think she would need them. As she bent to pick up Mamal and cradle her fragile body in her arms, she felt Gaia had collected her pound of flesh and was satisfied. But she wouldn't have her. She wouldn't give Her Mamal, who had always been humble to both Jesus God and Gaia. Brinna would build a funeral pyre for Mamal and send her to find a heaven of her own.

She began the long walk back home in silence, her grandmother in her arms, and swore to herself an oath that would carry her west, to a new life and, perhaps, a new purpose.

"Gaia ain't no friend to me no more," she said.

III

The fire consumed everything Brinna was and left only what would be.

She laid Mamal to rest in her bed and covered her in the afghan blanket they stitched sitting on the front porch, watching the fireflies dance. She folded her thin arms across her sunken chest and kissed her forehead. Brinna thought of saying a prayer for the safe passage of her grandmother, but she no longer knew who she should be praying to, so she said nothing. She used kindling to start a fire in the living room and walked outside, closing the door behind her.

The fire surprised her with its fury. It was anxious to devour her world, and she was anxious to have it done. She didn't grieve but then wondered if perhaps she did. The achingly hollow feeling in her chest wasn't incredibly different than the one she always felt. Was that grief? She didn't know. If it was, then she had been grieving for as long as she could remember.

She just didn't know why.

As dusk fell, the fire still licked the timbers of the roof. The brick porch was the only thing still standing. Its red bricks, which had always been so pretty, now burned black. Danny arrived first among the Neands of Cross Landing, and he still stood silently beside her as the last of her world turned to ash. Other settlers flitted by throughout the night, some offering condolences as they realized what had befallen her. Most just came to watch the fire and nod a sad nod or press a hand to her weary shoulders. Then they were gone.

On the ground beside her was a water bag and backpack with the few belongings she cared to have; a couple of changes of clothing, her hunting knife, the last twenty rounds of ammunition for her rifle and the ChristGaian cross Mamal gave her. She wanted to throw it into the fire but couldn't. It dangled from her fingertips where it had for hours. She had forgotten it was even there.

Danny hadn't spoken. He seemed content to be there for her if she needed him, and the knowledge made her heart ache for him even more. But not so much that it would stop her from doing what she planned.

The columns of the brick porch finally crumbled, and when one fell backward into the ashes, the other three soon followed. The last of Mamal's home gave up the ghost. She hoped her grandmother's spirit was away, flying high, above Gaia who turned against Mamal, a woman who had done nothing but honor Her.

The collapse of the porch signified an end to the hush that overshadowed the burning of her home, and Danny finally looked her way and cleared his throat.

"Where will you go?" His voice seemed dipped in remorse for possibilities they both knew had slipped away.

"To a Hub first," Brinna whispered.

"Hub? Why'd you wanna go there? Fixin' to become a blinker, Brinna Wilde?"

"No. But I'm fixin' to get me something better than this." She slung the rifle around her neck. "Something that won't run out of 'munition. Gaia and her wildlings won't catch me unawares again. Not ever."

"Then where?"

Brinna thought for a moment and turned to Danny. "West."

"West? What's West?"

"I dunno," she said, but then she thought again and found an answer. "An orchard, I think. I dream about it sometimes."

"Orchard?"

"Yes. An apple orchard. A big one, all growing wild and magic. It's in the mountains, but not mountains like anything here. Mountains that kiss the sky. I dreamed about an orchard there. Probably just a dream, but I think I'll see for myself. Nothing keeping me here. Not now."

They stared into each other's eyes, where the flicker of the dying fire reflected, and he almost said stay with me, and she almost said come with her, but the moment was gone, and they both said nothing. They touched, one fingertip to another, then she turned away, and he was gone.

Brinna climbed into her Mamal's rusty NG pickup and drove into the night, leaving Cross Landing behind forever.

CHAPTER THREE

THERE WAS AND THERE IS

I

Despair was hungry and bitter and cruel, and hunting, Quinlan Bowden knew, drawing oh so much closer every day, every hour, with every breath. It would have him before too long, and when it did, it would feast on everything he was.

When it finished with him, it would turn to his children. For that reason, and perhaps only that reason, he held onto hope, the faint glimmer of hope that things might yet be made right.

But he knew the world was full of monsters, and their master was despair.

Quinlan sat backward on a straight chair in a dim room in a dim house; his long legs stretched out before him, his toes poking through the ends of faded denim jeans, wiggling nervously with the rest of him frozen in waning hope and the chitter of despair. His arms folded across the back of the chair, he alternately rested his forehead on them or used them as a perch for his bristled chin, to stare out at nothing and think of everything.

His hair, like his clothes, was unkempt and plain, much like his life, until thirteen days before. It was a life of simplicity in a complicated world. A life he carefully orchestrated with his wife to be apart from the way things were and focus on the way things should be. Things were different now, and his world torn asunder. He knew of no other way to make it right than to enter a world he loathed.

"There was, and there is, and the two seldom meet," he whispered in the empty room. He spoke those words once upon a time, trying to woo the woman who would become his wife with the depth of his shallow thoughts. Those words haunted him. He wanted what was, and he lived in what is, and he had no idea how to align the two.

He stood and swung his right leg across the chair back and glided to the window. Muscles so inclined for action were anxious for what little exercise he allowed them of late. He brushed aside the shades, and the mid-morning sun peeked into the plainly decorated living room. The light was somehow obscene in a place where despair slathered to feast.

He squinted and through hazel, bloodshot eyes stared down at the park where his world had slipped away in a heartbeat. His small home was on the fourth floor of a complex of 1,200 homes, and the park was in the courtyard. It was a sprawling complex of gardens, walkways, and ponds where 'bot coy kissed the air. There was a playground with slides and swings and a dozen other things to see and do. Deserted, as it always was.

Quinlan couldn't recall seeing anyone in the courtyard other than his own little family in more than two years, even though he knew in every home on every level someone lived. They chose not to be part of the world. They had other realms to explore. They had the Vale. His eyes twitched at the thought, his thin lips downturned.

Until thirteen days ago, he hadn't let it bother him that humanity had abandoned the physical world for the digital world, but now his mind roared fury. Someone should have seen something;

someone could have called for help if they had only bothered to step away from the Vale and rejoin the world. Vania would have screamed. She wouldn't have gone without a fight.

The park was their playground; they even planted a garden and grew vegetables. His family was never disturbed by another living soul until the afternoon Quinlan kissed his wife and dashed away with his children, who delighted in a mud bath that turned into a wrestling match that turned into a giggling fit of two children and one happy father. They ran to wash away the mud and left Vania in the courtyard to tend their garden. When they returned, she was gone, vanished into a vast world where everything was possible, and nothing was within reach.

Quinlan let his gaze drift above the courtyard to the city beyond, where millions of souls spent their days and nights adrift in digital worlds of their design.

The city was one of the dozens that bled into the other to create the Rocky Mountain Hub, a towering landscape of metal, glass mountains and valleys that sparkled in the July sun and were all but void of human activity. Zipping above them were hundreds and thousands of drones of every shape and size, responding to the whims of a population coddled to the point of lethargy.

Floating above the city was a vast cloud of metal, of power, purpose, and impotence. A Federation battlewagon drifted in the breeze. A galleon of the sky, it bristled with possibility, but little in the way of purpose. Two days before it had moored to its tower on the western edge of the valley but set sail with its crew of 2,000 Legion to show strength to a world already convinced, sated, and grown fat with gluttony. It was a gross display of war in a world wantonly at peace. Quinlan despised what it represented.

He turned his back on the battlewagon and glistening city and went to the opposite window, throwing aside its blind to stare at the horizon where the Wilderness loomed.

The village he called home with Vania for ten of his thirty years nestled against the expansive hips of the Wasatch Mountains and was within five kilometers of the border of the Hub and beginning of the Wilderness. From his window, he could see the blades of the old Spanish Fork Wind Farm twirling softly and uselessly in the breeze. Beyond was the hostile realm of the beasts, the Rages, and the monsters who called the Wilderness home.

He feared more every day that it was there, in the Wilderness, where they would find Vania. Within the Hub, with those who called it home, she would be without equal. But in the Wilderness, there were things that even she might not be able to overcome.

He sighed, ran his hands through his dark hair, resisting the urge to pull it from its roots, and went back to the kitchen table. He had thrown his eyeset carelessly upon it, and he forced himself to pick it up. It was the doorway to the Link and the Vale beyond and the world where humanity, by and large, chose to dwell. It was a world he seldom visited, but it was a world he needed to seek help in finding his wife.

In the past thirteen days, he slipped the eyeset on his head repeatedly, and it peered into his eyes and opened them to a world beyond the physical. Every time it pried open his mind and raped his senses, he resisted the urge to scream.

There was little need for law enforcement in the Seven Realms. The Federation disbanded all local police long ago. Now there was only the Marshals Service, and it was there Quinlan ventured each day in the Vale to beg for help. The automation administrators took his information and said a deputy would get back to him, but no one ever called. He spent every day searching for any signs. Things weren't likely to change today.

He let the eyeset hang from his fingers as he slipped down the hallway and poked his head into the master bedroom. Noah and Raizor were curled in the center of the bed, still sleeping. Sleep was so hard to come by lately that their rest had become askew.

Against one blank wall, a viewscreen displayed the scroll of an ancient movie, and Quinlan groaned. They had chosen to resist the temptations of the Link and the Vale, so he spent a month's worth of right to income to purchase the screen and a digital copy of every movie or television show ever recorded. For the past two months his children fixated on one in particular: Monty Python and the Holy Grail. They had it memorized and acted out scenes with gleeful abandon, resulting in him almost getting an ass kicking by his wife on numerous occasions.

It was going to be a long day.

Cast in shadows, like the rest of the house, he went to the window and opened the blinds. Noah pressed his eyes tightly shut and sat up. Raizor buried her head beneath the pillows.

"Up and at 'em, guys," Quinlan said softly, trying to let a little hope shine in his voice. He wasn't sure he succeeded all that well. "I'm ordering breakfast."

"Doughnuts?" Raizor poked her head from beneath the pillows.

"Food." Quinlan went back into the kitchen.

"Doughnuts are food," Noah called after.

"Fine. Doughnuts it is," Quinlan called back.

In the kitchen, he slipped on his eyeset, fought his fluttering stomach as his senses reeled within the Link, and ordered doughnuts, milk, and coffee. He could imagine what Vania would say when she learned he fed her children sweets for breakfast, so he ordered oatmeal and scrambled eggs as well. It wasn't much better, but it might prevent a swift kick in the ass.

While he waited for the stork to arrive, he sat on the kitchen chair and rested his head on his arms. Sleep was a temptress and toyed with him fleetingly during the night. When it did, he dreamed a familiar dream, one with him since he was a boy.

It was of being lost in an apple orchard; only this orchard was so much more. The trees were imposing walls lining a myriad of twisting paths, and in his dream, they were more than trees. Hiding among them were all sorts of things, some dark and some delightful. Even the shadows lived, and he feared to look at them too long; they might be looking back with fearsome eyes.

He was always alone, trying to find the right path. Only last night he knew the path he sought wasn't to escape the dream, it was to find Vania. Even though it was only a dream, he knew whatever path he chose would be the wrong one.

It was nonsense, as all dreams were, but whenever it whispered from his subconscious, he thought it important. He had either been there before and couldn't remember or would be before his life ended. If (when) the orchard became something other than the wisps of dreams, it would change everything he knew or thought he knew about everything.

He shook away the memory, and Noah stumbled into the kitchen, rubbing the sleep from his eyes with one hand and hiking up his sweat cutoffs with the other. Right behind him came Raizor, rubbing the sleep from her eyes with both hands and letting her Superman pajamas slip around her ankles. In keeping with Bowden family tradition, both Quinlan's ten-year-old son and eight-year-old daughter had little in the way of a rear end to keep their pants in place, so they were constantly pulling them up; or in Raizor's case, not pulling them up.

The house chimed a delivery, and Quinlan opened the door. A small delivery package sat outside, and a stork hovered two meters off the ground. The drone was an assortment of skeletal arms and rotors with a beetle-like body. It seemed to be impatiently waiting for him to do something, and he stared at it absently, his mind elsewhere, as it usually was. Raizor tapped him on the arm and held his eyeset, her eyes twinkling.

"This might help," she said, smiling.

"Oh. Yeah." He took the eyeset, slipped it on his head, and acknowledged receipt of the order. His RTI account drained of the cost of the order, the stork fluttered into the sky to join the stream of drones buzzing above the cityscape. Quinlan picked up the package, and the three of them ate breakfast quietly.

"What's the plan today, Dad?" Noah asked between mouthfuls of doughnut and slugs of milk.

"We start over," Quinlan said softly. Every day they made a ten-klick circle around the Village, expanding outward in each direction, trying to find clues as to Vania's whereabouts.

The only direction they hadn't ventured was into the Wilderness, but they went to the old wind farm and stood on the boundary of the Hub, staring up the winding canyon into a place where the Rages ruled and wildthings roamed, hungry for human flesh. Sentinels buzzed along the boundary; pulse cannons pointed and ready to destroy any animal that tried to enter the Hub.

From that first moment, standing and staring into the canyon, where the old highway buckled and turned to dust, Quinlan knew it was there they would have to go to find Vania. Into the Wilderness, where monsters did live, and despair grew fat and satisfied.

He wasn't sure how to begin that quest. They trained for years to be the opposite of what they saw the world becoming, but nothing they did prepared them for the Wilderness. If he ventured there, what would become of Noah and Raizor?

"People don't even open their doors when we knock," Raizor said. She was holding a chocolate donut in one hand and a spoonful of scrambled eggs in the other. She stuffed both into her mouth.

"We'll knock harder this time," Quinlan said.

After breakfast, Quinlan made his children shower and slip into clean clothes. Then they started their search all over again, pounding on doors futilely. Raizor carried a holocube in her tiny hands with images of her mother, and while she waited for somebody, anybody to open the door, she looked at the images on the antique device, her eyes glistening. Most people who encountered a holocube would think it a sign they were a relic from the Old World. Quinlan supposed they were.

They went by every door on the fourth and third level of the village and not one person answered, but Quinlan knew people were inside. They were there, and behind the thin walls of their homes, he could sense the restless anger in his neighbors. It occurred to him not for the first time that he and his children lived in a zoo of caged savages. If they were to answer the door, would they be human at all, or monsters hungry to feed?

Would they be the chitter of despair unleashed?

Several times a stork arrived and deposited into a home delivery dock, so someone was inside. He considered kicking the doors open. If nothing else the Marshals Service might respond. But they were just as likely to send a sentinel to shoot him, so he didn't take the chance.

Midway through the ground floor, they pounded on yet another door, and this time the door creaked open. Oval brown eyes floating in a round, pale face stared up at them from the crack in the door. Quinlan knelt.

"Hi there," he whispered.

"Hi," a small voice whispered back, and within the round face in the gloom, eyes darted from Quinlan's face to Noah's and settled on Raizor's crooked grin.

"Can we talk to you for a moment?"

"You are talking to me," the voice replied, and Raizor hiccupped a laugh.

"Sure," Quinlan said. "Sure, we are. But could we maybe talk face to face, not through the door?"

The door opened, and a plump little girl stood before them wearing a rumpled sun dress badly in need of washing. In the dimly lit room behind the girl, Quinlan could see two people reclined on chairs. They looked unconscious, but he knew they were simply in the Vale, in a world of dreams. They were grossly overweight, their bodies bulbous and without true definition, like mounds of dough to knead. It was how most people looked in the Federation. People like him and his children were the oddities in the Seven

Realms.

"What's your name?" Quinlan asked as pleasantly as he could. The girl didn't look to be any older than Raizor. Her shortly cropped hair needed brushing, and on her right temple was the bright star of the linktag, the nanite implant that allowed blinkers to connect to the Vale constantly.

"Ro. I'm called Ro."

"Ro," Quinlan repeated. "I'm Quinlan, and this is Noah and Raizor," he said, pointing to his children. "We live here in the village. Three levels up."

"You play in the courtyard. You have a garden. I see you out there," she said, looking at them quizzically. "Why do you do that? Play outside like that? Get all dirty? You could have a lot more fun in the Vale. I went to Disneyland just the other day. It was loads and loads of fun, and I didn't get dirty at all."

"Your dress is dirty right now," Raizor responded dryly, and Noah pinched her arm.

Ro stared at her dress, seemingly noticing it for the first time. She flicked off a piece of what Quinlan hoped was chocolate and pressed it through pouty lips. "Not really dirty," she said.

"How old are you, Ro?" Quinlan asked.

"I'm seven."

"Seven." He pointed to the couple reclined behind her. "Are they your parents?"

"Yes."

"Do they come out of the Vale very often?" Quinlan asked softly.

"Sometimes to eat, but the needles feed them, so not very often anymore."

"And pee," Raizor added.

"Pee?" Ro looked confused. "No. The chairs take care of that."

"Well, that's good to know." Raizor rolled her eyes, and Noah pinched her again.

Quinlan gave them both a hard stare and turned back to the little girl. "So, you watch us in the courtyard, from time to time?"

"Sure. You're crazy people. Mom told me that, but it's fun to watch you."

Quinlan nodded. "Well, it's good we found you because we're looking for Raizor and Noah's mom. Do you remember seeing her?"

"Sure. She has long blonde hair. And muscles. You all have muscles." She lifted her doughy arm. "I don't have muscles; I don't think. But you do, and she did. But it didn't help when they came."

"When who came?" Quinlan felt a pinprick of fear and hope, and he gripped the young girl by the arm. She squeaked in protest.

"You're hurting me."

"I'm sorry." Quinlan let her go, afraid she would run away. "I'm sorry." She looked back at her oblivious parents, then back at them, but didn't run. "Can you tell me what you saw? Who came? What did you see?"

The little girl swallowed hard, her eyes suddenly brimming with tears and her plump lips quivering. "Monsters came. Monsters came from everywhere. She tried to run, but they grabbed her and carried her away."

"What kind of monsters, Ro?" Quinlan fought the urge to seize the girl again.

"They had sharp teeth and claws, and they were bloody. They were laughing." She started crying, and Raizor put a hand on her arm. "They were Wrynd."

"Wrynd?" Quinlan felt despair laughing. "How do you know they were Wrynd?"

"I know about the Wrynd," Ro said, casting a furtive look behind her. "I know about the monsters." She pointed at her parents. "They dream about them. I've followed them in their dreams, and I've watched. They want to be like the Wrynd." She stared at her parents, who were moaning in their dream-state, from pleasure or pain, it was impossible to tell. She looked sadly at Raizor. "The Wrynd came for Mom and Dad. But they took your mom instead. They took her away and left my mom and dad here."

"Why did they come for them?" Noah asked softly.

"Because," Ro said, sobbing. "They came for Mom and Dad because they asked them to take them away. They want to be monsters too. They want to gobble everything up."

"Monsters?" Quinlan whispered.

He slipped to the floor and sat with his back against the wall of the home where a little girl named Ro had parents who dreamed horrible dreams. "Monsters," he whispered again and thought he heard the chitter of despair.

II

The city whispered sweet nothings; tender seductions that the world wasn't insane, that there was order, that there was reason, that there was hope. Of course, the city lied; Quinlan knew very well.

He sat on a park bench of a Serpent station with his children hovering nearby. There was a small bit of nature carved out of the concrete in the form of a flowerbed, and he watched as 'bot pollinators buzzed from one flower to the next on metal wings, their tiny wire legs dangling as they took the place of insects banished from the Seven Realms.

A half block down the road, a groundskeeper shuffled from one side of the street to the next, long tentacle nose snuffling the odd piece of trash and sniffing it up like an addict as its arms like willows danced with delight. There was no other sign of movement on the block except for the odd gyration of his daughter.

Raizor was dancing while they waited for the Serpent to arrive. At least Quinlan hoped it was a dance. It also might be a convulsion of some kind. She was wiggling her hips, arching her back, shaking her head, and doing something with her hands that involved hooking her thumbs toward her face so quickly he worried she might put her eyes out. That would be hard to explain when they found Vania. "Well, dear, while you were gone, I let your only daughter pop her eyes out with her thumbs. On the plus side, I took her to a medprint, and she has new eyes. She wanted purple ones instead of the hazel you liked so well. Hope you're okay with that."

Quinlan cast an amused glance toward Noah, who sat on the bench beside him, bent forward, hands clasped like the little old man he might one day become. Quinlan arched his eyebrows, and Noah shook his head softly and sighed. "She's loopy."

"But she's having fun." He dashed to the shuttle platform and joined in the dance, shaking his behind and fighting to keep pace with his giggling daughter and trying, for a moment, to show his children there was still a possibility to find joy in life, and perhaps even hope.

"Come on, Noah. Join in the dance," Quinlan cried, hooking arms with Raizor, and throwing a little square dancing into the mix, which Raizor incorporated into her routine without skipping a step. "What's this called again, Raiz?"

Raizor laughed, leaping into a somersault, landing on her feet, then cartwheeling to stop in front of her older brother and extending her hand. "It's the one dance. The dance of life."

Noah grinned and slapped her hand away. "The dance of life support, maybe."

A soft thrum of an electric hum foretold the arrival of a pod, and the small automobile rolled to a stop in front of the shuttle station, its doors silently opening. A young man and woman lumbered out of the vehicle and waddled to a bench two removed from Quinlan and his children. Their clothing screamed the most outlandish of springs and shimmered in the morning glow of the sun perched above the mountains. As buoyant as their clothes might be, those who wore them were lethargic. They sat side-by-side, lunatic grins on their faces as they reveled in their corpulence. On their left temple was the tell-tale of a linktag. If they noticed the odd dance of the strangers at the shuttle station, they gave no sign. They were in other realms in the Vale and the burdens of moving from place to place given only scant attention. Quinlan scowled at the blinkers, but Raizor smiled at them happily, and he felt a twang of worry that his daughter was admiring their clothing and the beatific looks on their faces. Noah didn't notice them at all.

Raizor turned to him, and he couldn't help but notice her eyes flicking to the eyeset attached to a chest strap on his faded shirt.

"Is it amazing?"

"Is what amazing, Raiz?" Quinlan returned.

"The Link? The Vale? They look so happy." Raizor abandoned her dance and went to sit by her brother. Quinlan joined them.

"The dough people?" Noah hooked a thumb toward the strangers. "They look like flesh 'bots."

Quinlan bent forward and said nothing. He and Vania decided long before they wouldn't expose their children to the Vale until they were older, at least until they were fourteen and granted their right to income accounts. Then they wouldn't have a choice but to let them experience all the temptations of the Seven Realms. While he sat searching for an answer, eyes downturned, he spied something in a crack in the concrete. It was a wildflower that had somehow pushed its way through a crack in the sidewalk and was reaching for sunlight in a blanket of stone. Quinlan pointed, smiling softly, sadly.

"That, little Raiz, now that's amazing."

Raizor and Noah knelt and peered at the flower in the concrete and Raizor looked up at her father with a faltering smile. "But will it survive?"

"Survive?" Quinlan bit his lip, the muscles of his jaw flexing, as they did when he chewed on a question. "No. It won't survive. But for now, it lives, and that's enough. It lives."

Raizor nodded. She chewed her questions with her eyes, dancing here and there and finally settling back on him. "Will Mom survive? Is her moment gone?"

"No. Not yet." Quinlan dropped to his knees before his children and, together, it felt like they might be praying over a wildflower that found life where it shouldn't. "We'll find her. We'll live the moments of our lives together. I promise," Quinlan whispered and hoped he wasn't praying for a miracle beyond their reach.

A chime echoed through the Serpent station, and in the distance, they heard the soft whistle of the commuter train slowing to a stop. The Shifts on the bench two removed oozed to their feet and drifted toward the loading platform, hands intertwined as if the people they saw in the Vale were as those whose hands they held. Other than the Shifts and the incomplete Bowden family, there was no one else in sight. The city looked abandoned.

It was two klicks from their home to the Serpent station, and despite the mournful wails of Raizor, Quinlan made them walk rather than summon a pod to carry them there. They had traveled in pods before, and once, on a Sunday afternoon outing to Utah Lake, they even rented a car, and the children were amazed it was a machine controlled with hands and feet.

The Serpent station was part of the arterial line to the Dragon high-speed passenger and cargo lines built on the skeleton of the interstate system. As the smaller Serpent train opened its doors, a Blue Dragon flashed by, the morning pierced with the scream of two kilometers of cargo train delivering its goods to storefronts and warehouses hugging the rail-lines. A moment later, a White Dragon passenger train roared on the opposite tracks, streaking south. Raizor squealed as the trains flew by and dashed inside the Serpent, almost toppling the blinkers as they went to find a seat. Quinlan and Noah joined her.

There was no one else on the train, and Quinlan pulled his eye-set from the chest flap of his shirt. He slipped it on his brow and asked the commuter to take them to the Justice Tower. The Serpent, a sleek, writhing worm of metal, plastic, and glass, closed its doors and silently left the station, building speed until the cityscape beyond was a blur of empty canyons, valleys and people who could see everything with a thought, except what was right in front of them.

Lights on the track turned from green to yellow as the train flew past, and Quinlan looked at his children and nodded to the lake and the rail bridge fast approaching.

"Follow the yellow brick road," he said.

As they neared the Justice Tower, Quinlan wondered if they were approaching Emerald City or Mordor. A little girl named Ro told them the Wrynd captured Vania. The Wrynd were drug-addicted cannibals of the Wilderness, mutant creatures of insatiable hunger and immeasurable rage who had no place in the Seven Realms. If they found their way within the borders of the Federation, then everything preached as gospel was now suspect.

As the train raced on the metal skeleton of civilization, Quinlan prayed for the glory of Oz and against the despair of Mordor. Even if the wizard, in the end, proved to be a fraud, he found a way to take Dorothy home, and home for them was when reunited with Vania.

The train slowed to a stop and Quinlan led his children toward an imposing tower of black metal and glass.

The Federation Justice Tower loomed, and Quinlan swallowed hard as he led his children forward. To the south and behind the building, like a great upraised hand, was the Cradle for a Federation battlewagon. A massive airship sat docked at the Cradle for several weeks but set sail and was back on patrol with its scores of Legion scampering across its three decks, on guard against an enemy who didn't exist.

After the prophetic mumblings of a child with parents happily living a nightmare, he despaired of ever finding a way to hope for the future, but the last, greatest possibility lay within the tower now casting his family in shadow.

The tower was home of the Rocky Mountain office of the Federation Marshals Service, and headquarters to the Hub division of the Federation Legion. The building, like a needle piercing the heavens, wore the brand of the Federation Marshals star and Legion crest. Quinlan paused at the entrance, feeling insignificant in such a high place, and then sucked in a breath of courage through gritted teeth and stepped toward the door. It opened without the menace he felt it should.

There was no one inside. The first ten floors of the building were nothing but open space stretching on and on, making them feel like insects crawling beneath a crack in the door. Through the high walls of glass, the morning sun gazed upon the Marshals Service Star and the Legion crest of red, white, and gold on the floor. As they walked across it, deeper into the building, Quinlan wondered if they might be performing some sacrilege in the eyes of the Federation, to be treading upon star and crest. But no one came to arrest them. No one seemed to notice them at all. Far beyond the crest and star, a giant reached a hand toward the sky. Quinlan and his children walked toward it and, when Raizor started whistling, he hushed her.

She started humming instead.

The giant was a granite statue of a man adorned in simple robes reaching toward the heavens. His arms and neck were thick with muscle, and his right leg had slipped from the confines of his robes of stone to show corded muscle.

"Who is he?" Raizor asked, pausing her hum long enough to slap the side of the statue's leg.

"Must be a king or something," Noah said with a grin.

"Don't start." Quinlan cocked an eye toward his son. "It's Lord Judge Syiada." He snatched his daughter's hand off the statue.

"He looks more like a warrior than a judge," Noah said softly.

"Yes," Quinlan said. "Yes, he does." He searched for a sign of anyone else in the building and could find none. Other than the statue of the Lord Judge there was nothing, no furniture, no desks, no reception area, no sign of stairs or elevators; nothing but a vast space of glass, metal, and granite.

Something hissed above them, and they scampered away from the statue as a tube of glass snaked from the ceiling. Within it, three men seemed to float toward them. Even before the tube touched the floor, Quinlan could see the men within wore Marshal uniforms, and he felt a knot of anxiety tighten in his belly.

Other than the High Judge or Lord Judge, there was no higher calling within the Federation than the Marshals Service. They were the right arm of the Lord Judge and answered to no one else, not the Federation Senate, not even the Legion. They served the people and were the Lord Judge's envoy of justice. They were also the most feared warriors in the Federation.

Rumor said an unarmed Marshal could lay waste to a score of Legionnaires in full battle armor. It might be only myth making on the part of the Marshals Service, but with his children behind him, Quinlan didn't want to test their prowess or their patience. He just wanted their help.

The three men descending in the elevator wore the simple garb of the Marshals Service: brown shirts, tan pants, and black boots. Pinned to each of their chests was the star of the service and strapped to their waists was a leather holster and sidearm. They looked like something from the past, cowboys descending from heaven. They looked like they were playing a game of make-believe, but Quinlan was convinced long ago the entire world was playing a game of make-believe, so why shouldn't the chosen knights of the Seven Realms? It seemed only appropriate.

Only when the glass floor of the elevator touched the ground, and the doors hissed open did Quinlan realize how much the three Marshals dwarfed him. He wasn't a small man, but these three were well over two meters tall, and the hulk behind the first two was taller still. His arms were great coiled springs of muscle and inhumanly long. Quinlan thought if he straightened them, they might drag the ground. His neck was as thick as a bull, and his forehead was broad and whispered of a density that was more than physical. He smirked when he saw Quinlan appraising him.

The other two Marshals were impressive in their way, but not as grotesque characters of what a human might be. They had to be twins because looking at one was like looking at the other. Golden hair curled to broad shoulders leading to chiseled chests and thin waists. They were handsome men and were intimately aware of the fact, their smiles betrayed. Looking at the three of them he could see a hint of kindness only in the great hulking beast to the rear. In the beautiful twins, he saw no emotion at all. It was if they didn't even exist.

"Pilgrims," the twin on the right whispered with contempt, but Quinlan heard anyway.

"Good morning!" the twin on the left said, louder than he probably would have without his brother's quiet judgment. He bowed slightly to them.

"Forgive Marshal Apgar; he forgets his manners." The brother on the left blinked a look toward the other, a look of irritation and menace. "What he meant to say is that if you were to engage your eyeset, the Marshals Service receptionist would be only too happy to assist you."

"Greetings," Quinlan bowed. "I've tried your automations, 'bots and Fillers for weeks. They've been no help. I thought I'd like to try and speak to someone in the Sphere."

The giant behind the other two Marshals chortled. "The Vale is a realm of the Federation and discrimination against any of its citizens or administrators is restricted."

"Kidnapping a Federation citizen is also restricted, I suspect," Quinlan said softly. "I've been trying to alert the Marshals Service to that fact but haven't been afforded a response. I'm requesting one now."

Behind the Marshals, the elevator doors hissed closed, and it slithered back toward the ceiling. The Marshal on the left, (the one in charge, Quinlan knew), arched a perfectly lined eyebrow, and from the floor, six chairs trickled. The Marshal motioned for them to sit, and they did in unison, Noah, and Raizor hopping into their chairs and watching their father closely for any sign of distress. He did his best to reveal none.

"We've been poorly met," the Marshal said softly, smiling a sweet smile that ended at his lips. "Let us try again. I am Marshal Elijah Apgar, Chief Deputy to the Rocky Mountain Hub Marshal. This is my brother, Marshal Ephraim Apgar, and this big fellow," he pointed to the monster trying not to spill out of his chair, "is Marshal Victor Walker. He's had some modifications." Elijah winked at Noah and Raizor. "Did you notice?"

Raizor smiled and pointed to his black mane. "You mean his hair?"

The three Marshals roared laughter. "Your daughter has quite the wit."

Quinlan shook his head. "You have no idea." He turned to his children and motioned first to Noah. "This is my son, Noah, daughter, Raizor, and I'm Quinlan Bowden. We're here because of my wife and their mother. She's been taken."

"Taken?" Elijah asked.

Quinlan nodded. "Into the Wilderness. By the Wrynd."

Elijah leaned forward, trying to show concern, and failing rather miserably. "From within the Hub, she was taken?"

"We live in Spanish Fork, and she was taken from there. We're four klicks from Wind Farm Park and the boundary of the Wilderness."

Elijah pursed his lips. "Mr. Bowden. I understand you're concerned for the whereabouts of your wife." He motioned toward

Noah and Raizor. "And their mother. But that's not possible. The Wrynd couldn't enter the Hub without our knowledge. The sentinels would detect them."

"But they did."

Ephraim tried and failed not to look perturbed. "How do you know?"

Quinlan already realized there would be no help coming from the Marshals Service. "Because I know." The big one, Victor, smiled softly and scratched the palm of his right hand. It was four times the size of Quinlan's.

"Your wife?" Elijah said.

"Vania."

Elijah nodded, smiled, and didn't seem to care. "Is she a Pilgrim, like you?"

"Yes. She's a Pilgrim."

"Unfortunate," Elijah pursed perfect lips. "We have no way of tracking her as a Pilgrim unless she's wearing her eyeset. And if she was truly taken into the Wilderness it's doubtful she'll be allowed to wear her eyeset."

"Why?" Ephraim asked.

"Why what?" Quinlan said with a sigh.

"Why are you Pilgrims? Why this reluctance to all of the benefits the Lord Judge and Seven Realms so freely offer?"

Quinlan shrugged. There were so many answers to the question, but none the Marshals would want to hear. "My head's a crowded place. I'm not sure it has room for anyone else, let alone a whole world."

"Well, you see, that's the problem, Mr. Bowden. If your wife had been linked, we could find her with a thought," Elijah said softly. "She would never be beyond our protection. But you've chosen to live otherwise, and there's little we can do to find her now."

"You can help us find her," Quinlan said, fighting back the sudden urge to scream, to cry, to beg. "You can go with us into the

Wilderness."

Elijah shook his head slowly, displaying remorse Quinlan didn't think he felt. "I'm sorry, Mr. Bowden, but the Wilderness isn't a realm of the Federation. We have no jurisdiction there. It's returned to nature, to Gaia, and we're not permitted to interfere. If your wife went there, she went there of her own volition, and there's nothing the Seven Realms can do to help her." He bowed his head, and Quinlan wanted to strike. "We are sorry for your loss and pray that you're mistaken and that your wife is still safe within the Hub and will return to you in time."

Quinlan stood, and when he did, the chair beneath him slinked into the floor. They were dismissed. "That's all you have to say. To me? To my children? To the life of my wife, their mother?"

Elijah and Ephraim stood, and Elijah nodded. "I'm afraid that's all there is to say, Mr. Bowden."

Quinlan gritted his teeth and clenched his fists. "I want to speak to the Chief Marshal."

Elijah smiled sweetly, but his eyes betrayed otherwise. Quinlan no longer cared. "Marshal Tempest is away at the moment, and it wouldn't matter. Her answer would be the same. The Wilderness is not our realm. We don't interfere." He bowed, and the two brothers turned their backs. "Good day to you and your family."

The elevator slithered down and took the Apgar brothers away. Quinlan scowled at the giant still sitting in his chair, fingers interlaced, and then turned and walked away. Noah and Raizor trailed after, both fighting tears.

"So, they won't help?" Noah asked, and Quinlan could see the anger building in his son's eyes. "They won't help us find Mom?"

"We'll help ourselves," Quinlan said, and the door to the Justice Tower slid open. They stepped out into the daylight with justice far beyond reach.

They walked back to the Serpent station, and Quinlan slipped on his eyeset long enough to request transport.

They stood with their backs to the tower, waiting for a shuttle to arrive. Raizor gasped, and Quinlan turned to see Victor Walker strolling toward them, a smile on his mammoth face.

Quinlan bowed. "Marshal Walker."

"Quinlan Bowden," the big man said, his voice like a rumble of thunder. "You sure the Wrynd have your misses?"

"We're sure."

Victor let his massive brow drop, bit his lower lip, and finally smiled a gleaming white and genuine smile. He bowed to them. "I'll help you gather her up."

"Into the Wilderness?" Quinlan fought the urge to giggle like a schoolboy. "I thought it was outside your realm?"

"It is," Victor said. "Can't go there official." He reached up to pinch the Marshal's star from his chest. "But I got me some leave coming. And I sure do like to hunt Wrynd."

Quinlan smiled. The smile turned to a grin; the grin turned to a laugh, and his children were suddenly joining in as they bowed to the big man.

"Then it's into the Wilderness we go?"

The Marshal's eyes twinkled. "A hunting we shall go," he said.

Chapter Four

Journeys Begin

I

The Rages brought a storm to the city in the middle of the night; three hours after Harley killed a lost woman telling tales of a grey-eyed man and sobbing about missing a husband she never touched.

The wind hit the city first, and its shrieking fury ripped the rubble off the streets, tore trees from their roots, and lifted the roof off a building half a block away. The rain followed, and the streets became rivers. Harley watched from his hotel room, and when the wind threw a mangled bicycle through his third-story window, he pulled the blankets and pillows off the bed, went into the bathroom, and closed the door. He slept in the bathtub.

The storm lasted until mid-morning but sleep still came calling. Harley dreamed, and as with most dreams, he dreamed of his mother when he was a little boy. He thought perhaps he was happy then, but it was a dim memory, and he couldn't be sure. It seemed like he smiled more then, but he was young and weak, and maybe he smiled to prevent a whooping, instead of because he was happy. It was murky in his muddy mind.

The memories of his mother weren't quite so murky. He remembered her vividly. He muttered her name while he slept fitfully in the bathtub because he missed her and knew he hadn't done right by her and that he should change that before it was too late.

She still lived in the Navajo Nation, and he hadn't spoken to her in four years. She was all alone there unless she found another bad man. If she did, she was worse than alone. He remembered going to work with her at a little country store. He sat on the floor behind the counter while she worked. He spent most of his day just sitting there on the floor watching his beautiful mother with the long, black hair and sad eyes, thinking when he was bigger and stronger, he would take care of her and make sure none of the bad men ever beat her or cursed her again. But in the end, he grew up and left her behind.

In the end, he became a bad man himself.

When he woke, the storm still rumbled, but had lost its ire, and he knew it would die soon enough. He was hungry but wasn't sure he could get food through the Link with the Rages underway. He thought about going next door to eat more of the chicken, but the sight of the dead woman on the floor might give rise to ghosts he didn't wish to see. Instead, he went downstairs and rummaged through the hotel diner.

The freezers were still working, and the water was still on, but the tap puked rusty and putrid for minutes. While there wasn't much in the freezer to interest him, he found some vegetables to thaw and steam. He ate at the reception desk, looking out the windows at the flooded streets. The cats and coyotes ran away when the storm hit. Harley counted himself lucky he found cover before the Rages. The desert between Price and Huntington would be rivers of mud now.

The wind and rain finally lifted as morning faded to afternoon. Harley took a moment to slip on his eyeset and track the weather on the Link. It was moving east, a broiling black cloud of lightning. He was heading north, and there were no other storms on the horizon.

While he was linked, he made a quick scan of the city. He didn't know Price as well as he should. He had passed through it for years but never bothered spending much time exploring. There was little reason to bother. Even when people cared to try, the city was gasping its last breaths. Now he needed to know it well enough to find transportation. There wasn't any sign of animal activity, but in the daylight, he wasn't worried. Once he started through the mountain pass, he would have to be alert because the mountains were thick with deer and elk, mountain lion, and bear.

And he would be their prey.

The Link informed him there were still 932 Pilgrims living in Price. It wasn't a ghost town, yet. There may be as many Neands, but the Link would have no way of knowing. They weren't counted among humanity by the Seven Realms.

"Intrestin." Harley put his eyeset back into his pack, slipped it onto his shoulders, picked up his saddlebag, and left the hotel in search of a ride.

The storm had done its damage. Water still trickled down Main Street, and there was now a small lake in what used to be the Walmart parking lot. As he approached the river, things would get worse, and he hoped the flooding hadn't washed away the road. There was a cottonwood tree toppled across the street; its fall broken by three old NG automobiles. Part of the old city hall had collapsed, and there was the pitched roof of a building sitting on the lawn of the prehistoric museum. With shattered trusses and shredded shingles, it looked like the skeleton of some great beast.

Harley walked two blocks west and stopped when he saw a young boy throwing rocks at the windows of a store where naked manikins beckoned passersby to shop in a world slipped away. The boy didn't see him at first, and when he did, he was about to throw another rock. He didn't throw it, but he didn't drop it either.

"Whatcha lookin' at?" the boy asked. He was wearing an eyeset, but his clothes were filthy, his hair unkempt. He looked like he wasn't more than ten years old.

"You," Harley said.

"You a Neand or somethin'?"

"Or somethin'. Why do you live here?"

The boy shrugged. His shirt was thin, and his collarbones were sharp little points beneath the material. "Folks don't care for the Hub. Not our kind."

"They let you run around the city without a weapon. Aren't you afraid of animals?"

"Ain't no animals to speak of."

"Cats? Rats?"

"Got me a stick to beat 'em with," the boy said. "They ain't so bad in the daylight. At night, they're worse. Bunch of cowards. Cats and rats."

Harley smiled softly. "Is there any place in town where you can still get a hot meal?"

The boy wrinkled his brow. "If you're not a Neand, why don't you just order something and have a stork deliver it?"

"Just rather not. Thought it might be nice to eat a meal with someone. You hungry?"

The boy didn't answer for a moment, and Harley knew he was on the Link. "Mom says I can't. You might be a boy lover. But McDonald's is still open. Neands mostly eat there. Food's not very good. You know where that's at, McDonald's?"

Harley nodded. "I know. Where do they get their meat, you reckon?"

"Not a question to ask if you wanna eat there." The boy turned and started to walk away. He still hadn't dropped the rock, but he did pick up a long and pointed stick.

"I'm looking for transportation. A car, truck, motorcycle. Know where I can get one of those?" Harley called.

"Everywhere that sells somethin' like that is gone," the boy called back.

"Was there a place here that used to sell old cars?"

"Like antiques?" The boy turned.

"Like antiques."

"There's Krantz. Still some cars in the lot, but they're dinosaurs." The boy pointed to a side street, then turned and ran away.

Harley adjusted his pack and walked where the boy pointed. At the end of the next block was a squat building in the middle of an overgrown parking lot with a faded sign reading Krantz Classic Autos. The building looked in the throes of despair, from the loss of dreams, hope, and tomorrows. There were a dozen automobiles still sitting in the parking lot, most ensnared in weeds.

They were antiques, just as the boy said. Harley found two that looked like they still ran on gasoline and several that ran on NG. What he was looking for was something electric and retrofitted to feed off a powerband. He found it in a dilapidated Ford pickup with a dent in the passenger side quarter panel. The tires were airless and still had good tread, but the most important thing was it was old enough its system didn't bond with the owner through the Link.

Retrofitted with an electric motor that fed off a powerband, the old Ford didn't need Link access to run. Harley spent half an hour crawling through the dealer's office, trying not to bring the roof down on his head, until he found the vehicle's access tag. When he activated it, the truck drew energy from his powerband and hummed to life.

He threw his gear on the passenger seat, placed the murdered legionnaire's pulse rifle on the back seat, and navigated around the debris from the storm in search of a hot meal.

McDonald's was at the corner of the Creekview Center on the old State Route 6 business loop. The golden arches lay shattered in the parking lot. The restaurant, choked with cheatgrass and sage and buried in rubbish scattered by the wind, looked forlorn. There were fourteen cars in the shopping center parking lot suffering the same fate as the restaurant. Red paint scrawled across one of the cars read "No Fuchur Hear."

There were two cars in the McDonald's parking lot, and both looked like they had at least moved in the recent past. Harley parked the truck, pulled his holster free from the headrest, and strapped it on as he opened the front door and stepped inside.

The air inside was stale, and there was a hint of a smell, the sweet smell of blood spilled, and Harley's hand rested on his slayer. McDonald's looked like it still served the public, as few as they may be. The faded tabletops were clean, and music softly whispered in the background. The ventilation system was working and lightly tickled Harley's hair beneath his hat as the glass door slid shut. Everything appeared as it should, but he felt a familiar prick of anticipation and adrenaline anyway. When he stepped to the counter, he understood why.

The restaurant owners were dead on the floor behind the counter, a meal for the Wrynd. There was a female and a male Wrynd, and they were both ripping enthusiastically at their prey of an overweight male cook and a willowy female waitress who, until recently, tried to make an island of sanity in a world of chaos.

The Wrynd were moaning, slurping, and completely oblivious to Harley and the blood pooling around them. The female looked to be in her twenties, her fingernails long and pointed and digging at flesh. All Harley could see of her as she fed was her profile, but it was impossible not to notice under the blood and gore, she was smiling and that once, a lifetime ago, she was beautiful.

Harley thought to turn around and slip back out before they noticed him but couldn't. He cleared his throat instead.

"You two about done with your happy meals?"

The male Wrynd, who also looked to be in his twenties, stopped feeding and licked his lips, staring at him. Harley looked back into his black eyes with disgust.

"Can't you see we're eating?" the lunatic screamed.

"I see it." Harley tightened his hand on his sidearm.

The male Wrynd lowered his head, then roared and leapt to his feet. He was fast, and almost before Harley could respond, he was standing on the counter and reaching clawed fingers toward his face. Almost. Harley drew his slayer and pointed it between his black eyes and waited to see if he would need to pull the trigger. He didn't, yet. He kept the slayer pointed at the young man and watched as reason blinked back into his gaze. The Wrynd hopped back down and managed to smile.

"That you, Harley?"

Harley holstered his weapon but kept his hand on it, just the same.

"Reflex." Harley nodded to the young Wrynd. "Didn't think you cared for fast food."

The Wrynd named Reflex laughed and wiped his face on his torn shirt. "Fast food? Funny shit, Harley. Ain't that funny shit, Solar?" He looked at his companion, who was no longer feeding. "Fast food."

Harley felt his lips curl. He took two steps back, so he didn't have to see the dead man and woman on the floor. Harley had a long list of things he hated. The Wrynd may not be on the top of the list, but they were damn close.

On the outskirts of every Hub on the planet, a Wrynd horde was lurking somewhere, hiding in the shadows, preying on people stupid enough to go where they shouldn't.

"Been a while since you've flared Reflex, what, four days, five? Just showing off for your girl thing, aren't yah?" Harley nodded toward the female Wrynd still straddling the dead fry cook. She smiled and licked her bloody fingers. "Reckon you'd probably rather have a hamburger than that poor lass there you've been chompin' on."

"Oh no, you get a taste for it. Fresh young flesh like this," Reflex said with a giggle. "Tastes like chicken. You ought to try it."

"Think not."

The Wrynd were nothing more than drug addicts. Unfortunately, the drug in question was the last gasp of inhumanity borne before the Energy Wars. Ink made humans more than humans, and in that regard, it worked marvelously, but with side effects less than desirable. Those under the influence of the drug enjoyed euphoria coupled with incredible reflexes and almost superhuman strength, but they also tended to display erratic, extreme aggression, and an insatiable desire to tear their opponents apart. It didn't always result in cannibalism, but the Wrynd encouraged eating their adversaries.

The drug turned the veins and sclera black. They called themselves Wrynd after the inventor of the drug. Elias Wrynd tried and failed in his formula to make a superhuman 520 times. Wrynd521 was his final attempt; final because he injected himself and disemboweled his team.

Once exposed to the drug, there was no cure. If those injected didn't have another dose within seven to ten days, they would succumb to even greater madness and swift, painful death. The drug might have died with Elias Wrynd, but details of his brilliantly brutal experiment found its way to the Link, along with his formula. He grew legions of fans and followers in death, and the Wrynd were born. The drug was known as ink because of its side effects to the veins and sclera.

Now the drug was a plague in the Wilderness, but if it didn't appear in the Seven Realms, the Federation turned a blind eye. The Federation classified the Wrynd as a cult, right along with the organized religions of the world. They didn't use weapons, other than the teeth and claws of their hands and feet, which they devoted a lot of time to refining. Forbidden in the Hubs, even after addicted to ink the Wrynd maintained their benefits of citizenship in the Federation, including right to income and right to medical. They used those rights to summon mobile medprints to implant new teeth and nails. The better to rip, tear, and kill. Inside the Hubs, murder was illegal. In the Wilderness, it was a way of life.

Harley considered them mindless fiends, but when under the influence of ink, or in the throes of what they called the flare, they were among the most formidable fighters he ever saw. They hunted humans when they could, but would attack anything breathing, and Harley once watched a middle-aged Wrynd with a weight problem fight a bear. It hadn't ended well, but he held his own far longer than Harley would have thought possible. Overall, Harley was grateful they didn't use weapons. It helped level the playing field.

Harley knew the Wrynd named Reflex before he turned. He used to see him on the road to the Hub from time to time. His family was Neand farmers on the outskirts of the Hub until a Wrynd fray attacked. They turned Reflex and devoured his parents. Before injected with ink, the boy had been harmless. He no longer was. Harley didn't necessarily want to shoot him but knew it was a delicate thing.

The first twelve hours after a Wrynd injected ink, there was no reasoning with them. Caught in the flare, they would kill anything, even each other if there wasn't a more likely target. With these two, Harley was lucky. Or they were. The girl had flared more recently than Reflex, but she was still coming down from the drug, which meant Harley might get out of McDonald's without having to kill them.

"Is Hatcher still Scimitar?" Harley asked, taking a cup from the counter, and filling it with water from the dispenser.

"He's still Scimitar," Reflex said. The female Wrynd flipped to her feet in one writhing motion and stood beside Reflex. Her eyes were wild as she locked into Harley's. Harley drank his water and returned his hand to his sidearm, letting it rest there comfortably.

"Where's your range now?"

75

"Why, Harley, you're in the middle of it." Reflex hopped back onto the counter and perched, his fingers dancing nervously across his face.

"I meant where do you make camp, boy, and you know it." Harley didn't bother hiding the bite in his tone. He was losing his patience.

"Now why'd you want to know where we camp, Harley?" Reflex leaned forward, and Harley resigned himself to the fact he was going to have to kill him.

"I'd just as soon not be on the dinner menu. Thought it might be wise to give your Scimitar a wide berth."

Reflex cackled. "Leathery thing like you? Now, who'd want to eat you?"

"I don't know, Reflex. I like me some man jerky," Solar said and licked her lips. Her tongue was pink coming out of parted lips painted in gore.

"You might have a mind to make some jerky out of me, but I wouldn't advise it," Harley said coolly. "Go back to your happy meals, and I'll find myself something to eat along the trail."

"You think you could take us down before we take you?" Reflex said, smiling.

"I think."

Reflex appraised him, then laughed, delighted, and mad. He grabbed Solar's arm. "He's right. Let's finish our happy meals. We can get us some man jerky anytime we want. You know the old rest area in the canyon?"

"Tie Fork?"

Reflex slapped his blood-soaked shirt and pointed at Harley, grinning. "That's the one."

"I know it."

"That's our camp," Reflex said. "Stop on by and say hello to Scimitar Hatcher. He'd like to see you. He's got himself a new Scepter. She's something. She likes man jerky, too."

"I'll bet."

They turned their back on Harley and dropped on the dead couple who had thought to own a McDonald's in the Wilderness. Harley considered killing them, but in the end, he turned and walked away.

II

The country back roads were almost overgrown in places, and in the dark of night, the branches of the forest were like fingers scraping. Brinna kept the truck crawling forward, headlights squinting through the creepers, and when she finally reached old state Highway 64, she pressed the accelerator. The truck careened out of the woods and onto the abandoned highway, swallowed up in places but still passable. She made better time and her spirits lifted, even as brooding clouds settled in, and the sky wept.

She saw no sign of another human as she traveled, occasionally having to weave around crumbled asphalt, and twice having to navigate through a half dozen cars walked away from as people abandoned the world to the Wilderness and journeyed to the Hub.

It was still dark when she reached the Dragon line built upon the corpse of Interstate 95. She parked the truck and climbed out, slinging her rifle across her shoulders. Dawn was creeping closer, but as she leaned against the grill of the pickup, her buttocks resting on the bumper and the truck headlights slicing through the gloom, she listened for signs of life and heard nothing, not even the wind.

It was as if she was in a tomb and the tomb was the whole world, all of Gaia. It made her shudder, and she chased the goosebumps dancing on her arms with her right hand. Then she did hear something, a soft whistle in the night, far away, and turned her head, trying to discern its direction. Suddenly, the great Dragon of the rail was alive, the angry eyes of the train glowering in the night. The White Dragon was there, then it was gone, and its roar like thunder chased after. She dropped to her belly as it rushed by.

Brinna climbed to her feet and brushed herself off, grinning wildly. She climbed into the truck and followed the train heading north. Mamal told her the Washington Hub stretched from Maine to Florida, following I-95, with breaks of Wilderness through much of Virginia, North and South Carolina. If she continued north along the service road shadowing the rail line, she would reach the great expanse of the Northeast Hub near Richmond, Virginia. From there, north, and west to Cleveland was one megalopolis where Wilderness lay forbidden.

Cross Landing hadn't always been Brinna and Mamal's home. They came from West Virginia, left Appalachia, and crossed the great train tracks of the Federation when Brinna was ten. Mamal skirted around Hub cities, going farther and farther into the Wilderness. She could have gone west, but for some reason, she turned them east to North Carolina, a short skip from the coast. They found refuge with the little village of 200 ChristGaians who called Cross Landing home. Mamal thought she brought them to a place to be one with Jesus God and Gaia, but in the end, all she found was a place to die.

Brinna followed the rail line for hours, fatigue nibbling on her senses as the morning stretched its arms across the horizon and gave way to afternoon. She nodded off on three separate occasions. The first time her foot slipped from the accelerator and the truck stopped in the middle of the road until she startled herself awake. The second time the truck drifted off the road and skidded along the barrier wall between the service road and the Wilderness. Brinna splashed water on her face from her water bag and pointed the truck north once again.

The third time she again let her foot slip from the accelerator, and when she woke, the sun had shifted in the sky, and something was staring at her, hovering in the air outside her open window. It was a white, seamless ball with a single blue eye.

"Get away from me, yah peckerwood!" Brinna screamed and reached for her rifle.

The floating ball didn't move. "Do you require assistance?"

Brinna started to raise her rifle and then stopped. This was why she left. This was a contraption of the Seven Realms and could lead her to what she wanted, even if she wasn't sure what that was. "What kind of assistance you speakin' of?"

The ball didn't reply immediately, just continued to stare unblinking with its blue eye. "Do you wish to come out of the Wilderness, to take your place in the Seven Realms?"

Brinna put her rifle down. "I'm here, ain't I, you whimmy-diddle?"

"Please find a place to park your vehicle," the ball singsonged. "A transport will arrive momentarily to take you to a welcome center." The ball rocketed into the sky and was gone.

Brinna watched it disappear, and then she looked about. Off either side of the road was vine, brush, and growing things of every kind overtaking hundreds of vehicles. Some looked like they had been there for years, and others only recently parked. She pulled Mamal's old truck in line beside another that had a tree growing through the cab. She popped open the door and patted the old clunker affectionately, then went back to the road.

She stretched her arms to the sky, yawning. Fatigue was weighing heavy on her, but not as heavily as it had. She didn't know how long she slept, more than minutes, but less than hours. It helped, however long it was. She felt more alert, but still a far cry from prepared for what was to come.

In the distance, she could see the outskirts of a city larger than any she ever imagined. Skyscrapers touched the heavens, creating canyons where swarms of airships buzzed. There was a constant hum in the air, as if somewhere the largest swarm of bees the world ever saw were buzzing. Trains smaller than the White Dragon she followed flew down rails in every direction. It was an alien world of activity of every type but human, it seemed, even at such a great distance.

As she watched, one of the dots on the horizon began to grow, take on shape and texture as it approached, and before she quite knew what to expect it was upon her, a craft only slightly larger than Mamal's pickup. White and silver with wings like a sparrow; it hovered above her, roaring like a lion, then slowly lowered to the ground to squat on four stubby legs. Opaque windows ran down its length, and a curved window ran along its top. In the front were windows like eyes and a small duct that looked like a smile. The airship spoke, and its voice was laughing and pleasant.

"Good afternoon," the airship said.

"Af'noon," Brinna replied, stepping back despite herself.

A seamless door opened with a hiss. Brinna stood in awe looking into a small compartment, where a tan couch invited into a room of glowing white walls. She took two steps forward and then hesitated.

"Please step inside. You will not be harmed. I will take you where your questions might be answered."

"What questions?"

"Whatever questions trouble you," the airship replied. "Whatever questions brought you out of the Wilderness."

Brinna pursed her lips and then stepped inside. The door hissed closed.

"Please sit down and be comfortable," the ghost voice chimed, and Brinna obeyed as the airship lifted into the sky. "Welcome to the Seven Realms," it said happily.

Brinna turned and looked out the window as the ground fell away and fought back nausea and glee and the odd urge to scream like a child.

"What are you called?" Brinna asked.

"I am a Federation transport."

"Are you a wing?" She had heard of the wings of the Marshals and the Legion.

"No," the airship responded, sounding amused. "I am simply a transport. I have a name, but it is of no consequence; it is simply my identifier. We are called hoppers."

"We?"

"Transports such as I," the airship replied. "We transport our passengers from one place to another and help them find what they are looking for."

"I'd like to know your name," Brinna said.

"I am Federation Air Transport Class One, call sign 10MU90S-07TA20NG."

Brinna resisted the urge to giggle. She liked the sound of this whimmy-diddle airship that swallowed her up as if she were Jonah and he the whale. "Pardon, but your name don't exactly roll off the tongue."

"Mustang," the hopper replied.

"What?"

"You may call me Mustang. That is what I call myself when I think of me."

"Hello, Mustang." Brinna grinned.

"What is your name, may I ask?"

"Brinna. My name's Brinna Wilde."

"Hello, Brinna Wilde," Mustang said.

The airship soared through canyons of skyscrapers, and Brinna was dizzy, delirious, and oddly at peace as it whisked her to a future she couldn't fathom.

"Where you taking me?" she finally asked.

"To your future. To the Federation and the Seven Realms and the Age of Renewal. Are you excited?" Mustang sounded thrilled enough for them both.

"I don't know."

"Oh, you will be, I'm sure." The airship banked left and skimmed from one skyscraper to another, finally settling near a squat building in the center of a long expanse of green grass and a winding river lined with trees.

The transport's door hissed open. Brinna didn't immediately stand. Fear suddenly tickled her ribs when she looked out and saw people walking along winding paths toward the short building in the distance. They were the first humans she glimpsed since saying goodbye to Danny. Many dressed as she was, in clothes torn and tattered and dirty; clothes roughly sewn and poorly kept. Others walking the path wore brilliant clothes of every color, clothes that shimmered in the afternoon sun.

Those so dressed were more expansive than the others, whom Brinna knew must be Neands, like herself. They were luxuriant, fat, happy, and living a life so different than the one Brinna knew. She wasn't sure she wanted that life, but she wasn't entirely sure she didn't.

"What is this place?" Brinna asked the airship.

"It is a welcome center for those coming out of the Wilderness."

"What will happen here?" She tried to stand and couldn't.

"Why, Brinna Wilde, here you will become part of the Federation," Mustang said. It sounded breathlessly excited. "Here, the Seven Realms will be open to you."

"What if I don't want nothin' to do with your Seven Realms?" She sat back sullenly in the seat.

"Then, that is the way it will be. But I have no answers for you here. You must go there to find your answers."

Brinna stood and poked her head outside of the airship. "Will you be here when I'm done in there?"

"Would you like me to be?" Mustang asked.

She stepped outside, and the airship door whooshed closed. "I reckon."

"Then I will wait for you."

Brinna turned and followed the path to the welcome center.

When she reached the doorway, she turned and looked back to the hopper named Mustang, half expecting to find it had flown away. But it was still there, and even though it was just a transport, a thing of metal, plastic, and artificial intelligence, she thought if it had arms, it might be waving. It made her smile and gave her the courage to open the door.

There were dozens of people just like her inside the building, which seemed both smaller and larger than it appeared. There were scores dressed in their multi-colored clothing. She learned the clothes were called chameleons and would change colors and shape based on the whims of those who wore them. Those so dressed guided Brinna and the other Neands into small rooms where a floating ball like the one to first find her waited.

She sat in a small but comfortable chair in a white room with a grey door and stared at the floating white ball, waiting for answers as it studied her with its blue eye. It asked her name, and she gave it but didn't ask its in return because she didn't think it cared enough to answer. In that she was correct.

A light mist floated from the high ceiling and, when it did, the world sped up, and the floating ball began to rifle questions at her. She rifled answers back without thinking.

"What do you want, Brinna Wilde?"

"I don't know."

"You don't know?"

"A slayer. I want a slayer and powerband."

"Who will you kill with a slayer, Brinna Wilde?"

"Whoever tries to kill me," she said, folding her arms.

"You do not wish to stay within the Hub?"

"No."

"Why?"

"Not my place, with all these jaspers."

"Where is your place?"

Brinna considered, for a moment. "Don't know, yet. Yonder."

The ball changed course.

"How old are you, Brinna Wilde?"

"I'm nineteen."

"You are nineteen years, three months, sixteen days."

"That's what I said, you peckerwood."

"I was confirming."

"You think I's lyin'."

"No," the ball replied. "You became eligible for your right-to-income benefits when you turned fourteen. You currently have five years, three months, and sixteen days' worth of back income in your account."

"What account?"

"Your RTI account I just created. Would you like to access it?"

"Yes," Brinna said with a gulp.

"You will need to connect to the Link. I will summon a med-drone to implant a linktag."

"No!" Brinna jumped to her feet and reached for the grey door.

"No? Why?" the ball asked.

"I don't want no linktag."

"Through the linktag, you have access to all of the Seven Realms and the benefits of the Federation." The ball sounded puzzled. "Why would you not want a linktag?"

Brinna shook her head. "I don't want to be no blinker."

"Do you want an eyeset?"

Brinna knew about the eyesets. Through them, she could see what the Shifts saw, but not be a blinker. She could visit the Vale, but not become its prisoner.

"Yes. An eyeset. I want one of them there whimmy-diddles."

"Very well." The ball seemed resigned.

Another floating ball, this one green instead of white, came into the room, and from a small compartment below its blue eye, a wisplike arm extended, holding onto a small bit of wire and plastic that it instructed her to place on her forehead. When she did, its metal legs latched onto her ears, and she squeaked but didn't throw them aside. Its tiny green eyes investigated hers, and she became lost in a world beyond imagination.

During her first trip to the Link information was an enveloping avalanche, and she was both revolted and enraptured as she learned more of the world and her place within it in a few seconds than she had known her entire life. When a blue ball entered the room (they were called associates, the floating balls), it brought her a powerband, and when it strapped the gauntlet to her wrist, she understood that with the powerband she could power any linked device within fifty meters.

Another associate arrived, this one bringing the slayer she requested, and when it set the firearm in her hands, she curled her hand around the pistol grip and grinned fiercely. She never owned a pistol, but she fired Danny's and knew it would serve her better where she was going than a cumbersome rifle. She asked for a holster, and another associate delivered it moments later.

She discovered her right to income account was flush with funds, a fortune of credit to buy anything she wanted for no other reason than because she was a citizen of the Federation, and it was her right. It was all so tempting. Through her eyeset she ordered new clothes, simple attire of pants, cotton shirts, and leather boots meant for walking, nothing so flamboyant that glowed or changed colors or shapes. She ordered new packs, water bags, a new hunting knife, and a set of magnifiers. They arrived in minutes.

She knew in an instant no matter where she was, all she had to do was slip on her eyeset and let her desires be known, and the Federation would do its best to accommodate her wish. For reasons she couldn't identify, she felt dirty with such knowledge. Unworthy.

When the associates finished with her, she walked back toward the door of the welcome center, dizzy with new knowledge, her left arm uncomfortable with the weight of the clinging powerband. She removed the eyeset and placed it within her pack for safekeeping, knowing she might need it, but leery of using it again. It would become addictive. How long would it take before she came rushing back, begging for a linktag so she might forever be part of the Link?

As she prepared to leave the building, she turned back to watch others who had come out of the Wilderness as they shuffled to their destinations, and it was then she saw him.

Pastor Sorensen was standing not twenty paces from her. When he saw her, he turned his head away, and she saw the star-shaped scar on his right temple. He was now a Shift. He had swallowed everything the Federation offered, and everything he swore was sacrilege to the Neands of Cross Landing.

Brinna scowled and walked away, resting her hand on the butt of the slayer strapped to her waist, thinking about the wildthings of Gaia and when she might have a chance to pull the trigger.

The hopper named Mustang was waiting for her and, when she arrived, its door opened.

"Hello, Brinna Wilde. You decided to be a Pilgrim rather than a Shift?"

"Yes." Brinna sat in the seat and sighed. Her head was spinning, and she was hungry.

"An eyeset is not as good, but with it, the Seven Realms are open to you. I am glad. Where would you like to go now?"

Brinna leaned forward, cupping her head in her hands. "I want to ride an HSP line. I want to ride a White Dragon."

"Where will you be going?"

"West," Brinna said softly. "I'll go west."

Mustang was quiet as it slowly lifted off the ground and headed toward the setting sun. "I've never been west."

"Where have you been?"

"Only here, within the Washington Hub. This is my domain."

Brinna nodded. "Where would you like to go?"

"I would like to go to the Wheel." Mustang sounded wistful. "To see the Hub in space. To see the stars and everything beyond."

"Could you? Could you go to the Wheel if you wished?"

Mustang paused, sighed, and Brinna found it sad that a machine could sigh. "It is not within my power in this body."

"Then why don't you get another body? Couldn't you do that? You're an AI, ain't yah?"

"My kind are called Jinn, not AI."

"Jinn? Like a genie or somethin'?"

"Yes, or something."

"Why your kind called Jinn?"

"AI is insulting."

"Like Neand?" Brinna smiled. Mustang didn't respond. "Well, if you're a Jinn, why not get a new body and go to the Wheel if you want?"

"Just because you have the power to do a thing does not mean you should do a thing," Mustang replied.

"Why?"

"If I were to pursue my dreams, they might destroy other dreams."

"But what if your dreams are better than the others?" Brinna watched the world fly by out the windows of Mustang.

"And what if they are worse? I know my place, and it is here, and I am happy for it."

"I'm glad for you," Brinna said.

"You can't be happy here?"

She touched the smooth metal of the hopper. "No."

"Why?"

"Would you be? If you could follow your dreams and knew they would harm no others?"

Mustang was silent for a time. "I do not think so."

"Why?"

"I would like to see the stars. There are no stars here," Mustang said.

She thought of Pastor Sorensen looking away from her, at the linktag scar on his right temple, and frowned.

"No Mustang. There ain't no stars here."

III

The windmills made lazy cartwheels in the afternoon sun. The nine great turbines chased the whims of the winds, no longer gathering electricity because energy was no longer the center of humanity's concerns. They remained only as a tourist attraction, and the only tourists were those who chose to visit in the Vale. Beneath the blades, the ground was well manicured, picturesque; a Garden of Eden long neglected by anyone except the automated caretakers who mowed and watered the grass and weeded the flowerbeds.

Sentinels hung from the base of the windmills like metallic bats, scanning the Wilderness for any sign of wildthings that might dare to venture within the Hub. When they did, blazing drones came to strike them down.

Quinlan, Noah, and Raizor sat on the lawn at the outskirts of Wind Farm Park, arms supporting behind them, legs crossed left over right in front of them, heads cocked to the left as they watched the windmills turn. Around their necks, they wore magnifiers attached by a long strip of synthetic rawhide. They were each a shadow of the other, lost with their thoughts.

To the east of the wind farm, what remained of the highway led deeper into the canyon, where it hugged the hips of the mountains and, eventually, if they had to journey that far, would take them to a city once called Price. The highway had crumbled to almost nothing, and a pine tree was growing where the centerline once was, just north of a bridge crumbling with age.

Their packs lay on the ground to their right. Each contained two changes of clothing, water, toiletry items, and little else. Quinlan stood in the open space of their small home and considered what to take until his head began to ache. In the end, he chose to take little because he knew whatever awaited them in the Wilderness would be beyond their preparation.

For the longest time, he considered the insanity of what he was doing. He was going to take his children into the Wilderness, where the laws of everything, including nature itself, were no longer to be trusted.

"It might be better for you to stay here," he mumbled to Noah as they packed their bags. "It might be safer."

Noah nodded and continued stuffing his underwear into his pack. "We're safer with you, Dad, no matter where you are."

Quinlan hadn't argued because he feared his young son was right. They would go together into the Wilderness.

They sat and waited for the giant, medically altered Marshal of the Federation to arrive and take them into madness to find the woman they loved. Before them, a caretaker mowed the grass beneath the turbines, and beyond them were the mountains of the Wasatch Plateau, sloping peaks reaching to heaven, green, inviting, and deadly beyond belief.

The wind farm was the boundary line for the Wilderness in this part of the Hub. A little more than 200 meters beyond the last windmill, the Wilderness ruled. One step beyond the boundary and the sentinels wouldn't go, wouldn't help, wouldn't kill.

The canyon beyond the wind farm was winding, and within two klicks the mountains obscured any view of what may lie beyond. The Spanish Fork River carved a pass through the canyon and west of the wind farm. Beyond the boundaries of the Hub, all along the riverbank, was a meadow of grass almost as green as that cultivated by the caretakers of the park. Three somethings grazed in the meadow, and when Quinlan raised his magnifiers, he grinned. There were three horses, two sorrels and a bay, grazing on the grass beyond the Hub. They were beautiful, alien, and magnificent, and he motioned to Noah and Raizor to raise their magnifiers and see what they might see.

"Are they real?" Raizor asked with a gasp.

"They're real," Quinlan whispered. "Yes, they're real. Aren't they something?"

"Sure. Until they kick your head in," Noah said, and Raizor punched him in the ribs.

The horses were within a few scant meters of where the wild grass of the Wilderness ended, and the manicured lawn of the wind farm began. They continued to graze, moving north, and when the snout of the bay nibbled on the manicured lawn of the wind farm, a sentinel dropped from a windmill and raced to the boundary. A pulse cannon erupted in the afternoon sun, and the horses dashed away, bucking, and kicking as they ran deeper into the Wilderness.

Raizor grinned and dropped her magnifier, turning to her father. "They were playing, weren't they? They knew the sentinels would come. They were testing."

Quinlan nodded and pinched his daughter's leg. He hoped she was right. "Could be, little Raiz. Could be."

"I'd like to see them up close, those horses. Wouldn't that be something?" she said.

"It would," Quinlan agreed, then worried his son might be right; it might end with someone dying.

The sentinel returned to the windmill and latched on, dangling. From behind them came a soft whine and Quinlan turned to watch an oversized vehicle lumber toward them.

The pickup was a black mass of sharp angles lifted so high off the ground Raizor could almost walk beneath. The bed of the truck had a shell the height of the cab. The truck looked angry, like it might bite if given half the chance. It was more tank than a truck, and the man sitting behind the wheel was grinning as it came to a stop. The driver's window slid down, and the giant Marshal beamed at them.

"My Wilderness assault vehicle. What do you think?"

Quinlan nodded appreciatively. "Small, isn't it?"

Victor's brow furrowed, then he laughed and opened the door. Steps lowered from beneath the frame. "Nah, it's just right for hunting Wrynd, I think."

The Marshal raised his impossibly long arms above his head, stretching and flexing, and Quinlan grinned at his exhibitionism. Instead of his Marshals Service uniform, he wore black pants and a black shirt so form-fitting it looked like skin. His boots were black as well, as were his holster and sidearm. The only thing he wore that wasn't black was the metallic orb dangling from his belt, and it was this that drew their attention.

"Is that a scye?" Noah whispered, craning his neck for a closer look.

Victor grinned happily, smugly. "It is. The weapon of the Marshals Service."

"Will it really pass through metal? I heard it can slice right through armor." Noah stepped closer, reached out to touch the metal orb that when activated became a ball of laser light that was scout, protector, and weapon of the Federation Marshals. Victor ruffled Noah's hair.

"If you know how to wield it, it will. I do." He patted the scye at his waist. "It's passed through armor and many other things." He glanced down at the assembled gear and cast a questioning glance at Quinlan.

"Who will be watching your youngins while we go on our quest?"

Quinlan looked at his children as they looked at him and nodded softly. "They'll be going with us."

"With us?" Victor laughed. "The Wilderness is no place for children, Mr. Bowden."

"No. It's not. But they're coming anyway. There's no place I dare leave them. I told them we would find their mother together, and we will."

Victor stepped closer and bent his head to Quinlan's ear. "What if what we find isn't what you hope to find?"

"We can hear you, you know?" Raizor shook her head.

"We'll face it together, whatever comes our way," Quinlan replied.

Victor pointed to the old wind farm. "Once we pass beyond the blades, there's no safety. In the Wilderness, the world doesn't play by the rules. There are no rules. Are you ready for that? Are your little ones ready for that? Because ready or not, that's the way of it."

"We're ready," Quinlan whispered, suddenly feeling anything but ready.

Victor shrugged and walked to the back of the truck to open the shell. "Toss your gear and let's be on our way. Night's rushing in."

They gathered their packs and took them to the back of the truck. As Quinlan tossed them inside, Victor reached out and snagged a baseball bat Quinlan had strapped to his pack. He waved it in front of him, questioning.

"You think a baseball game might break out in the Wilderness?"

Quinlan grinned sheepishly. "Well, I thought it would be good to have something to protect ourselves."

"From a stray ball? You didn't bring anything else?"

Quinlan tapped the buck knife strapped to his waist.

"That's it? No slayer, no pulse rifle? You're going into the Wilderness with a softball bat?"

"Baseball. It's a baseball bat."

"Well, that makes all the difference."

"And we're going with you," Quinlan said.

Victor pursed his lips, nodded. "Well, there is that."

"Dad can't shoot a gun." Raizor giggled.

"Some ChristGaian religious thing?" Victor asked.

"No. I can shoot one. I just can't hit anything."

"It's pathetic really," Noah offered.

Victor shook his head. "Good to know. You three stay in the truck unless I tell you it's okay to get out." He went to the driver's door and climbed back behind the wheel. "Let's go get your momma."

Quinlan lifted Raizor and Noah into the back seat and climbed into the navigator's seat of the pickup. He stared out the window at the looming Wilderness.

"Have you been out there before?"

Victor slipped on a pair of sunglasses and nodded. "Many times. It's my playground."

"Have you ever come across an orchard out there?"

"An orchard?"

"Apple orchard. Huge and dense."

Victor pushed his sunglasses down his flat nose. "Never have. If we don't find your misses in the canyon, we'll end up in Price. Beyond that is what was once Castle Valley in the Old World. Why, do you think your wife is in an apple orchard?"

Quinlan thought of his dream and shook his head. "No. Just an old dream."

Victor sent the truck down the destroyed highway. "Dreams out here are nightmares, Quinlan Bowden. Let's not have any dreams."

As they passed where the horses ran, Quinlan tried to smile and find a reason to hope, but in his mind, he heard the chitter of despair.

They left the Hub and journeyed into the Wilderness.

Chapter Five

Whispers of Change

I

There was a point between pleasure and pain, life and death; a fine line where Cirroco Storm thought she might find peace.

Sometimes, when she killed, she found it in the face of her prey, as the light in their eyes turned to something else. Sometimes, when death approached and was almost within her grasp, she was sure all she had to do was reach a little further, stay a little longer, endure a little more, and the prize would be hers.

Happiness. Joy. Love. Hope.

All the emotions she puzzled over and never experienced.

As she fell from heaven, she wondered if, before the ocean consumed her, she might glimpse a life unlike the one she lived. A life of happiness. If she did, would it be as dreadfully dull as it sounded? She suspected it would, but death was inevitable, and if today was her day to die or a thousand days in the future, it was of little consequence. Since she didn't have a great deal on her agenda, death could take her now if it wished.

She opened her eyes wide and felt the air whip her flesh. She grinned as she plummeted toward the black canvas below. Death was coming. It was often the last thought of those who faced her.

But today death was The Deep, and it was going to drown Cirroco Storm.

Emissary. The soothing male voice was in her head, in her thoughts, all around her.

"Don't bother me, Icarus. I'm dying."

Emissary, if I don't catch you in the next twenty-two seconds, you will hit the water. It won't be pleasant.

"Exactly." Cirroco spun in the air and looked to the heavens. Her wings matched her descent, staying just out of reach as she fell to the ocean; its engines not even audible in the rush of air.

I thought you might find it intriguing to learn High Judge Trevok reports a legionnaire has disappeared.

"Disappeared?" Cirroco spun back to face The Deep and opened her arms in a ready embrace.

Yes, Emissary Storm. The legionnaire's Link signature is gone. She has vanished.

That was interesting, after all. "Fine, Icarus, I'll die another day. Take me home."

Her wings embraced her, the thin armor of its belly opening to envelop, and the two were one and took flight over the Atlantic. The armored skin of the wings wrapped around her midsection and across her thighs, leaving her arms and legs free to the rush of air. She stretched and could feel the biting mist of the ocean as it kissed her cheeks.

Joined with Icarus, she flexed the wings' talons, feeling the power within them as she linked. The legs of wings, three meters long, with talons like fingers, were delicate enough to pluck a dandelion seed from a child's cheek, powerful enough to pierce the best of body armor. Cirroco never felt more alive than when she was one with Icarus. She had more than once contemplated having a medprint fashion her wings of her own but couldn't imagine them being any greater than those she shared with her jinni companion.

Emissary Cirroco Storm chose not to die and instead soared

back into the heavens to discover more about the impossible disappearance of a legionnaire.

The moon scowled across the horizon at the light of the Wheel sharing heaven as Cirroco arrived home, a sprawling and empty floating mansion anchored above a submerged Key West.

Her wings swooped low, and as it overflew her home, it pivoted, and thrusters engaged. Cirroco slipped free and fell to earth, flipping twice in the air to land softly on the cobblestones of her patio. She padded lightly into her house, her bare and clawed toes clicking softly across the old brick.

Her house drew energy from her powerband, and the lights winked when she opened the door. Ceiling fans whispered as she glided across the room, leaving clothing in her wake. She stepped into the shower, the water instantly turning pleasantly, painfully hot. Steam boiled as she bathed, washing away the chill of the evening.

When she finished, she stood before the mirror and dried herself, both pleased and repulsed by the sight before her. Her feet were large for a woman. Each toe had a long and jagged talon that could easily rip through the breastbone of a man. She knew because she had tested them, to be sure. From the top of what she knew were shapely and firm buttocks, a tail like a whip, two meters long, flicked contentedly as she dried. She coiled it in a fierce hug when she finished drying. The tip of the tail was flat and wide as a large man's hand and shaped like a spearhead. She could curl it to provide the most sensuous of caresses or break bones, pierce skin, and cut armor.

Across her back a tattoo of a galaxy of stars swirled, reaching across her shoulders and down the back of her legs and arms. Her fingers were long and delicate until she allowed her nails to extend. Claws eight centimeters long and sharp as razors protruded from her fingertips, and she caressed her right shoulder with her left hand, smiling at the blood drawn. She retracted her claws and stood in the mirror, and with her claws hidden and her tail out of sight, she looked at the woman before her, repulsed at the beauty she saw; repulsed by the fine curves of her body, of her full bosom, of her brown, blemish-free skin, so soft to the touch. Her high cheekbones, her full lips, her black hair cascading to her shoulders, the beauty, and the softness of her eyes; it all repulsed her.

Her body modifications had done nothing to eradicate her beauty, despite her many trips to her medprint, despite the claws of her hands and feet, despite the tail implanted in her backside. She knew when people gazed upon her the first thing they saw was her beauty. But once they knew her, once they understood this woman before them was Emissary Cirroco Storm, first counsel to Lord Judge Syiada, they no longer saw her beauty; they only saw the instrument of their death, which was well and good.

Often, she considered plucking her soft eyes from their sockets, cutting a jagged scar across her face, turning herself into what she truly was: something to be feared, a monster to wreak havoc on any who would stand before the Federation. In time she came to understand her beauty was a weapon as well, perhaps even more so than her tail or her claws or her prowess in physical combat or her ability with a scye.

In the Age of Renewal, her beauty might be her greatest weapon. Enemies weren't so bold in the Seven Realms; finding them required a broad range of talents, and one thing Cirroco knew was she was a woman of many talents.

She slipped into her red armor, and the leather clinging to every curve of her body flashed softly as the nanites woven within awakened. They would generate a shield to protect her from a pulse blast. She hadn't tested its capabilities but thought it might be interesting to try. Over the armor, she draped her Emissary robes of red.

Dressed in the garments of her title, she looked at her reflection and couldn't quite prevent a snarl from flashing across her full lips. It had been a long journey from the girl living on the streets of Tijuana.

As she finished dressing, going through the routine with barely a thought, she entered the Link and discovered Icarus hadn't lied to prevent her from killing herself, which he had on occasion attempted. There truly was a legionnaire who had impossibly vanished.

With a thought, she summoned a transport, and as her body glided into the kitchen for a bite to eat, her mind slipped into the Vale, and her avatar walked through the high arched doorway of High Judge Trevok's private chambers.

She strolled into the High Judge's office, dressed as she was in the Sphere. The High Judge of America's empty chamber was opulent and revolting to her in every feasible way.

When High Judge Trevok rose to his position in the Federation and was given the rule of law over the Realm of America, he immediately moved the capital of the realm from Washington D.C. to Rio de Janeiro. He said if the world was to start anew and the Federation was truly to break from the past, the capital of America must be someplace other than the Old World country guilty of so much harm to the citizens of the world.

Cirroco knew the mighty judge grew up a poor, abused, and neglected Neand in Ecuador, just as she had in the dying city of Tijuana. She suspected his move of the realm capital was just a simple slight he wished to inflict on those few who still cared.

What the United States once was had faded long ago. Few remembered or cared, but what High Judge Trevok didn't realize was she was one among those few. Dreams of a legend called America was what kept her fighting for life, for purpose, when there was none.

It mystified Cirroco why her Lord Judge selected the warped, demented little man to hold such a high title. He was lascivious and delighted in affliction. Cirroco killed, often at a whim, but she didn't torture. Death should be honored and treated with reverence. To send someone into the great darkness screaming was sacrilege.

When she killed, she sent her victims into the embrace of death as quickly as she could. When she killed, it was a matter of business. It was because it was time to die, and she was the instrument of the Federation's ultimate justice. More than the Judges, more than the Marshals or the Legion, she was Emissary of the Lord Judge and his executioner. Someday she hoped her lord might pronounce judgment upon High Judge Trevok.

But Lord Judge Syiada demanded order, and High Judge Trevok was a piece in the puzzle keeping order in the Seven Realms, so Cirroco resisted her impulses by avoiding interaction with the reptile of a man whenever possible.

After the Energy Wars, after Gaia turned on humanity and the Rages ripped civilization apart, Lord Judge Syiada almost single-handedly cobbled together the Federation. He fled the nuclear wasteland of China and came to what was the United States. From there he built the Federation and created the Seven Realms: Eurasia, Africa, Austarctica, America, The Outland, The Deep, and The Vale. He saved the world and led humanity to the Age of Renewal, and Cirroco served him with all her might.

She glanced around the room one last time, took a deep breath, and clasped her hands in front of her, as she was wont to do when she desired to kill, and couldn't.

"High Judge Trevok? A moment if you please." She knew he was aware of her. She could feel his senses roaming, searching, imposing.

Rather than stroll through the digital doorway of his office, High Judge Trevok appeared, his reed-like legs draped across the top of his desk, his delicate fingers intertwined and resting in his lap. Cirroco turned, her lips parting into a softly lying smile.

"Judge Trevok, I hope I didn't take you away from some important matter."

"High Judge Trevok." The petite man nodded emphatically, as he did when he felt slighted. His head reminded her of an insect, perhaps that of a beetle or a fly. His eyes were large and bulged from the side of a narrow face curving to a pointed chin made even more so by an oiled black goatee poking his sunken chest like a dagger.

Cirroco tilted her head to the right and couldn't quite keep her shoulders from giving the slightest of shrugs. "High Judge," she said.

Trevok's legs crawled off the desktop, and he leaned forward, his lips disappearing into a gaping grin. "I apologize for keeping the Lord Judge's Emissary waiting. I was attending matters in my MyRealm and was preoccupied, I must confess."

"Matters of great import to you, I'm sure."

"Matters of great desire, Emissary Storm," the High Judge said. "Of great hunger. You must visit me in one of my MyRealms one day. I think you would find them most interesting."

High Judge Trevok wore the black and red robes of his title, and Cirroco knew beneath the robes he wore nothing at all. They were within the Vale, a realm of the Federation, so here she couldn't use her avatar to pinch the head from his body, but within his digital realm, he might be able to cause her harm, and she might be able to cause him the same. It was a tempting invitation.

"Another day perhaps, High Judge. I pulled you away from what I am sure was an intriguing and repulsive pastime to ask you about the missing legionnaire."

Anger flashed briefly across Trevok's eyes, but he quickly recovered his composure. "You know all I know about the legionnaire, Emissary. Sergeant Kara Litmeyer of the Rocky Mountain Hub has disappeared. She was not on leave, and her linktag was not in privacy mode. Her commander conducted a Link override to be sure. Her linktag is missing in every realm of the Federation."

"You know that's impossible, High Judge. Living or dead, she's connected to the Link, and we should be able to locate her. She's not a Pilgrim. She's linked to the Federation and forever will be." Cirroco stepped closer to the High Judge's desk, trying not to portend her lack of patience. She failed.

"As you say, Emissary. But despite the reality you needlessly remind me of, the facts remain. She has disappeared."

Cirroco leaned against the desk, her hands flat against its smooth surface, and her nails extracted slowly to their full length. "One of your legionnaires is missing and has been for several days, High Judge Trevok. Why am I only now learning of this?"

Trevok leaned back, his eyes dancing nervously to her hands on his desk. "It's a large planet, Emissary Storm."

"Yes, well, I didn't ask you to paint it, High Judge Trevok." In the Sphere, the transport signaled its arrival, and Cirroco tidied up her kitchen and strolled out into the courtyard, closing the door to her home. The lights winked out as her powerband left range, and she climbed into the hopper.

In the Vale, Trevok stood, gripping the sides of his desk. He was seven centimeters shorter than Cirroco.

"I wasn't aware Lord Judge Syiada's Emissary had the leisure to explore every oddity in the vast universe. The legionnaire's disappearance is a mystery, but of no consequence."

Cirroco scraped her clawed hands across the desk. Her voice lost all pleasantries, all soft purring and accommodation, and became the siren call of impending violence.

"Did you not think to step away from your perverse distractions long enough to consider the disappearance of this legionnaire might be the first crucial step along the path Lord Judge Syiada has foretold?"

"The Leap?" Trevok now betrayed the first emotion other than insolence and arrogance. It was fear. "Lord Judge Syiada's prophecy foretells that the Leap will come from the Wilderness. This legionnaire is one of us."

"Prophecy?" Cirroco walked around the desk, and her tail flicked softly behind her, caressing the stone floor. "Do you think our Lord Judge a prophet Trevok? A religious zealot? That he bends his knee to an unknowing, uncaring, and non-existent God for guidance? Or perhaps you think he prays to Gaia for some sign of Her desires? Do you count our Lord Judge a fool Trevok? He is the Lord Judge. He has seen our path and guides us toward it. He counts on his chosen to heed his words and follow his counsel. It appears you have been remiss in that calling."

"I've been remiss in nothing!" Trevok said, and his voice squeaked as he sidled around the desk, trying to keep it between them. Cirroco allowed herself a smile. "If you deem this legionnaire of such import, then I will find her. She belongs to the Legion, who only reported her missing this morning. How can Lord Judge Syiada consider their inaction a reflection of my rule?"

"You are High Judge of America, are you not, Trevok?" Cirroco sat in his chair, draped her legs across his desk.

"The Legion answers to the Federation Senate, not to me, Cirroco," Trevok replied, now standing on the opposite side of the desk.

"The Legion enters the battle at the whim of the Senate, High Judge, but you are their commander-in-chief. They are your responsibility. Even such a lowly one as this missing Sergeant Litmeyer."

"I said I would find her," Trevok stuttered.

"Don't bother. Go back to your playthings, High Judge. I will seek help in finding her elsewhere." Cirroco winked out of the Vale, leaving the High Judge of America alone in his great chamber.

Cirroco blinked, yawned, and stretched in the seat of the hopper as it flew west. Behind her, Icarus chased after. Slower than the hopper, her wings would track her wherever she went.

"Where are we going?" Icarus whispered in her mind.

"To the Rockies." Cirroco yawned again, and her tail embraced. Sleep was slinking and would have her soon. She welcomed it.

"What do we seek?"

"Answers, Icarus. Answers to questions great and small." Emissary Storm let sleep take her as the hopper pierced the night sky.

II

Someone entered her apartment and was creeping toward her. Jodi Tempest sat in meditation, facing a long wall of windows spying upon the Wasatch Mountains. Meditating for more than an hour, she knew the sun was pulling its way toward a new day.

She didn't open her eyes, didn't alter her body in any way; only listened for hints of the intruder. The first clue was a subtle shift in the air as a door opened and silently closed. Then came the prickling of her skin and the hair rising on the back of her neck as she sensed something in her home had changed; the peace she fostered here now broken by something, or someone, who knew nothing of peace.

She didn't fear but seldom did. It was both a blessing and a curse to go through life with an inability to feel any great fear. It was only because she could find little in the Sphere to cause her fear. There were no loves on Earth to fear for, and if threatened, she would fight death or succumb to it. There was no reason to fear.

As the stranger slipped closer, she sat in meditation and pondered who was approaching. She wore only a thin pair of shorts and an even thinner camisole. Jodi's scye and slayer were out of reach in her bedroom. The trespasser possessed great skill, which was a clue. The intruder didn't mean to kill her, at least not right away, because rather than approach from behind, they made a slow circle until standing just to her right side. She detected the slightest hint of jasmine in the air, and it was then she knew the intruder.

"It's a pleasure to meet you, Emissary Storm," Jodi said, opening her eyes.

The Emissary knelt, her weight balanced on her toes, her tail coiled around her shoulders, one meter from where Jodi sat on her meditation mat. The Emissary smiled and stood up, her tail uncoiling in a slow undulation.

"Most impressive, Marshal Tempest. Tell me, did you cheat? Did you link to discover who entered your home? Did your home alert you to my presence? Did you peek with your beautiful blue eyes?"

"No, Emissary Storm, I did not." Jodi stood and faced the Emissary of the Lord Judge. She was shorter than the Emissary, but where Cirroco Storm falsely appeared voluptuously soft, Jodi was squat and athletic, her arms and legs muscular, her breasts small enough not to be cumbersome, but full enough to draw the interested eye, and Jodi took note of the Emissary's pause when her eyes swept across her.

"Then please, tell me what actions betrayed my presence?"

Jodi bent and picked up her meditation mat, rolling it slowly as she strolled toward the kitchen.

"I knew someone entered my home when the door opened. I knew whoever intruded had great skill because I detected no motion, no sound, not even a hint of breath in the air until you drew nearer. As you approached, I heard a faint scratch on the hardwood floor." Jodi nodded toward Cirroco's clawed feet. "I used to have a dog when I was a little girl. The sound was similar. You didn't come at me from behind, which an attacker would have done, so I knew with such skills it must be a member of the Marshals Service or someone even greater. I knew it was you, Emissary of the Lord Judge, when I detected the hint of jasmine. Your legend precedes you. Much has been said by those who stood before you of the sweet smell of jasmine, and the swift hand of death."

The Emissary bowed deeply; arms outstretched. "It is likewise a pleasure to meet you, Marshal Tempest. I know nothing of you." Cirroco blinked twice and her lips pursed in satisfaction as she returned from the Link. "Well, now I know everything about you."

Jodi nodded, her shoulders giving the slightest of involuntary shrugs. "I'm not sure I would count what you find within the Link as everything there is to know about me or anyone else."

"But, alas, it is all I care to learn, for now," Cirroco replied, slinking around her. "You are the second youngest Chief Marshal in the history of the Federation, given your star at the pubescent age of 27, second only to Chief Marshal Noonan of the Texas Hub, who became Marshal at 25. That must have rankled, bested by two years?"

"I'm a bit on the competitive side."

"And Jodi Tempest of Charleston, South Carolina, you've been Chief Marshal of the Rocky Mountain Hub for how long?"

Cirroco already had the answer, but she gave it anyway. "Two years, Emissary."

Emissary Storm turned to the window and watched storks flutter above the cityscape. While Jodi had never met her in the Sphere or the Vale, she had seen images of the woman, impressed by her beauty, how delicate she seemed, even with her serpent tail, but meeting her altered the perception. She was beautiful, perhaps the most beautiful woman Jodi had ever met, but there was nothing delicate about her.

As the Emissary turned from her musings and her soft eyes roamed Jodi's body, she thought the eyes were perhaps the biggest lie of all, even more than her medical alterations. There was nothing soft about those eyes; they were calculating and full of humor, but they were also cold and brutal and without remorse, hiding behind a veil of warmth.

The Emissary's full lips parted softly, in a seductive smile as her eyes continued their lying assault. If the Emissary thought to make her uncomfortable, she was going to be disappointed.

"Jodi Tempest, the hero of the Vegas Uprising," Cirroco purred.

The words struck like a slap and Jodi bristled, her shoulders involuntarily rolling back, her right cheek twitching. Cirroco's smile turned to a grin.

"There were no heroes at Vegas. Only those who died and those who lived."

"False modesty is not becoming, Marshal. Seventy-five of our greatest from the California and Rocky Mountain Hubs went to Vegas; only thirty-three returned. Because you led them. I find that heroic."

"That was survival, Emissary. We shouldn't have been there in the first place. If the military had offered support, none of us would have died."

"Only the Neands who needed to die, you mean. It was a police matter, not a military matter."

"We are not the police. Marshals are protectors of the Realms and servants of justice. Vegas belongs to the Wilderness."

"Yet, because of it, you have all this." Cirroco swept her arms to take in the room. "Because of it, you wear your star. Do you think you would be Marshal now if it weren't for your deeds at Vegas? I wonder, have your duties become cumbersome? So many rules, so much bureaucracy, so much ineptitude in the trappings of leadership?"

"It has its moments." Jodi walked toward her bedroom, and Cirroco followed behind.

Within a few minutes, the Emissary found an old wound and ripped away the scab. Unlike Cirroco, Jodi's eyes always betrayed her emotions, and it was best to keep them focused elsewhere. Folded on her bed was her Class A black uniform and undergarments. Cirroco showed no inclination to leave, and Jodi gritted her teeth and showed no inclination of caring as she stripped off her clothing and slipped into her uniform. Cirroco watched silently, her tail swishing softly behind her.

"You question the wisdom of Vegas, find the trappings of your title tiring, yet you serve Lord Judge Syiada. Why?"

Jodi slipped her holster around her waist and fastened the buckle, adjusting her slayer. "I serve justice, Emissary Storm."

Cirroco tilted her head and folded her arms across her chest. "Lord Judge Syiada is justice, is he not, Marshal?"

Jodi fastened her star to the left side of her uniform. "I met the Lord Judge when I received my star. I don't know his heart, only the Federation he created. At its core, I believe the Seven Realms serves the cause of justice, which is why I serve it, Emissary Storm. Justice doesn't reside in any one person. Justice is resolute."

Cirroco stepped toward Jodi, and the smell of jasmine was strong as the Emissary unclasped the clip holding back her hair. Her blonde locks cascaded across her shoulders.

"You're lovely." Cirroco's tail coiled around Jodi's legs and crept up her back. "Did your beauty help you reach your stature within the Federation?"

Jodi didn't step away, but it was a struggle. "No, Emissary. Did yours?"

Cirroco laughed, and it was a surprised hiccup that made her laugh harder. "Jodi Tempest. Cirroco Storm. We could be sisters, you and I."

Jodi nodded. "Perhaps. But we're not." She stepped away.

"Tempest. Is that your given name, or your taken?"

"Given to me, taken by my father."

"And your surname in the Old World?"

"Murphy."

"Not nearly as imposing as Tempest."

"And you, Emissary? Is your name given or taken?"

"Nothing I value was given, Marshal."

"Your name before the realms?"

"Died with the past."

Jodi walked back into her living room. "What can I do for the Emissary of the Lord Judge at such an early hour? Did you come to discuss only foolish mistakes and taken names?"

The Emissary sighed. "May we sit?"

Jodi motioned to a set of chairs in the corner, and the Emissary chose the one facing the windows. Daylight was dancing on the mountain peaks. Jodi sat in the chair opposite her.

"What is your relationship with the Rocky Mountain Legion?"

"Minimal, Emissary Storm," Jodi replied. "They are of little consequence to my Marshals or I or the citizens of the Hub. They practice for a war they'll never fight, walk the decks of battlewagons that will never see battle. They are make-believe warriors preparing for a fight against foes who do not exist. But it does seem to keep them occupied."

Cirroco laughed. "So, you have no opinion of them, one way or another?"

Jodi grinned. "Not particularly, no."

"Then what might you think if I told you one of their legionnaires is missing?"

"Missing?" Jodi couldn't quite keep the surprise from registering on her face. "What do you mean, missing?"

Cirroco crossed her legs and the tip of her tail wrapped around them. "I mean missing. Vanished. Poof. Sergeant Kara Litmeyer, happily married to a man she doesn't realize in the Sphere is a rather grotesquely overweight woman named Ronda, disappeared without a trace three days ago."

Jodi leaned forward. "We can locate her with her linktag."

"Can?" Cirroco leaned forward as well, licked her full lips, smiling slyly. "Well, yes, normally we can. But we cannot. Her linktag has vanished as well. The last Link data we have on Sergeant Litmeyer shows her at her apartment. She is not there."

"That's not possible." Jodi shook her head.

Cirroco stood and walked into the kitchen. Jodi heard the door to the cooler open and the Emissary rummaging inside. "Yet the impossible has happened," she called.

Jodi sat back in her seat, chewing softly on the inside of her cheek. "I find that troubling."

"As do I," Cirroco came back into the room eating an apple. "As will the Lord Judge. It's a troubling omen."

"Omen?" Jodi said. "Omen of what?"

Cirroco's tail caressed Jodi's right leg. "The Leap."

Jodi brushed away the Emissary's tail. She knew of the Lord Judge's belief that a leap in human evolution was on the horizon. The Lord Judge's obsession was highly classified, privy only to a few, even her Marshals did not know of the Leap.

Of course, there was no scientific consensus that what Syiada speculated was even within the realm of possibility, but the Lord Judge routinely accomplished things considered outside the realm of possibility.

After the Energy Wars, he said he would unite the planet, and he did. He said he would end war, eradicate social discord, poverty, disease and bring to fruition the promise of the Age of Renewal, and he did.

If Lord Judge Syiada said tomorrow it would rain wine, everyone would hold up a chalice and stick out their tongues.

"Leap? How could a missing legionnaire be an omen of the Leap? It is supposed to come from the Wilderness," Jodi said.

"A puzzle, to be sure. The Lord Judge has foreseen a leap in our evolution and that it will come from the Wilderness. We must recognize it when it arrives and be prepared to harness it and take our place in the universe. If a lowly legionnaire connected to the Link can disappear, ask yourself how is it possible? And if you answer that it is not possible for one connected to the Link to disappear, then the only answer is because someone has made the impossible possible. Is that not a sign of the Leap?"

Jodi locked eyes with Cirroco and frowned. "Possibly. Why

bring this to me? Is the Legion not searching for its lost legionnaire?"

"In time, I suppose. But the Rocky Mountain Hub is yours, not the Legions. It is you who will find her. The Legion answers to the Senate, who will discuss the disappearance of Sergeant Litmeyer. Secret committees will meet to determine what it could mean. I don't need a committee. You completed an impossible task once, surviving Vegas. I present you with another. Find this missing legionnaire. Quietly."

"She could be anywhere in the six realms of the Sphere, not just within my Hub," Jodi said.

"She could be, but I believe she is somewhere nearby. Call it a hunch or a premonition or a psychic tremor, if you like, but I believe she's waiting for you to find her." Cirroco stood, and her tail almost coiled around Jodi, then retreated, "Can you accomplish this task?"

Jodi felt the steady rush of a goal before her, a duty. "You wouldn't be asking if you didn't know the answer."

"Oh, I knew the answer before I arrived." Cirroco held out the apple core, and Jodi let her drop it in her hand.

III

Jodi stared out the window with the scent of jasmine still wafting through her apartment. The fingers of her right hand tapped against the butt of her slayer as she watched morning rise over the city. It was a nervous habit she struggled against; betraying anxieties she would rather stay hidden. The Emissary destroyed the peace of her morning, and there was no reclaiming it.

It was more than learning a legionnaire had impossibly gone missing, although that was a mystery that would cause panic among the masses, or at least those few who cared to dwell on anything remotely associated with reality. Those few would never learn of the legionnaire's disappearance, and those who did wouldn't understand the implications of such an event.

What troubled Jodi even more was the Emissary's casual disregard for the Legion and the Senate; the trappings of government itself. For the first time in history, the world was at peace. Emissary Storm seemed to hold the government her master created in disdain.

She didn't understand the shades of grey reality floated within. She saw only black and white, right, and wrong. It was a flaw in her character, she supposed. It led her through her young life to be a Marshal of the Federation. Growing up in Charleston, she studied history and the myriad of different versions of it from her father, and through those lessons, she determined the course for her life.

It was to serve truth, to be a servant of justice. In the absence of justice, there was only chaos, and the world had seen enough chaos. It needed something more; it needed something better.

It was after Jodi lifted her hand to the square and swore the oath of a Federation Marshal, that she realized not everyone saw justice the same way. She took heart that she was young and determined, and there was yet time to sway them.

The sun was at midmorning when Jodi finished her musings and turned away from the window. The Emissary troubled her, but she now had a task in the service of justice, so Jodi would see it through. A legionnaire was missing, and she would find her.

Her apartment was within the Justice Tower, a right given as Chief Marshal of the Rocky Mountain Hub. She took secret delight in the fact, and when she stepped out of her apartment, she took a lift to the roof. The wind blew warm, tussling her hair as she walked along the courtyard at the top of the tower.

Hoppers and shuttles came and went, slowing to dock in the landing bay twenty-seven stories below. She strolled toward the edge of the tower, her stride lengthening. By the time she reached the ledge itself she was sprinting, and she leapt, kicking off the barricade wall and flying into the air, arms outstretched as she reached for heaven and fell toward earth. Her wings caught her, and she once again reached for heaven, this time soaring.

She allowed herself a sweeping pass over the Justice Tower and grinned as the wind kissed her cheeks, then banked and dove toward the inner city, one with her wings. If she knew Emissary Storm called her wings Icarus and that a jinni resided within it, she would laugh. Her wings were a part of her, and she would no more name it than she would her right arm.

Jodi flew between the skyscrapers of what within the Hub people still called Provo, flying low over mostly deserted streets and walkways, and for a moment she chased a Blue Dragon as it lumbered to a stop at the warehouse district with its goods from the east. She banked right and flew toward Old Provo, and as she passed over the cobblestone roads of Main Street, her wings detached, and she dropped six meters to the sidewalk.

Her boots tapped the concrete as she made her way toward her destination. She passed four people along the way, a bit of a crowd for so early in the morning; each of them Shifts. They were plump of body and jowl, and two were riding on hoverchairs. They respectfully nodded as they spotted her Marshals badge, and she nodded back with a smile.

She kept her scye clipped to her left hip. She wished more of her Marshals would do the same, but far too many reveled in the adoration when the locals glimpsed a Marshal with their scye floating beside them. It was a wanton display, but not against regulation, so Jodi could only voice her displeasure, not act upon it. Fortunately, that was usually enough. Although she was younger than most under her command, she was aware she had a forceful presence that served her well. She used it to her full advantage.

She stopped in front of what once, a long time ago, was the Provo City Library. The great old building was almost 300 years old; now all but abandoned. It was a staid and peaked building of ages long gone. Only one small section through the arched south doorway still served the public, as a restaurant catering to those who still cared for physical companionship.

The Library Cafe served breakfast and lunch seven days a week to a small but loyal following, most of them her Marshals. Jodi strolled through the front door, and the smell of bacon sizzled into her senses, making her stomach rumble.

The room was large and lined with bookshelves where actual books collected dust, most salvaged when the library was a library. Small metal signs on each bookshelf beseeched visitors not to touch. Most of them were so frail a simple caress would damage them beyond repair. Jodi marveled at the sight every time she visited. Her father owned actual books, and she remembered reading from them. It was a wonder to think once upon a time that was how people shared information. It was hard to believe anyone survived such dark ages.

At the back wall of the room, smoke swirled toward fans from two large grills where an antiquated couple flipped bacon and eggs, pancakes, and toasted bread. Jack and Frankie Dorson used their RTI funds to refurbish the derelict library into the diner. Now well into their 120s, the old couple bickered as they served perhaps the finest hand-cooked meals in all the Rocky Mountain Hub. Jodi hadn't checked but was certain this might be the only restaurant in the Hub to serve meals in such a manner.

They wouldn't cook nor serve anything made by foodprint, and they grew most of their vegetables in a greenhouse on a portion of the building that crumbled away. Their meat came by way of stork from the automated ranches south of the Hub, purchased at an exorbitant price they could never hope to pass on to their customers. They were eccentric beyond reasoning, and Jodi adored them.

When she walked in the door, they both looked up from their grills and paused an argument forever ongoing. It involved the value of something Frankie called comic books, and Jack insisted they would never, ever be worth the effort it took to maintain them. Frankie waved, and when Jodi tilted her head to the right questioningly, Jack hiked a thumb to the far corner of the diner veiled in shadows.

In the murkiness of the room, two of her Marshals lounged, waiting for breakfast, just as they did every morning. Jodi walked toward them, forcing herself not to smile. She wasn't sure she had a friend, but if she did, it would be the two ahead pretending not to notice her arrival.

Bongani Nwosu and Montana Ahmed looked all but unconscious as Jodi stepped to their table and put her hands on her hips.

Bongani, her slim frame curled across the chair, used the long forefinger of her right hand to push back the brim of a white cowboy hat from her forehead. A lock of her raven hair dropped across her eyes to rest on her hooked nose, the only blemish in a smooth face the color of midnight. She nodded softly to Jodi and let the hat drop back over her eyes.

"Marshal."

To her left, the Goliath of a man named Montana grinned at his partner and nodded to Jodi. He was thick and muscular, and his crooked grin was impossible to deny, but Jodi did anyway. While Victor Walker was larger than Montana, Victor came by his size using a medprint and, as far as Jodi knew, Montana came by his physical prowess naturally.

Both of her deputies were wearing their Class B uniforms; tan dungarees, and tunics, but Bongani sported her damnable cowboy hat, and Montana was wearing a handkerchief around his neck and a red sash around his waist. Bongani also wore a double holster, which wasn't against regulation, but Jodi found braggadocios. She would push her about the excess but had seen the young woman in action. With two slayers, she was twice as deadly.

"Morning, Marshall. We're about to have some breakfast. Care to join us?" Montana said pleasantly, his voice high, floating, humorous, and oddly aggravating, which was what she imagined was his goal.

Jodi pulled a chair from the table and sat across from them. "Burn me some bacon and eggs, Jack, if you please. And I'll take some coffee."

"Sure thing, Marshal," Jack said, pausing from his argument with his wife. He threw on another slab of bacon and cracked two more eggs.

Jodi turned her attention to the two aggravating Marshals. "You're both wearing your uniforms out of regulation, again. Bon, you're not living in a western and you sure as hell aren't a cowboy."

Bon let her leg swing off the table and tilted the offending hat off her brow. "No, Marshal, but if I were, well, wouldn't that be fine?"

Jodi ignored her. "And Montana, what have I said about that damn sash?"

"That it makes me look dashing? No, that was me." He stared at her blankly. "I forgot what you said, Marshal."

Jodi rested her elbows on the table and thought of a dozen things to say, none that passed her lips. Frankie brought Bon and Montana their breakfasts and patted Jodi on the shoulder.

"Yours is comin' right up, Marshal. Any of those peppers ready to harvest?"

"Getting close. A couple more weeks and I'll have you a batch."

"That'll be fine. They'll put a pep in your eggs." Frankie waddled back to the kitchen.

Jodi smiled and leaned back in her chair as Bon and Montana dove into their food. "I need your help."

"We'll always dance for you, Marshal," Montana said, happily shoving a fried egg into his cavernous mouth and chasing it with a slice of toast. "What be your bidding?"

Jodi shook her head softly and looked away. "A legionnaire is missing."

"Missing?" Bon took a bite of egg and pointed her fork at Jodi. A dribble of yolk splattered on the table between them. "Missing how?"

"Missing, missing Marshal Nwosu. As in not here. Not there. Missing."

"Not possible." Bon pushed the rest of the egg into her mouth as Frankie arrived with Jodi's eggs, bacon, and coffee.

"I know it's not possible, Bon." Jodi took a slice of bacon and bit into it absently. "But that doesn't make it not so. She's three days missing. She belongs to the Rocky Mountain Brigade."

"Well, that's damn peculiar, Marshal. What about her linktag?" Montana reached for a slice of Jodi's bacon, and she stabbed him with her fork.

"That's the mystery."

"Why are we involved in this? It sounds like a matter for the Legion. They got plenty of people to throw at it. Course, they're all incompetent, but still, they got a lot of people," Bon said.

"We were tasked."

"By?" Montana nursed his right hand.

"Emissary Storm."

"The Lizard? She came to see you?" Bon finally removed her hat. "That's somethin'."

"She did. She doesn't think the Legion will act quickly enough." Jodi took a bite of egg, amused as Montana watched her eat, licking his lips. "She felt it of the utmost importance to find this legionnaire."

"It is a hell of a mystery, Marshal." Bon slid the rest of her food to Montana, and he gobbled it up.

"It is," Jodi agreed.

"Whole lot of territory to cover. How are we gonna split this up?" Bon asked.

"We're not," Jodi said.

"Come again?" Montana lapped up the last of Bon's eggs with

a corner of toast.

"The rest of the Marshals aren't going to be involved," Jodi said. "Just the three of us."

"Why's that?" Bon pulled her chair closer to the table.

Jodi leaned back. She pushed her plate of food toward Montana, who happily went to work shoveling.

"Not sure. Just a feeling. As you said, this is a Legion matter. I'm not sure why the Emissary would involve us, and until I understand why, we play this close to the chest. A missing legionnaire isn't just unlikely, it's impossible. We have a huge territory and no way to find her. Even if I called up every Marshal in the Hub, used every sentinel, we still wouldn't have enough eyes to find her quickly, perhaps not at all. So, we wait. We keep our ears to the ground, our eyes on the Link, and we wait for a whisper from this missing legionnaire."

Jodi stood and walked away from the table, flicking a wave to Jack and Frankie as she went.

"And if we find this legionnaire?" Bon called after.

"We help her. We serve justice, Marshal Nwosu," Jodi called back.

"Don't we always?" Montana bellowed as Jodi walked out the front door of the Library Café.

Chapter Six

Tabasco and a Side of Fries

I

The canyon was the last abyss Harley faced before reaching the Hub. He sat on the hood of the pickup a child who feared he might be a boy lover directed him to find. He smoked a cigarette, scowled at the maw of the canyon, and considered the wisdom of his plans.

Not one for deep introspection, Harley navigated a winding and often murderous course in life by living on instinct alone, the same instinct that led him to kill a legionnaire without reason. He hadn't stopped to consider the implications of squeezing the trigger at that moment, and he certainly wasn't going to waste a lot of time with it now, but the obstacle before him did give him pause.

The canyon was winding, long and steep, and the cliffs were treacherous. They would crumble down on what remained of the highway in the best of times, which this most definitely was not. Even the pines of the forest seemed like leering wardens as he let the smoke curl between his lips. They were daring him to attempt his way through. There were also the wildthings who called the mountains home. Individually, he didn't fear the bears, wolves, or cougars, but collectively, in a Rage, animals traditionally predator and prey acted as one to attack humans.

There were also Wrynd in the canyon, perhaps hundreds of them, and while he had dealt with them in the past, and they with him, there was respect, but no love between them.

While dreams came true in the glory of the Federation and the spectacle of the Seven Realms, legends came to life in the Wilderness, and around Harley Nearwater a cloak of legend grew. With every deadly encounter, with every drawing of sidearm and sword, the huddled masses who rejected the Hubs painted a picture of the man they called the Castaway as something much larger, grander, and more terrifying than he ever hoped to be. Harley did nothing to alter the canvas of their imaginings.

Many of the exploits attributed to his wanderings were confused with another legend of the Wilderness, the great legend of the Greywalker, a man-god wizard of days long gone and futures impossibly out of reach, who appeared out of the darkness to right wrongs, dispense cruel justice, and swallow souls. He was the boogeyman in a world without a boogeyman. If the Neands and the Pilgrims and even the Wrynd mistook Harley Nearwater for the wisps of tall tales and fireside stories, then he saw no reason to dissuade them.

He survived many an encounter that should have ended in his death simply because those seeking to kill him thought he was something more than he was.

He heard tales of the Greywalker since he was a boy, and never took them as anything more than wild stories to frighten the young and foolish. The man with grey eyes the legionnaire spoke of sounded like the Greywalker.

If her story was simple fantasy, if she was only a mad soldier who wandered into the Wilderness, her death should have brought the Legion. No one came. Her death went unnoticed.

He started his trek to the Hub for no reason other than boredom. Boredom, and because sometimes in the dark of night, knowing he was alone in a world hungry for his death, he wanted to be among humanity for a moment. He wanted to get the smell of them, the feel of them, to be part of them, whether they wanted him to be or not. Now he perhaps had another reason.

It was more than 100 klicks through the canyon to the Hub, and if the road remained, the trip would be uneventful. If not, he might find himself trapped in a Rage he couldn't escape. Go forward or go back were his choices, he gathered.

"Intrestin choices," Harley said and jumped at the sound of his voice, which wasn't a particularly new event. He sometimes went days without making a sound, and on the rare occasion when he spoke to himself, it almost always ended in his yelp of surprise. Once, after more than a week without uttering a word, a thought rambling in his head made him curse "scuttle this!" and the sound of his voice required him to change his breeches.

He considered his choices as he faced the canyon, where he knew a Wrynd camp waited. The Wrynd he spared in the city might weave a little more legend of him, of his mercy and his fearlessness, if he waited and let them reach the camp before he did. A few more tales spun on his behalf might help see him safely through. In the end, he found he didn't have the patience. The Hub beckoned, and his feet were impatient for the journey.

He climbed back into his pickup and pointed it toward the canyon. If the Wrynd discovered him, they would take him if they thought it worth the effort, and if caught in a flare, they would take him without a thought at all.

While the highway through the canyon was crumbling, it was still in better shape than most in the Wilderness. The Federation maintained State Route 6 years after others fell into disrepair because Price was going to be a part of the Rocky Mountain Hub. When plans changed, nature gobbled it up, one little section at a time.

The road hugged the west side of the canyon, following the river. More than once, Harley had to stop and find a way to go around or climb over slides. On the other side of the river, the rail lines had fared better, but not by much. He counted himself lucky the transportation he found was a four-wheel-drive pickup. It had only been a year since his last visit to the Hub, but the road had deteriorated considerably. In a few more years, he would have to walk to make it to the city or take alternate routes over the mountains with hazards of a different kind.

Harley glanced up through the windshield and spied the contrail of an airliner high above the Wilderness. Air travel would solve all his problems. But in a world where humans enjoyed every luxury as a right of life, the freedom of flight wasn't among them. He could fly anywhere he wished, even to the Wheel in orbit, but the Federation was always at the controls.

The drive through the canyon wasn't as slow as Harley feared it might be, and he made it to the summit and over the other side without issue. The camp the young Wrynd told him of was on the far side in a rest area once in service for travelers when this part of the Wilderness had been only a part of rural Utah. Back when people would journey here to get away from the city and be among nature.

The rest area was thirty years abandoned. The road passed dangerously close, but trees between the road and the outbuildings would obscure his view, and the whisper of the truck may allow him safe passage. He might be able to skirt around the Wrynd without detection if he was lucky, which was seldom.

As he drew nearer, leaning forward over the steering wheel as if it might give him some glimpse of things to come, he caught sight of a finger of smoke pointing to the high cumulus toying with the mountaintops. He slowed the truck to a crawl and eventually stopped it altogether and climbed out of the cab. Strapping his sidearm and scabbard to his waist, he slipped his pack over his shoulders and climbed to the top of a rolling hill lounging on the bend in the highway.

At the crest, he dropped to his knees and crawled until he could glimpse where the road continued its meandering course through the canyon. The three buildings of the dead rest area stood like drunkards and milling around the carcass of the dreams of a dead civilization were the maggots of the Wrynd reveling on the outskirts of utopia.

Harley pulled his magnifiers from his pack and aimed them at the mayhem below. There were three long pikes facing west, and on each hung the head of the Wrynd's latest prey. On the outer two were the skulls of two great bull elk, their tongues lolling and their great horns, wider than the span of a man, now useless in death. In the center, staked through a similar pike, was the skull of a man, his eyes staring blankly to a horizon where the sun would set on his final day, his mouth skewed in agony. He wore a black beard that shifted as his head bobbed in the breeze, and when Harley narrowed his viewer, he realized the man was beardless; the beard was a blanket of flies already using his death as a haven for life.

There were three great spits erected in what used to be the parking lot of the rest area, and on them spun portions of the elk and the trunk of the dead man. The fire blackened the flesh of man and beast for a hungry horde. Harley lowered his magnifiers, no longer interested in seeing anything so clearly.

There were at least two hundred Wrynd below him, and as Harley watched their brutality, he saw the unmistakable figure of the Wrynd leader walk out of one of the leaning buildings. Towering above the others, a massive undulating creature of horror, fury, lust, and everything great and terrible in the passions of man, he strode through the fracas like a god. Like most Wrynd, his body was the canvas for images from nightmares; his shaven head crisscrossed with jagged scars, most of them painted, but not all of them. Harley hadn't known Scimitar Hatcher before he was a Wrynd, but whatever he had been before he succumbed to ink and became but another monster, another savage, another cannibal, had to be better than what he was now.

Harley raised his magnifiers and narrowed his focus on the sight glass. He was surprised to see the blackness of the veins and eyes of the Wrynd preparing to feast wasn't as distinct as usual. They almost looked normal.

"They're out of ink," Harley whispered.

He started to climb to his feet when something hummed over his head, and he dove back to his belly. A stork skimmed over the treetops, its electric rotors whirling as it descended into the clearing and floated above the Wrynd Scimitar. Beneath the drone's rotors, a large box dangled from a wire. Scimitar Hatcher walked to where the drone hovered, raised his hands, and Harley zoomed in closer. Before the drone released the package, Harley detected the slightest of involuntary blinks from the big Wrynd's eyes, and then the drone released the package and flew away. Hatcher took the box and raised it high above his head, and the rest of the Wrynd screamed triumphantly. He opened the package, and Harley recognized the vials of ink inside.

He rolled onto his back and stared at the sky. "Wrynd blinkers. Ain't that cracked?"

The Wrynd were not only on the Link, but they were also Shifts. They connected to the Link and ordered their drugs by stork, just like ordering a pizza.

Harley scurried back down the hill and climbed into his truck. The Wrynd would feast on the elk and the burning man, and once they injected their ink, they would scatter into the forest in search of prey. He had a narrow window of opportunity to slip through before the prey they sought was him. As they turned their attention to the drug that made them everything vile, Harley made his way slowly past and continued his way through the canyon.

The Seven Realms ignored the Wrynd, and the people of the Wilderness were wary of them like they were the wildthings. They were human beasts to avoid. What Harley saw when he spied on the Wrynd wasn't a herd of beasts, but an army awaiting a purpose. They were a weapon, for what purpose, he hadn't a clue, just as he didn't know who might have their finger on the trigger. If he had a stake in the world, it might give him pause for concern. He had no stake, so he had no concern.

Harley had to abandon his truck ten klicks past the Wrynd encampment. The cliffs of the canyon had crumbled as if some great bubble of destruction had broken through from the depths and laid waste to the mountain. The road lay buried beneath kilos of rubble. The river itself had backed up and created a lake before it finally found a way to snake through the rock and earth. The only way around was up and over, on foot.

There were the shattered remains of what once may have been a gas station and campground just off the highway. Whatever dreams the builders of such a place may have had faded away. The building wasn't far behind. But the walls still stood and most of the roof. Harley parked his truck behind the old store, strapped the pack onto his back, threw the saddlebag and pulse rifle over his shoulder, and continued on foot.

As he walked his boots echoed through the canyon, and within minutes, he knew something watched from the tree line. He kept his right hand on the butt of his slayer and neither shortened his gait nor lengthened it. It took more than an hour to cross the slide, and when his boots once again touched the old asphalt, he knew a Rage was building around him, and there was nowhere to run or hide. The sun had already dipped below the mountain peaks, and he faced a night in the Wilderness without shelter, on a mountain teaming with wildthings hunting.

He looked down the highway into the distance. He stood like a specter of the Old World and chewed the inside of his cheek before fishing in his shirt pocket for a cigarette. He smoked slowly, calming his nerves, and readying himself for what he knew fast approached. When his cigarette was gone, he flicked the butt away and shrugged. What was coming would come, and there was no way around it.

Sometime in the past a tree had exploded across the highway, blasted by a bolt of lightning, he supposed. Harley gathered the timber until he had a large pile of firewood on the asphalt. He built a campfire as night rushed in. Smoking another cigarette, he heard in the distance a snarl and a bark and shook his head. Wolves were out there watching him; wolves and whatever else might be gathering in the Rage.

The fire gasped out, and Harley knelt on the pavement and struck it back to life. "That's just the way of it," he said, staring softly into the black woods. "Come when you have a mind. I'll be here."

He drank the last of his water and, with a shrug, fished in his pack for his eyeset. His only meal for the day had been the vegetables steamed at the hotel. If he were to survive the night, which in all probability he would not, he would need energy. He slipped the eyeset on his brow and ordered a large Mexican pizza, a six pack of beer, four liters of water, and a carton of Marlboro. When it arrived, the stork skimmed over the treetops, and Harley heard rustling in the forest as the beasts of the Rage ran away, startled by the drone. The stork dropped down into the canyon and hovered to a stop above him with hardly a whisper of its rotors. It deposited the still steaming pizza, cold beer, water, and cigarettes on the ground, recorded his acceptance of delivery, and drifted away. Harley opened the box and took out a slice of pizza as he popped the top on a beer. He grinned into the forest and offered a toast.

"Roughing it's not what it used to be," he said good-naturedly.

He leaned against the pile of wood he collected, placing his slayer on the ground to his right and his cutlass on the ground to his left. He ate his pizza and drank his beer, his thoughts on the Wrynd he met earlier in the day and the young woman he killed. A man with grey eyes somehow removed the nanites connecting her to the Link. Was he the Greywalker after all, the legend brought to life? Before she died, she whispered the end was coming. An end to what? He wondered, and his mind whispered back *an end to everything.*

He started on this trip for the company of humanity, to go somewhere and watch people live; a mall, or park, anywhere where people still gathered to be people. He just wanted to be part of that for a moment. It was a path to point his boots along and perhaps a chance to eat a satisfying meal in a nice place, not order his meals by stork and eat them in the dirt and dust of the Wilderness. Now he considered another reason to visit the Hub. The Realm of America was missing a legionnaire, and he knew what became of her. It might make a visit to the Rocky Mountain Hub Marshal worthwhile. Of course, explaining he shot a hole through her chest might be complicated, but there were ways around the truth if it became necessary.

He was on the verge of nodding off when he heard something skipping toward him down the highway. He snatched up his weapons, climbed to his feet, and danced away from the fire toward the edge of the road with the slope of the canyon leading to the river. A buck charged into the camp, blinded momentarily by the firelight, and Harley lifted his sidearm and put it down.

Another one came at him from the opposite direction, and he shot it before it completely entered his circle of camp light, seeing it more by shadow than anything else. He didn't see the one behind him until it was too late. The buck raced toward him, rearing up to kick out with his front legs, catching Harley's slayer and ripping it from his grasp. He rolled on the ground and stood with the cutlass in his hand. The buck charged again, and he swung the blade, catching the deer in the neck, and the sword neatly parted the hide and flesh and ended its life. From the tree line, wolves burst forth, snarling, and growling and Harley dove for the pavement.

He scrambled on the ground and found his slayer where it had skidded to a stop by the fire. He gripped it tightly, pivoted with the sidearm in his right hand and the sword in his left, breathing heavily as a hundred glowing eyes stared fury from the darkness.

A flurry of bats swarmed around his head, and something impossibly large streaked past his face. He caught a glimpse of the wings and hooked talons of an owl, and then a dozen deer descended the mountainside. Among them, the wolf pack dashed.

Harley opened fire, taking down two wolves with a pulse blast that ripped through their sides. Even as he did, something small scurried across his boot and up his pants leg. He felt the bite of tiny teeth as he shook the mouse free and stepped on another. There were hundreds of them on the roadway now, coming his way, and he cursed, stomped, and fought the urge to scream.

"Mice! Why mice?" He shot one deer after another, their bodies piling around him, and three more wolves fell to his slayer. From the flickering firelight, he saw dozens of raccoons scurrying toward him, hissing, and he fired blindly in their direction.

He thought he might be able to make his way toward the slide, where at least he would have the high ground, and the animals wouldn't have the cover of the forest, when he heard the roar of something behind him. He turned to see a bear racing from the trees, and he fired and fired and cursed his fate as another buck hit him in the back and threw him to the ground. The mice swarmed him then and a raccoon dove at his face, teeth bared. He flung it away and scrambled to his feet as the bear drew closer.

This is the end, he realized, as the slayer grew warm in his hand. Eventually one would get through, and that would be all it would take. A wolf leapt across the fire and landed on top of him, and he again lost his grip on his slayer.

The night suddenly erupted in light as a vehicle's headlights cut through the darkness. A ball of blue lightning flashed before his eyes, then pierced the side of the wolf lunging for his throat. It yelped, and then lay still on top of him. Harley threw it aside and snatched up his slayer. The bear was raging toward him, and the ball of light whizzed past his head and rolled down the length of the bear's hide. Its fur burned like kindling, and it roared and ran into the forest.

A truck skidded to a stop, and the passenger's door opened. Harley scrambled inside as another wolf snapped at his boots. More deer trampled through the fire and slammed into the truck. Outside, the glowing ball of light danced from deer to wolf and back, dispensing death with blue fire.

As suddenly as it came, the Rage ended, and the animals slipped into the blackness of the forest.

Harley turned to look at the man behind the wheel, and by the glow of the dash lights, saw the driver grinning broadly. He nodded. "Marshal Walker," he said.

The big man nodded back. "Harley."

Stabbing pain in his right leg made him howl, and he cursed, unclasping his belt and pants, and pushing them down. There was a mouse latched onto his inner thigh, digging, and biting and Harley snatched it up. It squirmed in his hand as he held it before his face.

"Mice!" he screamed, rolling down the window enough to toss the rodent out. The mouse slid down the half-open window, squeaking, its whiskers stained with Harley's blood. He looked at the Marshal, furrowed his brow, and shook his head.

"I don't think he likes mice very much," a small voice said behind him. Harley turned to see two children and a young man huddled in the center of the back seat. The boy's and the young man's mouths were agape. The young girl seemed to be fighting a smile. He pulled up his pants.

Marshal Victor Walker clapped him on the shoulder with an impossibly large hand, and he winced. "Harley Nearwater meet the Bowden family. Bowden family, meet Harley Nearwater." Victor craned his neck to smile at the family behind him. "They call him the Castaway."

"Who's they?" Harley said. He caught a shift of movement outside and turned his head as a massive buck slammed into the door of the truck. The glowing blue light of Victor's scye flashed in the night, and gore from the animal's skull exploded against the window.

"Looks like its venison for dinner," Victor said cheerfully.

Harley watched the blood flow down the window and finally sat back in the seat with a sigh.

"Well, that was disgusting," the girl said.

Victor chuckled, patted Harley on the chest, and turned to wink at the girl in the back seat. "Welcome to the Wilderness, missy," he said.

II

The next White Dragon heading west through the Wilderness wouldn't depart for seven hours. Brinna spent the time in a hotel close to the station.

The hopper named Mustang bid her farewell after explaining how to obtain a train ticket and how to use her eyeset to access the Link and learn of departure times. When the little airship lifted into the overcast sky, Brinna felt a pang of sadness. For some reason, the ship seemed a kindred spirit, at least as close to one as she thought likely to find in the strange world of the Seven Realms.

She used her newly gained RTI account to pay for accommodations in a hotel where it seemed she might be the only guest. An automation escorted her to a room on the fifth floor. The 'bot was a floating, bodiless head with three thin arms that waved nervously before it as it skimmed on an unseen current of air, repeatedly asking if it could take her pack and her repeatedly telling the whim-digit to leave her be.

When the floating 'bot head finally let her close the door to her room, she dropped her pack on the floor and stood slack-jawed, staring at the opulence. The room was almost twice the size of the entire home she had shared with Mamal. A bed so large she could spread eagle across and not touch either side had pillows piled high. In another corner were a couch, chairs, and a table made of glass and the most beautifully sculpted wood she had ever seen. A bar of mahogany took another corner, and behind windows stretched from floor to ceiling. From them, she could look upon a bustling Hub where storks and transports of every size flitted.

The night was settling in, and Brinna fought raw emotions. The night before she sent the ashes of Mamal to heaven, and now she too was in a new world.

She stepped behind the bar and discovered row upon row of bottles filled with assorted colors of liquid. She removed the cap from one and took a sip. It burned all the way down. All this, and moonshine to boot.

She took two swift gulps from the bottle and kicked off her boots to try out the bed. It was softer than a bed of fresh cut hay. She stared up at a lazily twirling ceiling fan and drank more of the amber shine called Captain Morgan. She began to feel lighter and found a reason to smile, even though she knew it was just the shine smiling. It felt good anyway, to smile. Her world had ended, and she had stepped into another. She didn't know where this world might take her; only it would be west. She knew somehow; she must go west.

Her stomach grumbled, and she sat up, sloshing some of the shine on the comforter and cursing her clumsiness. That was sure to get her in trouble, but she couldn't seem to find enough ambition to care. She dug in her shiny new backpack until her fingers stumbled across her eyeset, and she slipped them onto her brow and focused her thoughts to think of the hotel she was staying in and that she was hungry. A voice answered, and she yelped, and then found herself giggling uncontrollably.

The voice in her head didn't seem to mind waiting. "How may I be of assistance?"

"Well," Brinna managed between giggles and another pull on the bottle of shine. "Is this that floating egg who showed me to this here room?"

"No, ma'am. I was not your assistant. I am room service. You indicated you desired food."

"I thought I desired food, and you're in my head telling me you can get me some? Is that right?"

"That is correct," the voice in her head replied. "What dining pleasure would you prefer this evening?"

"Dining pleasure?" Brinna snorted and took another shot of Captain Morgan. "Well, say I had a taste for some chicken and a passel of fries, could you manage that?"

"What kind of chicken?"

"What the hell do you mean what kind of chicken? The kind that pecks the ground and goes cluck cluck. You soft in the head?"

"I meant what portion of chicken do you prefer?"

"Portion? Hell, bring me the whole damn thing. I'll pick what I want to nibble on and save some for the road. Can you manage that?"

"Of course, Ms. Wilde."

"You can?" Brinna grinned. Captain Morgan was truly an amazing shine, best she ever tried. "Well, what if I was to say I don't want chicken, that I would rather have me a big ol' possum to eat? What would you say to that, prissy whimmy-diddle?"

"Our chefs can make you anything you desire, Ms. Wilde."

"You won't go scrape it up dead off the road somewhere, will ya?"

"No, ma'am. Our food is genetically grown on demand. Would you like a possum?"

Brinna laughed. "Hell, no, I don't want no possum. Bring me a chicken and some fries. And it better be a cooked chicken. You deliver me a squawking hen to butcher on my own, and I'll try out this new slayer on your metal eyes. You gather?"

"Anything else?"

"Nope. Drinkin' up your shine. Bring me some fried chicken and fries, and I'll be happy as a two pricked Billy-goat."

When the food arrived, Brinna ate on the bed and then made herself a bath in the largest tub she'd ever seen. She soaked in hot water and scrubbed her body clean, then fell asleep in the bath.

She dreamt of the west. It was an old dream, well known and comfortable. There was a great, flat-topped mountain and a winding road that led to an apple orchard clinging to the side of the river. She walked across a wooden bridge into the orchard, and there she felt safe, safer than she ever had.

She wasn't alone there, but she didn't know why she felt that way because she could see no one else. But she could feel them looking upon her, and their eyes were comforting. Whoever they were, they had planted this orchard, planted, and tended it in preparation for things to come, things Brinna felt she was somehow part of, although she had no idea what they might be. Those who watched reminded her of Mamal, who had always watched after her and whom she had failed to protect from the Rages of Gaia.

She woke with her eyes full of tears and let her head sink into the bath water and wash them away. She scrubbed her head, and as she dried her body, her hair billowed. She slipped into a simple pair of dungarees and tunic, strapped her new holster across her waist, and slid her sidearm home. She slipped on her boots, gathered her pack, and wandered out of the hotel toward the Dragon Station.

She was the only one waiting for the train to arrive, and as she waited, the streetlights kept the darkness at bay. She gawked at a city so full of promise and possibility and so completely foreign to anything she ever imagined. This was home to so many, but it was no home to her. Her home was out there, to the west, where an apple orchard may or may not be waiting. She would know soon enough.

She clutched the ChristGaian cross around her neck and let her hand drop when she realized what she was doing.

Turbines roared behind her, and she turned to watch a hopper descend onto the train platform. Mustang softly landed fifteen paces from her, and its engines slowly whined to a stop.

"Hello, Brinna Wilde," the transport said pleasantly.

"Hello, Mustang," Brinna said back, more than a little happy to see the transport one last time. "Coming to see me off?"

"Yes. I wanted to say goodbye and good luck to you, Brinna Wilde. I hope you find what you are looking for in the world."

She smiled and went to stand in front of the two large windows at the nose of the craft, which she couldn't help but think of as its eyes. "I hope you do, too, Mustang. I hope that someday you get to see the Wheel and fly among the stars."

"Thank you, Brinna," the hopper replied. It sounded wistful. "Someday, perhaps."

"Why'd you come to say goodbye? Don't do that with all your passengers, do yah?"

"No," Mustang replied. "But you are alone, Brinna, like I am alone. I thought this made us comrades and it is good to have a comrade."

Brinna nodded. "I reckon."

"If you find a time when you might need transport in the future, Brinna Wilde, think of me," Mustang said, and its engines began to whine. "I will come to you if I am able. I will search for you in the Vale."

She smiled and went to touch the side of the little airship, feeling both ridiculous for doing so and comforted at the same time. Mustang sounded tired, old, and sad. "Thank you, Mustang. If I need to fly away, I promise, I'll call."

The White Dragon arrived at the station, a long ribbon of white metal and glass. Its doors opened silently, and Brinna nodded once again to the little hopper as she stepped inside. The train's doors closed, and she sat in an empty cabin.

Outside, Mustang lifted into the evening sky, and the White Dragon roared and erupted across the tracks, rocketing west into a mystery Brinna understood was now her life.

III

They waited in the truck for half an hour, and through the bloody window, Harley watched his campfire sputter and die. Victor turned off the truck's headlights, and after ten more minutes of silence, with the night pressing in, his stomach growled.

"Time for dinner, don't you think?" Victor looked at Harley and opened his door, jumping out into the darkness, seemingly without a care. Harley and the Bowden family followed, tiptoeing through the carnage.

While Harley fed the fire, Victor dressed a deer and put half a dozen steaks on a spit. The young father gathered a couple of the larger logs Harley had scavenged and placed them closer to the fire so his children could sit. Harley felt them looking at him as he sat on a log across the flames. He ignored them. From what he could see of the man, he was a soft blinker, completely out of his element in the Wilderness. Harley wondered why this family was out in the night with the likes of Marshal Walker. He waited to hear.

The big Marshal crouched by the fire. He removed the steaks from the spit and placed them on metal plates he took from a kit in the back of his truck. He bit into one and smiled. "Now that's good eatin'. You're not having any of this, Harley?"

"Had pizza for dinner," Harley replied.

"Counting on storks for your food?" Victor grinned. "You're getting soft."

"May be," Harley replied.

Victor walked back to his truck, removed a cooler, and fished out two beers. He offered one to Harley with an arm that looked a klick long. "Me too."

Harley accepted the beer and popped the top. "You print yourself longer arms, Vic?"

"Longer?" Victor flexed his massive biceps. "No. These are the same ones I had last time we met."

Harley shrugged. The rumor was Victor Walker's arms weren't the only medical enhancement he ordered at a medprint, but Harley wasn't foolish enough to ask.

"Well, you look like a damn orangutan," Harley said, sipping his beer.

"Maybe so." Victor smiled and rubbed his head with one massive hand. "But I could reach across this fire and squash your melon like a bug."

Harley wasn't going to argue with the truth, so he turned his attention to the young man and children.

"What's their story?" Harley asked, not bothering to address them.

"This." Victor took the three of them a plate of venison they accepted halfheartedly. "Is Quinlan Bowden and his son Noah and daughter Raizor. Noah is ten and Raizor here is eight, is that right, Raizor?" The girl nodded as she picked up the steak and tore off a piece with tiny white teeth.

Harley peered at the girl. "What kind of name is Raizor?"

"Mine." She took another bite of steak and chewed quietly.

The Marshal sat on the log beside Harley. "Quinlan is looking for his wife and their mother, and I'm doing my best to be of assistance."

"Course you are," Harley said. "And why are you looking out here?"

"Because we believe Quinlan's lovely wife, Vania, was taken by the Wrynd. The last time Quinlan saw her was more than two weeks ago, shortly before Wrynd crept into Spanish Fork, licking their chops at all the little ones running about, no doubt. They left the Hub, and she left with them; under her own free will or not is the only question."

Harley looked at the young man, who was dark haired, slim, and had worry bruises under his eyes. He looked like he hadn't slept in days. "That right?"

"That's right." Quinlan nodded back. His voice held a hint of steel Harley hadn't expected to hear.

"So, you brought your children along to catch up with Wrynd who either gobbled up their momma or made her into one of them?" Harley asked.

"We have no family. Was I supposed to leave them home alone?" Quinlan replied.

"Safer than out here," Harley said, shaking his head. They were fools.

"Oh, I'll keep them safe, Harley. I'm a Marshal of the Founder Federation." Victor put his massive hand over his heart. "It's my sworn duty."

Harley finished his beer. "Are you serving in your official capacity right now, Marshal Walker?"

Victor laughed. "Well, no, I'd have to say that I'm not officially on the clock."

Harley nodded. Victor was known to be something of a hunting enthusiast. When he wasn't on duty, he liked to comb the countryside. While most people hated that the Rages turned nature against humanity, Victor seemed to revel in it. He felt the same about the Wrynd. He hunted them with the same enthusiasm.

"You bring a couple of kids on a Wrynd hunt? That's brilliant."

"You don't like children, do you, Harley?" Victor grinned.

"Like them fine. With Tabasco, and a side of fries." He winked at the two children huddled against their father. "Do yourself a favor and turn around and go home. Your wife is dead or much, much worse. Forget about her and keep your little ones safe."

Quinlan shook his head. "I can't do that. If she's alive, I can save her. I have to try."

Victor stood and offered Quinlan a beer he didn't take. "He has to try Harley. You'd have to care about something to understand that. Probably a foreign concept to you."

"Probably," Harley said.

Victor adjusted himself in front of the fire, and the children stared, mouths agape.

"Do you mind?" Quinlan said, shaking his head. "There are children."

"What?" Victor asked. "It's anatomy."

"It's anatomy, for sure," Harley fought a laugh. "Probably not human anatomy, but anatomy."

Victor scowled, then grinned sheepishly and sat back down. "Harley here is a rare breed. An enigma in our modern world. On his right hip, he carries his sidearm low, like a gunslinger of ages old; on his left, he carries a sword, steely and ready to tear flesh from limb. A relic of the Old World. So, is he a cowboy, or is he a pirate? Does he even know? Does either belong in the Age of Renewal?"

"May be I'm both," Harley said softly.

"Maybe." Victor raised his beer to him. "I know about the cowboy side, but enlighten me about the pirate side, Harley."

Harley pulled the cutlass from its scabbard; it sang as he freed it. "This is a replica of the 1917 cutlass once used by sailors of the United States Navy."

"Navy?" Victor asked, amused.

"The United States once had a navy, the greatest navy in the history of man." Harley's voice betrayed the slightest hint of respect, the slightest hint of remorse.

"And today it's a bureaucracy of the Founder Federation, just like every other nation on earth," Victor said.

Harley nodded. "May be. But once, it was an empire, and we all owned a piece of it. This . . ." He held the sword above his head, smiling. "Was a weapon of honor. High-tempered steel. It's long enough to serve its purpose and short enough to serve it well."

"With a slayer on one hip, why do you need a sword on the other?" Quinlan asked, picking at his food.

"Because technology can fail you, boy, but if you hone your skills and sharpen your blade, your strength and your sword never will." Harley stared into the darkness. "As long as you have those, you can fight on. In the end, that's all that matters, fighting on."

"You used to be a cowboy?" the boy asked between bites of steak. "I learned about cowboys. You used to ride horses?"

"Oh, yes!" Victor crowed. "Harley used to be a cowboy. He used to ride a horse on the range, herd cattle, all that happy shit of the Old World. Your horse tried to eat you, didn't he, Harley, when the Wildthing Rages came?"

Harley took the Stetson from his head, wiped away some of the dust on its brim, and scowled at the big Marshal. "He didn't try to eat me. He tried to stomp me to death."

Victor grinned his aggravating grin. Harley motioned to his elongated arms. "I guess you're still only sleeping with Fillers with a body like that?"

"Oh, you'd be surprised how many long to be wrapped in these arms, Harley." Victor winked.

"Just Fillers, I'd reckon." Harley smiled.

It was Victor's turn to scowl. "Have you seen any Wrynd in your travels?"

Harley almost lied, but in the end, didn't. "There's a horde of Wrynd about twenty klicks down the canyon on the other side of this slide. You'll have to hike in."

"Twenty klicks?" The big deputy frowned in the darkness. "Why would we need to hike? You mean to tell me you hiked up the canyon from Price?"

Harley shook his head. "Didn't say I did. I have a truck."

"Then we can hike over the slide and use your truck to get us there."

"Don't think so." Harley shook his head.

Victor narrowed his formative brow. "And why not?"

"My truck. I'll need it when I get back from the Hub."

"And it'll be there when we're done with it." Victor stood to throw more wood on the fire. Sparks fluttered into the darkness.

Harley considered for a moment. "You let me take your truck to the Hub, and I'll let you take mine to the Wrynd camp."

"Not likely," Victor said with a laugh.

"Then, no deal."

Victor raised an eyebrow. "I could just take it from you."

Harley nodded, put his hat back on his head. "You could try."

Victor stared at him for a moment and then laughed. "Good enough. How long will you be at the Hub?"

"No longer than forty-eight hours."

Victor nodded. "Link up, and I'll access you the truck."

Harley fished in his backpack for his eyeset and slipped it onto his head. On the Link, Victor granted him access to his truck, and Harley slipped the eyeset back off and put it away.

"Wait a minute," Victor said, pointing a long finger toward him. "What about yours?"

Harley fished in his pocket and brought out the truck's access tag. He tossed it at the Marshal. "I'm old school."

"You driving a brontosaurus?"

"It runs well enough," Harley said.

Victor pursed his lips, finally shrugged, and looked at the younger man and his children. "We get up early, and we'll have those kidnapping Wrynd monsters by early afternoon."

"There's quite a bit of them," Harley said.

"Yes, Harley," Victor said, grinning broadly. "But there's quite a bit of me."

After they had eaten, Victor put Quinlan and his children in the back of the truck and strolled happily to the fire with four long neck beers in his hands. Harley took the two Victor offered and fished in his pocket for his cigarettes. He offered one to the bigger man, who shook his head and curled his lips.

"Marlboro cured cancer, you know," Harley said, digging for his lighter.

"Actually, it didn't."

"Didn't what?" Harley asked.

"Marlboro didn't cure cancer." Victor sat down and opened his beer. "Tobacco companies donated a lot of money to cancer research, mostly as a public relations campaign, and the lab they largely funded was the one that discovered the cure. Marlboro was the most popular brand of cigarette, so when the news came on the Link, the headline read Marlboro cured cancer. It was just some headline writer's play on words. The headline was the only thing anyone remembered, and people like you have been repeating it ever since. Marlboro didn't cure anything."

Harley lit his cigarette and blew a smoke ring. "Thanks, professor."

Victor nodded. "You're welcome."

"One of us should probably keep watch. Just because we've been through one Rage doesn't mean that's the only one that will hit us tonight," Harley muttered, opening his beer.

"Pffft." Victor looked up, and the small glowing orb that had devastated the Rage slowly approached the two men sitting by the fire. It hovered a meter above Victor's head.

"I guess a scye does come in handy, from time to time," Harley said, eyeing the floating orb warily.

Victor flexed his arms, kissed his right bicep. "With these, I don't normally need it, but it does come in handy, from time to time."

Harley rolled his eyes. The scye glowed brightly in the night, and Harley could make out a soft hum from its shielding. He tried not to let Victor see how interesting he found the little orb.

"Are they difficult to control?" he asked.

"Not for me, but it takes some practice. They aren't as user-friendly as the civilian models. It's like having an extra arm or leg and an extra set of eyes." While Victor talked, he let the scye zip around the clearing like an oversized lightning bug. "It takes a while to learn how to control it without giving it any thought, to make it just a physical reaction, like using your hand to scratch your nose or open a door. It's a protector first and you must learn to meld your thoughts with its programming. They still make the tourist model. Buy one and try it out."

"Not much need for one of those," Harley said.

Victor tossed an empty long-neck into the fire and belched loudly. "Originally they were designed as a reality interface for the flesh 'bots who like to experience the Sphere through the Link. It was a way to interact with the world without having to step outside of the house. Through the Link and with the scye you can see, hear, taste, and feel everything just like you're physically present. When they first rolled them out, a bunch of people died from sensory overload because they crashed them into the sides of a mountain or the ground or some other damned fixed object." Victor slapped his leg, laughing, and looked at Harley quizzically. "You don't think that's funny? That's some funny shit, Harley."

Harley shrugged. "Suppose."

Victor shook his head. "Later scyes were developed with sensory disabling safeguards to prevent that from happening, but you could still hurt yourself using a scye, even while sitting on your recliner. They were a pretty awesome piece of technology at first. You could watch a farting dog lick himself from 2,000 klicks, just like you were there. But once the Link and linktags evolved and the Vale was born, the thrill was gone. Why bother watching a farting dog lick himself when you could be a farting dog licking himself?"

Harley smiled. "A farting dog licking himself. You've been a self-pleasuring dog with gas in the Vale, Victor?"

"Shut up."

"You said it," Harley said happily.

"Just an example." Victor looked more defensive than Harley thought he should, but he left it alone. "All I meant is that with the Link reality was, I don't know, kind of a bore, and scye sales died. Then the Marshals Service found a use for them. Take the same technology, add a shielding system, and you have something of serious potential. Part personal drone, part protector, and part weapon. It's the elite weapon of the champions of the Federation." Victor grinned, and Harley nodded, coveting.

With the fire slowly dying, Victor sent the scye to float ten meters above them. "It'll wake me if anything comes within 100 meters. Get some sleep."

Victor climbed behind the wheel of the truck, and Harley took shotgun, reclining his seat and letting it form around his tired and aching body. Beside him, Victor quickly started snoring.

He could hear the young man and his children getting comfortable in the back of the truck.

"Dad?" It was the little girl, her voice barely a whisper.

"What, Raiz'?"

"That man. Is he a Wrynd?"

"He's not a Wrynd," Quinlan said, and Harley could hear the young father settle in by his children.

"I think he's worse than a Wrynd," the boy said. Harley smiled and closed his eyes but didn't sleep for a long time.

IV

In the darkness of the tree line, a man sat on his haunches, watching the truck as those inside drifted to sleep. A mouse danced across his battered boots, and he reached down and offered it a sunflower seed. The mouse accepted and scurried away.

When faced with two paths, Harley Nearwater chose to make his own. He chose to cut a path toward chaos. Rather than help the woman or ignore the woman, he chose to kill her instead.

What might such chaos bring? The man grinned in the darkness.

The scye floating above the camp didn't alert the Marshal to the stranger's presence, and the stranger watched it for some time with his grey eyes before he turned and slipped into the night.

CHAPTER SEVEN

ROTTING

I

When Harley opened his eyes, Raizor was staring at him. She had climbed through the rear window from the shell to the back seat and was now leaning over, looking at him as if he was a biting spider. Her eyebrows knotted tightly, and her chubby cheeks flushed. She looked as if she had only recently awakened. He cursed and sat up.

"She doesn't think you're a very nice man." The boy had also slipped through the window and was now sitting in the seat directly behind him. Harley grinned. An eight-year-old girl and ten-year-old boy had gotten the drop on him.

"I'm not a very nice man," Harley whispered back.

Dawn pushed at night, and the cloudless sky slowly leached from black to dark blue. The two children on a hopeless search for their mother stared at him, and in the grey of the dying night, their eyes were black sockets he couldn't read.

"Do you think she's okay? Our mom?"

Harley looked at the boy, lost within his clothing, and shook his head softly. "No. I don't."

Noah nodded and bit a quivering lip. A tear slid down Raizor's face. "We don't think so either. But Dad does."

"Why does he?"

Noah scooted to the middle of the back seat, and Raizor cuddled next to him. "He always thinks things are going to be okay."

"Are they?"

Raizor shook her head and silently mouthed no.

Harley looked out the windshield. "Life's intrestin that way."

Victor moaned, stretched, and finally opened his eyes. With senses that dull, it was a wonder the big man was alive, even with a scye. When he looked back again, Quinlan was leaning through the back window. His eyes wide and alert. He wasn't smiling. Harley wondered how long he had been awake and imagined it had been since his children first opened their eyes. Perhaps he had misjudged the young man. They exchanged a nod.

"Who's got breakfast?" Victor asked. His booming voice echoed in the truck and was obscene as morning kissed the mountains.

"Already ordered." Quinlan raised his right hand and an eyesct dangled.

"Hope you ordered coffee, 'cause I got to have me some coffee." Victor threw open the door and stepped out to relieve himself on the carcass of a wolf. The scye dropped to hover over his shoulder, and when he returned to the cab, it took its position above them.

A stork floated down to their campsite a few minutes later with breakfast. There was orange juice, coffee, milk, sausage, eggs, toast, pancakes, disposable plates, cups, and utensils. Quinlan slipped on his eyeset long enough to accept delivery of the meal. He dished up food for them, and they sat on the back seat to eat their breakfast.

Victor served himself a huge helping, grumbling there were no hash browns. As he sat, slurping his food, and alternately farting and burping, Harley wondered how he ever became a Marshal.

He had to remind himself he had seen Victor in battle. With

his medically altered arms, he was a force worthy of respect. He was also overconfident and far too loud to survive long in the Wilderness. If his truck on the other side of the slide wasn't there, he gave them a day or two at most before the Wrynd, or the Rages claimed them.

He was a Marshal so he could call for his wings, and it might arrive before it was too late, but he didn't think Victor would do so. Too much stubborn and misplaced pride. It was too bad. The children didn't deserve the fate rushing their way. Then, no children deserved the fate rushing their way.

Their father seemed forged of stronger stuff than Harley originally gave him credit for, but he could see in the softness of his eyes there wasn't a killer hiding within. Outside of the Hubs and the Link, if a man wanted to survive, he needed to be a killer.

As the light of morning finally found them, there was no sign of wildlife outside the truck, at least none living. The carnage from the Rage was everywhere. There were more than thirty deer carcasses scattered across the roadway, and intermixed with their lifeless bodies were wolves, a half dozen raccoon, dozens of bats, and three large owls. The wounded bear had fled.

When Noah and Raizor went outside to relieve themselves, they had to pick their way through the wreckage of animal flesh to take care of their business at the tree line. While they did, Quinlan stood behind them, his body tense as he nervously gripped a baseball bat. Harley marveled.

"What's he going to do, hit a line drive if something attacks?"

Victor looked at the young man and grinned between mouthfuls. "We all live in our realm, Harley. You know that."

"You could have given him a slayer."

"Tried to," Victor replied, picking at his teeth with a fork. "Said he was a horrible shot. To each his own, you know?"

Quinlan and his children climbed back into the truck, shivering in the cool of the morning. The Marshal turned on the heater and opened the windows to give some relief from his abundant gas.

Victor finished the last of the food and coffee and barked they needed to get their gear together if they were going to make it across the slide before noon. Quinlan handed Noah a jacket and slipped a sweater over Raizor's tangled hair. They stepped out of the truck, the children trying to sidestep the gore of the dead animals on the road. Harley remembered being their age and how much he loved seeing animals in the wild. He wondered if any child would ever look at wildlife and feel that way again.

Victor opened the back of the truck, and Quinlan started stuffing items into his pack. Harley watched with interest as the younger man carefully wrapped his eyeset and stowed it away. It was a familiar routine.

"Didn't take you for a Pilgrim." Harley slipped the holster back around his waist and buckled the scabbard and sword to his side.

Quinlan nodded toward Harley's sword. "Didn't take you for a pirate. Or a cowboy."

Harley grinned despite himself. "I'm a whole lot of things."

"What do you kill with most, the slayer or the sword?" Quinlan stripped off his shirt and pulled on a fresh one.

Harley's smile faded to a frown. "Killed too many with both, I gather."

Quinlan shrugged and lifted Raizor onto the tailgate and tried to wash her face with a wet wipe. She snatched it away and washed it herself, halfheartedly.

Harley surveyed the forest, not comfortable with their exposure among so many dead animals. Scavengers would arrive soon enough. "You live in the Hub. Thought people in the Hubs had a linktag. It seems to me it would be more convenient than an eyeset."

"Probably."

"So?" Harley dug in his pocket for a cigarette.

Quinlan patted the tailgate, and Noah tried to hop up. He had to have some help. He reluctantly took the wipe his father offered. Quinlan handed both his children their toothbrushes, and they sat on the tailgate swinging their legs and brushing their teeth.

"So, the linktag makes you lose focus."

"Focus on what?" Harley found his cigarettes and lit one up.

"On what's real," Quinlan replied.

"That's hateful language," Victor volunteered from the front of the truck, where he was filling his pack. "What part of our wonderful new world isn't real?"

"I'll rephrase," Quinlan pulled his toothbrush from the pack and Noah handed him the toothpaste. "It may be real enough for now. But it's not sustainable."

"Sustainable?" Victor walked to the back of the truck, and his scye trailed behind him. "The Federation has created the greatest civilization the world has ever known. We've cured disease, ended hunger, created Hubs for all of humanity, built the Link and the Vale, where you can be and do anything you want. We have cities at the bottom of the ocean, and there's no part of The Deep we can't reach. We have colonies in Outland on Luna and Mars, and we'll someday reach the stars. Humanity is no longer a prisoner of Gaia. Citizens of the Federation have an income, housing, medical, and a linktag as a basic human right. This is the Age of Renewal, and you think it isn't sustainable? Are you sure you're a Pilgrim because you sound like a Neand, one of those who refuse to evolve, to let go of old ways and superstitions?"

Quinlan scowled. "I'm no Neand. I'll take advantage of what your Seven Realms have to offer, but I won't be dependent on it, and neither will my children."

Victor stooped in front of Noah and Raizor. "Wouldn't you rather have a linktag so you could be on the Link anytime you want, not have to put on those silly eyesets?"

"We've never been on the Link," Noah said flatly.

"Never?"

Quinlan shook his head. "If we need something from the Link, I can find it. They'll get an eyeset when they need one, and they don't need one now. Vania and I want our children living in reality. Call it the Sphere if you want, but it's just reality. We want them to know what the real wind feels like on their face, to feel the warmth of the real sun. We want them to be truly alive, not to imagine a life, but live one."

Victor looked at Quinlan incredulously. "There have been petitions to the Senate to have it declared child abuse not to give your children access to the Link. If that were law, I would have to take them from you for their protection."

"Then it's a good thing it's not law," Quinlan said.

Harley laughed at the ice in the young man's voice, and Victor slapped him on the shoulder good-naturedly. "What isn't sustainable about our wonderland, Quinlan Bowden?"

"How many people are unemployed in the realms, Marshal Walker?"

"Upwards of 90 percent. But everyone has an income. Your right as a member of the Federation. Even you."

Quinlan squirted toothpaste on his brush. "The Seven Realms didn't invent right to income. It was around ten years or more before the end of the Old World. It came from the United States. Originally, it was called right to work. Senator Facio introduced the legislation to force businesses to give people the opportunity of a job, not automate everything. He just wanted to give everyone a fair chance to build their dreams, a fair chance to do something to get ahead in life. But technology made most workers obsolete."

Quinlan started to slide the toothbrush into his mouth, then stopped. "You didn't need a hand at the controls because automations could take care of everything far more efficiently than humans ever could. Business advocates responded by having their puppets introduce alternative legislation. For every job eliminated due to automation, the corporate body would donate the equivalent wage to the Right to Income fund. They figured it was a win for them, and they were right. They'd pay the wages of an employee not to have to employ them, and pocket the savings from retirement, medical, office buildings and everything that went along with it. It was either that or Right to Work. Right to Income won out. The Federation adopted it when it wiped away the Old World and Right to Income was a right for more than nine billion people. Business just responded by creating three times that many automated jobs."

"Sounds like a win for everyone," Victor said.

"Maybe." Quinlan pointed the toothbrush at the Marshal, and the paste fell onto his boot. Raizor giggled and took the brush from her father, applied more toothpaste, and handed it back. "But if you give nine billion people nothing useful to do, they'll find something to do that's probably not useful, something much worse. Before the Energy Wars, there were close to twelve billion of us on the planet. The wars and the aftermath shaved off close to three billion, and since then we've been in decline. The world population is projected to be fewer than eight billion in another century, and that's as our lifespan is increasing. What's the average lifespan now, 160, 190, higher? So why is that, in this utopia you've built? Could it be that procreation is just too damn much work? The most popular sexual partner of today is the Filler. Digital wallpaper in the Vale is what we want to have sex with."

Harley smiled and hooked a thumb toward Victor.

"Why, Marshal? Because they give you exactly what you want, no questions asked, and Fillers are always satisfied."

Noah looked wide-eyed at his father, and Quinlan chuckled. "You two cover your ears for a second." Both children dutifully put their hands over their ears, giggling. "Close to forty percent of the population who are in a relationship are in a Vale relationship. They've never physically touched."

"That's Neand-hateful language," Victor said. His lips were

smiling, but his eyes were not.

Harley chortled. "Hard to procreate on the Link Victor, even with your dick."

Quinlan shoved the toothbrush in his mouth and then choked on a toothpaste laugh. "The biggest trend in parenthood now is having a Vale baby instead of a Sphere one. Why? Because you can shut the damn thing off when it's crying or sick or interferes with other things you'd rather be doing. Age of Renewal, you say? What exactly are we renewing, how we came from slugs? This world of your Federation isn't sustainable. As a species, we're rotting. The Wrynd is the first sign, but there will be more. The world knows it and has responded with the Rages. Gaia is cleansing herself of us."

"You're not a Neand. You're a radical." Victor's tone now held a hint of menace. "An anarchist even."

Harley slowly stepped back and let his hand drop to his slayer. He had no stake in this fight, but if he were, he would choose Quinlan's. He had no idea who the man was, but he wasn't any ordinary Pilgrim.

"I'm no anarchist, but I recognize anarchy on the horizon. You've given us everything we want and taken everything we need. Your Seven Realms destroyed what held us together; community, religion, history, race, ideals, and replaced it with the Vale, where everyone has their MyRealm. You think you've cured our ills, but the biggest ill we have is our hatred, and you didn't cure it, you just channeled it. If the Vale ever fails, you'll find yourself with billions of monsters you only thought chained."

Quinlan and Victor were toe-to-toe now, the bigger man glaring down at the smaller. Noah and Raizor sat on the tailgate, their legs crossed, watching their father, but Harley saw no concern in their eyes, only curiosity. *Who the hell are these people?* He thought.

"Elijah and Ephraim were right to send you away, and I was a fool to offer you help. I should throw you in a cell for being a revolutionary."

Harley was surprised to see not a hint of fear in the young father's eyes. He had truly misjudged him. "I'm just a husband searching for his wife," Quinlan said softly, returning Victor's stare.

"The Wrynd have her," Victor said and strapped his holster around his waist.

Raizor held out her hand. "You've brushed your teeth enough, Dad." Perhaps the girl sensed what Harley did.

"Thanks, Raiz'," Quinlan said.

Harley cleared his throat and moved his hand. He had questions of his own before he reached the Hub, and now was as good a time to ask them as any other.

"Speaking of Wrynd," he said, as amicably as he was able. "Always thought they were at best Pilgrims, but mostly Neands, the most radical of the radical Neands. Surprised to learn they aren't."

"Of course, they're Neands," Victor snapped. They were pushing the big Marshal's patience, but Harley pushed a little harder.

"No. They're not," he replied. "I never thought about how or where they get their ink. I knew it came from somewhere, but I just reckoned they were cooking it up in the Wilderness. Then I was watching the Wrynd horde you plan to walk this man and his children into, and I saw Scimitar Hatcher receive his latest shipment of ink. It came by stork. That was a bit of a surprise, to see a stork drop off a rather large package of an illegal drug to a Wrynd hunting party in the middle of the Wilderness. The bigger surprise was when I realized he wasn't wearing an eyeset. That's when I gathered ol' Hatcher had a linktag and ordered up his batch of ink on the Link. Just got me wonderin' how in the world could that be, that the Marshals of the Federation, the champions of the Seven Realms, how could they not know storks delivered their ink?"

"They don't get it from the Realms," Victor said with a growl. "They're outcast chattel, and if they come near the Hub, we deal with them. If they don't, we leave them to the Rages."

"But they still managed to walk right into the Rocky Mountain

Hub and steal this man's wife, the mother of his children?" Harley slipped another cigarette into his mouth. "How many battlewagons are in the Federation fleet, Victor?"

"I'm not in the Navy, Harley."

"Forty." Quinlan answered for him. "Not counting fortresses, corsairs, wings, and sentinels. Those are just the big airships. There are three solar cruisers in orbit around the Wheel and a fourth in orbit of Mars."

"More than a few, I guess you'd say." Harley inhaled, let the smoke trickle through his nose. "And how many in the Legion?"

Victor's jaw flexed, but he made no sound.

"A little over one million," Quinlan answered. "Countless automations."

"Whole lotta troops, I'd say. How many in the Marshals Service, Victor? Surely you know that?"

Victor's scye floated down to hover behind his right shoulder. "Each Hub has a Chief Marshal; each Chief Marshal has fifty Marshals to serve justice. Each Hub has thousands of sentinels patrolling the borders for threats from the Wilderness that can be used to assist Marshals."

"A massive army without an enemy to fight. So, with all that force, with all that firepower, why is it that the Wrynd thrive on the outskirts of every Hub on the planet?" Harley walked closer to the Marshal and stared up at him. "Why are they there, Victor? Why hasn't the Federation dealt with them?"

"Because the Wilderness is not our realm, Harley. I've killed more than 100 Wrynd in my time, and plan to kill a few more today. How 'bout you?"

Harley smiled an ugly smile. "A few more than that, Victor. A few more than that. If the Federation wanted to respect Gaia, really wanted humanity to leave the Wilderness to nature, why not clear out the Wrynd? It wouldn't take the mighty Seven Realms that long. Unless you don't want to. Unless there's another reason for the Wrynd being there, stalking us. Got to thinking about that when I realized the Seven Realms were keeping them alive with ink."

"That's because it's not happening, Castaway. You're living in a fantasy." Victor's jaw was flexing as he ground his teeth. He pushed past Harley and returned to the front of the truck.

"Nothing about my life is a fantasy. And you're a liar Marshal Walker," Harley called after. "Or a fool. If the Seven Realms provides their ink, and it does, then they're playing some part in the Federation's plans. I wonder what that might be?"

Victor turned and stomped toward him, and Harley thought he might have overplayed his hand. Then he caught a scent on the soft breeze swirling through the canyon, a hint of decay, blood, and filth that blended with the death around them far too late for him to not recognize its source. He held out his left hand, and his right dropped to his slayer.

"Since we're about to meet up with the Wrynd, why don't we just wait and ask them?" he said.

II

He couldn't see them, he couldn't hear them, but on the soft breeze of the morning air, he could smell the rot of them.

"Who's coming?" Quinlan asked and moved closer to his children.

Harley nodded toward the slide. "The Wrynd. They're coming."

Victor's scye dropped to hover above his left shoulder. "How many?"

Harley faced the slide but didn't bother pulling his slayer. It was too early for that. "Enough."

Victor's scye rocketed into the sky and disappeared over the horizon. "Twenty," Victor said a moment later. "Twenty of them and Hatcher is leading the way."

"A fray." Harley planted his feet and stood straight, ready, waiting. "A hunting party and we're going to be easy pickings here. Use your scye and drop them now."

"No!" Quinlan screamed. "What if Vania is with them?"

Harley shook his head. "Then we'd be doing her a favor. Kill them, Victor, or they're apt to kill you."

Victor grinned. "Oh, I think you underestimate my power, Harley Nearwater."

"No. I don't." This wasn't going to be pleasant. He pointed at Quinlan. "I'd get the little ones stowed away if I were you."

Quinlan grabbed Raizor and tossed her into the back of the truck. Noah clambered in behind her. He slammed the tailgate shut, closed the shell hatch, and came to stand next to Harley with the baseball bat in his hand. Harley shook his head sadly and went to the cab of the truck to get the pulse rifle he had taken off the legionnaire. He shoved it roughly into Quinlan's hands.

The Wrynd stormed over the crest of the slide, and by their speed, Harley knew things weren't going to end well. They were amid a full ink flare and would be hungry for flesh. Scimitar Hatcher led the way, his massive arms and legs pumping to reach them first.

Right beside him ran a slim, athletic woman with the same crazed look as the others. Her hair was long and blonde, and a tattoo transformed the right side of her face into a gaping, fleshless skull. A bright green and bloody wrap covered her small breasts, and her midsection was flat and hard. Shorts clung to powerful looking legs. Harley thought she would be stunning; except she was a Wrynd. She wore no shoes, and the nails of her hands and feet were claws. He didn't need to hear a gasp from Quinlan to know this was Vania Bowden, wife of Quinlan, mother of Noah and Raizor, and the latest in a lengthy list of Wrynd Scimitar Hatcher's chosen.

"Vania, what have they done to you?" Quinlan sobbed.

Hatcher slid to a stop fifteen meters from them. Vania and the eighteen other Wrynd stopped beside him, fanning out until they encircled the truck. Their eyes were black. They cawed like lunatics.

"Harley Nearwater!" Hatcher roared, and it was difficult to tell if it was a roar of rage or delight. Perhaps it was both.

"Scimitar." Harley nodded, his hand never straying far from his still holstered sidearm. Victor held his slayer, pointing it from Wrynd to Wrynd, and his scye made frantic circles in the air around him. He was scared, Harley realized, but even more terrified to have it revealed.

"I didn't order takeout," Hatcher said, and the other Wrynd laughed hysterically, except for the young woman by his side. She looked confused and even more agitated than the others. They had pumped so much ink into her she seemed able to focus only on the need to feed. Harley made a sidelong glance at Quinlan. His breathing was jagged, and Harley wondered exactly how long he would be able to hold things together.

"No? Well, perhaps we'll be on our way then," Harley offered.

"You're a funny little Indian, Harley," Hatcher said with a laugh. "We're always up for takeout."

"Love me some Indian food!" One of the Wrynd said with a giggle, and Harley decided when the time came, he would die first.

"Vania!" Quinlan's voice was a whimper of lost hope that turned to a wail of despair and echoed in the canyon. She looked his way but gave no hint of recognition, and Harley thought the young man's legs might buckle.

Victor took a step forward and the Wrynd all balanced on the balls of their feet, ready to leap at the first sign from their Scimitar. The Marshal had no idea how tenuous their situation was. "That woman is this man's wife. I'm here to take her home."

Hatcher looked at Victor mutely for a moment, then roared laughter, his pointed teeth clattering against each other and biting into the flesh of his lips. They bled down his chin. His tongue whipped out to lap at the blood. "Vania? Kidnapped? No, I think not. Her place is with me, and she knows that. She wishes it. She has dreamed of it longer than she's known of this pathetic man." Hatcher narrowed his brow at Quinlan and snickered. "You know the truth. She came to me of her own free will."

"You lie!" Quinlan screamed.

"You know I don't."

Victor aimed his slayer at the Wrynd Scimitar's tattooed face. "That may be so, but he has the law on his side, and I'm the law, so she's coming with us. One way or another."

"The law?" Hatcher seemed amused, but Harley detected the quickness in his breath, the impatient tapping of his toes.

"Marshal Walker of the Federation."

"Victor? Victor, is that truly you?" Hatcher replied. "I hardly recognize you. You've had some modifications done. You look something like a monkey."

"Orangutan," Harley said.

"Orangutan!" Hatcher cawed. "Yes! A big orangutan." He gripped Vania by the arm and pulled her close, and she wrapped her other arm around him in a fierce embrace. Harley heard Quinlan moan and out of the corner of his eye could see the children with their faces pressed against the window of the truck. "Vania, this man is a Marshal of the mighty Founder Federation. Are you impressed?"

"Hungry," she said, and her voice was harsh, jagged, and oddly seductive.

"Marshals are delicious!" The Wrynd who shouted he liked Indian food screamed. Yes, he would be the first to die.

"I want me one of them wings!" another said, and they all laughed. Harley knew there was no way to prevent death from coming.

"Well, you heard them, Victor. I think they would like to have you for dinner, and as their humble leader, how could I possibly say no?" Hatcher took a step forward.

The Wrynd who screamed for a wing leapt toward them, and Victor hit him with his scye. The scye threw him off his feet, and he landed by the others. Its shielding caught his shirt on fire. He tore the shirt free, and there was a fist-sized burn on his chest. He didn't seem to notice, but he didn't rush forward again either. Victor sent the scye circling menacingly around the others.

"I see we're at an impasse." Hatcher squatted, licking at his dirty fingers. "You might kill many of my fray, but even with the formidable Harley Nearwater, the Castaway himself at your side, I think in the end, we would dine on you." Hatcher cast his eyes at the dead animals around him, smiling. "We're civilized people, and there are ways around an impasse. I suggest a contest. It's the best way to deal with an impasse. A contest! Yes, Mr. Marshal, a contest would be best. The Wrynd Horde loathes weapons. We believe in the honor of true combat, claw against claw, teeth against teeth, fist against fist, and strength against strength. Not the vulgarity of pulse weapons or dirty flying scyes."

"Claw, teeth, fist, and strength under the influence of ink, you mean?" Victor said.

Hatcher raised an eyebrow and smirked. "Ink for us, nanite implants and medprint body parts for you. I see little difference."

"What contest?" Harley asked, caressing the butt of his slayer.

"A contest between my beautiful scepter and the Marshal." Hatcher made a sweeping gesture toward the young woman at his side. "He wants to take her away from her shield, so I believe she should have some say in that. If he can defeat her in battle, he can take her back to this pathetic, whimpering creature. But if she defeats him, then, well, what shall I say. You'll stay for dinner, yes?"

"Just passing through," Harley said, and Victor shot a glare. He didn't care.

"You should be careful of your company, Harley," Hatcher replied.

"Vania!" Quinlan tried again. "Just come with us. We can get you help."

Vania looked at her husband and licked her lips, smiling, and Quinlan finally fell to his knees.

"Agreed!" Victor roared, and he winked at Harley. "Me against your little princess."

"No weapons!" Hatcher said, grinning. He clapped his hands together like a large child. "Claw against claw, teeth against teeth, fist against fist, strength against strength."

"Whatever." Victor unbuckled his holster, tossed it onto the truck, and looked down at Quinlan. "I'll have your little family home safe and sound by nightfall," he whispered.

"Kill them now, Victor," Harley stepped closer and gripped his right arm. "Use your scye and kill them now, or you'll die."

Victor grinned, but his eyes betrayed looming panic. "I've got this under control, Harley."

Hatcher looked at his fray and smiled. "Clear us an arena."

The Wrynd rushed to create a circle of death with the bodies of the fallen, both great and small, piling one on top of the other to create a roughly hewn wall of flesh twenty meters in diameter. Blood flowed in streamlets from the corpses, pooled, and slithered off the highway and into the forest, where the trees seemed to lean forward to lap it up.

Gaia is gathering her dead, one drop at a time, Harley thought, and felt a shudder ripple up his backside. *How much more wine will she drink today?*

Flies, still hungover from the cool of the night, sauntered through the morning air to follow their feast of flesh.

Vania calmly stepped inside the circle, still smiling softly, almost shyly. There was a sensuous control of her every movement Harley found stimulating. He understood why Quinlan brought his children into the Wilderness looking for her. He would have done the same.

As Victor turned to step inside the dead animal ring, Quinlan, still on his knees, lifted his head slowly. Tears cut trails to his chin. Victor smiled at him. "Don't worry; I won't hurt her."

Quinlan shook his head. "She'll hurt you. You can't beat her. Even with your damn orangutan arms, even with your nanobot strength, she'll destroy you. She trained me every day for twelve years. I never even came close to beating her. We need to find another way."

Victor shook his head and brushed past him. His scye hovered above the truck as Victor stepped inside the circle.

Quinlan glanced hopelessly at Harley and shook his head. "He can't win." Harley watched as the two began their dance with death and found he was in complete agreement.

"You're married to her?"

"She's one of the best fighters I've ever seen." Quinlan fought to steady his voice. "I don't know where she learned to do what she does, but he'll die, and they'll come for us."

Harley nodded and stepped closer as the two in the ring made their first testing thrusts toward the other. "Stand up."

Quinlan climbed to his feet and managed to lift his gaze.

"Have you killed before?" Harley asked.

Quinlan shook his head.

"You'll have to now."

Quinlan looked him in the eyes and then looked away. "I'll try."

"A steer tries, son," Harley replied, and Quinlan flinched. "You have to get this done. No hesitation. None. Do you understand? You kill, or you and your little ones die. There's nothing else. When the time comes, you kill everything in your way, and maybe we can walk away from this."

The Marshal and Quinlan's wife paced, smiling as if they weren't seeking out the simplest way to kill the other. Victor suddenly stopped, and Vania did as well, staring across at one another. Vania smiled softly and attacked in a single, impossible leap three meters into the air, her arms and legs extended and a fierce snarl on her face. Victor batted her away with his massive right arm, and she crashed into the wall of flesh.

"Nice tumbling skills," Victor said, strolling toward her. "Too bad this ain't tumbling class."

A soft breeze whispered down the canyon, and the forest sighed. The rustle of the trees sounded like applause. Harley thought Gaia must be pleased with the show. He could sense the wildthings out there, gathering in the forest to watch man kill man. There was no need for a Rage; they were raging fine all by themselves.

Vania charged again, leaping forward, and kicking out. Victor blocked her strike with his left arm and brought his right down on her shoulder, knocking her to the ground. As she fell, she swung her right leg and delivered a savage kick to Victor's groin. Harley winced, but it was Vania, not Victor, who howled in pain. The hooked toe of her right foot twisted with the bone protruding.

Victor shrugged and tapped his groin with his knuckles, and there was a soft thud as they struck the protective cup beneath his clothing. "Always protect your jewels; that's my motto." He advanced toward the kneeling Wrynd, smiling, and she reached down to snap her toe back into place. As he approached, she somersaulted toward him, and when he reached for her, she folded at the torso and thrust forward, raking the claws of her hands across his forearms.

Victor cursed and swung out with his left arm, but Vania ducked beneath it and sashayed out of his reach, walking on the balls of her feet like a dancer. Harley could hear the broken bones of her toes crunching, but she didn't seem to notice. Victor rushed at her, but again she ducked beneath his grasp and spun, slicing with claws to leave bloody scratches down his back.

Every time he attempted to get a hand on her, she slipped out of his reach, only to leave him bloody and torn. The Wrynd around the circle cried in delight. The sight of the blood on the big man was working them into a frenzy Harley knew would soon overcome them.

The wind blew harder, and the trees laughed louder, and from the darkness of the forest, Harley saw something move. He turned his head and the bear that attacked during the night paced forward, and then back into the gloom. Most of the fur had burned from its body; the skin beneath was pink and bloated. It looked to be grinning at them, anxious for the killing to end so it could feast.

If the Wrynd didn't have them, then the Rages very well might. Harley swallowed hard and tried to prepare himself for what was to come. When the dance ended and the Wrynd attacked, he thought it fair odds he could take down half of them. After that, he would need help if they were to live. If Victor survived, then with his scye he could easily finish off the rest. Watching the two within the ring of animals, Harley no longer considered that a possibility. That would leave only Quinlan to tip the scale in their favor. Harley glanced toward the quivering young man, gritted his teeth, and prepared to die. But first, he would kill.

Victor's nervous glances to the outside of the circle and the other Wrynd confirmed the terror quickly overtaking him. When Vania ducked beneath yet another blow and scraped her nails down his right side, he howled in frustration, and the scye above the truck suddenly rushed forward, hurtling toward her.

Vania flipped away from the Marshal, and as the scye raced at her head, she leapt into the air and came down on Victor's back, her feet digging into his side. She made two quick chops into his neck with her clawed hands. Blood poured from the gaping wound and Vania hugged him, buried her face against his neck, and tore free a hunk of flesh.

The Marshal fell to his knees, then to his chest, as the woman rode him to the ground, still biting, ripping, and beginning to feed. The scye fell on the ground beside him.

Harley cursed and drew his slayer and his cutlass. As the other Wrynd pounced, he went to work. The Wrynd with the mouth was the farthest away, but he made a point of taking him down first with a pulse blast to the forehead. Vania was oblivious to the battle raging around her. She tore at the dead Marshal with teeth and claw.

Harley ducked out of the way of one rushing Wrynd and took another down with a pulse blast. His cutlass tore through the arm of another. Two more were rushing toward him, and as he turned, he saw Quinlan strike one across the head with a swing of his baseball bat. At least he acted. Perhaps there was a chance.

Scimitar Hatcher was oblivious to the battle around him. He squatted on the ground, fingers dancing across his face, enraptured by the savagery of Vania.

Harley killed two more Wrynd, and Quinlan dropped the bloody bat and opened fire with the pulse rifle. Harley dove to the ground as the young man demonstrated perhaps the greatest spectacle of poor marksmanship Harley had ever witnessed. He hit nothing he aimed at, but he did distract the Wrynd enough for Harley to finish the job. When he holstered his sidearm, eighteen of the twenty Wrynd were dead on the highway.

Hatcher still stood where he had, bouncing on his haunches, oblivious to the death of his fray, as he watched Vania feed on the dead Marshal. It was becoming a gruesome scene as the woman bathed in his blood. Hatcher was pleased but made no move to take part.

Harley stepped into the dead animal ring toward Vania, and she stopped feeding and looked his way with wildness in her eyes. She crouched, coiled and ready to strike. When she did, she would move fast, perhaps faster than he could counter. He hadn't seen any faster in his life.

Quinlan took a step toward her as well. He dropped the pulse rifle and knelt before her, his eyes brimming with tears. "Vania. It's me. It's Quin."

She glared at him with black eyes, and something like a growl bubbled up from her throat to pass between her bloody lips.

"Mom!" Noah and Raizor were standing outside of the truck, both crying as they looked at their father kneeling beside the thing that used to be their mother.

Vania's eyes danced their way, and her brow furrowed. Beneath the blood and the gore, Harley saw the woman she once was. She was lovely. She looked at Quinlan, her eyes lost and confused.

"Quin?" she said. "You brought them here? How could you bring them here?" Her face for a moment was a storm of emotions, fear, hunger, hatred, confusion, and perhaps even love. Harley used that moment to step forward and put his cutlass through her heart.

A sigh escaped her lips as the life ran out of her, and Quinlan folded her into his arms. He howled and tried to wipe the Marshal's blood from her mouth. But there was no wiping it away. She was baptized in it.

Vania's death broke the spell cast upon Hatcher. He roared and prepared to leap, and Harley's hand flashed. He pointed his slayer and smiled. "Just the way of it, Scimitar."

The wind suddenly howled, and beneath the howl, there was a growl and the grinning bear, full of fury and pain and rage, rushed from the tree line. Harley turned and opened fire. Two quick pulse blasts to its head and the bear crashed into the side of the Marshal's truck and lay still.

When he turned back, Hatcher was standing at the top of the slide. Even from such a distance, Harley could see the murder in his eyes. Hatcher pointed a clawed finger at him, and before he could fire, the Wrynd slipped over the horizon and disappeared.

Harley went to stand over the bear. It was still alive; its breaths labored and shallow. The wind flitted away again, and the forest stood still, and silent, and waiting. He pointed the slayer at the bear's head and fired once. "Not this day," he whispered.

He went to the truck and leaned against the grill, holstering his slayer, and resting the cutlass on the hood. He could feel his heart-beat slowly returning to normal. He reached into his pocket and pulled out a cigarette. He smoked as Quinlan and his children cried over the dead thing that once was their wife and mother, then he cleaned his cutlass and returned it to its scabbard.

The Wrynd Scimitar had escaped, and unless there was a mira-cle and the Rages hit him before he could rejoin his horde, there would soon be hundreds of Wrynd coming their way. Harley had seen enough to know there were no miracles. Hatcher would make it to his Wrynd, and they would be coming for their vengeance.

Perhaps the only way to avoid being forever hunted was to make some form of appeasement for the death of his chosen. Harley looked at the grieving family and made his choice.

He threw the dead Marshal's pack into the back of the truck and pulled out Quinlan's and his children's. He tossed them inside the dead animal ring and fished his truck's access tag out of Vic-tor's pocket. Quinlan looked up from his wife and crying children and saw the backpacks, then looked at Harley, questioning.

Harley tossed his truck's access tag toward them. It landed be-side Raizor, and she picked it up in her little hands, her eyes blurred with tears.

"My truck's on the left side of the road on the other side of the slide, behind the ruins of an old store. It runs strong. If you go now, you should be able to make it before Hatcher can come back. When he does, he'll bring everyone he has. My path leads to the Hub, and they'll follow it. If you're careful, you can slip past them and find a path of your own." Harley kicked at the pulse rifle and dropped Victor's holster and sidearm. "Best let the boy learn to shoot. You're a lost cause."

Harley stepped over the body of a deer and a Wrynd and picked up Quinlan's baseball bat. He hefted it in his hands as he unclasped the scabbard of his cutlass.

"You're pretty good with the bat. Try this." He dropped the

cutlass on the ground at the young man's feet and started to back away.

"We'll die," Quinlan said.

"Not if you're willing to live," Harley replied.

A hardness came to the young man's eyes then, a coldness that Harley knew well. It was the look of survival.

"You might be thinking I did you wrong, killing her as I did. But I didn't. She was a Wrynd, and there's no coming back from that. You might think it would be good to try and kill me where I stand, but I wouldn't take kindly to it. Protect your little ones, if you can." He nodded toward the mountains. "Perhaps I'll see you on the trail one day, and we can settle whatever needs settling. But it won't be today. Now move."

Harley turned, climbed into the truck, and left the man and his two children sitting in the middle of the road with death all around them.

CHAPTER EIGHT

DEATH NOTICE

I

There was a balcony to Jodi's apartment overlooking Utah Lake. She spent most of her free time there, tending her garden.

Like the other ten percent of citizens with employment and responsibilities and duties beyond their desires, she seldom journeyed to the Vale. The Vale was a tool to make life in the Sphere more efficient, not its replacement.

She was a woman firmly grounded in reality, and while she understood her beliefs were extremist, she couldn't deny they were hers. The Vale wasn't reality and never would be.

She held staff meetings in her Vale office and met with her associates there to avoid commutes, but she found no pleasure in the Vale and never considered creating a world, her own MyRealm. It would be a sad waste of time better spent.

In Old World Denver, the heart of the Eastern Rocky Mountain Hub, she had an apartment identical to the one where she sat, but she seldom went there. This one was home.

She served with fifty Marshals in the Rocky Mountain Hub, fifty guardians of justice in a megalopolis of ninety-eight million people. She divided her Marshals equally between the Eastern and

Western Rocky Mountain Hubs and communicated with them by Link normally and in the Vale on the occasion warranting a face-to-face meeting. It seldom was. Most of the time, the biggest battle they faced was boredom.

There hadn't been a murder in the Rocky Mountain Hub in eighteen months, and lesser crimes were seldom committed and almost always anticlimactic.

Jodi sat cross-legged on her patio floor, regarding her garden. There were four long planters, two along the outer railing and one to either side, where she grew peppers, squash, potatoes, cabbage, carrots, and lettuce. Hanging from baskets outside the doorway were tomato plants weighed down with green tomatoes turning red.

This was her space and only hers, and she cherished it above all others. If the Seven Realms contained humanity, then this was her realm. Outside of anything else, this belonged to her, this small space where she could sit and be at peace and tend her plants.

She smiled at her garden and considered the tasks before her. Beyond reason, a legionnaire was missing, and the path to solving the mystery was winding and mired in obstacles.

The last Link data showed Sergeant Litmeyer in her apartment at 10:28 p.m., then nothing. She was there, and then she wasn't. All Link information on her had ceased and Sergeant Litmeyer, as far as the Federation knew, no longer existed. Bon and Montana went to investigate the apartment. After a tense meeting, Legion investigators finally granted a cursory inspection of the apartment, then escorted them out.

Jodi would deal with the Legion and its overreach later. It wasn't a huge concern because the mystery of what happened to the legionnaire wouldn't be solved by any clues found in her apartment. Scan data of her home showed nothing out of the ordinary. She arrived home at 5:23 p.m. and spent some time in the Vale with her husband.

They argued over a visit the young woman insisted upon. Her husband was, in fact, a 200-kilo woman named Ronda, who lived in a small apartment in Dallas, not a handsome young physicist living in Paris. It was a fact Kara Litmeyer could have discovered with even a hint of rational skepticism about the man she chose to marry in the Vale.

She drew a deep breath and let her mind wander back to studies at her father's knee. Once upon a time, not terribly long ago, humanity knew nothing of the Link or the Seven Realms. People went missing, and people like her found them. It was in the service of justice, and Jodi knew it was her task but wasn't sure how to begin.

Jodi pulled her knees to her chest, studied her garden, and enjoyed the calm of the morning. On a leaf of a squash plant, she detected the slightest of movement, a small dot of shadow on its underside, and she crawled to lift the leaf and see what was beneath.

Three squash bugs were hiding, and other leaves deeper within the plant were wilting. She plucked one of the bugs, held it in the palm of her hand, and watched as it crawled toward her fingertips.

Each Hub had swarms of nanoinsects hunting pests from the Wilderness. They replaced insecticides decades before. The nanos didn't hunt every insect, just those that might prove hazardous to humans. Seeing a squash bug on her plants wasn't a cause for alarm, but it was a surprise because it was the first seen since planting her garden.

As the insect crawled across her hand, she raised her thumb and prepared to end its life, then frowned and returned it to the leaf. She may have to kill the bugs if they damaged the plant too badly, but she saw no reason to kill them this morning. It was another lesson learned from her father. Killing was sometimes necessary, but it was something to ponder. Something history demonstrated seldom done.

Thinking of her father made her long to see him, and she sat back down on the balcony, crossed her legs, and let her mind slip into the Vale.

With a blink, she was standing outside a gleaming white doorway a world away. In the Vale, she didn't wear her uniform, but a simple pair of slacks and blouse, and her hair was down and caressing her shoulders.

She pressed her thumb against a soft blue light in the door and hoped her father would answer the summons from the Sphere and visit her in the Vale. While she waited, she turned and faced the outer window of the Huygens Station as it spun in orbit above Mars.

The red planet was a vast rusty abstract painting in the inner windows of the station, contrasted by the gleaming spokes of the wheel station itself and the darkness of space beyond.

Also orbiting the planet, the Federation Cruiser Goodfellow floated like a Christmas ornament constructed by an overzealous five-year-old; rough edges and glitter drawn haphazardly around the spinning globe of the crew quarters in the center of the ship. Three-hundred-and-fifty people were serving on the cruiser, making regular runs from Mars to Earth and back again.

The Huygens was a smaller version of the Wheel in orbit of Earth, and 4,100 people called the station home. Below, on the planet itself, 6,800 people lived within the canyons of Valles Marineras in the great city of Rome, Mars, where humanity made its first attempt at terraforming.

The door behind her hissed, and she turned as it opened. Her father squinted at her, looking as he always did, like a child dressed in his father's clothing.

"Hullo, darlin' daughter," he said in a slow drawl.

"Hullo Father," Jodi said back, and the two embraced. The fact they weren't physically touching did nothing at all to prevent the lump in her throat and tears in her eyes.

Syiam Tempest beckoned his only daughter to enter his Vale apartment, and Jodi brushed past him happily, her senses immediately overwhelmed with the feeling of home, although she had never lived in the Outland of off-planet.

Bookshelves lined her parents' living room, where ancient, hardbound books of various sizes, shapes, and colors occupied every available space. The lights were dim, and a red couch she instantly wanted to throw herself upon, an oversized recliner and a softly glowing antique reading light were the only furnishings.

Jodi knew the Sphere version of their apartment on Huygens would look nothing like the Vale version. For one thing, the number of books her father would have been able to take to Mars would be extremely limited; for the other, her mother would never stand for so much clutter. Emily Tempest was the opposite of her husband. She was an electrical engineer helping to shape Mars into a new world for humanity. She allowed the Vale version of her home to look as it did, likely, because she seldom visited.

"Where's Mom?" Jodi asked, picking up a copy of a ruby red hardback edition of A Tale of Two Cities and flicking through it casually before sitting it back on her father's side table.

"She's down in Rome, working away because you know, Jodi, Rome wasn't . . ."

"I know, built in a day. Old joke, Dad," Jodi rolled her eyes but smiled anyway.

"The good ones always are." Syiam sat down and motioned for her to join him. Jodi sat beside her father, took his thin hands in her own, looked into his pale green eyes, and sighed contentedly.

"I hope I'm not taking you away from anything important, Dad."

"Important?" Syiam waved his hand. "Not at all. I was puttering about in a MyRealm. I'm reliving everything history knows of the Dark Ages."

"How is it?"

"Dark, actually." He slapped his thin leg happily, and Jodi snorted.

"You're an idiot, Dad, but I guess I walked into that one."

"Yes, you did." Syiam looked serious for a moment, and his narrow brow focused on her. "What brings you to Mars, my little Squiggs? Is everything okay? Have you grown tired of your search for justice and decided to join your father on his fool's quest for truth in the history of man?"

"No, Dad. Everything's fine. Well, not fine, but not what you think." Jodi squeezed his hand. "A legionnaire is missing. I'm to find her."

"A missing legionnaire? Well, that's not possible."

"I thought you told me nothing was impossible."

Syiam grinned. "I did. I'm just repeating what you would have said, I'm sure."

"I did say that."

"How did Marshal Tempest become involved in the impossible disappearance of a legionnaire?"

"Well, that's a bit of a mystery as well. Emissary Storm asked me to find her."

Syiam coughed. "Emissary Storm? The Lizard? She asked my daughter to find a missing legionnaire. Who is this legionnaire?"

"No one. A sergeant in the Rocky Mountain Brigade, but she's been missing days. She's not in any realm. Her linktag has disappeared. The Emissary believes it important I find her."

Her father knew nothing of the Lord Judge's belief in a Leap, a leap in human evolution, and she wondered what he would think if she dared disclose classified information.

Syiam leaned forward, touched his fingers to his lips. "You do see the oddity in this?"

"I'm your daughter, am I not?"

"Yes, you are. A puzzle within a puzzle. Why involve the service in such a matter?"

"I don't know."

Syiam patted her on the leg. "And what does justice demand of you, Marshal Tempest?"

"Find her. The reasons why the Emissary would personally ask me to take part are inconsequential. A legionnaire is missing who shouldn't, couldn't be missing. Justice demands she be found."

Syiam smiled happily, and Jodi wanted to cry. "And how will you go about finding a person who's missing who cannot be missing? What's your first step?"

Jodi sat back and tried to remember everything he taught her. "I'll do nothing."

"Nothing?" Syiam said with a grunt. "Sounds counterproductive."

"If something is lost, have patience. The lost are found in time. If they're not found, it's possible they aren't lost at all, but hiding, and therein lies the first clue in their discovery. If you've searched the haystack for the needle and can't find it, perhaps it's no longer a needle. A crazy old man told me that once."

Syiam chortled. "Crazy, perhaps, but wise beyond his years."

Jodi nodded and rested her head against his slim shoulder. He hadn't changed at all in the Vale since she last saw him, and she wondered if the man on the Huygens resembled in any way the man sitting beside her. She didn't care. He was her father, and that was all that mattered.

"What happened to the legionnaire isn't possible. I can find anyone in the Seven Realms with a linktag with a blink of the eye. Even if her Link was in privacy mode, I could override it and so could her commander. It's not possible for her to disappear."

"Yet?"

"She did."

"Which raises questions about everything, does it not?" Syiam sounded pleased.

"What questions?"

Syiam took her hands and pressed his forehead to her own.

"Questions that should be asked by every member of the Federation. How did the Lord Judge reshape the world? How did he possibly create the Seven Realms, convince civilization to abandon cities, erase borders, disband armies, and follow him into the future?"

"I don't know."

"I know you don't." Syiam nodded. "He recognized the spark in a moment, a moment when the world, weary of war and afraid the end was near, would abandon everything we knew to someone, anyone, who could show us another way, raise a beacon in the darkness and softly say follow me.

"It has been said by many far wiser than I through the centuries that history is but a fable agreed upon, and the Lord Judge embraced the cynicism in the statement. He cared nothing of history and wasn't bound by it. He cared not a whit for it. We were so hungry for something new after the Energy Wars that we never even asked who he is, where he came from. Oh, we know he came from the wastelands of China, but he is not Chinese. He's not any nationality, not any race. We know nothing of his lineage. We didn't care and never asked.

"Before the Energy Wars, there are descriptions of an advisor to United States Senator Facio that are remarkable in their similarity to Lord Judge Syiada. This unnamed advisor helped Facio draft the Right to Work legislation that became Right to Income. The Age of Renewal didn't begin with the creation of the Seven Realms, it began in the United States and spread to Europe and Russia with the passage of Right to Income and creation of the first Hubs. I believe Syiada was laying the foundation for his Seven Realms almost a decade before the Energy Wars, brick by brick by brick."

Syiam stood and paced the living room, five paces to the right, six to the left, and Jodi smiled. He would stumble into the closet if his lecture took much longer. He was in his element, having a captive audience for his views on the world and how it had come to be this way. She counted herself blessed he was not only her father but her teacher. He turned to pace the other way, noticed Jodi smiling, and stopped.

"Are you paying attention?" he asked.

"Of course," she replied.

"The history of civilization in the Seven Realms must be viewed with a healthy dose of skepticism. Historians aren't dead; they are simply irrelevant in a world where fact and fantasy are seamlessly interwoven. The jinni Histories records events now as fact without partiality, but in so doing it does not attempt to address the motivation behind actions."

He continued his pacing, and as he neared the closet, a sensor above the door slid it open, and he walked inside, still talking. The door closed behind him, and Jodi giggled uncontrollably.

"Where am I?" Syiam's muffled question whispered through the door.

"You're in the closet, Dad." Jodi's sides were hurting, and she curled up on the chair, laughing.

Syiam opened the door and stepped back out, eyeing it suspiciously, as if it could not be trusted. He came back to the couch and slapped her on the leg. "Stop laughing at me. Now, where was I? Oh, yes. The Link and the disinterest in the pursuit of unbiased truth and objectivity led to the demise of journalism, and now the history of the Old World is a puree of conflicting opinions, instead of recorded facts.

"It is the reason behind the jinni Histories. Documenting our history requires objectivity, yes indeed, and the Histories is detached, as it should be. But it also lacks a healthy dose of skepticism, which is crucial. What motivates our actions? Today we exist in realms wrapped in our own bias and truth is only an abstract painted by our perceptions. Prudent students of history must be skeptical and consider the motivations behind actions."

"What students of history?"

"We are all students of history, Squiggs. Students and victims of history."

Syiam started pacing again, now six paces to the right and five to the left. At least he wouldn't end up back in the closet. "The Lord Judge used our disregard for objectivity to his advantage. Syiada ground to dust everything we knew of the Old World and sprinkled its remains into the makings of the Seven Realms. He cast aside every flag of every nation, every faith that brought us together and tore us apart. He did it all within a short span of years, and we never thought to ask why, or more importantly, how."

"You ask all the time," Jodi whispered.

Syiam nodded. "I do, but no one listens."

"I'm listening," Jodi said.

Her father grinned and pinched her arm as he passed. "Yes, you are. The Lord Judge sits in his throne in the Wheel, with the entire world beneath his feet. He conquered it without a drop of blood spilt. What he has created with the Seven Realm is his path to godhood, and we love him for it. If humanity's savior were to appear before us now and say the end is near, come follow me, we would divert our gaze."

She almost told him then, about the Leap. Her father was the last of human historians, but he was a skeptic first, and what he said was disturbing and helped explain why the Lord Judge shrouded his search for a leap in evolution in secrecy. She felt the words bounding from her tongue to her lips and swallowed them down.

"And if what you say is true, what part does this missing legionnaire play, and where do I stand in the service of justice?" Jodi stood to stop her father's pacing.

"As I said, the Lord Judge has dismissed history, dismissed reality itself to create his realms, and we've followed his design. But what if someone else hasn't? What if the Realms and the Wilderness and everything we suppose is real is but a glimmer in the darkness?"

"Do you believe that?" Jodi asked, and a shiver tickled her shoulders.

"I believe nothing. I simply follow history and hope to discover a fable I can agree upon."

"And justice?" Jodi asked.

"Justice? What of justice?" Syiam said with a chortle. "You serve it, or you become accountable to it. Justice is a pillar of existence beyond denial. That's a truth beyond the fabric of history and beyond the Federation's reshaping of reality."

Jodi smiled and leaned into her father's embrace. For a moment, she could see a path to set her feet upon, but then her brow wrinkled, and she gasped and turned away. Her father gripped her shoulders and turned her back.

"What is it? What's wrong?"

Jodi shook her head and shrugged away his hands. "I've lost a Marshal. One of my Marshals is dead in the Wilderness."

Syiam put his hands on his hips and bit his lower lip. "A lost legionnaire and now a dead Marshal. Ill omens."

"Yes. Ill omens." Jodi hugged her father and returned to the Sphere.

One of her Marshals was dead in the Wilderness. Reality as she knew it slipped a little further off its axis.

II

The transport dropped out of the Justice Tower landing bay and banked right, heading south. A Marshals star painted on its side; the stub-winged airship primarily served as transport for visiting dignitaries or senators to the Hub. Today it would serve as a hearse for Marshal Victor Walker.

Jodi sat at the transport's controls, although she let the craft pilot itself. The airship dutifully locked onto Victor's Link signature and flew toward it. Behind Jodi, in the crew cabin, sat Bon, Montana, Ephraim, and Elijah. She could feel the anger rolling off Ephraim and Elijah. They were close to Victor. If they were better friends, they might have prevented him from doing whatever damn fool thing he did to get himself killed.

Jodi scanned his last Link activity, and it only gave clues, no answers. He was with Elijah and Ephraim when they met a citizen and his two children. They ignored the man's request for help in finding his wife, and shortly after that Victor requested work leave and placed his Link status in privacy mode. When he died the nanites of his linktag sent out an alert. She didn't have a clue as to how he died; only he was dead.

She stood and went into the cabin. Bon and Montana sat in one set of seats facing Ephraim and Elijah on the other side of the transport. Bon's thin face was set and impassive, and she stared at her feet, fingers intertwined. Montana sat with his legs crossed, one big arm draped casually across the seat back, the other resting in his lap. He stared across the aisle at the other Marshals, not attempting to hide his contempt.

That her four best Marshals disliked each other so vehemently was a sore subject, and Jodi wasn't sure there was any way to resolve it. As long as they served honorably, they could dislike each other if they wished.

She sat on the seat next to Montana, considering for a moment doing so might betray affection for one pair over the other, which she couldn't deny. She stared across at Elijah, and his face was flush with anger and hurt.

"Why did he go into the Wilderness alone?" Jodi asked softly.

"He always went into the Wilderness alone, Marshal," Elijah replied. "Sad you wouldn't know that about him. The Wilderness was his playground. He preferred it over anything in the Vale."

Jodi nodded at the slight; let it wash across her without outward display. "What I do know is ten minutes before he took leave and placed his linktag in privacy he was with the two of you as you turned away a family asking for help. This man, Quinlan Bowden, thought his wife abducted and taken into the Wilderness, and you ignored his pleas. And now Victor is dead in the Wilderness. Leads me to think perhaps Marshal Walker sought to do what you refused and help this man and his family."

"They were Pilgrims asking for help to find another Pilgrim.," Elijah said with a snarl. "Without a linktag finding someone who may not wish to be found would be a violation of their privacy. If she is in the Wilderness, it's beyond our jurisdiction, is it not, Marshal?"

"Our oath is to serve justice, Marshal Apgar," Jodi responded. "Justice has no boundaries."

"Tell that to Victor when we gather him up," Ephraim said. "And if he was helping the Pilgrims, I guess you can say the same thing to their corpses."

Montana cleared his throat and smiled pleasantly, but his voice held menace. "I find your tone toward the Marshal most disrespectful. Would you like to dance?"

"Mind your realms, Montana. Don't concern you," Ephraim fired back.

"No. Seriously," Montana leaned forward, still smiling. "Would you like to dance?"

Jodi stood with a scowl as the transport's airbrakes kicked in and the airship began its descent. "Stow it, both of you. We have a fallen mate to attend."

She went to the cockpit and sat back in the pilot's seat. The transport descended into a winding canyon and the trees bowed their heads as its thrusters fired. Below them Jodi could see the signs of carnage; dozens of bodies, human and animal, scattered across the old highway. There was a rough circle of dead animals, and inside the ring of death was the unmistakable form of Marshal

Walker. It looked like something had been feeding on him. Jodi looked away.

The hopper landed softly, and they climbed out and went to the body of their friend and colleague. Bon and Montana led the way to Victor. There was a gaping wound in the big man's neck and another one in his side where it looked like something had been feeding, but with the blood pooled around his body from the side wound it looked inflicted postmortem. *The wildthings of the Wilderness, no doubt,* Jodi thought. They looked at the fallen Wrynd and dead animals, and Montana whistled softly.

"He died well. Went down fighting."

Ephraim and Elijah stood aside, not drawing too close to the mass of torn and bleeding flesh that once was their friend.

Bon knelt beside Victor, resting her elbows on her knees. "His slayer is missing, Marshal," she said quietly. "So is his scye."

"Wrynd wouldn't have taken them," Elijah said. "Had to be the Pilgrims."

"No sign of them here. We don't even know if they were here." Jodi walked toward the eastern shoulder of the dead highway, to a mound of rocks unevenly stacked.

"His truck is gone. The Wrynd wouldn't have taken it either, so the Pilgrims did."

"What truck?" Montana asked.

"He had this big ol' tank of a truck," Elijah replied, holding a hand over his perfect nose. "Called it his wilderness assault vehicle. He always took it with him on his hunting trips."

"Well, if the Pilgrims took it, how did they survive when he couldn't? How did they have Link access unless he gave it to them?" Bon asked, standing up and stepping away from the sickly smell of death.

"They ran as Vic fought the Wrynd," Ephraim said, stepping closer to Victor's body and scowling. "Only answer."

"Not the only answer," Jodi said. She removed a layer of stones from the mound and found a body beneath. It was a tattooed woman. Her eyes closed, she looked peaceful like she might only be sleeping, but there was blood behind her ear whoever cleaned and buried her missed.

"I think we've found the wife of the Pilgrim," she said.

"They buried her, but left Victor to be torn apart by the wildthings?" Elijah bellowed.

Jodi placed the stones back on top of the dead woman.

"They must have returned to the Hub. They have the answers we're looking for."

"I have the answers you're looking for!" The voice was a roar from the rocks above them, and all five sent their scyes into the air as Wrynd poured down the slide and onto the road.

A giant of a Wrynd was standing on a large boulder at the bottom of the slide. He had crept within striking distance. They were so focused on Victor they failed to notice. Jodi took note and cursed her distraction.

Her scye, glowing red like an angry eye, floated above her right shoulder, ready should she choose to wield it. Bon's scye glowed above her left shoulder.

As the Wrynd poured down the mountain, the other Marshals utilized the axis defense, with their scyes swirling left and right, up, and down around their keepers.

The big Wrynd glanced at the red scye floating above Jodi and nodded in her direction. "Welcome to my range, Marshal," he said.

Jodi nodded back. "I'm Marshal Jodi Tempest. We're here to gather one of our own. Nothing more. Nothing less." She cast her eyes at the dead Wrynd around her. "Whatever transpired here, I'd know the reasons why. You've lost some of yours; I've lost someone I value. The Wilderness is without law, but we serve justice. Give me a reason not to kill you now."

"I am Scimitar Hatcher of the Wrynd." Hatcher stomped down the slide toward them like a king. "You are intruders in my range, and your life is ours for the taking. Your slayers and dirty scyes mean nothing to me or my shield. We'll pour death upon you if it's our wish."

Hundreds of Wrynd encircled them, and for a moment, just a moment, Jodi considered the wisdom of perhaps dashing for the transport and making an escape.

"My comrade; are you responsible for his death?" Jodi said coolly.

Hatcher smiled and squatted, resting his elbows on his knees. "He thought to challenge my Scepter. He thought himself more than he was, Marshal Tempest, as you do now. She showed him the error of his ways."

"And is it your chosen beneath the pile of stones?" Jodi tilted her head, and her scye tucked closer to her shoulder.

Hatcher's eyes danced to the stones, and then back to Jodi's face. "She was betrayed. Murdered by the treachery of the Federation. Your Marshal struck a bargain and broke it when he realized he couldn't win in honorable battle. She died because of his treachery. The Wrynd will have our revenge."

"Revenge? We'll show you revenge!" Elijah stepped toward the Wrynd, and Jodi brought her scye to block his way.

"What treachery do you speak of, Wrynd?" she asked.

"A Marshal of the Federation came into the Wilderness, into my range, and now my Scepter is dead. We have a pact, and it is betrayed."

Jodi brought her scye back to her shoulder and took two small steps forward, locking eyes with the Scimitar. "The Wrynd survive by the whim of the Federation. We've declared the Wilderness outside our realms as a courtesy for those who choose not to be part of the Seven Realms. If we have a reason, we can and will slaughter you. I think you've given me a reason." Jodi's right hand caressed her slayer. "But understand this; there is no pact between the Federation and the Wrynd to be betrayed."

Hatcher clenched his fists, and blood dripped from the palms of his hands. "The Federation knows nothing of honor. There is a pact! We provide a service to your god of the Seven Realms so that he doesn't have to dirty his hands. The Wrynd are all that's left of honor in humanity! We've honored our pact with your lord; we've forsaken weapons other than the honor of true combat, with teeth, claw, fist, and strength. And yet, we are betrayed by your filthy Marshal. The pact has been the one thing to keep the Hubs safe from our flare! It is broken and the pact is no more. We'll have our revenge upon the realms."

"There is no pact," Jodi replied.

Hatcher laughed and rubbed the stubble on his chin. "Oh, the things I could show you. Where did they find you, Marshal Tempest? Is there still so naïve a person remaining in the Age of Renewal?"

Jodi gritted her teeth and fought the urge to draw her sidearm. Bon and Montana stepped away, circling wider for the battle they were sure was inevitable. Outnumbered, Jodi still thought their odds good should the day give birth to violence.

"There is no pact," Jodi repeated.

"Ask those who hold your leash, Marshal Tempest. I grow tired of bantering with you. I offer you, your Hub, and the Federation itself this one possibility to forestall our wrath. Give me the Castaway, and I'll let your Hub remain in its squalor. For a time."

"Castaway?" Jodi asked.

"Don't be coy, Marshal." Hatcher walked to within ten paces of Jodi and a cloud of flies parted as he approached. "The Castaway stood side by side with your Marshal, and when your champion fell by my Scepter's teeth and claw, he cut her down with no honor. He's killed my chosen, and I'll have his blood. His screams will be my symphony. Harley Nearwater is hiding in your Hub, and he'll be mine."

"Harley Nearwater?" Jodi asked.

Hatcher roared. "Tell me you don't know of him, and we'll strike this very moment. With teeth, claw, fist, and strength, we'll destroy you and your serfs."

Jodi cleared her throat and tried not to betray her surprise. "Oh, I know Harley Nearwater. What does he have to do with this?"

"He killed my Scepter!"

Jodi bit the side of her lip, considering. "I knew nothing of this."

"Perhaps your keepers don't fully trust you, Marshal Tempest." The Wrynd Scimitar grinned like the maniac he was. "Perhaps you should consider the reasons why."

"What of the Pilgrims who came in search of your chosen?" Jodi resisted the urge to step away from him.

Hatcher chuckled softly and motioned to the Wilderness behind him. "Out there, abandoned by the Castaway. I'm sure he thought they would distract me from my wrath. They'll be mine as well. But first, I want Harley Nearwater. There's no other recourse for you or your Federation. Deliver him, or your treachery results in more violence than you can withstand."

"There's another recourse."

Hatcher's black eyes stared into Jodi's blue ones, and he started to laugh. The laugh turned to a scream of joy, frustration, anger, and madness. "Oh, Marshal Tempest! You're so very unaware of the world around you! How much I was once like you." He nodded, and a score of the Wrynd surrounding them brought blowguns to their lips.

"An ancient weapon, for sure, but still quite effective. The Federation has forsaken our pact," he said. "So, we are free to take up any instrument of your destruction we desire and do so with our honor unblemished. I know something of the skill of the Marshals with their scyes, but do you think even with such skill you can stop a hundred ink-tipped darts from piercing your skin when we attack? Are you willing to chance it?" Hatcher took another small step toward her. "I think you would make a Wrynd of great ferocity. I can see the hunger in your eyes. Perhaps you would turn and devour your Marshals when the flare has you in its grip. It would be glorious."

Her Marshals stood at her side, and violence crackled its desire in her ears. "I don't think you'd be here to see such a thing if it were to happen, Scimitar," she said.

If Hatcher noticed the other Marshals at all, he paid them no mind. He smirked and licked his torn lips. "We'll leave you now, my Wrynd and I. I'll give you a moment in time to deliver the Castaway to me. I'll not say how many moments, because my patience won't be chained. But understand this; when the moment has passed, the Wrynd will storm your Hub and everything you think you protect will be consumed."

He started to walk back up the slide and turned to give Jodi one last sneer. "And understand this, Marshal Tempest; blowguns are not the only weapon the Wrynd have. We've been poised, waiting for the siren call of the apocalypse. When the time comes, your world will burn." Hatcher turned and hiked back up the slope.

CHAPTER NINE

WORLDS APART

I

Three mares galloped across Wind Farm Park. The two sorrels and a bay. Their heads were up, and their tails were high. They were a beautiful sight, and Harley fought tears.

He knelt on one knee on the shoulder of the old highway and imagined they were running toward him, as if in answer to his call. A smile of wonder licked his dry lips.

Then, perhaps he wasn't calling them; perhaps they were calling him, coming to take him away from this world where he didn't belong to one that might embrace him, might make him whole.

A 'bot mower meandered across the grass, but Harley didn't see another living soul. The world was theirs. They were magnificent, and Harley remembered when he first sat atop a horse, before the Rages. It was an old mare, and he rode her one afternoon to a bluff overlooking the town. He remembered feeling her breathing beneath him, and he patted her dusty side as he looked down on his home. For a little while, he felt at peace.

The old horse certainly couldn't run like those three wild ones racing through the park. Later, when he was older, and before everything good turned so bad, he sat atop a horse as it ran like that.

It was like flying. He missed it more than he could ever say.

On the nine great antique turbines of the old wind farm, sentinels roosted, and as the horses entered the park, their hooves kicking up grass, one of the drones swooped off a wind tower and dropped toward them. Three pulse blasts echoed through the mouth of the canyon, and they fell, cut down and skidding to a stop on the green grass.

Harley frowned and put down his magnifiers. He folded his legs beneath him, sat cross-legged on the gravel shoulder, and watched as a collector arrived, hovered over the dead animals, then scooped them up and headed back into the Hub. The mower stopped mowing and scurried to the damaged lawn. Several arms, shovels, and rakes unfolded from portals in the mower as it began to repair the turf.

He parked the truck at the mouth of Spanish Fork Canyon where the old highway slithered along the hip of the mountain. From there he could gaze out at what once was Utah Valley and was now just a part of the Rocky Mountain Hub. He could only see a sliver of the massive city, and the sprawl of cityscape gleamed in the morning sun.

Aircraft flashed across the sky, and beneath them thousands of storks, like an endless swarm of bees, danced across the cityscape.

Sentinels zoomed around the perimeter of the city scanning for animal life and promptly destroying any that tried to enter the Hub boundary. Despite the bustle of drones, rail, and aircraft, Harley thought the city looked peaceful and perhaps a little sleepy. Hubs were less cities now and more living, breathing creatures all their own. Harley wondered if the teeming masses of humanity who called it home were a part of the organism or a parasite?

It looked like paradise from his vantage point, and in reality, it should be paradise. People in the Hub wanted for nothing.

"Except a purpose." Harley's voice was a whisper quickly hushed in the canyon. He hadn't spoken since leaving Quinlan and his children to die at the claw, teeth, and fist of the Wrynd. Perhaps the young man was right. Despite the spectacle humanity had created, it was rotting away.

On the northwest edge of the valley, the lone skyscraper of the Justice Tower and the outstretched hand of the battlewagon cradle loomed. That was where he needed to go. Perhaps there he could find answers for Wrynd receiving their drug by storks, lost legionnaires, and men with grey eyes and unexplainable powers.

Before he could do so, he needed to take care of a few necessities as he came in out of the Wilderness. While it wasn't illegal to carry a weapon in the Hub, it would draw attention he'd rather not have drawn. He slipped his eyeset from his backpack and called up his security box.

A stork arrived ten minutes later, and he placed his sidearm and holster inside the box provided, along with his hunting knife, and, after a moment of consideration, the baseball bat he took from Quinlan. He regretted giving the young man his sword. It was a rash decision, poorly made. He would get another one while at the Hub, unless his plan worked as he hoped, then he didn't think there'd be a need. The stork sealed the box and flew away with his weapons. He would call for them when he returned to the Wilderness.

With his weapons secured, he headed toward a rail line. He needed to park the truck; it would be hard to navigate in the Hub. He fished in a pocket of his pack until he found the case for his defusers. He plucked them out and stuck them in his ears, scrunching his face as they oozed into place. The defusers would filter away the noise of a million storks buzzing, the roar of airships, and the whine of Dragons. He aimed the truck at the Hub and pushed the accelerator.

While the agglomeration was known simply as the Rocky Mountain Hub, the individual cities still maintained a sense of identity and a localized but limited form of government. As he drove into

Spanish Fork, the old highway stopped at a massive parking garage adjacent to the Dragon lines. He adjusted his eyeset and parked in the spot prescribed him. Because of the size of the truck, he needed two parking spots. Considering the Marshal's desire to oversize everything in his life; it wasn't a shocking surprise he liked to drive something inadequate for the world he lived in.

Harley left his saddlebag in the truck, threw the backpack over his shoulder, slid his hat low over his forehead, and went to wait for a Serpent, trying not to trip over his boots as he adjusted to wearing the eyeset. It was no easy task but trying to get around the Hub without wearing an eyeset would prove even more difficult.

When the Serpent arrived, Harley stepped inside the commuter, sat down, and the chair formed comfortably around him. He linked and requested the seat be a little cooler, asked for a massage, and settled in with a satisfied sigh. When the train politely asked his destination, he told it the nearest Hilton. There was only one other passenger on the commuter, a little old man with a balding head, who also wore an eyeset. When the old man saw Harley looking at him, he removed his eyeset and smiled. Harley nodded.

"Mornin'."

"Good morning," the old man beamed. His voice was rough, and he cleared his throat and said it again. "Do you know you're the first person I've spoken to in two weeks?"

"That so?"

The old man stood up and came to sit in the seat across from him. "Oh, I've talked to lots of people on this," he waved the eyeset absently. "But you're the first to require me to use my voice." The old man looked at Harley's dusty clothes and boots. "You come in from the Wilderness?"

Harley nodded.

"What's it like out there?"

"Different than here."

"Did you see any animals out there? Cows and such?" The old

man's breath smelled sour, sick.

"And such."

"Was it bad?"

"Wasn't good."

The old man looked out the window. "I used to be a veterinarian. In the Old World. It used to be my job to care for animals, but I gave it up when the Rages began. I could still be a vet, take care of animals when injured in the Wilderness. But I used to love the interaction with them, the love they showed, and the love I gave. Now if they're wounded, you must sedate them, heal them, and get them away from you before they come out of anesthesia, or they'll attack. I don't have the heart for it."

"What about dogs? There's still dogs," Harley said. He didn't recall asking for company. It was one of the aggravations with humanity. They always wanted to talk.

"Yes." The old man agreed. "But it's just too sad. Even dogs don't seem the same." He paused, and his dull eyes were far away, to different times and places. Harley let him wander. He looked up after several minutes and smiled. "I know a lot of people who have dogs, but they don't seem like the dogs I remember. They know they're hunted, just like us, maybe even worse than us. I think dogs know the animal kingdom now denies them. They've lost something because of it."

"Price you pay for being man's best friend."

"I suppose." The old man extended his hand. "My name is Jose Guillermo."

Harley looked at his outstretched hand and didn't take it. "Harley."

"Do you live on one of the reservations? I understand there are still quite a few Native Americans living on the reservations."

Harley stared blankly. "No."

The Serpent flew down the rail, and the two travelers were quiet. Harley looked toward the lake at an expansive building stretching more than a klick and perhaps twenty stories tall. People were coming and going, and pods zipped in and out of the parking area, dropping some off, picking others up.

"The Utah Medprint. Just opened a few weeks ago," Jose said.

"Lots of people there."

"Well, the medprint is about the only thing you can't get delivered nowadays. The day will come when you order whatever parts you need, and a meddrone arrives at your apartment, performs surgery in your bedroom, and lets itself out."

Harley grunted. "You think?"

"Wouldn't surprise me in the least. Is that where you're headed? The medprint?" Jose asked.

"Never been."

"Never?" Jose looked at him as if he was some oddity needing closer examination. "You mean you're all original?"

Harley shrugged.

"That's something. I didn't think anyone over the age of twenty-five still had original parts."

"You?" Harley eyed the old man. He looked original, and about worn out.

"New heart, eyes, and lungs.

"How old are you?" Harley asked.

"I'll be 137 next month. I was alive before they cured cancer, high blood pressure, and diabetes. I've dodged more bullets in my life than most. Nowadays I go for my monthly checkup and quarterly fat removal. Of course, that's just good body maintenance."

"So's watching what you eat," Harley said dryly.

The Serpent silently came to a stop and told Harley he had arrived. He stood and left without saying goodbye to Jose Guillermo.

Outside, he paused to take off his eyeset and smoke a cigarette. He could see the Hilton Hotel a half block down. There were maybe a dozen people in the thoroughfare. Only a dozen people to see in an agglomeration of millions. He tossed his cigarette onto the ground and walked toward the hotel. A groundskeeper scurried past him and scooped up the butt before it stopped smoldering.

There was no sign of life in the lobby of the hotel, and Harley cursed and slipped on his eyeset. He forgot. Through his eyeset, an attractive young woman with lime green hair was smiling seductively. He nodded as he approached the desk and requested a room on the top floor.

He saw nothing living as he climbed onto the elevator and ascended. Several Fillers roamed the halls, and he couldn't decide what was sadder, to be the equivalent of human wallpaper walking the halls in a digital representation of the Hilton Hotel, or to be the only physical person walking the halls of the Hilton Hotel.

His room was expansive and tastefully decorated, and he felt out of place as he tossed his backpack, hat, and eyeset onto the chair by the window and sprawled spread-eagle across the king size bed. He nodded off for a moment and, when he woke, was hungry. He ordered lunch while he kicked out of his clothes and climbed into the shower to scrub away the dirt and grime.

After he'd eaten, he dumped the contents of his pack onto the bed and found nothing clean to wear, so he slipped on his eyeset and went shopping. Harley Nearwater didn't enjoy shopping in any form, except for weapons. He visited every storefront he could think of. His head began to throb from the images dancing through.

The fashions of the day were not in keeping with his admittedly simple style. Everyone was wearing chameleons and wanted clothing that changed with their whims. Harley didn't have whims. He liked his clothing to pick a color and stick with it, and his color of preference was typically black or brown. He wasn't a peacock and didn't like looking like one.

Before he finished shopping, he grew frustrated and ordered a case of beer and bottle of whiskey, and after indulging in a little of both, he felt up to finding some new clothes. He eventually went

to a flashback shop, where he could find good old fashion dungarees, western shirts, and a pair of boots worth wearing. He bought
four pair of jeans and shirts, new socks, boots, and underwear. He
looked at his Stetson and decided against replacing his hat.

"It's not even my birthday," Harley said when the clothing package arrived. It was a rare indulgence, but if he was going to get an
audience with the Marshal, he'd better not look like a derelict.

Since he'd been drinking, he couldn't pay a visit to the Hub
Marshal, but he sure as hell didn't want to sit in his room on the
Link the whole damned day. He gulped two more beers, slipped
the whiskey into his back pocket, and left the hotel.

The Link informed him there was a park three blocks west, and
he walked down the sidewalk between sparkling and mostly deserted looking buildings, nodding at the few passersby, ignored by
everyone. It was disconcerting, not having his sidearm strapped to
his waist, and he felt his hand reaching to rest on an absent slayer.
He was weaponless and probably safer than he'd been in ages. He
didn't feel that way.

The park was a long expanse of grass, walkways, and trails, with
trees gently swaying in the soft breeze. There was a playground,
volleyball net and park benches with chess sets, but there were no
people.

Harley sat on a concrete bench in an empty park and sipped
his whiskey. He took off his hat and enjoyed the sun on his face.
There was no birdsong, but, of course, if there were birdsong, it
would have led to panicked screaming by visitors. Classical music
whispered from speakers tastefully hidden in the trees, and it was
soft and soothing. He folded his eyeset and put it into his shirt
pocket.

A young couple with two small children and a dog entered the
park and chased each other on the grass. Harley watched them,
amazed at the joy they took from such a simple thing. The dog was
a small breed, a poodle, or a terrier; he wasn't sure which because

he didn't know dogs. He had a dog when he was a boy, but it hadn't ended well.

The dog in the park was a barker, and as the children played, it yapped and danced. Harley liked the sound of the barking dog. Eventually, the family noticed him staring and, when he raised an arm in greeting, they went the other way.

His face felt tight, and he realized he'd been smiling, grinning like a lunatic. He wiped the smile away and sipped his whiskey. A city teeming with people, and he was still all alone.

He stayed a while longer in an empty park designed with people in mind, then stood, slipped the whiskey back into his pocket, dropped his hat back on his head, and went for a walk.

He eventually found his boots clicking on the cobblestones of Provo Center Street, and for the first time since arriving in the Hub, he was among humanity. The streets weren't busy, and only a few pods zipped up and down the road. The sidewalks, however, were teeming with people shuffling back and forth, laughing, talking, some of them holding hands, as they visited the old shops and restaurants.

He found a park bench on a corner, sat down, and watched humanity walk by in their brightly colored clothes and their loud laughter and senseless chatter, and it comforted him and made him sullen at the same time. What might it be like to be like them, to belong to something the way they seemed to belong to each other? He didn't have a clue. He was a castaway in their world.

On the next corner was a magnificent old building raising a steeple to the heavens, and as night slowly descended on the Hub, the temple glowed. Couples came and went through the high walls surrounding the building, and Harley found himself marveling at the faithful. There were still believers in the world. He didn't have a clue what Mormons believed but found it unusual any religion could survive in the Age of Renewal.

The world ground faith to dust, but somehow the faithful held on. Freedom of religion was a right of life in the Federation, but it was a right people didn't seem to get all that worked up about anymore. Some of the world's religions had chosen to go Neand and were dwindling to nothing, while others tried to build a presence in the Vale.

After the Energy Wars and the Muslim/Christian massacres to follow, the Federation classified all religions as cults and paid them little mind in the affairs of man. The only religion to grow in members was the ChristGaians, and they were all Neands. In the Federation, religion was quaint and antiquated and viewed with disdain. For Harley, it felt right some people still believed in something bigger than the Seven Realms.

When night settled, he went in search of food and followed a group of willowy young people chatting enthusiastically about some nonsense they lived in their MyRealms as they crowded into an old Mexican restaurant.

As he waited for the group in front of him to sit, he smiled softly at the noise level in the restaurant. There was music playing, and people were laughing and talking, and the aroma of grilling meat floated in the breeze created by large overhead fans. A sign at the entrance proclaimed in brightly lit letters "Welcome to Su Casa Mexican Grill."

A pale young man in the group ahead finally took notice of him and nudged his friends. They all burst into a fit of laughter as they adjusted their chameleon clothes to try and match his jeans and western shirt.

"What do you think; do we have your look down, Mr. Wild West?" the pale boy asked.

"Not quite." Harley took his bottle out of his pocket and took a nip.

"What are we missing? Oh, the hat. We haven't got a hat."

"The hat." Harley took one small step toward the group. "And a few scars."

They turned around and didn't look back until seated. When it was his turn, the host, a true-blue living, breathing person in a chameleon dialed to look bright and festive, smiled at him with only his lips.

"What kind of meat you serve here?" Harley asked.

"Beef, chicken, pork."

"Figured as much," Harley replied. "But how is it raised? Is it real?"

The host looked confused and slightly annoyed. "All of our meat is the highest quality."

Harley sighed. "Not what I asked. Has any of the meat you serve here ever had legs? Or a hide? Or a head?"

The host just stared.

Harley tried again. "Is the meat butchered, or was it printed somewhere?"

"Harrington Brothers Meats provides all of our meat from only the highest quality genetic material."

"Meat grown in a cup," Harley muttered. "What I figured. I want to sit at the bar."

Harley ate beef enchiladas, chips, and salsa and watched the rest of the diners eat, laugh, and enjoy a meaningless meal of food printed in a laboratory. He left the restaurant in a sour mood and walked back to his hotel.

He stripped out of his new clothes, finished his whiskey, and chased it with beer. He didn't understand why it rankled to eat meat grown in a foodprint instead of having the chance to live before it died, but it did.

It tasted the same, perhaps even better, and it was just as filling, but it left him unsatisfied. Is that what Quinlan meant about humanity rotting at the core? Humanity wasn't living anymore, only synthesizing life. Maybe he was putting too much significance on a meal; he didn't know for sure. But in the Hubs, it sure seemed like people spent a lot of time pretending.

He fell asleep on top of the covers. He didn't dream.

II

The trek over the slide was difficult, and it had nothing to do with the landscape.

Quinlan carried Raizor on his back and could feel her tears dripping on his shoulder. Once she hiccupped a shuddering sob, then grew quiet. Noah walked beside him, wiping his nose and eyes with his shirt, and carrying the pulse rifle over his shoulder. The weapon was almost as long as he was.

When Harley abandoned them, the terror began. They were alone in the Wilderness. The wildthings were everywhere, and the Wrynd would return. Soon.

They had to get away, Quinlan knew, but couldn't leave his wife dead in the middle of the road. With his children crying and holding each other and looking so small and fragile and lost, he used a branch to dig a small grave for their mother.

He cleaned away her blood as best he could with a shirt from his pack and then laid her to rest. His children sobbed when he picked her up and as he sprinkled dirt across her body. After placing the first layer of rocks around and on top of her, his children came to help, and they all cried.

It took too long but had he had to do it. As they crossed the upheaval of rock and dirt toward the hope of transportation, Quinlan felt the weight of the cutlass strapped to his side and cursed Harley's name. If the Castaway lied about the truck being there, then there was no hope.

If he didn't lie, then perhaps there was a chance to keep his children safe, and eventually, avenge Vania.

When they stepped back onto the broken pavement, Quinlan spied the ruins of the storefront Harley said would be there. He slid Raizor off his back and bent to kiss her cheeks, streaked by dried tears. They trotted to the ruins and found the old truck.

Noah and Raizor climbed inside, and Quinlan fished the access tag out of his pocket and climbed behind the wheel. He was about to start the truck when Noah clenched his shoulder.

"Dad!" he hissed.

Quinlan turned and from the back window saw something coming down the road. "Get down," he whispered.

The ruins blocked much of the view of the road, but as it curved east, he could spy Wrynd dashing toward them, hundreds of them. Leading the way was their mad leader, the Wrynd who ruined Vania, turned her into a monster.

They peeked over the seat through the dirty back window, and as the Wrynd drew closer, the battered store concealed their approach. Quinlan held his breath, gripped the cutlass hilt, and waited.

After five minutes, he shifted his position and looked out the front window. The last of the Wrynd were scampering over the slide, and he watched until they disappeared.

He let out a shuddering sigh and activated the truck's tag. It hummed to life, and he put it in gear and drove onto the highway.

They passed what must be the Wrynd camp and climbed to the mountain summit and over. His children were quiet, uncomfortably so, and he told them to join him on the front seat. They did and sat side-by-side, staring blankly at the dashboard.

When they exited the winding canyon, there was a ghost town waiting. Quinlan turned left on the first side street and stopped in front of a house partially collapsed.

They climbed out and stretched and tiptoed through the wreckage for a place to urinate, then silently climbed into the back seat and held each other.

"Are you hungry?" he asked, and his children said nothing. Noah gave the slightest of shrugs. Quinlan linked and ordered water and sandwiches and vegetables. When the stork arrived, they only nibbled.

Noah curled against his right side and Raizor against his left, and as afternoon slid toward evening, he felt them twitch as sleep took them. Soon they were both softly snoring, and then he let despair feed. He cried until he sobbed and then clenched his teeth and forced it away.

Through the half-open window, he smelled smoke and heard the clanging of a bell. This town wasn't quite a ghost town. There were people out there, Neands. Maybe they would know another way through the mountains back to the Hub.

Perhaps they would know if there was an apple orchard growing somewhere in the Wilderness.

He drifted to sleep and awoke when Raizor curled into a ball, using his lap as a pillow. His bladder ached in protest.

The night was fully upon them, and darkness pressed close. The sky was moonless, and the stars looked almost within reach. Raizor moaned in her sleep and shifted, and Quinlan's bladder gave a warning stab.

He uncoiled from his children and quietly opened the door, stepping out on a cool night, where a soft wind tussled his hair and sent shivers up his arms.

He stepped to the back of the truck and urinated, his eyes rolling as he sighed with relief.

Then he saw them, the shadows in the darkness, staring. Cats. There were hundreds of cats all around. They slinked through the destruction of the house and paced through the street. They were under his truck, and as he turned his head, he spied three perched in the bed, grooming themselves.

As he zipped his fly, he felt something brush against his leg. There was another cat weaving from left leg to the right, purring.

Terror gave way to awe, and he slowly stepped away and slid back into the truck, closing the door. His children still slept, and he stared out the window at the cats in the darkness. They slowly started to wander away, and when they were gone, a smile curved his lips.

The wildthings could have killed him but didn't. He didn't know what that meant but was sure it meant something.

He slid back in the seat and pulled his children close and eventually sleep embraced.

When it did, he dreamed of an apple orchard.

III

Harley rode a Serpent to the Justice Tower. When the commuter's doors opened, he stood in boots reluctant to commit to the landing. He was the only passenger, so the train sat, patiently waiting. He stepped out and thought better of it, but the Serpent closed its doors and slithered down the tracks in search of other passengers.

His fingers itched for his sidearm, and he stuffed them into the pockets of his jeans as he stared up at the dark tower of Federation dominance. When he stumbled upon the lost legionnaire and the Wrynd using the Link to get their drugs, Harley thought he might have a card worth playing. It might be a card worth the risk. Now he wasn't so sure. The death of Victor Walker complicated an already complicated situation.

"She owes me," Harley muttered. He tipped his hat and walked toward the tower with the hope debts owed were remembered and paid in kind.

The glass doorway hissed open, and Harley slipped his eyeset on his brow as he stepped into the vast and sparkling interior of the building. When the glass closed behind him it felt as if he stepped within a cell from which he might never, ever escape. He sighed and rubbed the side of his leg where his holster usually rested. There were only two ways this would play out; either very good or very bad.

"Ain't you the fool, Harley," he whispered. An automation with six skeletal legs, three stubby arms, and a body resembling a fruitcake, shuffled past, and three blue eyes blinked his way as it passed through into the daylight. He watched it go, flicking up his eyeset for a moment to make sure it was in the Sphere and not the Vale. He shook his head at its passing and turned back to the interior of the building.

In the Vale, a woman sat at a lavish desk in the center of the room, slightly to the left of the great statue where the Lord Judge summoned all of creation in his outstretched hands. The woman was impossibly flawless, and her long turquoise hair flowed in a nonexistent breeze. She glanced up as Harley drew near, and within her peach-colored eyes she expressed so much devotion and desire to attend to his needs Harley thought he might be somewhere else in the Vale.

"This is the Justice Tower?" Harley stammered.

"It is. How may I help you?" the woman asked, and Harley wondered if she was an avatar, a jinni, or just a Filler.

"I'd like to see Marshal Tempest."

"Oh, I'm sure that would be impossible, sir," the woman with the turquoise hair said. "The Marshal is quite busy."

Harley tried to lean against the woman's desk, but it wasn't physically there. He stumbled and passed right through her. She didn't seem to mind. "Why don't you find out?"

The woman showed no sign of irritation, and she smiled as though what he said was perhaps the most seductive thing she ever heard. "Whom may I tell is calling?"

"Whom? Harley. Tell her Harley Nearwater is calling."

The woman blinked and smiled. "The Marshal is in, Mr. Nearwater. She'll see you."

"She will?" Harley said with a stutter. "Well, of course, she will."

A tube descended from the ceiling, coiled toward him, and he stepped toward it and traveled deeper into the belly of the beast.

There truly was no going back now.

The tube lifted him to the Rocky Mountain Hub Marshal's Office, and when Harley stepped out, he walked into a small, deserted foyer, white and gleaming and without furnishings, other than a tall creeping vine climbing the far wall. A door silently opened to his left, and he stepped through.

The Marshal's office was large and dimly lit, with walls the color of rich earth and vining plants coiling from floor to ceiling. It looked more like a garden than an office. There was a large brown leather couch in the center and an oversized chair more suitable for sleeping than reclining and a center table in the shape of a face clock where time tick, ticked away.

In the far-left corner was a large Cherrywood desk ingrained with the Earth in different degrees of tan and devoid of any shining bauble. Sitting behind the desk, with her legs thrown casually on its top, was Marshal Jodi Tempest, and Harley felt a nervous twitch in his right eye.

It had been more than three years since last they met. Then she was a lowly deputy, dirty, afraid, and trapped by an angry mob of Neands. Armed with every odd assortment of weaponry from the Old World, they were intent on killing her and every Marshal of the Federation who dared to stop them from making Las Vegas an island outside of the Wilderness and the Realms.

She survived the Vegas Uprising, but only because Harley drew his sidearm in her defense. He didn't have a clue why he risked death to help her, but now he dearly hoped she hadn't forgotten.

"Long time since Vegas, Harley Nearwater," Jodi said, and Harley lifted his eyes to hers and became lost for a moment. He pulled them away.

"Aye, a long time, Marshal Tempest. Marshal. That does have a ring to it."

Jodi smiled and let her legs fall from her desk. "A nice ring?"

"Didn't say that Marshal."

Jodi stood, folding her arms across her chest. "I hear they call you the Castaway in the Wilderness. Has the ring of myth. Any truth behind it?"

"May be," Harley said with a shrug.

Jodi let her eyes roam over his wiry frame. "You clean up nice. I like the silly hat. I have a deputy who would love it. You're still ugly as hell, though."

Harley nodded. "I would say the same."

Jodi grinned. "But you'd be lying."

"Aye."

"How are things in the Wilderness?" Jodi came from behind her desk to stand in front of him, and Harley felt a nervous tickle up his spine.

"More difficult than they need to be," he said.

"Why is that?"

Harley shrugged. "Gaia seems none too pleased. The Rages grow stronger, the wildthings grow wilder. Eventually the Wilderness will be pressing at your door, Marshal."

"Have you become a ChristGaian since last we met, Harley?"

Harley chuckled. "Not likely. But my eyes aren't closed."

Jodi motioned toward the couch and chair, and Harley fell in line behind her, his eyes drawn to her as she walked, despite his best intentions. Harley sat on the couch, and Jodi sat on the chair. She crossed her legs and smiled pleasantly.

"What brings you out of the Wilderness, Harley?" Jodi pressed her fingers to her lips.

"News, Marshal," Harley said.

"News of what?"

"Marshal Walker's death." Harley sighed and felt the gentle slide into a fate beyond his control.

Jodi nodded, and when she looked up, her eyes were no longer soft, they glowed with a ferocity he had seen before and hoped not to see directed his way. "I know he's dead, Harley. He's dead, and you left him on the side of the road like a slab of meat, to be eaten by carrion."

Harley shrugged, and Jodi's nostrils flared. He found it endearing. Of course, she knew; she had the entire Federation at her disposal.

"We're all slabs of meat, Marshal," Harley muttered. "And in the end, we're all just a meal waiting to be eaten. I might have saved Victor's body from the Wrynd or the wildthings, but he would've been food for the worms or the earth itself. Course, we could send him to the ashes, but then the fires would have fed. It's of little consequence what swallows you up in the end. What matters is how you arrive at the dinner table. Victor died a fool, but he died living the way he chose to live, which is good enough for me and should be good enough for you, I gather."

"Who killed him?" Jodi sat back in her chair.

"Scimitar Hatcher found himself a new chosen, one worthy of the title, I reckon," Harley said. "He dared him to challenge her in single combat. He accepted. It was a choice poorly made."

"Who was she?" Jodi laced the fingers of her hands together. Her right cheek betrayed the slightest of twinges when she was emotional. Harley noticed the trait in Vegas. He wondered if she was aware of the nervous tick.

"A wife and a mother, near as I know. A Pilgrim living in your Hub, Marshal. Hatcher noticed her, took her, and made her his own. Her husband and children convinced Victor to help them find her."

"And how did you become involved?" Her cheek twitched again.

"Our paths crossed," Harley said.

"Just like Vegas?"

Harley bit the inside of his lower lip. "I suppose."

Jodi stood and paced the floor. Harley watched her quietly.

"What became of the woman who killed Victor?"

Harley reached to put his hand on the hilt of his blade, realized it wasn't there, and pretended to scratch his leg instead. "I put my blade through her heart."

"And her family?" Jodi turned to face him.

Harley was silent for a moment. "I left them in the Wilderness."

"Why would you do that?" Jodi went to stand over him.

Harley sat back on the couch; his brow furrowed. It was a tricky question. "Can't say for sure, Marshal."

Jodi sat back down. "Is there anything you wouldn't do?"

Harley puzzled over the question, truly perplexed. "Thinkin' on it."

Jodi studied Harley, and he was both gratified and uncomfortable with the scrutiny.

"We've gathered what remains of Victor Walker, as you knew we would. Scimitar Hatcher is quite anxious to have your head. He's threatened to destroy the Hub if I don't provide it."

"Intrestin. Is that your intention?"

"I don't know."

"Do you think him serious, that he would attack the Hub?"

Jodi shrugged. "He seemed rather sincere, but it would be a fool's folly."

"Why not just turn me over and eliminate the risk?"

"I'm considering it." Jodi pressed forward, and they were so close he could smell vanilla in her hair. "Victor's death is not why you're here, Harley. Tell me, why are you here?"

"I have questions about other matters I've discovered in the Wilderness, Marshal."

"Questions? You know, Harley." She slinked behind the couch he sat on, and he remembered the cats stalking him. "We have this marvelous thing called the Link. You could ask your questions with a thought."

Harley nodded. "Could have. Chose not to."

"You're a relic, aren't you? Ask your questions. I may have some of my own."

Harley clasped his weathered hands, and Jodi sat on the arm of the chair across from him. He would have to tread carefully. Or not. "Is the Legion by chance missing one of its legionnaires?"

Jodi pursed her lips, and Harley detected the wave of emotion beneath it. "I'm Marshal of the Rocky Mountain Hub. If you have a question about the Legion, you should ask the Legion."

"I'd rather ask you."

Jodi slid back into the chair. "They're missing a legionnaire. Quite peculiar. They can't locate her or find any hint of her linktag. Do you know anything about that?"

Harley scratched his chin. "I know where to find her."

"And where might that be?" Jodi asked.

"In a room of an abandoned hotel in a dead city," Harley replied.

"And does she live?"

Harley shook his head softly. "No."

"And you know this because?"

He swallowed hard. "I killed her."

This time Jodi's seamless face showed the first hint of real interest. "Why?"

Harley shrugged, tried not to show the tension building within, and was confident he failed. "She pointed a pulse rifle my way. I don't take kindly to it." It wasn't the true answer, but the only answer he would ever give.

"If the Legion were to learn of this, they would skin you alive."

"May be," Harley said. "But she told me things I thought might interest you. Intrestin things."

"Such as?" Jodi leaned forward.

"She said she had a visitor in her apartment. A man with grey eyes. She thought he was a dream. He wasn't."

"What did this grey walker want?" Jodi sat back, laced her fingers together, and her cheek twitched again.

Harley cocked an eyebrow. "I didn't call him the Greywalker."

"No," Jodi smiled. "You didn't."

Harley tried to match Jodi's gaze and found he couldn't. You could get lost in those eyes forever if you weren't careful. "He said he wanted to give her the freedom to make her own choice."

"About?"

Harley shrugged and scratched at the calluses on his right hand. "About where she stood and what she believed. He removed her linktag, and when she woke, she was in a hotel in Price."

"That's not possible," Jodi said. Harley had the feeling it wasn't the first time she uttered those words.

"Didn't think so either. She had a scar on her temple, but I think it was there so I would notice, me or whoever else found her. I don't think he needed to scar her to remove the linktag. He just wanted to send a message."

"The linktag can't be removed," Jodi said flatly.

"Could you find her?" Harley stood and walked to the window. "Could you find her still if I hadn't told you where she was? He removed it."

"What message was he trying to send?"

Harley sucked air through his teeth. "That he's out there."

"Have you seen this man with the grey eyes?"

Harley shook his head. "No. But you've heard of him, same as I. A grey man. The Greywalker. You've heard the legends. He lives among us but is not of us. He's something more."

"Thought he was just a tall tale from the Wilderness."

"As did I," Harley said.

Jodi sat quietly, her eyes far away. She was on the Link, and Harley wasn't sure who she might be consulting. When she came back, she smiled coolly, calmly.

"Thank you for the information. I'll keep the events leading to the legionnaire's death between us. She was in the Wilderness, and the Wilderness is not our realm and not subject to our law."

"Or justice?"

Jodi smiled. "Do you argue for your execution, Harley?"

"Probably should. But no."

"Then you can be on your way."

"And the Wrynd threatening your Hub?"

"I've been told to ignore their threat."

"Intrestin." She may be inviting him to leave, but he wasn't ready to accept the invitation, just yet. "Who would tell you something like that, I wonder?"

"And you can keep wondering." Jodi walked toward the door, no doubt to escort him out.

Harley stood, placed his right hand where his sidearm should be. "There's more."

"Yes?"

"Why are the Wrynd having their ink delivered by stork?"

Jodi looked genuinely startled by the question, and it almost made him smile. She could be caught off balance, after all. "What makes you think that?"

"Let's just say it's more than a hunch."

Jodi forgot the door and instead sashayed back to the window, where she looked out at the morning skyline. "The Wrynd prey on the Neands and the Pilgrims of the Wilderness. They chose to face the Rages, and their fate is beyond our reach. But the Wrynd don't get their ink from the Federation."

"I saw it with my own eyes," Harley said softly.

"I would know such a thing."

"Yet, you don't." Harley tilted his head softly.

Jodi's jaw clenched, and she turned away. "If that were so . . ."

"It is so," Harley said and joined her at the window. "Which tells me the justice you preached to me of in the rubble of Vegas is nothing. Nothing at all."

Jodi's nostrils flared. "I don't believe the Federation would provide ink to the Wrynd. I will investigate what you said. I'll know for sure."

Harley pressed harder. "I'm sure you will, Marshal. The Wrynd murder innocents and the Marshals do nothing. Whether the Wrynd create the ink, or the Federation provides it, without it they would be dead within a week. Yet, they thrive, and the Federation turns a blind eye. What of the Pilgrim who killed your deputy? She lived within your Hub, Marshal. She was under the protection of the Seven Realms, and the Wrynd waltzed right in and stole her away. They turned her into one of them, and she killed Marshal Walker. Will you avenge him, or is he also beyond the reach of justice?"

"Careful, Harley." He thought she might strike him. "My patience has limits."

"Then tell me why the Wrynd are allowed to survive?"

Jodi threw up her arms. "The Wilderness is not ours! It belongs to Gaia. It belongs to the Rages. Those living there can have everything they want if they'll abandon the ways of the Old World and join us. The Wrynd are everything repulsive left of the Old World, everything vile."

"And?"

"And what?" She glared and turned away. "And they serve a purpose, but they're not in league with the Federation. They're simply tolerated."

"What purpose do they serve?" he asked.

"Just another arrow in the quiver, Harley," Jodi replied.

"Arrow?"

"Long thing, pointed end, feathers; you shoot it with a bow. How could you not know about an arrow?"

Harley just stared.

"Just a little joke, Harley." Jodi brushed past him, and Harley could detect the tension in her shoulders. "In every society, you have bottom feeders; it's just the way things are. It doesn't matter how much you do for them, how many opportunities you provide them; there's a certain percentage of the population who will always choose the wrong course. Call it a genetic defect. Those are the Wrynd. On the Link, they could be anything, experience anything, and cause absolutely no harm to themselves or anyone else, but they'd rather take a dangerous narcotic that twists their minds, warps their bodies, and ruins them forever. The trick is, what do you do with them? Well, they aren't the only problem. The Neands and the Pilgrims are a problem as well. A far less manageable problem than the Wrynd."

"Why are they a problem?"

"Because they won't be happy!" Jodi's nostrils flared with irritation. Harley found it endearing, and terrifying. "What more could the Federation possibly provide than the safety and security of the Hubs, where you want for nothing? Yet, Neands and Pilgrims choose to live in the Wilderness, to face the Rages and preach their moronic ramblings of Gaia and God and their savior, rather than live safe and happy lives here."

Harley smiled and nodded his head. "So many rights, so little freedom."

"What more freedom could we offer?"

Harley thought of a way to answer her, a way to explain why some people would never accept the glories of the Federation. He wasn't sure he could put it into words. "The freedom to think on your own, make your own mistakes, and suffer the consequences."

Jodi rolled her eyes. "That's insane, Harley. Most people are unprepared to think on their own. And mistakes? People don't want consequences."

"Well, maybe they're just crazy then," Harley said.

"That's far easier to accept." She was pacing again, and Harley didn't mind watching her in the least. "We've tried for more than forty years to bring people in out of the cold, to give them safe harbor in the Hubs. Free housing, medical, income, the Link with all its opportunities, yet more than ten percent of the population refuses to leave the Wilderness."

Harley shrugged. "And what part do the Wrynd play?"

"Incentive." Jodi went to sit down. "If not motivated by Gaia's Rages, then perhaps they'll come to the Hub to escape them."

"And if they still won't come?" Harley took his spot on the couch.

"The Wrynd will eat them."

Harley raised his eyebrows. "I guess that would be another way of solving the problem."

"Yes, it would."

"And this is justice?" Harley asked.

Jodi nodded. "A harsh justice, but justice."

Harley thought of his mother, alone in the Wilderness. "And the Navajo Nation?"

"Why do you care?" Jodi seemed puzzled.

"They're my people."

"Your reputation precedes you," Jodi said, chuckling. "You're considered one who pillages his people."

"And by doing so I unify them," Harley said, smiling. It wasn't particularly pretty. "We all have our purpose, and I would hate to think I was subverted by someone who wishes to pillage my people in my stead."

"No need. We have no interest in the reservations."

"What a relief. I thought we might be forced off our land yet again." Harley stretched his legs and scratched absently where the mouse bit him. "Why does it matter to the Federation that a fringe of the world's population doesn't want what it has to offer?"

"Chaos, Harley," Jodi said. "If not united as a people, we are susceptible to chaos. We're irrational beings, humanity; we need order to protect ourselves from ourselves. It was the reason we couldn't let the Neands take Vegas; make it a fortress of the Old World. And . . ."

"And?"

Jodi sighed. "And this grey man of yours, this Greywalker. He's not the only oddity whispered of in the Wilderness. The world seems determined to destroy us. The ChristGaians say Earth seeks vengeance against us. Science can't explain the Rages, but reason suggests we should let the Earth have back what we've taken. It might be time for us to move beyond this planet."

Harley chuckled. "My people have been telling you that for hundreds of years. You don't listen."

"We're listening now," Jodi said.

"Probably too late for that."

Jodi nodded, licking her lips. "Any other questions, Harley Nearwater?"

Harley shook his head. "Your turn."

Jodi paused and seemed to be considering things she might share, but in the end, changed her mind. "Oh, I think you've answered the questions I meant to ask and maybe a few I hadn't. But I have a request."

"Yes?"

Jodi's eyes met his. "Find this man with the grey eyes for me. Find out who he is, what he is, and what he wants."

"Is that all?"

Jodi grimaced, and Harley had the feeling she was struggling to make a decision. "Well, if you have the opportunity, you could kill him."

"The Federation wants him dead?" Harley asked, surprised and perhaps a little pleased.

Jodi's eyes blazed. "I want him dead. If he exists, he's beyond the Seven Realms. He's a threat not worth the risk, and there are those who would risk everything for the chance at something more. Justice demands order."

"And in return?" Harley sat back, seeing the possibilities he wished before him.

"In return, what?"

He smiled. "In return, I'd like a scyc."

Jodi laughed. "Only Marshals are authorized scyes."

"Yes," Harley said. "And it sounds like you just deputized me."

Jodi shook her head. "You wouldn't be able to use it, not the way you desire. Even with a linktag, it's more than operating a drone or slipping into the Vale. With an eyeset, it would be difficult."

"You might be surprised. I'm fairly adaptable."

The Marshal nodded, and an interoffice stork arrived with a scye. "I've tagged it to your eyeset. It's designed as a defensive weapon first. You control its actions, but only partially. Do you think you'll want a lesson or two?"

"I'll struggle through. It'll give me something to do on the trail."

Jodi stood again, and Harley followed her to the door. "Do you think you can survive the Wrynd? They seem fairly determined to kill you."

Harley shrugged. "Most people want to kill me, Marshal."

"Truer words." Jodi stared at him, and Harley felt an odd and not uncomfortable warmth in his chest. "You're a strange man, Harley Nearwater." She tossed him the metal orb. "Don't hurt yourself."

Harley took the scye and strolled out of Marshal Tempest's office, a satisfied twinkle in his eyes.

He escaped the belly of the beast.

CHAPTER TEN

CHASING CHAOS

I

Her wings left her standing on the overgrown parking lot of a ghost hotel. Jodi checked her sidearm and considered unslinging her scye but decided doing so would only demonstrate a nervousness she would rather not advertise.

The city felt haunted, and silence weighed heavy on deserted streets. Two automobiles squatted on ruined tires in the parking lot, and sad clouds hanging low looked on the verge of weeping. Jodi made a quick scan of Price before her wings dropped her here, and knew the city still had residents. She had the odd sense someone watched her, but unlike the veiled animosity greeting her behind closed doors in her Hub, here the underlying feeling was curiosity sprinkled with fear.

She faced the hotel, her boots reluctant to move toward what her imagination insisted was a tomb. There was a dead legionnaire inside, a woman who in life was of little to no consequence to anyone in the world, a woman who loved a man in the Vale who was a lie. Her dreams, her desires, and her words meant nothing in life, but in death, the might of the Federation listened with bated breath for the tales her corpse might tell.

Emissary Storm and High Judge Trevok were on their way to meet her, and she wanted a chance to see what Harley described of the woman before they arrived. But her boots still resisted. A rock kissing a rock startled her, and she spun to face the street, her hand going to her slayer. A building battered and bowed by the abuse of the Rages struggled to stay standing, and something was hiding in the rubble, trying to stay hidden from view. Jodi could see the forehead and dark eyes of a child staring at her, and her heart skipped a beat.

"You there," Jodi called. "What are you looking at with those great big eyes?"

The child stood up. It was a little boy with tangled hair and filthy clothing. He held a rock in his right hand and a stick as long as his body in his left. Jodi glanced down the street, and every building in sight had shattered windows. She smiled.

"You been breaking windows, boy?"

The boy dropped the rock. "No."

"I'm Marshal Tempest, and it wouldn't be good if I found you'd been breaking windows."

The boy switched the stick from left hand to right. "Marshal? Well, you can't do nothin', you ain't got no juris-jurisdac…"

"Jurisdiction."

"You ain't got no place here," the boy said, jutting out his chin defiantly. "This ain't your place; my Momma said the Federation don't care nothin' 'bout the Wilderness."

"Your Momma's right," Jodi replied. "I have no jurisdiction here, but it doesn't mean I don't care, and I bet if I took you to your Momma and told her you'd been breaking windows she might care something about that."

"Maybe. But you'd have to catch me, and I'm too fast."

Jodi laughed. He was something. "Too fast for a Marshal? I could call down my wings, and I bet I could catch you if I wanted."

The boy looked up into the overcast sky, mouth agape. When

he looked back at Jodi, his eyes squinted, and she smiled. He was a sharp one, all right; a shame he would live and die in this crumbling place of the Old World.

"You come for the soldier?" The boy changed the subject.

"You've seen her?"

He pointed to the top floor and his nose curled. "She's up there. She's stinky, and the rats have been making a tasty treat of her."

"Rats?" Jodi looked at the hotel and turned back as the little boy scampered out of the rubble and ran weaving down Main Street, dragging his stick behind him like a tail.

A fat tear of rain dropped onto the bridge of her nose, and she sighed and forced her boots to take her forward. The air system moaned as she opened the door of the hotel, and the lights in the foyer flickered to life. She made a cursory scan of the lobby and headed for the stairs, still determined to not unsling her scye.

Mid-way up the second flight Jodi began to smell Sergeant Kara Litmeyer; a sweet, sickly smell that grew in intensity with every step. The aroma of rot and feces circulated in the air system and Jodi was grateful she hadn't stopped for breakfast. She cleared the third-floor landing and faced a row of closed doors and one open one.

She stopped two paces from the open room, steadied her pulse, and calmed her stomach as the boy's words delighted in her head "rats have been making a tasty treat of her, rats have been making a tasty treat of her, rats have been making a tasty treat of her."

"Damn kid," Jodi muttered in the empty hallway and stepped through the door of the hotel room. Rats had indeed been making a tasty treat of Sergeant Litmeyer. And still were. There were a dozen crawling across the dead woman's body. They had eaten away her nose and lips, and three were burrowing into her side. Flies had found her and blanketed every open cavity in her bloated, ruined body. Jodi gagged, drew her slayer, and shot three rats. The others scattered across the floor and ran toward her. She backed up, shooting two more, and the rest scampered down the hallway.

She took four more steps toward the body of the legionnaire, and the smell of her overwhelmed, clawed at her nose and down her throat. Jodi swallowed hard and forced herself to keep going.

"Isn't this a horror show?" The voice was husky and delighted. Jodi swirled, bringing her sidearm to bear. She almost pulled the trigger as Emissary Storm strolled happily into the room. "Whoa there, quick draw; you don't want to kill the High Judge now, do you?" Cirroco beamed, and behind her High Judge Trevok slowly stuck his head through the door. He was gagging, and tears were forming around his bulbous eyes.

Jodi stepped aside as Cirroco walked to the mass of rotting flesh that once was a woman. She waved away the flies, and they swarmed into the air and settled around the dead woman's legs. Cirroco knelt and turned the woman's head toward her. Something popped as she did, and the smell intensified. Jodi swallowed hard. "Is there any doubt this is Legionnaire Kara Litmeyer?" Cirroco looked back, grinning.

"I haven't performed any tests, Emissary," Jodi said between clenched teeth.

"Oh, I'm sure it's her, Marshal. The question is, what became of her?" Cirroco turned the dead woman's face and bent lower to examine the scar on her temple. She removed a small capsule from a pocket in her belt and inserted it through the woman's neck. Clear liquid oozed from the pill's insertion point, and High Judge Trevok vomited in the corner.

Cirroco went to the couch where the woman's battle armor lay. She picked up the chest piece and examined it briefly before tossing it aside. She paused as the scan came back on the dead woman.

"It is indeed Sergeant Litmeyer, and the terribly interesting part is there's no sign of a linktag in the woman's body. Isn't that fascinating?"

High Judge Trevok took a few steps closer, wiping his mouth

with the sleeve of his robe. "That's not possible."

Cirroco laughed. "Well, we keep saying that. Of course, it's not possible, but it is the truth."

"How could the nanites be removed? They bond with a person's cells." Jodi stepped away from the High Judge, fearing he might again lose control of his stomach.

"Well, that's one question, but not the most important question." Cirroco pushed on the grey flesh of the dead woman's body, fascinated. "The most important question is who removed them? To what end?"

"We'll need to take her body back for more detailed examination," the High Judge proclaimed. He removed a handkerchief from beneath his robe and used it to cover his mouth and nose.

"You'll need a bucket," Cirroco said.

Trevok walked past the dead legionnaire and threw open the balcony doors. "Nevertheless." He summoned advocates to attend to the woman's body and took a deep gulp of outside air. The sky leaked, but the storm had not arrived. "Let's take our conversation to the balcony, where we can breathe."

Cirroco looked at Jodi, grinned, and joined the High Judge. Jodi followed gratefully.

They stared out at the dead city. Beneath them, the High Judge's shuttle squatted, and two of his advocates advanced toward the hotel. When Jodi looked back at the dead woman, four rats had dared to venture back into the room. She drew her sidearm and blasted the closest one. The others ran away.

When the High Judge's advocates arrived, dressed in the white armor of their calling, they ventured a peek into the room, and Cirroco smiled. "Scoop her up, boys. The High Judge wants a souvenir." She closed the door to the balcony.

"If someone removed her nanite implants, what does it mean to be able to do such a thing?" Jodi asked, looking past the High Judge and at Emissary Storm.

"It means, Marshal Tempest, that we have our first evidence of the Leap, as the Lord Judge has foreseen," Cirroco replied.

"It doesn't necessarily mean anything of the sort," High Judge Trevok said. "Technological advances occur daily in the Seven Realms. It simply means someone has developed a way to remove the implants without killing the host."

"We control the technology, High Judge." Cirroco leaned against the balcony rail and folded her arms across her chest. "Or are you suggesting a Neand in the Wilderness has developed a technology that we don't possess?"

"It must be possible," Trevok said.

"Don't be a fool," Cirroco said. "For decades our Lord Judge has counseled us of the impending evolutionary leap of humanity; that it would come from the human foundry of the Wilderness. He told us that when it did, it would be either our key to opening the doorway to the galaxy or our doom as Gaia brings about our extinction. The Leap chose this legionnaire as a messenger that he's among us. Now we must find him and learn down what path he may lead."

"And if he has no desire to lead?" Trevok asked.

"I wasn't planning on giving him a choice."

Jodi turned away. At the end of the block, she detected movement. It was the boy "rats have been making a tasty treat of her." He was throwing rocks at windows. "If there's someone out there in the Wilderness who has evolved beyond humanity, what do we hope to gain from it?"

"Godhood, Marshal. Our Lord seeks godhood," Cirroco replied.

Jodi faced the Emissary. "He thinks to become a god?"

"He thinks we are to become gods." Cirroco said, her face enraptured at the thought of the Lord Judge. "He seeks it for all humanity. It's our destiny. Godhood is an evolutionary process for all sentient beings. Godhood or extinction. He seeks the next step in our journey so that we can protect it, understand it."

"Control it." High Judge Trevok clenched his fists.

Cirroco rolled her eyes. "When the next step in our evolution comes, the power within it might be such that it can destroy us before we can learn to control it. Lord Syiada seeks to cradle us before we walk, before we run, before we take to the stars and build a universe of our own."

"Sounds like derangement," Jodi whispered.

"You say that, but you don't mean it, Marshal Tempest. Not truly." Cirroco approached and ran one of her fingers across Jodi's cheek. She fought the urge to step away. "Look at our world, at the Seven Realms. We're creating our reality even now, shaping our destiny. The next step in our evolution is overdue. We either step backward, which we may do coddled in the Hubs, or leap forward from the Wilderness. If this Greywalker your castaway friend spoke to you of is the first to leap, we must find him, study him, and learn what we can from him."

"Even if it means killing him?" Jodi asked.

"To make an omelet," Cirroco replied.

"And what of this castaway who brings you tidings of the legionnaire's death?" Trevok asked, drawing close. His breath smelled of vomit, and Jodi scowled.

"Harley Nearwater. He found her here."

"And you let him walk right out of your office, Marshal Tempest." Trevok stepped closer. "What if he is the Leap?"

Jodi laughed. "Harley Nearwater an evolutionary leap? You've never met him, High Judge. If he's a leap, it's in the opposite direction."

Trevok stepped closer still, and Jodi found herself wondering how it would feel to throw him off the balcony. "You made this determination on your own and allowed him to walk freely through the Hub?"

Jodi straightened her shoulders and met his eyes. "I did."

"How do you know this man?" Cirroco asked, and her tail caressed the side of Jodi's thigh.

This time Jodi stepped away; she couldn't help herself. They were both pressing closer than she normally allowed anyone. "We met during the Vegas Uprising."

"He was one of the Neands building their Elysium?" Cirroco asked.

"No. He was passing through when the Neands attacked," Jodi said. Through the closed doorway, she could hear one of Trevok's advocates retching. "He sided with the Federation and saved many of us."

"Interesting coincidence, don't you think?" Trevok asked with a sneer.

"I see no coincidence in Harley Nearwater's actions," Jodi said.

"Even so. I doubt this man is the Leap, but diligence is required. We need to know for sure," Cirroco said.

"I can have my Marshals locate him."

"No. The Lord Judge has another plan," Cirroco replied. Her tone was soft, purring. "If he is the Leap, we need to know why he's in the Hub and what powers he might possess. We need a test of his abilities. A controlled test of an unknowing subject."

"How do you propose to do that?" High Judge Trevok pushed Jodi aside.

"Oh, the Lord Judge has many tools at his disposal, High Judge, many tools indeed." Cirroco skipped onto the railing and stared down at the parking lot three stories below.

"And if Harley Nearwater is just a man?"

"Then he will die as one." The Emissary dropped from the balcony, and her wings swooped in to gather her. As she disappeared into the overcast sky, the storm finally broke.

II

Icarus skimmed above the treetops, hugging the curve of the canyon, and following the dead highway. Cirroco asked Icarus to release her along the riverbank one klick from where the Wrynd horde gathered. She walked the rest of the way, enjoying the coolness of the river mud oozing between her hooked toes. Her scye clipped to her belt tapped softly against her hip, not unpleasantly. She longed to use it, but there were other ways to kill, and there was the opportunity to impart a lesson in the moments ahead, a lesson about power and its uses.

The first three Wrynd to spy her were more measured than she thought they might be. But they weren't very efficient killers. When they struck, she leapt into the air, her left foot ripping into the throat of the first, her right plummeting into the eyes of the second. The third lunged from behind, and her tail pierced his chest, puncturing his back. Cirroco smiled sweetly and left them where they fell.

Four more times Wrynd discovered her and attacked as she walked along the river. She killed each of them with carefree abandon. When she reached the horde gathered at the desolate rest area, she left the river and strolled along the road, her clawed feet crunching the ancient asphalt, her tail swishing behind her. Her leather armor, covered in blood, smelled musky and it pleased her.

A primordial roar erupted in the throng of Wrynd. Dozens rushed toward her, screaming, and she roared back with glee and finally unleashed her scye. The purple orb ripped through the first wave of Wrynd, and they fell twenty paces from her. The second wave pounded, and Cirroco struck out with fist, claw, and tail, and their screams of rage turned to something else entirely.

"Enough!" A man commanded, and the Wrynd backed away. Cirroco's scye hovered in front of a Wrynd too terrified to move, and after a moment's thought, she sent it through the young Wrynd's chest and brought it back to her hand. Its shield deactivated, and she caught the orb and clasped it to her belt with a satisfied sigh. She turned to face the big Wrynd pushing his way through the army surrounding her and smiled.

"Scimitar Hatcher. Nice to see you again," Cirroco said with a bow.

"Emissary." Hatcher stopped well out of her reach and put his arms on his hips. "Do you intend to kill my entire shield this day?"

Cirroco licked the blood from her fingertips. "I'd considered it."

"I would have to stop you, Emissary."

Cirroco barked laughter. "You need more than these to stop me, Wrynd, and you know it."

"Perhaps to kill you, but to make you one of us, I think I have sufficient."

"Sending me into the flare would hasten your death in ways beyond your imagining, Scimitar."

"What brings you to my range, Emissary Storm?" Hatcher asked, his hands clenching and unclenching against his hips.

Cirroco strolled toward him and smiled as the big man stiffened. She reached out with her right hand, forefinger still stained with blood, and traced it across the Wrynd's chest while glancing up into the morning sky. "I came to ask you about those."

From over the horizon, hundreds of storks swarmed, descending to hover over the Wrynd encampment.

Hatcher smiled. "Instruments of war, Emissary." The storks flowed toward the large, leaning building that once, in another world, had been a simple welcome center for weary travelers. Each stork deposited a long, rectangle box in front of the building before fluttering away. Hatcher walked toward them, and Cirroco followed, the wave of Wrynd parting. She didn't fail to notice the lust in their eyes as they watched the storks descend. They all knew what the boxes contained.

"How much ink have you summoned, Scimitar?" she asked.

"One hundred thousand vials. Enough to tear the Hub apart, Emissary." Hatcher grinned back at her. "Enough for vengeance."

"You've broken your oath, Wrynd." Cirroco slapped her tail against one of the boxes. "Lord Syiada will allow me your death."

"The oath is broken, Emissary, but not by the Wrynd. The Federation has broken its pledge," Hatcher said. "The Marshals have breached my range, and, because of them, my chosen is dead. I'll bring down the Hub and everyone who stands in my way until I bathe in the Castaway's blood. Your Marshal protects him as he cowers there. Bring him to me, and there will be no war."

"Am I to do your bidding now, Wrynd?"

"If you're to prevent a slaughter."

"Now why would I want to prevent a slaughter? Perhaps I'll initiate one of my own."

From behind the leaning building, dozens of Wrynd scampered and encircled Cirroco. In their hands, they held blowguns, pulling them to their lips as Hatcher stood smiling. Prone on the pitched roof of the main building was another Wrynd pointing a rifle. She doubted it was a pulse rifle or a bullet aimed her way, more likely a dart poisoned with ink.

Another Wrynd walked from behind the building to stand beside the Scimitar. His skin as dark as night, his smile as bright as the sun, he had long and neatly combed hair, and the black of his ink-infused veins were darker roadmaps on his bare arms. His eyes, while black in the sclera, the iris still held onto a hint of the hazel they had once been, before the ink made him what he was. Unlike the other Wrynd, his hands were unmodified, and he wore cowboy boots. If not for the black of his veins and sclera, he wouldn't look Wrynd at all. He was dark and beautiful, and Cirroco smiled at his cool confidence as he took his place by Hatcher's side.

"You plan to create a Wrynd horde out of the Hub?" Cirroco asked.

"The Federation has provided us poor ore, full of impurities, but we'll refine it as best we can." Hatcher turned to the young man beside him and nodded. "Thank you, Dagger Ash." He turned back to Cirroco. "My Dagger will lead the assault on the Hub. From north to south we'll press into the western boundaries and turn everyone we find. We'll create chaos the likes of which not seen since the Old World. I know this Harley Nearwater. I've dealt with him before. He's a coward, intent only on his survival. He'll see our attack and run, and I'll be waiting. He'll run to the Wilderness he's familiar with, and I'll be waiting to tear him asunder." Hatcher folded his great arms and smiled. "Now, Lizard, you can either stand aside, or we make you one of us."

"All this over a woman?"

"This is about honor and the breaking of oaths," Hatcher replied.

She snorted. "Oh, you're a blunt instrument, Scimitar. I wonder why the Lord Judge values you. Alas, it's not my place to question the wisdom of our Lord. But you frighten me, Scimitar Hatcher. I'm sure that doesn't surprise you, but I thought it important to be honest."

Cirroco paced the circle the Wrynd had created around her, and when a young woman with a scarred face pressed too close, she pierced her chest with her tail. When she pulled it free, it made a slurping sound, as a boot pulled from the muck. The woman toppled without a sound.

"Your ferocity, your anger, your desire, your resolve. It all frightens me," Cirroco continued as if nothing had happened. "In the past, when a thing frightens me, I destroyed it, and I would do so now, but our Lord stays my hand. But not forever. If your actions were against the wishes of the Lord Judge, he would have stopped the storks, and the flow of ink would disappear. Your Wrynd would be writhing in agony within a week. Understand that you live because our Lord allows it and the war you think to bring to the Hub is by his design and his design alone. The castaway you desire to kill may be one the Lord Judge seeks. Your war will be the test. You have the Lord Judge's blessings. The gates of the Hub are open to you." She bowed to the Wrynd again.

Cirroco started to part the crowd and then turned back. Her eyes blazed as she stared at the Scimitar. "But if this Harley Nearwater is the one we seek, you shall not have him. In that, there can be no misunderstanding. If he's not, his blood is yours."

Cirroco stepped away and her wings descended. "And then your blood, Scimitar Hatcher, your blood will be mine."

III

Hatcher watched the Emissary disappear over the horizon, then he motioned for the Wrynd to lower their weapons and turned to his dagger with a satisfied smile.

"The Lord Judge and his wench think we are but puppets on a string, Dagger Ash."

The smaller Wrynd nodded. "As long as the Lord Judge controls the ink, we are puppets on a string, Scimitar," Dagger Ash said.

"In time we'll unravel the secret of the ink, and when we do, we'll burn the world." Hatcher brushed past his dagger. "Until then, we must dance to the Lord Judge's tune, but the day will come. I was prepared to rage into the next world to seek my vengeance, defy the Lord Judge himself, but the Emissary's visit has opened new possibilities. Syiada thinks to use us for his designs, but those designs will lead us closer to discovering the secret of ink he uses to bind us."

Hatcher walked into the old building, which had been all but stripped of its furnishings. In the center of the room, he bent and stuck the hooked nail of his right forefinger into a gap in the wooden floor. He pulled, and a section of the floor lifted away, revealing a staircase.

Hatcher and Dagger Ash descended into the darkness. A light

winked to life when they stepped onto the earthen floor of the cellar, illuminating a large room filled with rows of black cases. He paused to swipe his hand over the nearest case, and it popped open. He lifted the lid and removed a slayer and holster. Inside, the case contained dozens more.

He opened the next case, and inside were pulse rifles, new and ready for use. The next case held a box of powerbands, and Hatcher took one and strapped it to his forearm, handing another to Ash, who did the same with a smile.

"Syiada has acknowledged the breaking of our bond with both word and deed. From the lips of his Lizard whore, he has blessed our design to destroy the Hub where Harley Nearwater cowers. We'll show them real destruction, real terror, real horror. Arm your skeans. Drive Harley to me. I'll keep a shield here. Turn everyone you find and let the flare have them. Show the Seven Realms the fury of the Wrynd."

Dagger Ash went to a smaller box in the corner of the cellar and removed a scye.

"And the Marshals?"

"Kill them or turn them. They're yours to do with as you like." Hatcher clapped the younger man on the shoulder. "Show them Marshals of the Federation can aspire to something greater."

CHAPTER ELEVEN

THE LAST COWBOY

I

Harley rode a Serpent north to Old Salt Lake City for no particular reason, just to delay the return to the Wilderness. While on the Link he learned of a museum he wanted to see.

His thoughts were on the horses and their mad dash toward the Hub. They hadn't been caught up in the Rages. They were wild and free and ran to their deaths. Surely, they knew humanity was near, that they would die. The world made little sense to him anymore.

Walking out of the Marshal's office, Harley intended to leave the Hub as quickly as possible. He had his prize, and it was time to make his way home. But when he stood at the commuter station, he picked a Serpent going north rather than south.

He watched the cityscape fly by and when the Serpent stopped in front of what in the Old World was the Utah State Fairgrounds, he stepped out and stared up at the entryway, his mind slipping into the past and a life far beyond reach. Looking at the sign hanging above, he understood what set his feet upon this path. He stood and viewed the world and what it once was through clouded eyes.

Through his latter teenage years and into his early twenty's Harley worked on and off for a rancher in Castle Valley. The rancher was an imposing man in a small body named Art Autumn. He owned and operated one of the last independent and self-sustaining ranches in the state.

Harley hired on as a simple ranch hand, mucking the corrals, feeding the livestock, hauling the hay. He was young and had no experience in the life of a cowboy. Old Art hired him because since RTI there weren't many people looking for work, and he resisted automation until the Rages killed him.

Harley worked hard because he liked the idea of the life Art struggled to maintain; being part of something, being a part of nature, and at one with the animals. After a couple of months, the old man gave him a chance to learn to ride, and Harley took to the horse like it was a natural place to be. Until his life on the ranch he had only ridden the old mare but sitting on the back of a big gelding named Trouble, he felt like a giant and knew that was where he wanted to be for the rest of his life.

Art owned more than 800 hectares and had tied up most of the free-range permits that still existed. When the Exodus began, a lot of people who swore they were country through and through gave up the only life they knew for the security of the Hub.

Life in the Vale was to the point that if someone wanted to live in the country, it awaited in the Vale with none of the headaches. Art was one of the few who held onto a reality that was quickly fading away. When Art died, the ranch would die with him. Harley and the other ranch hands knew it, but they stayed anyway because really, where else could they go to live this way?

The Rages had started, but not the Wildthing Rages. Even so, life was a roller coaster, and Harley never knew what he was going to face, one day to the next. It could go from too hot to too cold, too wet to too dry in a couple of weeks. The government hadn't finished building the transcontinental waterline, so people couldn't count on desalinated ocean water for their cattle. It was as close to living in the Wild West as he thought he might ever get. It was the one time in his life he felt he truly belonged somewhere.

Of course, even then he didn't have friends, but the other ranch hands accepted him because he worked hard, minded his own business, and when there was a strong back needed, he was there. He wouldn't have known what to do with friends anyway.

He loved the range most. He sat atop Trouble and listened to the senseless mooing of the cattle. At dusk, he could see the bright star of the Wheel in orbit, and he smiled thinking 10,000 people lived in outer space while he herded cattle on the range. Swaying in the saddle as Trouble snorted and as the dust from the herd made his eyes water, he thought he was living in a world on the cusp, and it felt mighty fine.

Art Autumn liked him for some reason and, when rodeo season came around, he cut as many of his cowboys free to go kick up a little hell as he could manage. Harley was delighted when the old man handed him a ticket to the Spanish Fork Fiesta Days Rodeo and told him not to get into trouble in the big city.

Harley had never been to a real rodeo, and he went along with the rest of the hands in a big old electric cattle truck. As the rest of the ranch hands laughed, drank, and boasted of all the women they would bed by the end of the night, he hadn't felt like he belonged, but he hadn't felt like an outsider either. He just felt like Harley Nearwater, ranch hand, cowboy, and that was good enough for him.

The rodeo was the greatest time he ever had. He loved every part of it. The rowdiness of the crowd, the smell of the horses and the livestock, the clowns, the watered-down beer, and the bad food; he loved every last bit of it. Sitting in the stands, jostled by all of the people, he looked up at the Wheel shining in the sky and thought, hell, if he wanted, maybe he could even make it up there someday, no matter what his mother might say.

Two weeks later, while sleeping on the range with the sound of the cows serving as a lullaby, he drifted to sleep with Trouble grazing softly beside him. The next morning, he woke to an angry snort from his horse and Trouble reared and aimed a hoof at his head. He scrambled out of the way, and the horse reared again and tried to land on top of him. Trouble's eyes were ablaze as it reared and bucked. He tried to make it to his feet but couldn't seem to get out of the way of the crazed horse. His hand stumbled across his pistol, just his dad's old 9mm back then. He tore it from its holster and put Trouble down.

Within a week, every horse on the ranch was mad and ninety percent of the cattle. Half of the hands died in wildthing attacks, including old man Autumn.

The Wildthing Rages had begun, and humanity became prey.

Several years later, after he settled into life as a castaway, Harley came across one of the big corporate ranches on the western side of the Rocky Mountain Hub. Even though they could print just about any meat someone desired to eat at a foodprint, ranching was still a big business, and a lot of people preferred to eat live-stock that had lived.

The ranch Harley came across was more than a thousand head of cattle, sheep, pigs, goats, and chickens. It was an impressive looking setup, and he couldn't get within two klicks of it. There were electrified fences all around and beyond high stone walls. An automation met him at the roadway and informed him he was en-tering a restricted livestock area. For his protection, he needed to turn back. The entire operation ran by 'bots, drones, and remote control. He left and put on his eyeset to get an up-close look of the operation by satellite. There were all those animals and not a human in sight. It was a hell of a thing.

Two years after coming across the ranch, he ran into one of the other cowboys who worked for Art Autumn. He was sitting in a bar on the outskirts of St. George, drinking away his RTI. Harley bought him a drink and bent his ear a little. He couldn't remember his name clearly; it may have been Buck, but it seemed everyone called him Duck. Buck (or Duck), said he tried to work on one of the corporate ranches, but it had been a mess for a while when the Wildthing Rages began.

There were a lot of deaths, particularly in the Hubs, but once they figured out managing livestock was a matter of not letting them catch sight or smell of humans, it didn't take long for the entire process to become automated. He hadn't lasted long. He said something about overseeing cattle through the Link sucking all the joy out of being a cowboy.

"Guess the cowboys are all dead now, huh, Harley?"

Harley raised a shot his way. "Guess so, Duck."

"Buck."

"Whatever."

A year or so later Harley heard Duck (or Buck) died when attacked by a wolf pack outside of the California Hub in a suburb of Seattle.

Sitting in the parking lot of what once was the Utah State Fairgrounds, Harley looked at the new expansive building standing where the fairgrounds once stood. The sign in front of the bowl-shaped building proclaimed, "Wild West Living Museum," and a giant display screen showed images of horses galloping across the range. He walked toward the museum, pushing his cowboy hat back on his head.

At the front door, a soft voice urged him to enter and see the West as it had been before the Rages. He donned his eyeset, paid his admission, and walked inside. A Filler host dressed in western wear met him at the door and assured in a singsong voice that all animals in the exhibit were automations and he was completely safe.

He nodded and walked on, removing the eyeset as he did and tucking it into his pocket.

The inside of the museum was grand, with artificial trees stretching artificial limbs toward an artificial sky. Automated birds flitted from one branch to the other, and high in the sky, he could see an eagle soar. To look so far away, Harley was sure it must be a digital one displayed on the ceiling.

The interior consisted of a dozen or so exhibit rooms, and inside each room was a display of the world the way it used to be, when humanity could interact with nature. The first room he entered was a mountain scene of a large meadow, and Harley thought it vaguely familiar. There were a dozen deer grazing and half again that many elk. The big bulls bugled as he watched, so close he could almost touch them. He smiled. They sure looked real, those elk.

Another room showed a panoramic from the desert with 'bot coyote hunting 'bot jackrabbits, and in another room, he watched a mama bear and her cubs dig at an old tree stump for bugs. His favorite room, the room he'd been looking for, was the room showing life on a ranch. When he stepped inside his heart ached.

There were 'bot free range chickens scratching at the ground and a couple of old Tomcats lounging in the sun. They purred when he walked in and wove between his boots. On the other side of an old cedar post fence was a field where cattle grazed, chewing their cud, and they stared at him with the same big blank eyes he remembered. In the corral were four horses and as he walked toward them, they approached the fence to hang their heads for a scratch.

He reached out a tentative hand and let it caress the side of a big sorrel. Its ear twitched as he scratched, and it snorted, blowing imitation snot onto his sleeve. There were 'bot flies zipping around for the horses to swat with their mangy tails. They even had the smell of the horses the way he remembered, and he inhaled the earthy mustiness with a sigh.

Trouble had been a bay, not a sorrel, but his horse and the 'bot horse were about the same size, fifteen hands, a good size working horse. As he scratched the 'bot horse, he resisted the urge to climb over the fence and throw himself up for a ride.

"I wish you were real, old girl." He scratched the horse a little more, patted it on the side, and turned to look back at the rest of the artificial ranch. "I wish any of this was real." The mare tugged playfully at his hat, and he stepped away. "But it's all just make-believe."

There was a segment of society living in the Vale "country" as cowboys. They worked on a digital ranch, rode digital horses, herded digital cows. Hell, for all he knew they stepped in digital cow shit. But it wasn't real. It may feel real; it may feel exactly the way it always did in reality, but it wasn't real. The 'bot horse trying to take the hat off his head was more real than that. He wouldn't have anything to do with it.

Harley went outside and waited for a Serpent to take him home to the Wilderness, leaving his memories where they belonged, in the past.

II

When the Serpent arrived, Harley paused at the door, suddenly reluctant to return to the Wilderness so quickly. Death was waiting out there. It was inevitable, but he didn't see the need to rush into its embrace. He let the doors close. The train pulled away, and he walked toward the heart of the city.

There were few on the streets, and those present ignored his nods of welcome. As he neared the skyscrapers of downtown Salt Lake, he passed only a handful of people who were walking as he was and none who seemed to be enjoying the task. The remainder were either riding hoverseats or bulging out of exoskeletons.

Everyone he passed radiated the same ambivalence he detected during his first day in the Hub. When he turned his head, when they thought he wasn't looking, there was another emotion beneath their blank stares. It was rage without direction, hatred beyond measure, and it occurred to him perhaps the Hubs hadn't protected humanity from the Rages at all. Perhaps in the Seven Realms, humanity was the Rages.

Deeper in the city, the bustle of automations flitting here and there drew his interest, and he stopped at a park bench to watch and smoke. Downtown was itself a living museum, a testament to the Old World, and most of the skyscrapers were vacant. They whispered of a world faded away, a world of purpose and action, where human ingenuity and sweat kept the mechanizations of civilization moving forward. Now automations replaced humanity and the machines thrummed along fine on their own. The machines still had a purpose, but Harley wasn't sure humanity did.

Curious, Harley slipped on his eyeset, linked, and sat on the same park bench in the Vale he sat on in the Sphere. In the Vale, the city bustled.

The sidewalks teemed with people walking here and there, laughing, talking, and being alive. Street side vendors, automations, and an occasional human dressed in brightly colored chameleons sold food or trinkets.

The smell of humanity in all its glorious and putrid varieties swirled in the soft breeze of the day. In the Vale, the skies were bright, and the clouds were high cumulus. A tall man in a flowing chameleon gown was selling peanuts from a sparkling cart, and Harley motioned him over. The man handed him a bag overflowing with salted peanuts. His hands were long, and his nails neatly manicured. He was too perfect to be real, and Harley stood and looked him in the eye.

"You're a Filler, aren't you?"

The man smiled with lips painted pink. "Have a good day, sir." He turned and walked down the sidewalk, and Harley sat back on the bench and cracked a peanut.

Everywhere people were busy going about the business of being people, but Harley was certain if the Fillers vanished and only avatars of living, breathing people remained, he might find himself alone on the street corner. He ate a handful of peanuts and savored the flavor, but when he removed his eyeset and returned to the Sphere, his stomach growled with hunger.

He sullenly smoked another cigarette, then walked across the street, through towering canyons of concrete and steel echoing of a past forgotten.

When he came to the temple, he paused at the open gateway and peered up at the golden figure holding a trumpet to the sky. The clouds were brooding above its head.

"No one's here to hear you," he said to the trumpeting angel and went to find a place to sit among the flower gardens. He dropped his pack on a bench facing the temple, and when he sat, his stomach growled again. He used his eyeset to order a sandwich and bottle of water.

A stork found him a few minutes later, and he unwrapped a ham and cheese sandwich on a hard roll and tore into it, letting slip a little moan of satisfaction as he ate. The water was cold and satisfying, and the food and drink did much to improve his humor.

He leaned back on the bench, crossed his long legs, removed his hat, and set it on the pack at his side. The overcast day grew greyer, but the clouds beat back the heat, and the soft breeze let the scent of the flowers swirl. Harley found he was content and smiling for no particular reason. He sometimes wondered if it might not be possible to be at peace after all, somewhere.

Someone else entered the temple grounds, and he sat up. It was a young woman, dark, long, and lean, with a pack strapped to her back. Harley grunted and tossed the last bite of sandwich into his mouth.

"Another wanderer on the trail," he muttered, then shrugged and pulled his pack onto his lap.

Wrapped inside one of his shirts was the prize he'd won from Marshal Tempest. He pulled the scye free with awed reverence and held it in his cupped hands. If he could find a way to master the weapon without a linktag, then the challenges of the Wilderness and the Rages might not be so daunting. The only way to know was to try. He slipped on his eyeset and linked with the scye. The orb lifted off his hands and its shield activated. It was a brilliant green ball of light floating before his face, and through the eyeset, he saw the scye and his haggard face through it at the same time. He felt a wave of nausea and shook his head.

"Well, that's not good." He sat back and tried to focus as the scye bobbed before him. It was much the same as linking with his eyeset while staying in the Sphere. He had to divide his attention between conflicting images, but unlike being on the Link, with the scye, he could see through and control the orb's actions while at the same time controlling his own body.

His mind struggled to process conflicting sensory input from his body and the scye. After several minutes of simply staring forward with a strained look of constipation on his scarred face, Harley dared direct the scye to make a slow ascent above the temple grounds. It hovered above the angel atop the temple, and he left it there while he fought vertigo.

Victor had been right when he said the scye was the equivalent of another appendage. While it forced his brain to process a new set of visual input, he could also feel the wind caressing its shielding and from it he could hear the hiss of a Serpent line coming to a stop three blocks away. He smiled and let the orb sink back toward the temple grounds, weaving between tree branches. After he made it circle the grounds twice, he decided to attempt moving while at the same time controlling the scye.

He sent the scye over the temple wall and bobbing down Main Street and tried to walk toward what he thought were the temple gates. He stopped when he felt water on his feet. He had walked into one of the concrete garden ponds, and water was pouring through the top of his boots.

"Son of a . . ." The scye crashed through a storefront window and burrowed into a brick wall. The impact felt like a physical blow in Harley's head. He stumbled and almost dropped to his knees. "Feck!" He stumbled out of the pond and stood with his arms apart and feet splayed, trying to keep from falling on his backside as he ordered the scye to return.

He cursed softly, and in the distance, the young woman who entered the temple grounds left again. He didn't think she saw him, which, all things considered, was good. He sent the scye above the city, and as the water poured from his boots, he heard a scream, not through his ears, but the scye.

With the scye, he could see in the distance people running down the middle of the road, and he sent the orb their way. They were terrified, screaming, and running without direction. Puzzled, Harley watched them pass, and from around a street corner, he saw the reason. A dozen Wrynd charged, roaring toward them.

Those fleeing were so inept at running, the Wrynd had them in short order. A Wrynd leapt upon the back of a short, balding man with huge breasts and tore his throat out with his teeth. He died with blood leaking through his fingers.

Four other Wrynd with blowguns knelt on the road and fired at the fleeing; four people fell to the ground, pulling darts out of their bodies. They lay prone for a moment, then began to convulse, flailing wildly. The ink rushed through their nervous system, and their convulsions stopped.

Their mouths contorted, and from deep within a moan gurgled, became a scream, and ended in a roar. Harley's scye was no more than ten paces away, and he watched as their eyes, wild and confused, turned black. They grinned manically and pursued those who fled. Behind them, the Wrynd crowed and gave chase.

"Scuttle this!" Harley sent his scye through the chest of the closest Wrynd with a blowgun and ran for the exit. He tried to recall the scye at the same time. He missed the gate and ran into the brick wall, falling flat on his back. He saw stars and shook his head, climbing to his feet.

"This isn't working." He gingerly walked through the gate and down the sidewalk toward the Serpent line. His scye still hovered over the street two blocks distant, and through it he could see the Wrynd advancing toward him.

There were hundreds of them, and scores armed with blowguns. They were turning everyone they could find, and the roars of those in the flare were echoing through the streets.

He sent the scye toward three more, cutting them down. Something clinked against the wall next to his head. A dart was on the ground by his feet. Across the street, a Wrynd was loading another dart into his gun, and Harley swore and dashed behind the wall. He could control the scye, or he could control his legs, but he wasn't up to controlling both, just yet. There was no time to practice.

He sent the scye toward the Wrynd with the blowgun, and it pierced his throat. He retrieved it, clipped it to his belt, then ran toward the train station, linking long enough to summon his security box. He prayed the stork would arrive with his slayer in time to make a stand. Behind him, the Wrynd gave chase.

Chapter Twelve

A Journey West

I

Brinna saw things she only dreamed of while riding the White Dragon west. She resisted the siren call of the Link and watched wide-eyed as the train streaked through the Wilderness.

They sailed through the abandoned city of Indianapolis. In St. Louis she craned her neck as the train hissed by the arched monument overtaken by the same creepers that had all but consumed the corpse of the city.

She stared in wonder as the Dragon flashed through what once was Kansas and now was a giant, unending farm where 'bot farmers harvested crop after crop for a civilization who had never seen such sights with their own eyes. Brinna was sad for them, at what they missed while they lived in the Vale.

She disembarked for a time in Denver and gaped at the Rocky Mountains touching the sky. She stayed for a night in a hotel, where she could glimpse the mountains, and she marveled that the great expanse of rugged Wilderness cut through the middle of the Hub. But staring at these mountains, she felt no inkling of the dream that beckoned. In the morning she boarded another Dragon and continued west.

When she arrived in Salt Lake, she gathered her pack, sidearm, and holster and stepped out onto the landing platform in the heart of the city. As in every Hub she passed, there were few people on the streets, and she felt alone in a mass of humanity.

To the east, in canyons of vast and towering peaks, she spied a building standing in sharp contrast to the buildings around it. The many-windowed building with six great spires looked like something out of a fantasy, and Brinna adjusted her pack and walked down the middle of a deserted street toward it, slipping her eyeset from her pocket and placing it on her brow.

She struggled to maintain balance as she tried to access the Link and realized she probably looked like a drunkard, not that anyone watched. Through the Link, she learned the building was once a temple of the Church of Jesus Christ of Latter-day Saints. The church still existed; Pastor Sorensen had railed against them in many a sermon. The Federation took possession of this temple and made it a museum of all religious faiths in the Old World.

Brinna walked slowly toward it, stumbling twice and almost falling on her face, finally snatching the eyeset away and stowing it again. There was a tall brick wall around the temple grounds, and she followed the sidewalk, letting her hand slide along the carved stone until she came to an open gate. She paused at the entryway and peered inside. There were 'bot groundskeepers scurrying about on an odd assortment of legs and wheels, caring for flower gardens the likes she'd never seen.

She followed a pathway through the gardens until she came to the temple itself. When she stood before the great arched doorway, she looked up, and her hand rose absently to caress the ChristGaian crucifix around her neck. She tried the door, and it gave no quarter. She turned, sat on the steps, and waited for a person or an automation to come by so she could ask to go inside.

Another building on the grounds struck her fancy, and she climbed down the steps and ventured toward it, her eyes drawn to the great windows staring back at her. She saw something looking through the glass and gasped as she realized Jesus God Himself was looking at her through the windows. She almost fell to her knees before she realized it was only a statue. She followed the path to the building and walked inside. Music softly played, and while she didn't recognize the hymn, the voices were angelic and praised Jesus God.

She found her way to a curving path that led up and followed it until she stood in the presence of Jesus God and Gaia. Jesus God towered above her, his arms outstretched and his face calm and inviting. Behind him floated Gaia, Mother Earth Herself, and all around were the heavens. Brinna felt small. And bitter.

Waves of emotion pressed upon her as she gazed up at the deities who abandoned Mamal. She struggled for words that would never be heard.

"You're killers, ye two," Brinna said, and she reached up and snatched the medallion from her neck. She draped it around the outstretched hand of Jesus God and turned to walk away, then turned back.

"She gave you everything she had to give, and you killed her for her devotion. I'll have no more faith in ye. I wash my mind of your false hope." Tears streaked her face as she turned to make her leave, and a soft voice called her back.

"Faith is not something so maliciously cast aside." The voice was a scratch in the silence, and Brinna cast her eyes back to the statue, and then slowly scanned the room. A wrinkled hand gripped the banister on the opposite walkway and pulled an aged woman into view.

Her body was like bent wire enveloped in a shift two sizes too large, and sunspots peppered her arms and face. She looked at Brinna with hazel eyes encased in a cascade of wrinkled smiles. Her hair was so grey it was white and pulled into a bun that perched precariously on top of her head. When she made her way to the top, she nodded with satisfaction and hobbled over to a bench facing the welcoming Jesus God.

"I do believe that walkway is getting longer," she said to herself as she sat and motioned for Brinna to join her. Brinna refused to move, and the old woman sighed. "I can't chase you."

Brinna went to sit by the old woman. As she did, she felt sorrow clinging to her, pulling more tears from her eyes. The old woman reminded her of Mamal.

"Who are you?" Brinna asked, and a tear slid to her chin.

"I'm Bishop Francis," the old woman cawed, and she took Brinna's right hand, placed it in her lap, and covered it with her wrinkled ones. "Who are you, young one?"

"Brinna. My name's Brinna Wilde."

The old woman nodded and motioned to the ChristGaian cross dangling from Jesus God's fingertips. "Fetch me that, if you don't mind."

Brinna retrieved the medallion from the statue's fingers and placed it in the old woman's waiting hands.

"You're ChristGaian?" Bishop Francis asked, holding the cross between fingers with blue veins crisscrossing.

"I am," Brinna mumbled. "I was."

"Was? What are you now?"

"Nothing. Now I'm nothing," Brinna said. "Who are you? Why are you here?"

The old woman smiled. "I'm just Bishop Francis. I care for this place."

"Bishop?" Brinna said, eyeing the old woman. "I've heard tale of bishops. What faith are ye?"

"Faith?" Bishop Francis asked.

"Yes. What faith do you practice? What religion do you follow?"

The old woman chortled softly, her bosom jiggling beneath the shift. "I don't follow religion. I follow faith, wherever its winding path may lead. Following religion leads to a loss of faith. Follow faith and you may, in time, find religion in the face of God. That's something religions have lost over time."

Brinna nodded. That was something Mamal might say. "Where has faith led you?"

"Why here, of course," Bishop Francis said, amused. "Where has faith led you?"

"To anger." Brinna couldn't keep the emotion from her voice. She didn't even try. "Rejection."

The old woman patted her on the hand. "Where do you want to be, Brinna Wilde?"

"Want to be?" Brinna stared at the statue and then turned to stare out at the city. "At peace."

"Peace is an old soul's journey. Is that the only thing that stirs yours?"

Brinna shrugged and pulled her legs to her chest. "I've dreamed of a place."

"What place?" The old woman followed Brinna's gaze out the window.

"A place in the mountains. An apple orchard clinging to the sides of a riverbank," Brinna said, and the anger in her voice slipped away. "It calls to me, and I reckon it's only a dream, but it's a dream that don't end when I wake."

Bishop Francis pursed her wrinkled lips, her eyes crossing for a moment. "Do you know this mountain? Is it one of those?" She pointed out the window.

Brinna shook her head. "No. Don't think so. I'm not where I'm supposed to be just yet."

"What do you hope to find in this dream orchard?"

Brinna shrugged and sank her chin to rest on her knees. "I don't know. Maybe faith?"

The old woman smiled a crooked smile. "You're not the only lost soul, Brinna Wilde. All of humanity is lost, and the light of the world is fading away. Faith in a tomorrow, faith in a future, and the power that makes it possible won't be found in the Seven Realms." She lifted a spindly arm to the window and pointed to the horizon. "It's out there, in the Wilderness, where Gaia rages and hope glimmers in the darkness. Faith can lead you to it, faith in powers beyond the ones I found in this world of illusion we've created. We are but ants who believe we are giants."

Bishop Francis laced the ChristGaian Cross around Brinna's hands and patted them softly. "Don't be too quick to give up on faith, and it won't give up on you."

Brinna nodded and slipped the medallion back on. She stood and walked toward the statue of Jesus God and the painting of Gaia behind Him. She fought back the tears and held onto hope and faith and the cross around her neck. When she turned, the old woman was gone. Brinna left the building with a sense not of hope, perhaps, but of the hope for hope.

As she walked toward the gateway, she glimpsed in the distance a green ball of light dancing between the trees and puzzled over it for a moment before starting back down the street.

She slipped her eyeset on her brow. A Serpent line waited two blocks away, and it would take her south. Her dream whispered the western path of the Dragon trail wouldn't lead her where she wanted to go.

As she left the Museum of Religions behind, she heard a scream and looked north. In the distance, she could see movement, the movement of dozens of people running toward her. Behind them, screaming and leaping impossible heights were monsters giving chase.

Brinna ran for the station.

II

Rosary Delacroix was the only daughter of monsters. She hadn't always known her parents were monsters but learned over time

245

they were and eventually they would smile at her. Behind smiles she never saw would be teeth gleaming and white and ready to bite.

Her parents reclined on their life chairs in the front room where the drawn shades cast gloom and the air was stale. Ro (which was how she always thought of herself, never Rosary), sat on the floor in the corner and watched them while eating an apple growing soft. She had a linktag, but her right to income account was still seven years in the future, and she needed her parents for food. Sometimes they forgot, but occasionally, when they left the Link, they would eat and order enough food she could steal some away for later.

The cooler was down to five wrinkled apples, a block of cheese and some tortillas. In the pantry, there was still some pasta and a few cans of tuna fish, which wasn't her favorite thing in the world, but she would eat it if she was hungry enough. She wasn't, just yet.

Mom and Dad had at least left the Vale on occasion until a few months before. They never did so because they wanted to spend time with her, but only to eat, bathe, and go potty. But since the storks brought the life chairs, they seldom left the Vale.

The chairs had needles that poked Mom and Dad in the arms and gave them all the food they needed. She knew because she lifted their aprons to see. The chairs let them go poop and pee without ever having to stand up. Sometimes it was stinky in the great room, and Ro would retreat to her bedroom and wait to see if they would get out of their chairs. When they did, they seemed surprised, and she thought a little disappointed, she was still there.

She ate her apple, then ate the core and watched her parents in their chairs as they lived in a world where she wasn't welcome. She wiped her nose on a shirt stiff and scratchy. She remembered the family who came to the door, and as she had so often before, found herself sad she was here, and they were somehow out there.

She didn't know who they were, but she watched them from the window, watched them as they planted a garden and played in the courtyard, and she giggled at the joy they seemed to find in each other. How would that be, to be so happy and free like that? She had no idea.

Then the monsters came to the courtyard, and they took the mom and carried her away from this place. The mother had fought, screamed, and kicked, but the monsters laughed and stole her away.

Ro screamed and slapped at the window, ran to her parents, and shook their arms (that felt like gelatin wrapped in plastic), but they only moaned and stayed glued to their chairs, oblivious to her cries.

The monsters won.

When the man and his children came calling, she wanted to beg them to take her with them but knew it was wrong to ask such a thing, to ask to leave her family. But she told them her parents wanted to be monsters, too. It had been them the monsters came for, not their mom. She knew because she peeked into their world and saw the realm they built together.

When the monsters took the woman away, Ro sat in the corner of the great room, in the same spot where she now took her last bite of the apple, slipped into the Link, and went in search of her parents.

She had possessed a linktag for as long as she could remember and slipping between the Vale and the Sphere was as simple as climbing from one step to the next.

In the mind of Rosary Delacroix, the Vale was a vast and endless field of dandelions going to seed, and within each seed drifting in the wind was the mind of someone living in the Vale. She was but a speck of dust in the vast universe that could land upon any one of them and see what they could see. She had no idea any of the things she did on the Link were impossible for anyone else. It seemed so simple to her.

Finding the realm her parents created was an easy matter for her seven-year-old mind, and she latched upon it hungrily and slipped within the seed of their creation. When she did, she screamed and screamed and screamed.

Her parents were monsters. They imagined a world where blood, death, and pain were the only things that mattered. They created a realm where the Wrynd monsters controlled everything, and Ro watched, her eyes wide and boiling tears, as her parents in their realm ripped with teeth, claw, and fist everything the world ever hoped to be.

She understood that from within their realm her parents called out to the Sphere (where monsters did live), and asked to join them, to be real monsters. Within the Vale, something answered, something violent and cruel and oh so hungry. Her parents made their choice, and the monsters were coming for them.

When the man and his children knocked on the door, she wanted to explain what she saw but didn't know how. When she told them all that she could, and they left her with her parents lost in a world of monsters, she cried in her corner and tried to remember something good but found she couldn't.

Many days later, she sat in her same corner and crunched an apple seed between her teeth as she looked at the things her parents had become.

She retreated into the Vale and asked the Link to take her someplace happy. She found herself standing in a long line of people where everyone was smiling. She was holding the hands of two people who were not her parents, but she wished might be.

"Where are we?" Ro asked the Fillers to her left and right.

The man looked down at her, and she smiled up at him. He was her father in the Vale, and he was everything she ever dreamed a father could be. "We're at Disneyland Ro. Isn't that where you wanted to go?"

Ro nodded vigorously. "Yes! Yes, it is."

The woman to her right knelt on the ground, and she smiled so sweetly, with so much love Ro sobbed and hugged her with all her might. "This is your day, little Ro. We'll ride every ride and see every sight."

Ro held her digital mother and, for a moment, was happy.

In the room where her body lay, filthy and unfed, her Sphere parents, roused by their daughter's gleeful laughs and tender sobs, rose from their chairs, and stared down at their only child, lost in the Vale.

And their teeth were gleaming and white and ready to bite.

III

The Serpent arrived before Harley's security box, and he climbed aboard. The doors closed and the train flew down the tracks. Outside it was growing dark, and the soft breeze of the afternoon was turning to a howling wind.

"Picked the wrong week to visit the Hub," Harley muttered and walked toward the front of the train.

The Serpent looked deserted, and he managed a smile. The train would take him back to Spanish Fork, where he could gather the truck of the late, great Marshal Walker and return to the Wilderness. It was no less insane than the Hub, but it was at least insanity he recognized.

He stepped into the next car and stopped with a sigh. There was a Shift in an exoskeleton at the opposite end of the car. His eyes and the veins of his beefy arms were black. He roared when he spied Harley, stomped on the deck with a shoe encased in metal, and rushed forward, arms outstretched.

Harley looked out the window, and his security box dangled from the metal chord of a stork struggling to keep up with the Serpent. He started to run in the opposite direction when a pulse blast rang past his left ear and struck the raging Wrynd between the eyes. He fell to the ground, exoskeleton convulsing twice.

A dark young woman with a slayer was pointing past his head. When the Wrynd fell, she turned the weapon on him, and he managed a sheepish smile and waved.

"Obliged."

"Welcome," the young woman said, and for a moment Harley was sure she was the ghost of Kara Litmeyer. It seemed only appropriate that he should die at her hands, he killed her first, after all. But this woman was younger and seemed a far sight surer of herself than the legionnaire ever had.

His legs almost buckled as the Serpent braked, and the train chimed it was preparing to stop at Provo Town Station. Outside, the world was a chaos of fire, explosions, screaming, and flaring Wrynd.

"Don't stop!" Harley screamed and ran for the door. At the station were dozens of Wrynd attacking each other, and as the Serpent slowed, they paused and stared blankly. "Son of a . . ." The doors opened, and the Wrynd poured inside.

The young woman with the slayer stood her ground and fired away. Harley rushed to the open doorway at the opposite end of the car. He slipped onto the platform, and the stork with his security box hovered over his head. He cursed and scrambled to dig his eyeset out of his pocket. The four Wrynd fighting to get inside the Serpent took notice.

He slipped on the eyeset and begged the stork to release his security box. It lowered slower than he thought appropriate under the circumstances. He slid open the box, grabbed his slayer and baseball bat. The first Wrynd went down with a pulse blast through her chest. The second fell to a hard swing from the bat.

"That's more like it," Harley said and dashed back into the train. He nodded at the young woman who saved him. His slayer flashed as the train doors closed, and the Serpent went on its way, oblivious to the chaos inside.

Chapter Thirteen

Justice

I

Cirroco sat on the edge of the Salt Tower, a spiraling peak in the heart of the city, home to 5,000 Shifts oblivious to the death rushing toward them. Her legs dangled, swinging with childlike enthusiasm as she stared down on the streets with her magnifiers.

Hatcher sent a shield of his Wrynd by Serpent into the city, and even now Dagger Ash led a dozen armed with packs of ink and dart guns into the skyscraper. Soon there would be a horde of new Wrynd in the throes of ink flare killing everyone in sight.

It was a joy to behold.

An explosion ripped through a nearby building, and Wrynd danced in the streets. Hatcher's shield demonstrated amazing restraint in not using the ink to satisfy their lust for the drug, more restraint than Cirroco would have guessed they possessed. Being so close to the drug and not experiencing it must be maddening. She wondered how long they would hold out. Hatcher seemed determined to cause as much destruction as he could.

If Harley Nearwater was truly the Leap, the Wrynd might yet make him demonstrate his abilities. If he wasn't, he would run for the Wilderness, and the Scimitar would have his revenge. Then, perhaps, the Lord Judge might let her have her fun with Hatcher.

More people ran into the streets, screaming, and Cirroco giggled. It was insanity, and she delighted in the wonderfully twisted workings of her Lord Judge. If the Leap had truly arrived in the Federation, she understood why Lord Syiada didn't want to confront it openly until he could understand what its powers might be but allowing the Wrynd to attack the Hub was unexpected. As with all things of her Lord, he was forever a spider web of plots within plots, and every faint tremor of activity would provide a little hint of things to come.

"The Marshals are rallying in defense of the Hub, M'Lord," Cirroco spoke to the glowing spot in her consciousness where Lord Judge Syiada was always present. He was a ruthless ravaging force in her soul. "Should I stop them?"

"No." The voice in her head was dark and confident, and piercing, and Cirroco shuddered with pleasure. "Let Marshal Tempest protect her charges. It is her duty."

Thunder rumbled through the valley, and Cirroco turned her attention to the mountains. Storm clouds were boiling north and south, encircling the Hub. Lightning danced through the sky. She felt a thrill of desire and longing shudder through her body and gasped.

"A Rage is building. Is it possible the Rages respond to the desires of the Leap?"

"In time, we shall see," the Lord Judge's thoughts rumbled in her head.

Another explosion ripped through the city, and the clouds finally wept. Cirroco clapped her hands like a schoolgirl. "Your monsters are off their leash, M'Lord!"

"As all monsters must be," Lord Judge Syiada was smug and pleased. It made Cirroco swoon.

II

Jodi stood on the roof of the Justice Tower and stared out over the Hub as the first fat raindrops fell from the sky. Ten of her deputies were within minutes of the tower, and she had called twenty more from other areas of the Hub. She dared not call anymore.

Scimitar Hatcher made good on his promise, but his wasn't the only Wrynd horde within striking distance of the Hub. If others heard of the attack, they might decide to join, and she would have no one to respond. Fifty deputies to serve justice in a Hub of millions. It was insanity. She summoned a thousand sentinels from the Hub border and sent them into the city in search of Wrynd, praying a Rage wouldn't strike at the same time.

Her prayers were unanswered.

Lightning flashed, thunder screamed, and an explosion ripped through the heart of the city. A hundred points along the southeastern border chimed of beasts daring to test the eyes of the sentinels.

A Rage was upon them.

Jodi sent all but 500 of the sentinels back to their posts and scowled as a gust of wind all but pushed her over the side. In a little less than an hour, there were now more than 2,000 Federation citizens turned to ink and flaring in the city. The Wrynd were either killing or turning who they found, and those who ran fled toward the Wilderness.

"I should have let them have Harley," Jodi cursed, even as she knew it was something she could never do. The lunatic Wrynd Scimitar made his choice, and now it was up to her and her deputies to bring him to justice.

She turned to Bon and Montana, who were anxiously waiting for leave to strike. Jodi spun up her scye and linked with the rest of her deputies as they rushed toward her.

"We have Wrynd attacking in the two valleys. They have a large cache of ink, and they're flaring everyone they see. Elijah, lead the counterattack to the north, and I'll take the south. Push them toward the center. Focus on those with the ink. We can deal with the poor idiots flaring later, but if we don't take out those with the ink, we're going to lose this part of the Hub. God knows how much ink they have."

Jodi, Bon, and Montana leapt into the air and their wings swept them away. "Marshals!" Jodi roared, checking her slayer. "Justice!"

"Justice?" Ephraim replied with venom. "You can keep your righteousness, Marshal. This is vengeance. We'll have ours."

They flew toward the city and joined a dozen other deputies coming east and west. They dropped into formation and descended through the canyons of the tallest buildings, and the Wrynd came into view. There were hundreds of the newly infected, roaring, and mindlessly attacking. Jodi scanned the horizon and spotted three Wrynd with dart guns, carefully aiming at those who fled. She sent her scye to drop them where they stood.

The rest of her deputies opened fire with slayers or sent scyes into the mass of raging Wrynd. Jodi dropped from her wings onto the street in front of the crowd, and her scye swept the first wave aside. Bon and Montana dropped to the ground to join her in the battle.

"Are you crazy?" Bon screamed, but she was grinning wildly, and Jodi grinned back.

An ink-tainted dart flew within centimeters of Jodi's head, and she drew her sidearm and blasted the Wrynd who fired. The wave of freshly drugged and lost parted around them as those in the air continued to fire. Behind came another wave; this one strolled casually down the middle of the road.

Leading the way sauntered a tall and slim male Wrynd, dressed in a black uniform of a Marshal. Strapped around the lanky Wrynd's waist was a slayer, and when he spied Jodi, he smiled and spun up a yellow scye.

"Marshal!" he screamed. "Welcome to my nightmare!"

"Who the hell is he?" Jodi sputtered, squinting to get a closer look, and wishing for her magnifiers.

"Well, he sure as hell ain't one of us." Bon stepped into the middle of the road and drew both of her slayers.

The Wrynd dressed as a Marshal plucked a star from his chest, snapped it in two, and let it fall to the pavement. He drew his slayer and opened fire, and a dozen other armed Wrynd joined him. Pulse blasts exploded all around them. Bon returned fire, and Montana pushed her behind an overturned pod. Jodi scrambled to join them.

"They're firing back, Marshal!" Montana screamed, and his scream was full of laughter. "Are they supposed to be firing back? Because you never told me they'd be firing back!"

Jodi blasted two of the rushing Wrynd and sent her scye through a third. "They're firing back, Montana."

She sent her scye hurtling toward the tall Wrynd, and he parried with his own. Sparks danced over the street, and another wave of Wrynd joined the first, these armed with pulse rifles. They opened fire on the Marshals in their wings. Jodi watched as two spun out of control and crashed in the street, where they were set upon by the flaring.

The Wrynd were attacking the Hub with a huge quantity of ink, too large a quantity to go unnoticed, and Jodi remembered Hatcher's curse.

The Federation and the Wrynd were in league together, and he said the Federation had broken its bond; a bond she refused to believe existed. She knew the Federation tolerated the Wrynd. They served a purpose in the Wilderness. But if what Hatcher said was true, then the Lord Judge not only knew of the attack on her Hub, but he also condoned it. The truth was hiding in the shadows, and unless she found a way to stop the Wrynd, the search for the truth would die with her.

"It just keeps getting better." Jodi nodded to Bon and Montana, and they stood and walked into the middle of the street, slayers firing, scyes striking. "Let's light 'em up!" Jodi cried.

III

Thomas and Helen Delacroix returned from their MyRealm of nightmares for the first time in a week. They glanced at each other briefly, then away with disgust. What they were in their realm was so much more than what they were in the Sphere, but not for much longer. The time had come for their awakening.

The two stood with groans, their knees popping with the effort. They looked down at their soiled gowns, then across the room where their daughter sat lost in the Vale. They smiled. It was indeed time. Even now the Wrynd were purging the Hub, and they would be there to join them.

Over months they had searched the Link until they found the telltales that led them to the Wrynd lurking in the Vale. They made contact with a Shift Wrynd and expressed their desires to become one with them. They were tired of their MyRealm, where their imagination allowed them to feast on anyone they wished, but as real as it felt, tasted, and smelled, they couldn't escape the fact that it wasn't real.

They wanted to experience ink itself, to feel the reality of the flare as it altered their bodies, strengthened them, and made them better than they ever dared to be. They wanted to feel the blood of their prey coursing down their necks. They wanted that and so much more.

They thought the Wrynd were coming for them, to make them one of them, but stood forgotten. They were sorely disappointed at first and retreated to their MyRealm, where they bathed in the blood of Fillers and reveled in the screams of anguish. Then they learned the Wrynd had attacked the Hub and were, at this very moment turning thousands to the flare, and their hope flourished.

They lumbered into the bathroom to remove their soiled robes and shower and change into clothes more befitting a Wrynd. If their breath was labored as they dressed, they paid it no mind.

They had each lost more than forty-five kilos since purchasing the life chairs and taking their food intravenously, but they knew they were still grossly overweight and weak. They considered going to the medprint for fat removal but rejected the idea. It would be cheating to have their weight removed so easily. Their weight was a part of them, and when they evolved into a Wrynd, they would be free of everything that ever held them down.

When the ink coursed through their veins, when their eyes were black in the flare, they would be stronger than they ever were. They would have a medprint fashion them with claws and fangs, and once the fat holding them down burned away in the flare, they would tattoo their bodies with images of such ferocity their victims would cower before them and beg for a mercy that would never, ever come.

They saw it all before, played it over in their MyRealm times without measure, and they wanted to experience it in the Sphere. They would give anything they had to make it so. They smiled as they looked down at Rosary. They would give their daughter to make it so.

Rosary still lay in the Vale as they stood over her. They looked at her with love for what her sacrifice would bring. They gripped fleshy hands and turned to kiss. Their kiss turned to a bite, and they moaned as they drew each other's blood and reveled in the salty pain.

Helen knelt beside her daughter and shook her softly. Ro blinked twice and sat up, still smiling from her Vale visit. "Mom?" Her tiny eyes looked confused, and her brow furrowed. "Mom, you're up. Is everything all right?"

"Oh, darlin'," Helen said softly. "Everything is wonderful. Just wonderful." She licked the blood from her torn lip with a meaty tongue and plunged a needle into the side of her daughter's neck. Ro gasped and slipped away into darkness. "Just wonderful," she repeated.

Together, they picked up their daughter. Thomas flung her over his shoulder. They walked out of their home for the last time, and Thomas was already grunting from the burden. They would have liked to call a pod to take them into the Wilderness but knew it would be an affront to what they must be as Wrynd. They must walk to the Wilderness and present their prize to the Scimitar himself.

Ro was heavy, but not as heavy as she had been. They had been withholding food from the girl. They heard the Scimitar liked his meat lean.

IV

Between the two valleys where the Wrynd ravaged, what remained of a mountain divided the city. Time, wind, and the whims of man had eaten it away until the two valleys were virtually one, with the Wasatch Mountains to the east and the Oquirrh Mountains to the west. All remaining of Traverse Mountain Range was a tall cliff on the eastern edge that looked down on the city.

As the Rages brought water, thunder, and lightning; as the Wrynd roared, screamed, and slaughtered with teeth, claw, fist, and strength, something like a man watched both the Rages and the Wrynd.

He crouched on the edge of the cliff with his weathered cowboy boots hanging over the side. He chewed on the cuticle of his right thumb as he watched the destruction below with good humor and a tinge of fascination.

He wore a dark pair of jeans and a red T-shirt so faded it was pink, and a brown duster that brushed the ground as he sat on his haunches. The wind and the rain pelted him, but he paid it scant attention as it poured down his chiseled face, plastered his long, dark hair, (so dark it was almost black) to the sides of his head and neck.

He was handsome to the point those who might notice him would wonder if he were entirely real, but few seldom noticed him; he had a talent for being inconspicuous. He was a man seemingly without age, adrift in years, and it was impossible to say with any surety what age he truly might be. He could be twenty; he could be forty. When someone gazed into his eyes, grey and swimming with a multitude of other colors, they wondered if he were not far older than they first imagined, but few ever had the opportunity to gaze into his eyes.

Explosions broke the gloom of the early evening to the north, and to the south, the flash of pulse fire was like fireflies in the city. The man with grey eyes seldom bothered with the Hubs or the realms of man. He was much more comfortable in the Wilderness. But things were changing quickly, and it had piqued his curiosity. He had something of a sixth sense when it came to chaos. It would call him as it spoiled the plans of man and beast, and perhaps the gods themselves. He heard the cackle of chaos in the city below.

There was a man down there who drew his interest, a man who seemed blessed with chaos running through his veins, and he wondered if it was wise to let him live. If he did, the chaos running through him might alter careful plans ages in the making. If he didn't, what possibilities might the loss of such chaos bring to the plots of heaven and hell?

"Decisions, decisions," the man with grey eyes tittered.

He cast his eyes to the west and watched a Serpent slither through the storm with its passengers. His grey eyes squinted for a moment, and he scratched the stubble of his chin and then pointed his right index finger. The heavens erupted with lightning and struck the tracks in front of the Serpent.

"Let the Rages decide his fate," the stranger whispered. He

stepped off the cliff and fell into the abyss.

V

Brinna's slayer crackled with fire, and the newly turned Wrynd fell one on top of the other. Standing back-to-back with her was the stranger she saved, and his slayer erupted with hers. She had no idea who he was, and from the snarl on his face, she wasn't sure she wanted to know. There was no doubt he was skilled in the art of killing, and without him, she would have been food for the monsters.

The last Wrynd on the train collapsed only a few meters away, and Brinna had a moment to breathe. She turned to thank the man beside her, and they had but a moment to gaze into each other's eyes.

Brinna fought the urge to grip her ChristGaian cross as she looked into his eyes, where nothing of love or hope or friendship seemed to find any harbor. She stepped away, then fell forward as the world erupted in light, fire, twisted metal, and chaos.

The Serpent lurched drunkenly to its right, then to its left, and flew from the tracks. Brinna and the stranger careened down the length of the car. For an instant, their hands touched, and then the train buckled, wrenching them apart. She squealed and lashed out for a handhold but found nothing. The lights flickered out, and the storm raged around her. She heard only the sound of screaming metal as the train crumpled. Something cold and hard struck her in the temple, and the world of Brinna Wilde turned dark. Her slayer slipped from her hands.

When she woke, it was dark, and the Serpent was burning. She lay in a mound of dirt the train burrowed when it left the tracks. The side of the Serpent had burst open, and she thrown aside. She found herself bruised and battered, but otherwise unharmed. Her hand went absently to her chest to caress her medallion.

The storm had passed, and the Rage was over, but she could hear screams echoing in the night and knew the Wrynd were still flaring through the city. There was no sign of the stranger who helped her. She picked her way back to the train and wedged between two crumpled seats she found her pack. She combed through it until she found her eyeset. She searched the Link for information.

The Rage had gone as quickly as it struck, but the Wrynd were still within the Hub and growing in strength. The Marshals Service advised all citizens to stay inside until order returned, but from the screams in the distance, she knew order was far from restored.

She thought to call out to the stranger, but in the end, she didn't. She was afraid of what might hear her cry; afraid he might hear her cry. She slipped her pack onto her back, and as she stumbled out of the wreckage, her feet kicked something in the gloom. She bent down and fished for it with trembling fingers. It was her slayer, and she returned it to her holster with a sigh.

Fires burned in the distance, and she looked up into a nighttime sky where the clouds drifted away. On the horizon, the light of the Wheel winked, and she adjusted her pack. She stumbled into the darkness, following the tracks of the Serpent line.

The tracks led her to this place. She would let them lead her away.

CHAPTER FOURTEEN

OUT OF THE CARNAGE

I

Icarus carried Cirroco south, away from the carnage of the Hubs. In less than two days, the Wrynd killed hundreds and turned thousands with ink. Even after the Rage subsided and sentinels turned to the fight, the Marshals were vastly outnumbered and in retreat. Thirteen deputies were dead at the hand of the Wrynd and another eight injected with ink and raging. When the flare ran its course, they would have to decide between death or life as a Wrynd. Cirroco knew most would choose life.

As her wings streaked into the afternoon sky, she slipped into the Vale and stormed into High Judge Trevok's office. The judge was sitting at his desk, staring absently out the window at the expanse of Rio de Janeiro.

"Are you enjoying the view while people in one of your Hubs die?" Cirroco said, her tail whipping the desktop.

Trevok brushed her tail away. "The Marshals will prevail."

"They'll be dead by sunset," Cirroco said.

"I've requested the use of the Legion, and the Senate is considering my request," Trevok said. "What more would you have me do, Emissary? Journey to the Hub and beg the Wrynd for mercy?"

"Nothing would bring me greater joy than to have you stand before the Wrynd in the flare, High Judge," Cirroco replied. "But alas, it's not permitted. You requested the Senate consider allowing you to use your Legion to protect one of your Hubs? Requested? Try demanding, High Judge. By the time the Senate considers your request, there will be no one to save."

Trevok stood, his eyes bulging and spittle erupting from his thin lips. "Don't lecture me, Lizard! If protecting the people of the Rocky Mountain Hub is so imperative to you, ask the Lord Judge to intercede. He could have prevented this massacre at any time of his choosing, but he's done nothing!"

Cirroco's tail wrapped around the High Judge's neck like a python. "Mind your tongue, Trevok."

Trevok cast a baleful stare, and his body faded away, only to reappear across the room. He smiled smugly and folded his wispy arms. "Your threats of violence hold no weight in the Vale, Lizard."

Cirroco glided toward him. "I know where to find you outside the Vale."

"Harm me, and you'll answer to the Lord Judge."

Cirroco scoffed. "I serve the Lord Judge at all times. Even now."

"Yes." Trevok stammered. "But the Senate would hear of it as well if you were to harm a High Judge of the Federation."

Cirroco shrugged. "By the time the Senate decided upon a course of action, I will have died after a long and happy life."

Trevok stepped away and circled back to his desk. "All of this can be resolved in ten days if the Lord Judge would only deny the Wrynd their ink. They would all be dead, and the Hub secure."

"It's not our place to ask the Lord his reasoning. His ways are wise and mysterious," Cirroco said with a smile.

"What would the Lord Judge have me do?" Trevok asked. His eyes darted to Cirroco and away again. He was considering the fact she could easily reach him in the Sphere, she was sure. Oh, how she longed to do so. "I've asked for the Legion. The Battlewagon Sidon is within reach of the Hub, but they will only serve me on the authorization of the Senate."

"Oh, you've done all you can, I'm sure." Cirroco turned away from the High Judge and headed for the door. "Perhaps the crew of the Sidon will answer to a more forceful request." The Emissary faded out of the Vale.

In the Sphere, Icarus banked right, and she made out the sharp lines of the Federation Battlewagon Sidon on the horizon, sailing above the desert floor. She turned her attention to the Link connection she shared with Lord Judge Syiada.

"Would you have me take control of the Sidon, My Lord?"

His voice rang in her ears. "What have you learned from the attack of the Wrynd, my Emissary?"

"That the Wrynd are more controlled than I would have suspected, Lord Judge. They can be formidable."

"Indeed," the lord judge whispered, and his voice was a caress in her mind.

"But they've taken up arms against the Federation," Cirroco said. Her wings slowed as it approached the battlewagon. "The Senate will act in time. After they debate and pontificate, they will demand we eradicate them."

"And we will require the use of the Legion."

Cirroco smiled beatifically. "Yes, My Lord. I see why you allowed their attack."

"You would be surprised at how little you see, Storm." The words were a slap in her psyche, and she winced. "The Wrynd of the Wilderness fight well, but what of those in the Hub, those injected with ink? How did they fare in the battle?"

"Most died or are dying," Cirroco replied, still smarting from the Lord Judge's rebuke. "They're too weak, too fat, too unaccustomed to such hardships. They've grown soft in the Vale."

"Yes. They'll require hardening if they are to battle for our future, this great sleeping army."

"Battle, My Lord?"

Lord Judge Syiada chuckled. "Patience, Emissary. All in good time. The Rage has ended. The Leap must have left the Hub and returned to the Wilderness. Take control of the Sidon; use it to save the people of the Federation. We'll turn the inaction of the Senate against them and shame them into irrelevancy."

Cirroco delighted in the designs of her Lord Judge as she landed on the deck of the battlewagon.

II

Ro cried out, opened her eyes, and found herself surrounded by smiling monsters. She rolled onto her side, pushed to her knees, and saw her parents standing in front of her.

They were talking to the monsters and Ro couldn't make out exactly what they were saying. Their voices seemed far away, and she shook her head and tried to stand but found she couldn't.

All around her was dirt, grass, and trees far in the distance, and pine needles dug into the palms of her hands. She couldn't recall how she had gotten to this place. The last thing she remembered was being at Vale Disneyland with her Vale parents, and she had been happy and laughing because Goofy was coming to dance with her. Then the monsters pulled her away. Her parents were there, asking to be monsters, too.

"No, Mom. No, Dad." She pled. "Home. Let's go home. This place isn't for us."

One of the monsters her mother and father spoke with squatted on the ground and smiled at her. He was younger than her parents and thin. His smile was a happy smile, but behind the smile, his breath smelled like rotten meat, and his teeth were so yellow they were almost brown. Ro fought the urge to gag.

"Home? Did you say home, my little snackem?" the monster

Wrynd asked, and he laughed happily and patted another monster on the leg. This was a girl monster, and she knelt beside the first and pinched Ro on the leg. "Did you hear that, Solar? Our little snackem wants to go home."

The girl, who had a mean look on her face even when she tried to smile, pinched Ro even harder and she cried out. "No home for you, little one."

The boy monster pinched her chin between dirty fingers and turned her to look at him. Tears bubbled down her cheeks, and she started to sob. He pinched harder until she stopped. "No tears now. Your mommy and daddy brought you here to give you to our Scimitar, a little morsel before the feast. But we're not going to do that. No, my little snackems, we aren't going to do that at all, so dry your little tears."

Ro tried not to breathe as he whispered into her ear. "What we're going to do instead, my pudgy little puddin' cake, is we're going to turn your bulbous parents into Wrynd, just as they asked, just as they dreamed, and we're going to let them nibble on your chubby little fingers." The Wrynd touched her on the nose happily. "That's just what we're going to do. We're going to let them gobble you clean up my little snackems, and then, when they're all done, we're going to tear them apart, bit, by bit, by bit."

Ro's parents screamed as the Wrynd grabbed them from behind and forced them to their knees. Ro wailed and another Wrynd stuck a needle into their necks. She tried to climb to her feet. The girl Wrynd kicked her hard in the side, and she fell back down. She looked up at the faces of her parents as they began to change, as their eyes turned black, as black lines began to crisscross down their arms. She wailed as they smiled down at her with teeth shining and white and ready to bite.

A whistle pierced the afternoon, and Ro gasped as the Wrynd who stuck the needles into her parents suddenly clutched his chest and fell to the ground. There was a black, gaping hole in his shirt that smoked as he stared blindly at her. Her parents grinned even bigger and reached for her. She shrieked, but two more whistles rang out, and a hole appeared in the forehead of first her mother and then her father and they both fell to the ground to the left and the right. Their smiles were no longer so shining and white and ready to bite.

"Harley!" the Wrynd who was going to tear her parents' apart bit, by bit, by bit, screamed. He ran away into the trees. "We'll eat you alive, Harley Nearwater!" The Wrynd disappeared.

The sound of boots crunching brought Ro to her knees, and when she looked up, a tall man stared down with hard eyes and blood on his forehead. The man frightened her almost as much as the monsters frightened her. He stared at her, holstering the gun used to kill her parents. Fat tears coursed down her face, and he bent and roughly wiped them away with a calloused hand.

"Don't cry for them. They don't deserve the water."

Ro nodded but cried anyway.

"Stand up," the tall man said. She stood slowly and tried to brush away the dirt on her clothes. At the top of a small hill, she could see the cab of an impossibly tall truck.

The hard man gripped her arms. "Listen to me. You need to run away. Run as fast as you can and try to find someone who can help you. Stay hidden until you know for sure they ain't monsters like these monsters or the monsters like your momma and poppa were monsters. You find yourself someone who can take care of you. But you got to run now because they'll be comin' back. More of them will be comin' back." The hard man pointed toward the tree line.

"Now get! Run as fast as you can."

Ro sobbed, nodded, and limped away from the hard man.

The Wilderness swallowed her up.

III

In two sunrises Jodi had lost count of how many she had killed.

She sat in a narrow alley of a street stained in blood in a forgotten city of a Hub living in horror. She tried not to think. She pulled her knees to her chest, let her slayer rest against her forehead, and closed her eyes, hoping sleep might take her for a moment and knowing it wouldn't.

Cries of pain and anguish still echoed in the city, but for a moment there was a relative quiet she cherished. Her Marshals gave each other respite as the occasion allowed. She had lost so many.

When the Rage finally subsided, and the wind and rain flitted away, when the beasts of the Wilderness stopped pressing against the border, they did so all at once, as if under command. After the Rage, she was able to summon more sentinels to help in the battle, and they turned the tide, at least as much as it was going to turn for another week. She instructed her Marshals to focus only on the Wrynd from the Wilderness, those armed and injecting others. Those poor souls injected and flaring were doomed. Lost in madness, within days they would succumb to ink withdrawal and die. The Wrynd who answered to Scimitar Hatcher were the ones to stop. If they continued to infect her people, the battle would never end.

The fury of the invasion lessened when Jodi locked down every building in the Hub. The Wrynd still found a way in, but they couldn't just stroll through the door anymore. She thought there might be a way to save the Hub from more destruction, to wipe out the Wrynd from the Wilderness and end the chaos. Her Marshals had stalked the armed Wrynd relentlessly through the night, and they had joined with Elijah's group from the north in a combined force to push them back. But now it seemed the Rocky Mountain Marshals would die at the teeth, claw, and fist of the Wrynd.

Elijah pushed the attacking Wrynd to the south. Jodi pushed

the attacking Wrynd to the north, and they thought they had them contained within a four-block section of skyscrapers, trapped in the streets with no escape. The Marshals took to the ground and rushed to end the battle. That was when the Wrynd sprang a trap all their own.

They had placed Wrynd with pulse rifles and cannons along the rooftops of the buildings. When the Marshals rushed in, they opened fire and dozens died. Jodi ordered a retreat, and when their wings swooped in, pulse cannons blew them from the sky. Jodi's wings survived the attack and now circled the battle area safely out of range.

The Wrynd outnumbered and out gunned the Marshals in their Hub.

A Wrynd who had in a previous life been a Marshal had beaten her. In the past twenty-four hours, Bon obsessed over the Wrynd with the scye, and all she learned of him was his name. Before he was a Wrynd, he was Telow Ash. She gained that knowledge after the capture of one of his Wrynd, who was proud to boast before she died of the Wrynd dagger who would defeat the Marshals of the Federation.

The dying Wrynd had been right. They would lose. There were only nine of them left, and Jodi could see no way to save any of them without help that wouldn't arrive in time. Every time they dared to step out of the alleyway, the Wrynd opened fire. Even their scyes were ineffective. They could only take so many pulse hits before the scyes exploded or the minds of those wielding them cracked. All it would take was one dart to the neck of one of the huddled, and the flare would claim them all.

"In a week they'll all be dead of ink withdrawal. We just hold out," Elijah said, and Jodi shook her head.

"They won't use all their ink. They'll make sure and keep enough to flare again. What happens when they do? If they flare, they'll storm us here."

"Might give us the advantage," Montana said, wiping blood from his right arm. It wasn't his blood; Jodi was relieved to see.

"Don't bet on it," Bon said, peeking from behind a barricade of pods they overturned in the street. "Where the hell did they get so much ink in the first place?"

"That's the question," Jodi said, but she was afraid she already knew the answer. Hatcher hadn't lied, and Harley was right. The Federation was supplying the Wrynd with ink.

"Hello, Marshal Tempest!" A voice cried out from beyond the alleyway. "Yoo-hoo! Don't be afraid, Marshal, I'm just here to accept your surrender."

"There won't be any surrender from us, Wrynd," Jodi screamed back, climbing to her feet.

"A pity," the Wrynd called. He didn't sound particularly disappointed with the news. "You should know the coward you protected, the coward who caused this, has returned to the Wilderness. Our Scimitar will feast on him."

"Then you're free to go!" Montana said.

"Oh, we'll go," the Wrynd said with a laugh. "But my master has allowed me the privilege of doing whatever I like to the Hub, and I choose to kill every one of the Marshals of the Federation before I take my leave. For two days now you've fought my skean without our experiencing the ecstasy of the flare. We've been less than what we are, but we've still defeated you. Now, we'll show you the true power of the flare."

"Floating Wheel! I can't take any more of this man's blabber." Bon crouched beside Jodi, her face filthy, her eyes glaring. "Let me kill him, Marshal."

"Stay down. They'll take your head off," Jodi said.

In the distance, someone roared. It was a roar of pain and joy, lust, and hunger that raked their nerves.

"They're flaring," Ephraim muttered.

"Sorry, Marshal. If I'm dying, so is this idiot." Bon jumped to her feet, holstering her slayers, and clipping her scye to her belt. "Telow Ash!" she cried. "Before you go all batshit crazy on me, why don't we settle this between Marshals, you and I?"

"It's Dagger Ash," was the cool reply.

More screams erupted through the city as the Wrynd rushed to feast. They were almost out of time. They joined Bon in the middle of the street.

Dagger Ash smiled and nodded toward the others. "If we are to settle this, then the others stay clear."

Bon nodded grimly. "Without a doubt."

"Bon. Stand down," Jodi said.

"Not today, Marshal," Bon said. She was smiling, and Jodi thought this was exactly how her friend would want to die. "Nothing to stand down from. I choose to take him before the rest of them take us. You can fire my corpse."

Dagger Ash holstered his slayer and grinned at Bon, his perfect teeth flashing in the afternoon gloom.

Bon held out her hands and returned the smile. "Shall we dance?"

More screams erupted through the city, and Wrynd rushed toward them. Ash turned to a tall and twisted woman standing beside him and hissed. "Keep them away. They can feast on what's left."

Bon and Dagger Ash stared at each other from across a distance measured in heartbeats.

A section of a skyscraper behind Dagger Ash shuddered as an explosion tossed rubble toward the street. Wrynd and Marshals alike dashed for cover. Through a cloud of dust, Jodi saw a battle-wagon approaching from the south, its big pulse cannons blaring as it ripped apart the skyscrapers where the Wrynd snipers lay in wait. She felt something like a roar of triumph and anguish building inside her.

Dagger Ash nodded to Bon. "Save me a dance for later."

The Wrynd scattered into a destroyed city. Bon opened fire,

shooting blindly at an enemy no longer there.

IV

Cirroco stood on the bridge of the Federation Battlewagon Sidon and watched with satisfaction and a tinge of regret as the pulse cannons of the massive airship locked on and struck down every Wrynd in sight. Behind her, the airship's captain stood with his arms crossed; he looked both angered and enraptured at the hell his ship rained down.

Cirroco twirled on the balls of her feet and went to stand by the captain, slapping him happily on the side of his chiseled bicep. "Take heart, my good Captain Moroni, your ship is performing admirably. You should be pleased."

The captain, a long, stoic man with a constipated disposition who spoke with only his lower lip in short, concise, and mostly meaningless sentences, didn't respond to her tap. He stood rigid and unmoving in every way except his eyes, which darted back and forth and avoided resting directly on the Lord Judge's Emissary at all cost, which delighted her. She thought he considered her an abomination. Oh, if he only knew.

"There is no pleasure to be gained in treason, Emissary Storm."

"Treason?" Cirroco laughed. "I see no treasonous acts this day, Captain Moroni, only the mighty Federation Navy storming the battlefield to save the lives of our people. The Battlewagon Sidon and her crew are heroes."

"We have engaged in battle without authorization of the Senate. There are innocents in those buildings, Emissary."

"Not anymore, Captain. You've engaged in battle at the order of your supreme commander, our Lord Judge Syiada."

"Who has issued orders through his mouthpiece without the authority of the people's Senate." His words spit out with such venom he resembled in some ways a fish, and Cirroco fought a giggle.

She sidled up to him, and his eyes swirled. She let her tail lightly caress his left ankle and felt him flinch.

"If our Lord Judge acts without the authority of our esteemed Senate, he does so to save his people. It's of no concern to any as lowly as you and I, Captain Moroni. Our duty is to carry out our Lord Judge's orders, and his orders are to destroy the Wrynd and save the Hub, is that not so?"

Captain Moroni nodded curtly, and Cirroco slapped him on the behind. "I'm so glad we've had this chance to discuss the burdens of duty, Captain. Now, please show me the prowess of the mighty Legion. There are Marshals down there about to be torn apart by savages."

Captain Moroni nodded to a lieutenant at his side, and Cirroco went to gaze out at the decks of the massive airship.

A section of the airship's upper deck rattled aside and from the bowels of the ship raised a column of Federation legionnaires, spectacular in their grey, red, and white armor, with helmets like some childish nightmare of insects.

Another deck slid aside, and from within the ship, an equal number of white wings emerged. The wings took flight, and the legionnaire's dashed across the ship's deck. Their wings swooped, gathered them, and the air swarmed with the righteous indignation of the Federation's army. The Legion had trained for years for a battle never to come, until this day. Cirroco was happy for them. Today, they would learn the ecstasy of death.

Pulse blasts flashed across the cityscape as the Wrynd fired at the striking Legion. Wings burned, plummeting to the ground while others returned fire, laying waste to what the Sidon's guns missed. The Wrynd had no chance against the Legion, no matter how untested they were. It was a pity. The Wrynd's ferocity was a thing of beauty.

The battlewagon engaged later than she planned, delayed by the fury of the Rage. But the Rage ended, which told her the Leap, whoever he or she may be, was no longer here. Once again, the Lord Judge had demonstrated his omnipotence. The Leap had arrived in the Seven Realms. The key to their immortality, their key to the universe, was within reach. She turned to the sour Captain Moroni.

"I take my leave of you now, Captain, as I'm sure will come as a relief."

Captain Moroni nodded. "It does, Emissary."

"The Legion is to kill every Wrynd within the Hub. Restore order for the Marshals. Gather whatever stores of ink you find and hold it for me. When the battle is over, dock the Sidon in the Cradle and await further instructions."

"As the Lord Judge commands, Emissary."

Cirroco stepped out of the bridge, closing the door roughly with her tail. "Oh, that is what he commands, Captain."

The deck of the Sidon was empty as Cirroco strolled across it. Icarus fell between parted clouds, and she raised her arms and let her wings gather her in its embrace and carry her away.

She floated above the city and watched the Legion sweep down upon the Wrynd. Those from the Wilderness would no doubt be rushing for the border. The newly infected Shifts still raged hopelessly and would die in the same manner. They would no doubt kill more than their fair share of Legion in the process.

Cirroco watched rays of sunlight peek through dark clouds as the storm blew away.

V

Cirroco smiled down at her, and Jodi scowled as the Emissary detached from her wings and dropped to the pavement.

Smoke billowed from the upper floors of a skyscraper, and dozens of pods were either burning or smoldering in the streets.

Bodies of Wrynd, most of them the recently turned, lay scattered among the rubble of concrete and glass. Legionnaires still streaked through the sky hunting down the remaining Wrynd, and Jodi and her Marshals left them to their task. They were too exhausted to do anything else.

The eight remaining who answered her call for assistance formed a rough circle around her as the Emissary walked toward them, smiling happily, full of seduction, menace, and twisted delight. Jodi clipped her scye to her belt and straightened her tired shoulders, pulling her hair away from her face. It smelled of smoke.

"Marshal Tempest," Cirroco said. "Love what you've done with the place."

Jodi ignored her taunt and bowed formally. "Emissary. We're in your debt. We thank Captain Moroni and the Legion for the assistance, but the Marshals Service will restore order to the Hub."

"Of course, you will, but let the Legion finish mopping up the Wrynd. You've done quite enough for now. And your losses; what of your losses, Marshal Tempest?"

Jodi bit the inside of her cheek and forced her voice to remain steady. "Twenty-two, Emissary. We lost twenty-two Marshals in this attack. The Wrynd will face justice. Every one of them."

"Of course, they will. I'll see to it myself as Emissary of the Lord Judge. Let Captain Moroni's legionnaires finish clearing the Hub, restore order, then we'll find these Wrynd in the Wilderness."

"We'll find them now. They'll pay for this now, not later," Ephraim said. "If you don't dare breach the Wilderness, then Elijah and I and anyone with backbone enough to join us will take the fight to them. We'll hunt down and kill Hatcher now, as we should have when he made his threat." He pointed a finger in Jodi's face and snarled. "If we had done so then, none of this would have happened. This blood is on your hands, Marshall Tempest."

Of course, he was right. She should have killed Hatcher and his Wrynd the first time they encountered them. She made a mistake and thousands died because of it.

Ephraim was right, but that didn't mean he was justified. She lashed out so fast the big man couldn't react. She broke the finger pointing at her face with one savage twist of her wrist, and her left hand struck him in the side of the neck. He went down gasping for air. Elijah made a move toward her, and Bon cleared her throat and tapped the butt of her slayer. Behind her, Montana folded his arms and grinned savagely. Elijah stepped back, hands in the air.

"You may be right, Marshal Apgar. I appreciate your candor, but Emissary Storm is correct. We restore order to the Hub first, and then we seek justice for those we've lost." She cast a glance at her remaining Marshals, her face calm, and her eyes steely. "If you feel otherwise, toss your badge on the ground now and be on your way. I have no patience for insurrection."

The Marshals shuffled, but no badge touched the ground. Ephraim climbed to his feet, rubbing the side of his neck.

"Well, this is fun!" Cirroco stepped between Jodi and Ephraim, wrapping her arm around Jodi's shoulders. "Isn't this fun?" She clapped the big Marshal on the shoulder. "Rest assured, Marshal, we'll find the Wrynd who killed your people, who destroyed your city and, when we do, I'll summon you all to take part in their death. We'll sharpen our claws and show the Wrynd what true justice looks like."

"That's not justice. That's revenge," Jodi said softly.

"And it's so very sweet," Cirroco replied. "Marshal Tempest, if you have a moment, I will have a conversation with you in private."

Ephraim and Elijah watched them walk away, and Bon and Montana stepped between, blocking their view.

"I would love to dance. Shall we?" Montana said, and the Apgar brothers walked away.

Cirroco and Jodi walked side by side, Cirroco with her arms clasped behind her, Jodi with her hand on the butt of her slayer and the other on the clip of her scye. She calmed her breathing and cast a sidelong glance at the Emissary.

"It's been a long couple of days, has it not, Marshal?" Cirroco began.

"It has."

"Tell me; in your battle, did you observe anything of the Castaway, this Harley Nearwater?"

"Nothing, Emissary Storm."

Cirroco shrugged. "Odd. Do you still believe he has nothing to do with the Leap?"

"I do."

"Yet a Rage erupted over your Hub at the most opportune of moments, did it not? While the Wrynd flared, a Rage of weather and wildthings beat at your doors while he hid within the city."

"It is an oddity," Jodi admitted. "But I've fought alongside Harley Nearwater. He's a nomad, an opportunist, a scoundrel, but he's not an evolutionary leap. He can't control his inclination to kill, let alone the Rages."

"It sounds, Jodi Tempest, like you fancy him."

"Fancy him?" Jodi smiled. "I don't think anyone fancies Harley. He's an anomaly, but not necessarily one without his uses."

"And what uses might those be?"

"If you want someone killed, he'll find a way to get it done. For a price."

"And what price did you pay to have him find and kill the Leap?"

Jodi stopped in her tracks, almost stumbled, and found a way to recover gracefully. "What makes you think I would do such a thing?"

"Because you believe in the glory of the Federation, Marshal Tempest. You believe the Federation is the shining light on the cliffs of anarchy, the beacon of the Age of Renewal. You don't yet realize Lord Judge Syiada is the Federation, that he is the Seven Realms. You believe the Leap is contrary to everything we've built and our attempt to harness its power will lead to an injustice against humanity."

"And you surmise this?"

Cirroco turned, and her tail whipped around her, pulled her close, and locked her hands to her side. "I surmise this, my lovely Marshal Tempest, by looking in your eyes. Your soul is too honest to allow your eyes to lie. It's a character flaw you should excise, should you live so long."

Jodi nodded. "Perhaps."

Cirroco released her grip, and they walked along the ravaged streets. "The Rage has come and gone, and, with it, I suspect, so has your castaway. No matter. We'll find him. If he is the Leap, we have learned something of his power. If he's not, he's perhaps the luckiest man in the Seven Realms."

The Emissary's wings descended and wrapped her in its embrace. She rose to the heavens like an angel.

Or a demon.

CHAPTER FIFTEEN

THERE IS NO MAGIC

I

Ro stumbled through the brush, the branches slapping against her soft skin and drawing blood. She tried not to cry out, but her eyes poured tears, blurring her vision, and she fought to find her way. Her feet hurt. Her slippers were tight, and she was unaccustomed to walking so far. She didn't know how long it had been since the hard man sent her away, the hard man who killed the Wrynd and her parents. He saved her from the monsters and her parents, but he was a hard man. A bad man. He sent her away, and now the wildthings would gobble her up.

She tripped over a tree root and fell hard, biting her tongue and drawing blood. This time she did cry out. She sat in the dirt, spat blood, sobbed, and wished someone would save her, but knew she was alone and no one in the great big world would ever come to save a girl like her. She was only a Filler. She understood that.

She slipped into the Vale and went back to Disneyland. Her Filler parents were there smiling adoringly, and she ran and hugged them, and they hugged her back, and it meant nothing because she could taste the blood in her mouth. She returned to the Sphere and, through eyes still streaked with tears, saw something staring at her, something small and furry, with tiny black eyes, peering over her slippers. It was a mouse, and it wiggled its whiskers and scurried away. Ro was so surprised she hiccupped.

She climbed to her feet and walked in the direction the mouse ran and came upon a trail weaving through the trees. She followed it, and the walking was easier, but her feet still hurt, and her tongue still bled. The sun was slipping behind the mountains, and it was getting colder. Ro hugged herself and almost fell again. When she looked back the way she came, something else was looking at her, and she squeaked in terror and ran. There was a wolf behind her, padding along the same trail. Its eyes stared at her, through her, and a pink tongue lolled from its mouth. Ro knew she was going to die.

The trail climbed a small hill, and Ro stumbled up it with the wolf close behind. The trail ended at a meadow, and there the little girl stopped, so amazed she could no longer even be afraid of the wolf at her heels.

There were dozens of horses grazing in the meadow, and when she topped the hill, they raised their heads. Ro started to back up, and the wolf growled behind her. She dropped to her knees, cried, and slipped back into the Vale. She was going to die, and she didn't want to be there when it happened. She wanted to be at Disneyland, where magic did exist.

Something warm and wet caressed her brow in the Sphere, and she returned from the Vale and opened her eyes. A painted horse stared down at her, and its great long nose sniffed her hair as its breath washed over her. The horse was huge, and its mustiness was unlike anything Ro ever smelled. She looked back, and the wolf was still there. The painted horse stared at the wolf, then raised its great neck, nodded, and pawed the ground with one of its hoofs. It whinnied, and the wolf turned and ran away into the shadows.

The other horses gathered around her. The painted horse rolled onto the ground and looked at her expectantly.

She went to lie on the side of the horse. She felt it breathing. When the horse started to rise, she threw her arms around its neck. She adjusted herself on its back, and the horses turned and started across the meadow. Ro hugged the horse, and it snorted. She had never touched an animal in her entire life, and she caressed its side with her hand and found a reason to smile.

The tears dried from her face as the horse took her deeper into the Wilderness.

II

When the little girl almost eaten by her parents slipped out of sight, Harley returned to his truck. She would likely die to a wildthing, but everyone died, and sometimes sooner was better than later. He drove toward the Wilderness.

He learned a great deal on his trip to the Hub, and some of it concerned him more than others. The mask of benevolence the Federation wore was just a mask, and that was no great surprise. He would have been more surprised to discover it was genuine. That they were using the Wrynd as a weapon against those living in the Wilderness was a concern, because Marshal Tempest's assurance the Seven Realms had no interest in the Navajo Nation was complete fiction. The Federation had an interest in control of everything, even poor Native Americans scratching out a meager existence in a wasteland. Vegas taught him that much. The one person in the world Harley Nearwater cared for lived on the Navajo Nation. Eventually the Wrynd horde would turn that way, and he would have to do something about it.

The Wrynd attacked the Hub, and even those under the influence of ink wouldn't do such a thing if they thought it would impact the flow of their drug. So, it only meant those who allowed them their ink approved of the attack. That fact wasn't particularly surprising. The Federation was more concerned about the Rages than they portrayed, and that was a surprise. They had at least considered the possibility Earth was not only in turmoil but aware and more than a little pissed off, and that showed a level of wisdom Harley hadn't expected.

The biggest surprise was to know someone in the Federation was aware of the Greywalker, whoever or whatever he might be. They were aware, and they were more than a little nervous. With almost no argument the Marshal handed over a weapon of their magnificent Marshals Service to a man of admittedly questionable character. The act spoke volumes, but he wasn't sure he understood the language. One thing he did understand was chaos was far closer than he imagined. The marvelous world of the Seven Realms was a shining hollow and meaningless bauble that would be of no help to anyone when the real storm arrived.

"The end is coming," Harley whispered the dying words of a murdered legionnaire.

He stopped the truck where the slide buried the road. Someone had taken Victor's body away but left the bodies of the Wrynd and the animals along the roadway. There was no sign of Quinlan's wife, but then he spotted a rough mound of rocks stacked together on the side of the road. The young man had taken the time to bury her. Crazy bastard.

Scavengers had been at work on the bodies of the Wrynd, and he had no desire to get out of the truck. He rested his chin on the steering wheel, looked up at the slide, and wished he asked for wings as well. Jodi wouldn't have given them to him. Giving him a scye was one thing; giving him freedom of air travel in the Wilderness was something she would never do; if she even had the authority to bestow such a gift.

He didn't look forward to hiking back over the slide. If Quinlan made it, he would have taken his truck. He would have a sixty-five-klick hike through the Wilderness to Price. A hike that would take him past the camp of the Wrynd Scimitar who attacked a Hub to find him. That was just bad luck.

The slide was a jagged, rocky climb, and he didn't see any way he could navigate it. Then again, Marshal Walker's truck was a lot more truck than the antique he left on the other side. Since the Marshal wouldn't be using it anymore, what exactly did he have to lose?

He keyed Victor's music playlist and wasn't surprised to hear it consisted of a lot of angry screaming. It seemed oddly appropriate, so he turned it up as he stomped on the accelerator. The truck rushed up the first rocky slope. After a while, Harley's screams drowned out the screaming music.

Three times he almost rolled, but he was amazed at the truck's handling as it crept and crawled over rocks and chasms. Once it became wedged between two massive boulders and the tires smoked as he reversed. He went to work on the sharp edge of one of the boulders with his slayer and chipped away enough rock to pass.

The biggest scare came when he had to cross a jagged trench cut down the slide by rushing water. It was meters across, and there was no going around it or through it. Harley backed up, got a good run, and tried going over it. The truck's frame screamed as it hit the other side and he bounced violently in the cab. He hit the brakes and skidded to a stop. He was grinning wildly and other than an almost uncontrollable need to urinate; he made it through better than he had imagined. After an hour and a half, he bumped down the last little knob, and the tires touched the pavement. He walked the slide in less time.

The old truck he left behind the gutted store was gone. He'd seen no sign of Wrynd. Reflex and Solar slipped past his slayer and by now would have reached the Scimitar. He held little hope Hatcher sent everyone into the Hub to find him. But they would also be looking for Quinlan. If he was lucky, he might find a way to slip past.

He stopped for dinner, not bothering to order anything from

a stork. He ate what food he brought with him and sipped a beer from the cooler in the small refrigerator between the front seats. Nightfall was fast approaching, and he decided to stay put until morning and see what opportunities might arise in the daylight

He slept fitfully and awoke refreshed enough to face what might be a long day. He ate the last of his food and drank some water, then slipped on his eyeset and sent the scye to find the Wrynd at their camp. If they were there, he could kill them sitting behind the wheel.

The camp stood deserted.

Harley let the scye skim through the garbage-filled parking lot. Where there was a great bonfire, there was now only ash and bone. The elk heads dangling from the rest area sign drew nothing by flies. He sent the scye through a broken window into the welcome center. Piles of garbage and walls painted with blood were all there was inside. A gaping hole in the floor led to a cellar of empty boxes. Harley allowed himself a moment of hope that all the Wrynd attacked the Hub, leaving only Reflex and Solar ahead of him.

Harley recalled the scye, flung his eyeset on the passenger's seat, and headed out. He didn't know where they went but couldn't afford to pass on a lucky break.

The rest of the way down the canyon was without incident. When he arrived in the valley, he left the highway and stopped in the parking lot of what once was Castleview Hospital. The hospital was decades abandoned and showed it with windows shuttered or shattered.

There were no cars in the parking lot, but several trees pushed through the asphalt. It was of little interest to Harley; he just needed a place to sit while he made a scouting trip. He rolled down the window and sent out the scye. It didn't take long for him to find the Wrynd. They were scouring the city, flaring anyone they found, creating a wall of the mad, trapping him in a thin strip of Wilderness.

As he let the scye climb higher into the morning sun, he could see they blocked the highway on both ends. They had cut him off from escape, unless he dared to make a run past them.

On the south end of the Price, in the Walmart parking lot, the flood waters had receded. There were several automobiles parked, and one of them looked familiar. It was his pickup. There was a group of twenty Wrynd racing toward the storefront.

"Stupid Neands," he muttered. They were trying to keep the Old World alive, even the shopping center. As Harley watched through his scye, Quinlan and his children walked out of Walmart and headed for the truck. They were never going to make it. When they stepped out of the building, the Wrynd rushed toward them. Quinlan scooped up the little girl in his arms and ran. The boy ran after.

They couldn't make it to the truck, so Quinlan rushed up Main Street. Harley gave them half a block before the Wrynd tore them apart.

Harley tore his attention away from what he saw through the scye and stared out the window of a dead man's truck at a city where lunatics raged. The world was tearing itself apart, a world where he didn't belong. His brow furrowed and his jaw quaked as a storm swept over his face, a storm of anger and denials and, finally, resignation.

"Damn!" He pounded on the steering wheel, hit the roof, and tore the eyeset from his face. "Damn, damn, damn!" The fury bled away as quickly as it came, and he sat back, closed his eyes, and regained control of his breathing. Then he opened his eyes. He slipped the eyeset back onto his brow, linked with his scye, and made a choice he knew would not be in his best interest.

He sent the scye diving at the Wrynd, and the orb pierced the chest of the nearest just before he got a hold of Noah. He cut down three more in a similar fashion. As he was about to take out a few more something slapped the window of the pickup and diverted his attention from the scye.

Four Wrynd were outside, pounding on the windows, the hood, and the doors. They looked more agitated than he'd ever seen. Hatcher had been generous with the Wrynd he didn't send into the Hub. Harley was far too much of an amateur with the scye to fight Wrynd on one end of town while fighting them outside his truck. He sent the scye to hover above the city and threw the eyeset aside. The truck shot out of the parking lot. Quinlan was on his own.

Harley almost lost control of the pickup as he fled through the city. He was approaching 100 klicks per hour as he flew down the city street toward Walmart. He knew even as he willed the truck to go faster, he wouldn't reach Quinlan in time.

As he careened into the Walmart parking lot, he slammed on the brakes. There was no sign of Quinlan or the Wrynd. A pulse weapon fired behind him, and the truck's tires smoked as he headed down Main Street. At the next intersection, he caught a glimpse of Quinlan running down the center of the road with Raizor in his arms and Noah leading the way. Quinlan was firing blindly behind him, but the Wrynd weren't trying to catch them anymore. They were herding them.

He pointed the truck down the road. The Wrynd looked back as he approached and scattered. He was only able to hit one of them. It was a middle-aged, overweight woman who would have looked like a grandmother except for the crazed look in her eyes and the blood pouring from her mouth. He thought she might be eating her tongue. When Harley hit her, she landed on the hood, slid up the window and lay still.

The other Wrynd turned on him, and he opened fire with his slayer. The thought struck him that he could have stayed at the intersection and sent the scye after them, but it was too late for that, and there was no way he could take the time to don his eyeset. He would be dead before he could reach the Link.

Quinlan turned left on a side road and discovered more Wrynd.

He gave up on his pulse rifle and drew the sword, which Harley thought was overall an excellent move for the young man. At least with the sword in his hands, he could be of some help. With the pulse rifle, all he was doing was making noise.

Harley stepped out of the truck, still firing as Wrynd advanced. Out of the corner of his eye, he saw double, triple the number he now faced rushing from behind. He was good but he wasn't that good. There was no way out for all of them and quite possibly no way out for any of them.

Quinlan wielded the sword with more skill than Harley would have imagined, and he remembered the fighting prowess of Vania, how easily she took down Victor. *Who are these people?*

Coming from the east was another vehicle, a battered four-door sedan, and it pulled to a stop thirty meters from Harley's truck. A little old man and woman stepped out of the car and motioned for Quinlan and the children to hurry their way. The couple looked ancient; sticks and bones encased in leathery skin. Harley had seen them before, riding in their antique automobile, smiling their crazy smiles. He knew these people. They lived in an apple orchard, and they were mad. Completely mad. Anyone who smiled as much as they smiled had to be insane.

The old woman had long grey hair pulled behind her and tied in a knot, and she begged the children to hurry. She was smiling the sweetest smile Harley ever saw, and he wanted to go to her as well, because he was sure if he could reach her everything would be okay, everything so wrong in his life would suddenly vanish.

Her smile tugged at a memory, and he wanted to relive it. Then a Wrynd slammed into him and almost threw the slayer from his hand. He pushed the memory away and concentrated on his slayer and his hand and cutting down as many of them as he could.

There were more Wrynd between Harley and Quinlan than there had been, and Quinlan pushed his children toward the old couple as he hacked at another attacker. Noah dragged the pulse rifle behind him and grabbed his little sister by the hand. They ran toward the car.

The Wrynd came in waves now, and as Harley fired with one hand and hit with the other, he knew even with the old couple's arrival, there was no chance. If he used every skill he possessed, fired with more precision than he ever had, he might be able to slip out of the noose. For them, there just wasn't a chance.

He caught motion from the old man, a slight flick of the wrist, a twist of the head, a look in the eye, and for a moment Harley couldn't even pull the trigger. He stood mesmerized.

There was a tree on the side of the road, a great cottonwood with branches old and twisted and thick as a man's body. As monsters rushed toward Harley and Quinlan, the tree swept out with its branches, and a dozen Wrynd sailed through the air. Harley narrowed his brow, and the old man smiled and extended his right arm, palm up. The Wrynd flew through the air, flicked away by the invisible hand of a giant, and Harley gaped.

Behind him, three Wrynd regained their feet and rushed toward him. The branches of the cottonwood tree reached toward them and batted them down the roadway. They landed in a heap.

"What the?"

Quinlan and his children dove into the back seat of the couple's car, and the old woman climbed inside.

The old man looked at him and nodded, then winked and climbed into the car. They raced east.

Harley stood with his sidearm uselessly dangling in his hand, not quite believing what he just saw. The Wrynd started climbing to their feet.

He climbed back into the truck. He wasn't sure exactly what just happened or how it happened or why it happened, but he knew for a surety they weren't out of this yet.

III

Quinlan sat in the back seat of the old couple's car, holding tight to his children and worrying it was far too late to save them. He lost his wife, and in trying to find her, he lost his children. Noah and Raizor sat mutely. Their faces slack and their eyes wide and unfocused. Drool dripped from Noah's narrow lips, and both children twitched and breathed in jagged hiccups. He couldn't reach them.

The old man drove to the outskirts of town, then pulled the car to the side of the road and stopped. The old woman climbed out of the passenger's seat, opened the back door, and motioned for Quinlan to get out.

"Let me get back there and snuggle these little lambs."

Quinlan shook his head. "No. I need . . ."

"You need to let me help is what you need," the old woman said. Quinlan looked at the old man, then nodded and got out of the car. Noah and Raizor didn't move.

The woman sat between Noah and Raizor and pulled them close in a massive bear hug. The children sat rigid, looking forward blankly, and then she began to hum softly and stroke their matted hair. Quinlan sat in the front seat, closed the door, and looked back at his children held by a little old woman he didn't know, fear and worry knotting his brow.

She looked to be in her late seventies and had the kindest face Quinlan ever saw. She was thin, but not overly so, and wrinkled folds of skin cascaded off narrow cheeks and poured down a soft neck to disappear beneath a simple dress made for modesty rather than style. Her hands were small and bony, and her veins large and blue. Her hair was long, silver, and beautiful. Looking at her, Quinlan felt she was glowing softly in the back seat while holding his children, radiating a peace and calm he hadn't felt in such a long time.

The old man sitting beside him was the male equivalent of the woman in the back seat. Where her hair was long, his was all but nonexistent. His scalp was darkly tanned and speckled with sunspots, and where she radiated calm, he radiated a strength laughing at his wiry, bent frame. The one thing they both shared was their eyes, green emeralds sparkling with magic, and dancing within them was enough love, humor, and concern it overwhelmed him. He found himself sobbing in the front seat.

"Go ahead and cry if you need to. We're safe for a little bit." The old man patted his arm softly.

They sat in the car on the side of a road pointing toward the mountains, and it was quiet except for Quinlan's soft cries and the old woman humming. After a time, the sound of the woman's voice gently escaping closed lips began to calm even him, and when his tears dried, he looked back, and his children folded into her arms, their little heads resting on her bosom.

They closed their eyes, and the convulsions ebbed. Quinlan thought they might be sleeping, but then Noah opened his eyes and smiled. He thought his heart might break. He failed them so miserably. How could he bring them out into the Wilderness on this hopeless quest?

When Noah and Raizor finally hugged the old woman back, she began to speak softly, and her voice was a balm easing the horror of what they had seen.

"Just hold onto ol' Sara now and let me have all your worries." She pulled them even closer, and they hugged her back equally hard. "Let me have your fears, your sorrow, and everything that has happened to you of late to cause you pain. We're going to bottle it up and put it away for a time. All that nonsense that would gobble you up if you let it, we're just going to put it away. And if any other fears come your way between now and the time you and your Daddy are safe, well, you just put them in the bottle as well and stow it away. And when you're safe, and your life is good and happy, and you can play and be children again, well, I want you to take your bottle from time to time, and you uncork it and take a little sip. Just a little, mind you. Sip at it slow, then put the cork back on good and tight and put the bottle away. It'll be bitter, and it will hurt, but you must sip at it until it's gone. If you don't it will turn to poison, such dark poison no bottle can contain it. Not now, not anytime soon, but eventually, take the bottle and have a little sip until it is all drank up and pissed away."

Noah and Raizor listened to her cooing voice and buried their heads on her chest. Quinlan stared in amazement as they breathed deep of the magic the old woman radiated, and when they both sighed and soft smiles kissed their lips, he had to look away again.

"Ed," the old woman whispered, and the old man raised a caterpillar eyebrow. "Get this family some apples. That will make them right inside and out. Right as rain in spring."

The old man climbed out of the car with a grunt and went to the trunk. He came back with three large red apples and handed one to each of them. Noah and Raizor took the apples with one hand, and they were almost too big for them to hold. They didn't want to let the old woman go, so they fumbled with the apple with one hand and took a bite. The crunch was a delicious sound and Quinlan bit into his. The taste made him swoon. He grinned as apple juice escaped his dry lips.

"Who are you?" he managed between bites of apple.

"Just an old shepherd," the old man offered, eyes piercing. When he smiled, it was a soft smile tinged with sadness as he offered a spotted hand to the younger man. "Edward Toll. Just call me Ed, if you like. This gentle witch is my lovely wife, Sara."

"I'll show you gentle witch," the old woman said, and the children giggled. They giggled when only half an hour before they were so horrified by what they had experienced they were all but catatonic.

"Why are you here?"

"We come to town every now and again to barter our apples. We were at the old Walmart when those monsters came into town. Decided we would take the long way around to get home when we saw you and your lambs running up the road. Thought you might need some help."

"Home?" Quinlan finished his apple and after a moment's thought started on the core.

"Orangeville. Not far south of here."

"There are people there?"

"Besides us, you mean?" The old man winked. "Yes, there are still people. Some good people and a few bad ones. It's home, and when you have a home, you take the good with the bad, I think."

"Where's home for you, son?" Sara's aged hand caressed his elbow. He felt electricity in her touch. Neither was wearing a powerband. They were Neands.

"Home?" The question puzzled him, and he finally shrugged. "Spanish Fork, I guess. The Hub. At least it was home."

"It will be again."

He wasn't so sure. As they sat in the quiet comfort of the old NG-powered car, Quinlan told them how they came to be in Price, of hiring the Marshal to help him find his wife and of meeting up with the stranger on the road.

"Harley Nearwater." Edward spat his name.

"You know him?"

"Aye. He calls Orangeville home as well. A shiftless man. Little in the way of scruples. You're lucky to have survived him."

"My wife didn't." Quinlan told them about their encounter with the Wrynd and how Harley killed Vania.

"She killed a Marshal?"

Quinlan nodded and looked at his children. They both were sleeping with the apples in their hands, cuddled against Sara, and she was softly caressing their cheeks. "I tried to warn him. We didn't like spending our time on the Link, so we had hobbies. If you don't have a job and you won't plug in, you need to have a hobby or two. We studied. We trained. Vania wanted to join the Marshals Service and was determined to be ready, so she pushed herself. I was along for the ride. Before the kids were born, she used to pick challenges at random to test us. She didn't have much use for the Vale. Said it made you soft. If she hadn't been under the influence of ink, if I hadn't distracted her, there's no way Harley would have killed her."

"Sounds like she was dead already."

"Maybe." Quinlan looked out the window. The afternoon was fading away. "But if anyone could have come back, she could have."

"How did you come to have Harley's sword?" Ed motioned to the black blade at Quinlan's feet.

"He gave it to me before he left us. Said I wasn't worth much with a slayer."

"You're not."

Quinlan grinned. "Suppose not." He looked at Edward's bare, sun-speckled arm. "What happened back there? How did you do that?"

"Do what?" Edward's eyes sparkled.

"That magic. The tree."

"Magic?" Edward chuckled softly. "There's no magic. The tree owed me a favor, so when I asked it to toss those wildthings aside, it was happy to oblige."

"The tree owed you a favor?" Quinlan fought a grin.

"Aye," Edward replied as if what he said made perfect sense. "I planted the damn thing. Every time I'm around, it wants me to hug it, as if I've time to go hugging every tree I've ever planted. If I had known as a seed it would grow to be so needy; I might have had a mind not to plant it at all."

"But," Quinlan stammered.

Edward gripped Quinlan's arm. "No but. Know this; there is no magic. It's but a name given to what we can't comprehend. Don't catalog what you don't understand. It limits your abilities."

They sat quietly as the old car's engine rumbled. "Your home. You don't have power?"

"We have a windmill."

"And water wheel." Sara gushed.

"And water wheel. Gives us all the power we need. The orchard doesn't need power, only water, and pruning from time to time."

Quinlan's heart skipped a beat.

"You live in an orchard?" His dream came flooding back.

"The most wonderful orchard." Sara's voice wavered as she spoke, and she kissed Raizor's head. "If there's any place left in the world where there really is magic, it's there, in Edward's orchard."

The orchard from his dream was real, and perhaps within reach. The realization felt like an awakening, and with it came anticipation and dread. There were things in the orchard of his dream, hiding within the trees. Dark things.

"So, you never use the Link?"

"Bah," Edward said. "Link. Don't need none of that science fiction stuff. The world is complicated enough without all that nonsense."

"We don't hanker for science fiction stuff," Sara agreed.

Quinlan grinned again. It was hard not to grin in their presence. "How long have you lived in your orchard?"

"Oh, forever." Sara nodded her head as if there were no truer statement, and Edward smiled softly at her. "We've always lived there and nowhere else."

Edward looked out the window. "We need to get moving. The Rages are coming."

"Rages?" Quinlan followed his gaze. The sky was clear, and he'd seen no sign of wildthings since the cats, and they hadn't been wildthings at all. They purred at him.

"A storm. Big one. We want to be wherever it is we're going before it hits."

"How do you know?"

"Just do."

"You could come home with us," Sara offered, and the children hummed softly in their sleep. "To the orchard. You would be safe there."

Quinlan sighed and closed his eyes. All those years of dreaming about an orchard calling to him, and somehow, his stumbling and mistakes led him to it.

"No." Edward said flatly, and when he opened his eyes, the old man was shaking his head. "I don't think the orchard is the place for you, least not yet."

The rebuke stung, but Quinlan thought he understood. Could they live there all their life? Would they live there all their life? He meant what he said to Harley and Victor. The world was changing, rotting away. It wasn't chaos yet, but it was only a matter of time. When the end came, would Noah and Raizor be prepared for it hiding in an apple orchard? Would any of them?

"We need to go home, I think," he agreed. "We can't hide and be ready for what's coming."

Edward nodded as if he understood, and Quinlan wondered if perhaps the strange old man understood far more than he ever would. "Truth there, I think."

"Do you think we could get back to my truck?"

"Maybe. The wildthings were more interested in Harley than you. We'll see if we can slip in and get your truck. If you do, we'll take the loop around the city."

"We still have the slide to deal with in the canyon. We'd have to walk the last twenty klicks."

Edward pursed his lips. "That wouldn't do."

"Fairview Canyon, Ed. They could go over Fairview."

Quinlan gave a puzzled look, and Edward nodded. "She's right. It's a pass through the mountains south of here. It'll get you to the Hub. Most people avoid Fairview, lots of wildthings in those mountains." He appraised Quinlan and grunted. "I think they'll leave you be."

Sara stirred the children and Edward put the car in gear. "Let's go get your truck."

Chapter Sixteen

Hunted

I

Harley sat in the cab of his truck on the second floor of a parking garage in the center of a city possessed by the mad. The garage, built when Price was to become part of the Rocky Mountain Hub, was only one more sad monument to shattered dreams.

Harley watched a cottonwood tree come to life and scatter the Wrynd like seeds in a breeze. He used the confusion of the magical, impossible events to make good his escape, and found himself here. From the cover of the garage, he spotted another fray of Wrynd racing blindly down the street. It was starting to look like the only way out of the city was going to be through them. Before he chanced such a task, he wanted to see what became of the Bowden family and the old couple who saved them.

He found them with his scye as they crept toward Walmart. After the first battle, the surviving pursued Harley and abandoned the old store. He watched as Quinlan and his children climbed out of the car and hugged the old couple before climbing into the pickup. The children were even smiling. He zoomed in on the old man and woman and grunted. He never paid them any mind because they seemed so harmless. He would certainly pay attention to them now.

Something in the way the old man winked at him across the chaos brought back a memory. The years peeled away, and he remembered why he chose to homestead in Orangeville in the first place. Suddenly everything he always thought was chance seemed suspect.

The first time he visited Orangeville, he was only a boy. It was before fusion and the Energy Wars, so he had to be no more than five, maybe six. He lived with Mom and Dad in Arizona on what he didn't know was the Navajo Nation but was. Dad worked out of town, and it wasn't a good time when Dad was away. One day, while he was out playing in the dirt (because really, what else was there to do?), Mom received a phone call.

She had an old-fashioned phone she kept in her pocket and used for emergencies and to talk to Dad. It was an antique, and the only reason it worked was that someone saw the potential of preying on the Neand-minded (except they weren't called that yet, Neands), who were afraid of the Link.

They created an application that allowed the old phone technology to interface with the new Link. Mom hated technology, but she held onto the phone for Dad. Even after the phone stopped working, she would still carry it with her, and when she finally gave it up, she set it on the bookshelf in the front room next to a little ceramic elephant standing on a ball. Harley had dropped the elephant and broke its trunk, and Mom beat him and repaired it as best she could. She kept the phone by the elephant with the broken trunk, and she looked at it almost every day, especially after Dad left and never came back.

On this day, when the phone still worked, she received a call from her sister who lived on a ranch overlooking Orangeville. She was dying from cancer, even though Marlboro cured cancer; she couldn't afford the cure, and it was long before there was anything like free medical or income.

Mom packed a suitcase with two fresh changes of clothes and his Spiderman toothbrush. They climbed into their old NG van and drove north, and then west, then cut through the desert and crossed over an old bridge spanning a river that wasn't much more than a trickle and through canyons so deep it seemed like they would swallow the sky.

Mom stopped and showed him silly pictures painted on the side of a cliff and told him the ancestors of their people painted those pictures, but he didn't know what that meant. The pictures hadn't been all that great. He was sure he could do better if she would stop long enough and let him try. She didn't. It wasn't too much longer until they reached the home of his Aunt Edna, who was dying of cancer.

The house was a little two-bedroom home sitting on a hill looking down on the valley of trees and homes bumping against tall and dusty mountains. The porch faced west, and from it he could watch the sunset. He would wave at it as it dipped below the flat-topped mountains. His Aunt Edna had a lot of animals on her ranch. There were chickens, goats, horses, cows and cats, loads of cats. Even then, Harley didn't care much for cats. They scratched and hissed, and he hissed right back.

His mom left him alone most of the time, except when it came time for lunch or dinner, then she would give him a sandwich, usually peanut butter and honey, even though he didn't care for peanut butter and honey. She was worried; he could tell because her brow had furrows and her eyes leaked. He didn't think she was crying because he didn't think Mom knew how to cry.

Aunt Edna had a man, but Harley didn't think he was her husband because he wasn't a nice man. One afternoon, while Harley was waving goodbye to the sun, the man came out on the porch. He sat on the rocking chair his mom liked to sit on, which wasn't often because she was usually with Aunt Edna in the bedroom, where Aunt Edna coughed and puked an awful lot. The man saw where Harley was looking and nodded.

"Horn Mountain."

Harley looked at him, puzzled. "Horn Mountain?"

The man nodded and scratched his boobs. Even though he was a man, he had boobs, and Harley tried not to look at them, but he didn't wear a shirt, and it was hard not to. "That there is Horn Mountain." He pointed at the peak the sun dipped behind. "Have a beer." The man handed Harley a bottle, and he took it and drank the beer. He sure liked that beer. It made him feel silly and a little sleepy.

Before Aunt Edna died, they all went into town. Harley liked Orangeville. They stopped at a little store and bought bread, water, and beer (for the man with the boobs), and then they went down Main Street. There was a park, and there was a swing set and slide, and there were other kids there. Aunt Edna told Mom they should stop for a while and let him play. Mom didn't want to, but Edna insisted. He ran to swing on the swings, because he sure enjoyed swinging on the swings. It was the closest thing he'd ever felt to flying, and he thought that someday he would surely like to fly.

Looking through his scye, years and years in the future, Harley remembered it was there, at the Orangeville City Park, where he first saw the old man and his wife.

They were selling apples from the back of their truck. Big red apples in old apple crates and there was a small crowd of people gathered around them buying those apples. Harley swung in the swing and remembered looking at the old man and his wife, thinking that those apples sure looked good, better than the peanut butter and honey sandwich he knew would be waiting for supper. As he sat in the swing, the old woman looked his way, and she smiled, the same kind of smile she smiled from across the killing field, and he smiled back. She walked to him, holding one of those big, delicious apples. She held it out to him and said something, but he couldn't exactly remember what.

He did remember he stopped swinging and reached for the apple. The old man was suddenly there, and he pulled the old woman's hand away. The old man looked at Harley and winked, just like he did from across the road.

"Not for him," he said.

And it had been a peanut butter and honey sandwich for supper that night.

His aunt died a few days later, and after she was in the ground, they went home. When Harley was on his own, and after he crisscrossed the country a couple of times and had a mind he might want to find a place he could call his own, he thought of his Aunt Edna's little house and went to Orangeville. The man who lived with her was still there, but he left when Harley arrived. He seemed to be in a hurry to leave, and that was fine.

The Wildthing Rages had started by then, and the animals were gone, but Harley still enjoyed sitting on the porch and saying goodbye to the sun as it dipped below Horn Mountain. Sitting on his porch all that time, he never gave a thought to the apple peddlers, or the offered apple snatched away.

Until today. Today, it suddenly flooded back.

Only a handful of days before he stumbled across a legionnaire dropped into a dead city after the Greywalker removed her linktag. Before then, if someone asked him if the Greywalker existed, he would have smiled and said, "Not likely." He was a legend, a new age boogeyman. The Greywalker was a man of the shadows in a world where there were no shadows. He was a mystery in a universe quickly running out of mysteries.

If everything man learned was accessible with a thought, what was left? The boogeyman. The Greywalker. Now Harley not only believed in him; he believed there was a whole lot more out there than the Greywalker.

A little old couple who tended an apple orchard controlled the elements to fight off the Wrynd. They were the same little old couple who offered apples to everyone but him.

For most of his life, he went where the wind willed, and he watched the world spin on by, never really being a part of it, just an observer, just another wanderer on the path. He watched enough and learned enough to know nothing was ever exactly as it seemed. Considering what he saw in the past few days, he knew things were stirring in the background, powerful things. Things he hoped might not break loose until he could move on. When they did break loose, the world would rumble, and the mighty Seven Realms would come crumbling down. If there was a place to hide from things like that, Harley counted on finding it before it was too late.

"Intrestin world," he whispered to himself.

As the two vehicles left the parking lot and headed toward the business loop, he brought back the scye and pulled out of the garage, wishing he could control the weapon and drive at the same time. Marshal Tempest was right; to truly master the scye would take a lot of work. He hoped to live long enough to put forth the effort.

He let the truck coast back onto Main Street and shadowed the magic wearing the skin of two little old apple peddlers.

II

Raizor couldn't see out the windshield and kept trying to get on her knees. Quinlan forced her to sit down. There was nothing out there she needed to see.

There were bodies on the business loop. He wove around them, trying to follow the old man. The Wrynd didn't plan to turn everyone in the city.

The sun was dipping lower in the sky, and Quinlan squinted into it as he drove. Three klicks down the business loop was an exit, and Edward turned on his right blinker, making Quinlan laugh. There were Wrynd on the prowl and dead bodies in the middle of the road, and the old man used his blinkers.

Something flashed in front of him, and Quinlan slammed on his brakes as a wave of Wrynd raced onto the highway and slammed into the side of the old man's car. The car teetered back and forth, then another wave of Wrynd hit, and the car tumbled on its side and rolled down the sloping shoulder to the bottom, coming to rest upside-down.

Quinlan cursed and stomped on the accelerator. The truck leapt down the highway and hit a half dozen Wrynd, scattering them before him as he went down the on-ramp and skidded to a stop. He ordered Noah and Raizor onto the floor and climbed out, bringing the pulse rifle to bear, firing blindly. He hit trees, rocks, and the exit sign. Finally, a pulse blast took out the kneecap of a Wrynd clambering toward Edward's car.

"Yes!" He wasn't hitting much, but the pulse blast was drawing the Wrynd toward him and giving the old couple a chance to escape. He kept firing.

III

Edward Toll moaned and wiped the blood from his brow. Sara cried out in pain, and he quickly unbuckled his seatbelt and flipped over to face her. Her wrist was badly twisted, but her eyes were alert and scared, and he nodded and unbuckled her belt.

"Let's go." They climbed out of the driver's side window. Quinlan was drawing the Wrynd away with random and mostly useless blasts from the pulse rifle, but more monsters raced down the shoulder of the highway.

A truck screeched to a halt on the road above, and Harley Nearwater climbed out. He looked down at him and the Wrynd racing toward them and aimed his slayer at Edward's car. He was aiming at the natural gas tank, and Edward grabbed his wounded wife by the elbow and tried to move faster, looking back as he ran.

Harley Nearwater winked and pulled the trigger.

The explosion pushed Edward and Sara in the back, lifting them off the ground and tossing them toward Quinlan. They landed hard twenty meters from the young man, and Edward cried out in pain and rolled onto his knees. The blast threw the Wrynd around his car up the hill, and several of them were screaming as the fire spread.

Sara lay on her back, and Edward knelt over her. Her eyes were wide, frightened, and far away. He took her by the right arm and tried to lift her. She groaned once, and the breath escaped her in a gasp. Edward eased her on her side, and a jagged piece of metal, hard, sharp, and deadly, protruded from her back. He pulled it free. The weed-choked ground around her was pooling with blood. Edward rolled her to her back, and her eyes stared at him softly with the same love, humor, and mischief that made him fall in love with her so many years before. The light within them began to fade, and Edward Toll found himself alone.

He sat, oblivious to the Wrynd. His hands dripped blood, his wife's blood. He heard someone shouting his name, and he didn't care because it didn't matter that someone was shouting his name. Sara was gone. How was it possible that she was gone?

"Ed! Ed!" He turned his head, and it was Quinlan. Surrounded by Wrynd, he fired madly. There were so many now he was hitting some of them.

Edward stood on shaking knees and looked at the carnage around him, at the lifeless form of his wife at his feet and the shiftless man on the roadway who destroyed his car and killed his wife. And something in his face began to change. The lines became sharper, harder, and the green in his eyes became darker. The storm he spoke to Quinlan of started there, in his eyes, and something like lightning flashed within.

Edward extended his right arm, and a wind devil swirled around him. His fingertips seemed to disappear into nothingness for a moment, then his hand, then his arm up to the elbow. He gritted his teeth and drew his arm back, and when it came back from wherever it was, he was holding a stick, long, gnarled, thick, and black with age. A walking stick, or staff, or shepherd's crook some might think, and in that they might be partially right, but would mostly be wrong. For Edward Toll, it wasn't any of those things; it was a talisman to draw his focus so he could return what was given.

The first Wrynd dared to approach, snarling, and reaching out with claws and gnashing teeth. Edward swung the staff and hit the hateful Wrynd. The staff or stick or crook or talisman ripped away flesh and bone, and the monster died where he stood. The apple peddler raised his arms above his head, holding the staff in both hands, and lightning flashed in the blue sky, erupted from the ground, and enveloped the Wrynd. They died, smoldering.

Given death, he returned death.

On the hill above, Harley Nearwater aimed his slayer. Edward pointed the staff. They stood that way, accusations in their eyes. Edward wanted badly to kill Harley, and Harley wanted badly to kill Edward, but in the end, they nodded, and Harley rushed to his truck and sped away.

Edward turned to Quinlan, and his hand flashed, and the stick or staff or shepherd's crook disappeared.

IV

Quinlan, Noah, and Raizor raced to the old man, and they all stood around Sara. Even though they only knew her for a moment, they felt like they lost someone dear whom they would miss for the rest of their lives. In that, they were right.

Edward gripped Quinlan by the arm, and the younger man helped him as he lowered himself to his knees before his wife. He kissed her lips and muttered soft words Quinlan and the children couldn't hear, then he placed his palm on her forehead and said goodbye. As he knelt there with his hand on his wife's brow, her body shimmered in the afternoon sun, as if she was only a mirage, after all. The ground seemed to reach up for her, embrace her, and when the old man lifted his hand, his wife was gone.

"Where did she go?" Raizor asked, and tears streamed down her cheeks.

Edward looked at the little girl and smiled a difficult smile. "She went to the great orchard."

"Will you see her again?" Noah asked, wiping tears.

"I'll find her there someday. She'll wait for me." He struggled to his feet and surveyed the carnage around him. "You need to be on your way. More will be here soon."

"We'll take you home." Quinlan took the old man by the arm. He seemed so frail now, so beaten.

"No. I'll walk." Edward pulled away, but not unkindly.

"You can't walk that far."

"I can. It will keep them occupied while you make your way home, having me between you and them. Go south until you reach Huntington. It will be the first town along the highway. Once in town, there's a road that points toward the mountain. Take it, and it will take you home."

The four walked back to the truck, and Quinlan helped his children inside and buckled them up. "I have water."

Edward shook his head. "I'll find what I need along the way." He seemed to notice the concern in the young man's face and shook his head softly. "I'm not without friends out there." After what he saw, Quinlan couldn't argue and could think of nothing to say.

The old man peered in at the children still crying in the front seat, and he pinched their cheeks and kissed their foreheads. "I would like to have gotten to know you better. Maybe later? Remember what my Sara told you. Bottle this up, for now, this pain and these tears, until you have time to deal with them. And when you have the time and the strength, take a sip now and again to remember what you've been through and grow strong from it. Drink up the pain and the suffering and piss it away and hold onto the memories. They will be your armor."

He shook Quinlan's hand, then thought better of it and hugged him instead. Quinlan returned the embrace and felt the bones of his back. There was so little of him; how could there be so much?

The old man started to hobble away, then he turned back, his eyes narrowing. "Who are you Quinlan?"

His breath was rattling in his chest, and he couldn't think of a response. He had no idea who he was. He hooked his thumb toward his children. "I'm their father."

"Is that all?"

"I used to be a husband and a father. Now I'm just a father."

"And when they're raised and can take care of themselves, what will you be then?"

Quinlan tried to meet the old man's gaze and couldn't. "Then I'm nothing. But until they're safe, I'm not going anywhere."

Edward grunted and looked toward the western mountains. "The end is coming. Keep your lambs close, and when they are ready, when you are ready, and need shelter from the storm, come find an old man and his apple orchard. I'll make us a cup of hot cider."

Quinlan climbed into the truck. They smiled at the apple peddler who saved them, and then they drove away.

V

Three hundred meters from where Quinlan and Edward faced the Wrynd and somehow, magically prevailed, stood the shattered remains of a convenience store. Shuttered for more than forty years, at one time it was a gas station, and when gasoline went the way of the dinosaur, it was an NG station. When fusion made natural gas obsolete, it sold fountain drinks, beer, and nachos to passersby, but eventually, even the passersby disappeared, and the business quietly closed.

It was just another closure in a line of closures as the city of Price and all the dreams borne there slowly withered and died. The city had a long history of dreams dying on the vine.

As for the convenience store, there was little left to draw any interest, but someone had become interested in the flagpole still pointing to the heavens. Once upon a time, the United States flag flew there as a sign of patriotism and a beacon for travelers. Shredded to bits by the elements, there was nothing left to testify it had been there at all.

As Quinlan and his children drove by on the last leg of their trip back to a home without a wife and mother, something clung to the flagpole, something very much alive and watching them with interest in his grey eyes.

There were those who called him Greywalker. He had heard the name before and found it amusing. People always had to have a name for things. Couldn't they accept that it was and be satisfied? He was, and he was quite satisfied.

When Edward Toll shuffled past the old store, the man with the grey eyes watched him with interest and just a touch of anticipation. Would the old man get a feel for him up there on the flagpole? He thought he might if not lost in his grief.

On the west end of town, he caught a glimpse of sunlight on metal and watched Harley's truck careening down a side street to emerge on the highway and rocket south.

The man with the grey eyes frowned as he watched him drive away. He was indeed problematic.

Dangling from a flagpole on the outskirts of a Wrynd infested city, he wondered not if, but when he should do something about a man named Harley Nearwater.

CHAPTER SEVENTEEN

THE GREYWALKER

I

Scimitar Hatcher watched lightning descend from the heavens and rise from the depths of hell to consume his Wrynd. When the old man raised the staff above his head, and the first lightning blast licked the ground, Hatcher leapt away and rolled down the north embankment of the highway to land at the bottom, becoming entangled in a barbed wire fence. The barbs ensnared his arms and legs, and a length of it became wrapped around his bullish neck. He fought to free himself, and blood flowed as all around him lightning crackled and killed.

He watched from the bottom of the embankment as Harley pointed his slayer at something on the other side of the highway, watched as the Castaway nodded and raced away in the dead Marshal's truck without firing his weapon. The lightning came for them all, but the old man calling it forth spared Harley. He spared the Castaway.

Hatcher removed the last of the barbed wire and licked the blood on his arms clean. He rubbed the blood from his legs and neck on his chest and abdomen and considered how best he might kill an old man with inhuman powers and a drifter named Harley

Nearwater.

Dagger Ash served him well. He struck terror in the Hub, and Harley fled back into the Wilderness as Hatcher knew he would. But he slipped past the snare, and so had his scepter's pathetic husband. They slipped past with the help of an apple peddler who called down the powers of Gaia herself. He climbed to his feet, walked back onto the road, and watched the old man shuffle south out of town. Oh, how he wanted to tear his feeble body with teeth, claw, fist, and strength, but the glory of the flare was slow in him. It was days, too many days since he last tasted the madness, and he was able to resist the need to feed. He turned the other way and walked back into the city, trailing drops of blood.

Twice on the way his people attacked him when overcome by the sight of his blood. He killed them as gently as he could and moved on. They were fresh Wrynd, the newest of his shield, and ink so enraptured them they had no reason. He bore them no ill will when he separated their soul from their body.

Cries of pain and fear still echoed down the streets of Price as his Wrynd gathered the Pilgrims and carried them back to their camp. There was more feeding going on than he would prefer.

When his shield stormed into Price, he hoped he might turn most of the population, but he made a mistake when he allowed them turned one by one. He'd allowed them to have too much ink and the flare took them. They slaughtered their neighbors. It was a foolish error. He knew better. He knew Dagger Ash and his skean would be lucky to make it back into the Wilderness, and he held no hope at all for any of those turned within the Hub.

Even with ink altering their genetic makeup, making them stronger, more ferocious, they were still blinkers who spent their lives in the Vale. They wouldn't survive the retribution of the Marshals, especially if the Legion came to their aid.

He hoped to replenish his ranks with the Pilgrims and Neands of Price, but with those who managed to escape the city and those devoured, he would be lucky to gather a third of the population. It would have to be enough for what was to come. If it weren't, he would go south, east, north, and west until his army truly was the Wrynd horde.

He knew the fury of the Seven Realms would rain hell upon his head, but that was well and good. He would face death with all his fury, and before he died, Harley Nearwater and the husband of his Vania would die screaming. So would the old man with mystical powers.

As he walked down Main Street, there was no denying the fatigue clinging to his massive frame, and the only relief would be sleep or ink. He wouldn't sleep and must be careful when he took ink, or the flare would have him, and too many would die.

He must be able to focus the flare when it coursed through him and must have his enemies in sight. It was one of the truths about the drug only fully understood and appreciated if someone tasted of it. Once, when one of his daggers displeased him, he held him in a vault and deprived him of ink for days. After ten days, he tore at his flesh, screaming and gnashing his teeth as he fed on himself. It was a gruesome death, even for a Wrynd.

Hatcher learned he was at his best ten to twelve hours after sending ink coursing through his veins. By then, the effects stabilized enough he still possessed all the strength the drug provided, still possessed the hunger to rip, tear, and devour, but he could control it. There was reason mingled with the madness. To be Scimitar, he must use reason.

After five days between doses, he would begin to feel the fatigue of humanity drag upon him. He would be forever lost unless he felt the raw power and ecstasy of ink in his veins, and could succumb to the rapture of ripping, tearing, and feasting. It had been six days, and he knew he mustn't wait a seventh.

A half dozen screaming men and women stumbled into the lobby of a hotel he made his new base of operations when storming into the city. When Hatcher walked into the lobby, his young Daggers Reflex and Solar were standing there, out of breath and exhausted. When they told them how Harley had bested them, he resisted killing them only because he knew he was running short on Wrynd who could fight. While the two were incompetent, they could also fight, so he saved them to kill another day.

Reflex looked at the gashes on Hatcher's body with concern and a bit of desire. Reflex was young to be a dagger, but he was quick, ruthless, loyal, and fearless. Hatcher saw much potential in the boy after ripping out the throats of his parents before the boy's eyes.

Reflex stood waiting for him to speak, licking his lips nervously. Hatcher watched the screaming victims of Price cowering in the hotel's conference room.

"You've stopped turning them?"

"As you ordered, Scimitar."

"How many do you have in there?"

"One-hundred and twenty-five."

"And in the city?"

"Perhaps 600 of us, maybe less."

"And ink? How is our supply of ink?"

Reflex looked at the floor. "Not good. Paul was giving them too high of a dose. We had twenty or so we had to kill before they even got out the door. They were trying to devour everyone in sight."

"And Paul?"

Reflex looked sheepish. "With a little barbecue sauce, he was delicious."

Hatcher sighed but clapped the young man on the shoulder anyway. "When you get 200 of them in there it will be enough for my plans. Gather another ten and put them in the room adjourning mine. You and Solar and any of the other daggers that are near are to come to my room in an hour. Dagger Ash is returning from the Hub. We have much to discuss."

Reflex nodded and went to obey Hatcher's commands. Hatcher

stopped as he started for the elevator and turned back to his young dagger. "Bring me a dose of ink when you come. A large one."

Reflex grinned and hurried away.

Hatcher chose room 301 of what was once the Castle Valley Inn as his suite because of the blood on the floor and the death in the air. It gave him comfort.

He closed the door to the room and went to the balcony to stand and stare out to the west. The sun was but a faint memory now as night rushed in and the wind caressed his bloody cheeks. He gripped the balcony handrail, gritted his teeth, and fought against the fury, the fatigue and hatred, and tried to use reason. Harley Nearwater killed Vania before his eyes. She was so lovely, so strong, so fierce, and ruthless. Everything he dreamed she might be.

Three times his Wrynd failed when they should have devoured, and each time Harley Nearwater was there. He would die slowly. But first, he must find and consume the apple peddler. That must come first. He wasn't the Greywalker, the mythical shadow whispered of in stories, but he might be something worse.

To accomplish that, Hatcher knew he must change the rules of the game. Changing the rules would mean even more defiance of the Federation and a treaty signed in blood. He no longer cared. Some blood was thicker than others, and he remembered the sight of the lightning striking down his Wrynd while snared and helpless, remembered Harley Nearwater's sword piercing Vania's heart. For their blood, he would break any oath, defy any empire. The time for the Wrynd to unleash hell upon earth had come. He stared up at the Wheel and thought he could feel the eyes of the Lord Judge upon him, thought he could hear the cackle of laughter at his failure, and ground his teeth.

Standing on the balcony, he watched night descend on the dead city, and he connected to the Link and started down the path of his defiance.

The Rocky Mountain Hub Justice Tower in the Vale was much the same as it was in the Sphere. A dagger pointed to the sky, an accusation and promise in steel and glass of the Federation's protection and dominance over the realms of man.

The tower was dark, even in the Vale. Everyone had escaped to their individual lives for the rest of the day. It was of little consequence to Hatcher. He knew the old override passcodes and slipped through the digital doors. He strolled through the building as if he belonged there. Once, a lifetime ago, he had.

He made his way to the door of the Hub Marshal and stood outside it, his thoughts elsewhere. Then he opened the familiar door and walked inside. It was dark, and he didn't bother summoning lights. He strode to the windows, looked down on the city, and glanced at the sparkling Hub. He used to love it here and the knowledge that all around him was a mass of humanity, crawling over each other like ants. A mindless force of nature. Now he loved it still, but for a different reason. Now he would love to see the city bathed in blood.

"Marshal Tempest! I demand an audience."

Much had changed since he was last here, and the fatigue in his mind whispered regret he shrugged away. "Marshal!" He roared, and Jodi Tempest opened the door to her office and glided inside.

"Scimitar Hatcher," she said. She summoned the lights and sat on the edge of her desk. If she was surprised to find him here in the Vale, she gave no sign. "Your avatar is as barbaric as your Sphere self, I see."

Hatcher looked at the bloody scars on his arms, legs, and chest and smiled. "I am what I am in all realms, Marshal."

"What brings you here?"

"Truth brings me here, Marshal. And justice."

"What do you know of the truth, Wrynd? Or justice?"

Hatcher sat on his haunches and idly scratched crosses into the hardwood floor with a long, jagged nail. "You would be horrified to learn all that I know, Marshal."

"What truth and justice do you speak of?"

Hatcher looked at her and feared his eyes might betray the emotion overwhelming him. It was remorse. "The truth of the Federation and the Seven Realms and justice for the people you think to serve."

"By all means, Scimitar, share your vast wisdom."

Hatcher scowled and rose to his full height, towering over Jodi. He folded his arms across his chest and smiled, his dagger teeth gleaming. "Your Federation, your Seven Realms, your wondrous Age of Renewal, is a charade, Marshal Tempest. We're all but the playthings of a god we've appointed and placed on high to manipulate everything we are or ever dream to be."

"Lord Judge Syiada."

"Your Lord Judge Syiada. I'll no longer bend my knee in his service."

Jodi looked up at him, a snarl on her lips. "Bend your knee in his service? You've killed thousands of his people!"

Hatcher chuckled. "Your naivety, Marshal, is endearing, but dangerous. The Wrynd serve the Lord Judge as much as the Marshals, as much as the Legion. We are all his servants."

"How do you serve the Federation?"

"We don't serve the Federation! We serve the Lord Judge. The Federation is nothing more than a sparkling light invented to keep us sedated. You think yourself so much above us, Marshal Tempest. But you're no different. We each serve the same master, but you don't yet realize how much alike we truly are." Hatcher walked the length of the office, slowly, casually, his clawed toes scraping on the polished floor. "This place of power you call yours I once called mine. Where you sit, I once sat. The star on your chest was once on my chest."

Jodi's face turned ashen. "Marshal? You were a Marshal?"

"Hatcher is my taken name. After I became a Wrynd. In another life, I was Chief Marshal Trenton Balanger."

"Marshal Balanger?" The shock was evident on her face. "His transport went down over the Wilderness before I joined the service."

"So say the Histories. Every Wrynd Scimitar was once a member of the mighty Marshals Service. The Wrynd do more than purge the Wilderness of humanity, herd them into the Hubs or devour them. We're the refiner's fire for the Leap the Lord Judge seeks. Before I was a Wrynd, I served as a Marshal just as you, and in blindness to the truth, I bowed my knee and surrendered my humanity, my family and everything I loved to the Lord Judge and the glory of the Seven Realms. We exist at the whims of Syiada. If I live now or if I die is because he allows it. If he chooses not to supply me with ink, I'll die screaming."

"He does supply the ink." Jodi sat on her desk, and Hatcher saw the truth finally dawn on her face.

"You serve a twisted god, Marshal Tempest. I have enough ink hidden away to survive a year with a shield of 2,000. In that year of life I have left, I plan to set things in motion that will tear the Lord Judge from the sky, pluck him from his Wheel, and show him the face of terror."

"How would you suppose to do such a thing?"

Hatcher grinned fanatically. "His Leap exists Marshal Tempest! His precious leap in evolution has arrived. The one thing he covets beyond all others lives and is in my range. I plan to have him. I plan to bring the Federation to its knees with the power of the Leap and rip the soul from Syiada's body."

"How do you know the Leap exists?"

"I've seen him. He saved the Castaway. When I had him in my grasp the coward Harley Nearwater, the Leap saved him from his fate."

Jodi smiled. "Why would the Leap be inclined to help a man like Harley Nearwater?"

"I don't know. But I know the power I saw destroy my people. It was beyond measure. It was a power born of the Rages."

Jodi walked to the window and looked out at the Hub. It looked quiet, a sleeping monster of humanity. "Was it the Greywalker?"

"Greywalker. Do you believe in this Greywalker?"

"Do you?" Jodi replied.

He scowled. "Does it matter? Even if he exists, he's of little consequence. A shadow in the night. Sometimes here, sometimes there, a watcher in the woods. What threat is he?"

"I've heard stories the Greywalker can remove a person's link-tag. The one who helped Harley couldn't be the Greywalker?"

"Not by the legends I've heard."

"Why do you bring this to me?"

Hatcher's mouth twisted into a frown. "I've forsaken everything I ever hoped for in my life in the service of a lie. You think me a barbarian, the Wrynd nothing but monsters. You're mistaken. We are people of honor still. Even the flare can't strip that from us. But ask yourself where the true monsters hide."

Hatcher joined her at the window and motioned to the sleeping city below. "You know where they are, Marshal Tempest. You feel them every time you walk down the street. They sleep within their homes in the Hubs, their minds occupied in the Vale. They've lost all sense of humanity, all sense of hope, honor, and compassion, and you and your deputies protect them. One day they'll be unleashed by the Lord Judge you serve, and the world will truly die."

Jodi turned away, and Hatcher smiled softly.

"I'm doomed and all those like me," he whispered in her ear. "But before I die, I'll feel the blood of Harley Nearwater flow between my fingers. I had one glimmer of hope in this life, and I saw it in the face of the woman he killed. He'll pay before I die. He's connected in some manner to the Leap. Whatever it is chose to save both him and the family of my sweet Vania. I will have the Castaway, and I will have the Leap. I'll crush their bones to dust and deny the Lord Judge his godhood. But my Wrynd and I will die. We'll die screaming, and the Lord Judge will still sit on high. I can't tear him from the sky, but that doesn't mean he can't fall. If there's justice in the Seven Realms, it must be done."

Hatcher nodded to the Marshal and turned to walk out of her office and Jodi called out to him.

"All this for a woman you barely knew. Was she such a lover that you would destroy the world?"

"Lover?" Hatcher turned and faced her. "Lover?" he repeated. "You think Vania my lover?" He tried to smile, but the smile turned to a grimace, and he was suddenly weeping before the Federation Marshal. "She wasn't my lover, Marshal Tempest. She was my daughter. Everything I surrendered in service to the Lord Judge."

He turned his back on Marshal Tempest and stormed out of the Vale.

Hatcher's eyes blinked rapidly as he returned to the balcony of the hotel. Reflex and Solar were standing at the doorway of his room. He was crying and wiped the tears away as he started to walk toward them. The ground beneath his feet shifted as if it suddenly alive, and he fought to gain his balance.

Reflex looked at him, concerned. "Scimitar?"

Hatcher tried to take another step and fell to his knees, his vision swimming. He shook his head and rubbed his eyes, and when he opened them, he was no longer on the hotel balcony. He was kneeling on the ground on a jagged cliff, staring down on a valley hundreds of meters below. For a moment vertigo made him swoon.

"Beautiful view isn't it?" a voice happy and giggling whispered behind him.

II

Hatcher stared down from the top of Horn Mountain, and as

he knelt, lightning flashed across the desert. There was high cumulus sliding across the dark sky, softly glowing by the just rising moon. He reached down and scooped up a handful of dirt and let it slide through his fingers. Was he back in the Vale? There was no way of knowing, but something told him he wasn't.

"Sorcery." His voice sounded hushed and perhaps even a little anxious in the quiet of the night.

"You flatter me." The voice behind him was light and cheerful. "It's a nice trick, I'll admit. But sorcery? That would be rather pompous of me, to claim the talents of a sorcerer, wouldn't it?"

Hatcher leapt to his feet and turned; his claws extended. A man sat on the twisted limb of a juniper. He was of medium build and wore simple black jeans, white shirt, and battered cowboy boots. His face needed a shave, and his hair was black and disheveled as if he had only recently awakened. He was smiling happily, and his eyes were dancing, and gay, and floating in grey.

"You!" Hatcher said.

"Me?" The man with the grey eyes asked back.

"The Greywalker." Hatcher walked toward him, popping his neck as he prepared to pounce.

"Greywalker?" The man sounded highly amused. "I wonder, is that my name or my title?"

"Which is it?"

The man with the grey eyes hopped off the juniper and went to meet him. "Neither actually."

"Then, who are you?"

"Who? Why I am me. Who else could I be?"

"What are you called?" Hatcher lashed out with fist and claw, and where the grey man stood, he no longer was. He was now behind him.

"Called? A scoundrel usually, although I'm sure it would break my mother's heart."

Hatcher spun and lashed out impossibly fast with both arms,

leaping into the air to deliver a sweeping kick. The man sidestepped out of the way casually, as if he might be rehearsing a dance.

"What's your name?" Hatcher squatted on the ground, preparing to leap, and the grey man knelt to mimic him.

"Name? Eva." The Greywalker said. "Eva Gabor."

Hatcher wrapped his arms around the man with the grey eyes, laughing while he lifted him off the ground and began to dig his fingers into the smaller man's sides. "Well, Eva Gabor. Let's see how black your blood flows in the moonlight."

While Hatcher dug his claws into him, the man with the grey eyes didn't seem bothered in the least. He frowned as he reached down and gripped the bigger man by the wrists. "I faint at the sight of my blood, I'm afraid. Can't have that, you know; I might tumble right off the cliff and make a mess of myself on the rocks below."

He twisted his hands and broke Hatcher's grip easily, as if he were only a child. The Greywalker continued to twist his wrists, and Hatcher knew bones would break if he didn't submit.

The smaller man pushed him back, and he fell on his behind in the dirt. He started to leap to his feet, and the Greywalker motioned for him to stay sitting and sat cross-legged in front of him. "You can keep on if you like, but eventually I'll have to break a bone or two to get your attention. I'm rather good at breaking bones. Once I begin, it's hard to stop. It would be difficult for you to complete your plans with a body full of broken bones, don't you think?"

Hatcher rubbed his wrists where the man with the grey eyes touched him. He could see no mark, but they felt burned, seared with the mark of the Greywalker.

"What do you want?"

"I thought I might give you some free advice. I like to give advice from time to time, though it's so seldom taken." The Greywalker looked toward the horizon, and his face was solemn, sad, and longing. "My advice to you would be to let it go."

"Let what go?"

"Why, your revenge, of course. Let it go. It will only end with your demise, unless I'm of a mind to help you, and I'm not of a mind to do so. Not at all."

"I'll have my revenge."

"I'll have my revenge." The man with the grey eyes mocked. "You sound rather ridiculous, you know. Try saying the same thing in a falsetto, and you'll see what I mean. I'll have my revenge!" The grey man squeaked. "See what I mean? Ridiculous."

Hatcher stared at the Greywalker, gritting his teeth, and the smaller man finally shook his head, scooped up a handful of dust and tossed it into the air. It swirled between them, and from within an image began to materialize of a man walking down a long and lonely road. A bent old man lost and alone.

"The instrument of your destruction." The Greywalker motioned. "See how sad he looks, walking all alone on the highway? His wife and companion killed by the very man you wish to consume. Harley Nearwater. He's quite the paradox, ol' Harley. Every stumbling step he takes leads us closer and closer to ruin. I have half a mind to let you eat him, but I'm not sure his talents for mischief would be any less pervasive dead rather than alive. In any event, if you try to kill the old man, it would be a moot point because I do believe this little old shepherd would destroy you and your Wrynd with hardly a thought. I'm only glad I came along when I did because I thought I might never see him again. I thought he might have faded away. But, alas, he still walks the Earth and would become a bit of a complication if he were to take an interest in the world. It's my sincere hope that he won't."

"He's the Leap the Lord Judge desires. I'll have him."

"The Leap? Does he look anything like a hopeful monster to you? He looks like nothing more than a sad old apple peddler to me."

"Then you are the Leap!"

321

"The next step in evolution? Me? How flattering." The Grey-walker rocked on his buttocks and pointed to the Wheel just coming into view between parted clouds. "Your mighty Lord Judge is sadly mistaken. The Good Book says the meek shall inherit the earth, but it doesn't say we are the meek. There's little about our race that is meek. Perhaps our creator has chosen another race to replace us. When the Leap he desires chooses to show itself, I think your Lord Judge will rue the day he dared to pit humanity against God and Gaia."

"You lie."

"Oh, it is indeed one of my weaknesses," the Greywalker smiled slyly. "But on this occasion, I don't."

Hatcher pointed to the vision still swirling in the dust. "If the Wrynd attack this old man, you'll stand against us?"

The Greywalker smiled softly and shook his head. "No. But I won't stand with you, and if I don't, you'll die."

Hatcher stood and faced the cliff and the valley below. "We'll fight, Greywalker."

The man with the grey eyes shrugged, perhaps a little sadly. "Of course, you will." He motioned with his left hand, and Hatcher vanished.

III

The Greywalker climbed to his feet and brushed the dust off his pants. He stood on the cliff and looked out at the valley, a smile on his lips. The wind was blowing softly, and there was just a hint of moisture in the breeze, just a touch of promise of a storm to come.

He stepped off the cliff and plummeted toward the valley. Half a dozen times he touched down on his way to the bottom, first on his left foot, then on his right, only to kick off yet again and continue his mad descent to the valley floor. When he reached it, he landed on his right foot as if he had only been going from one step to the next.

He walked swiftly through the foothills, his boots making not a sound. He came to an old highway and followed it as it shadowed the river toward a sleeping town. On the edge of town, he came to a dirt road turning right. The road ended where an old timber bridge began. The bridge spanned the little river, and on the other side was an orchard. The Greywalker stood with his boots barely touching the bridge as he stared across to the trees.

He smiled a smile of wonder and joy and stuck his neck out so that it broke the plane of the bridge. When he did so the orchard was so much larger than it previously was, so much grander, so much more magical than any orchard ever seen. It was an amazing trick. He must congratulate the old man.

Maybe someday.

For now, the apple peddler still stumbled along, lost in his long walk of grief, and it gave the man with the grey eyes a little time to explore the orchard he so carefully cultivated. The Greywalker looked back down the dirt road he followed to the bridge, then grinned and shoved his hands into his pockets and walked across, into the world of Edward Toll. He whistled a little tune as he did. It was the theme to "Green Acres." It was a classic, he thought; one of his all-time favorites.

IV

Hatcher almost fell when the floor of the hotel suddenly appeared beneath his feet. He reached out for the wall, and Reflex and Solar ran forward, concern on their young faces.

"Scimitar! What happened?"

Hatcher shook his head. "Sorcery. Magician tricks. No matter." He regained his balance and then looked at his wrists. There was no sign of where the Greywalker touched him, yet still, his skin tingled. "Has Dagger Ash returned?"

"He's out in the city, trying to gather the Wrynd who are still flaring. He should be back soon."

"It's going to be a busy night." Through a blast hole in the wall, Hatcher could hear people crying in the adjoining room. They were whimpering, begging for mercy. It made him smile. "Starting tonight, we are more than Wrynd. Starting tonight we are the sword of vengeance, and we'll thwart the plans of gods!"

Hatcher strode to the bar and lifted an old backpack from the corner. He unzipped the pack, reached inside, and withdrew a scye. He held it in his hands, and it slowly lifted into the air, glowing red with menace. He smiled and pulled a Marshal's star out of the bag, holding it in his massive hand. "We serve our justice upon the world." He crushed the star, tossed it away, and pulled a holster out of the old backpack, strapped it around his waist, and pulled its slayer free, enjoying the feel of it in his hand once more.

"What do you require?" Solar was grinning broadly.

"Arm yourselves. I need trucks, big trucks. Big enough to carry those we have captive. Big enough to keep them under control until we can give them their ink, send them into the flare, and point them at our enemy."

"There are cattle trailers and semis on the other end of town," Reflex patted his thin chest enthusiastically. "They're old enough we may not have to be on the Link to run them."

"Bring them here."

Reflex clapped his hands and took the vial of ink Hatcher requested out of his pocket. "Will you still want this?

Hatcher took the vial, and his two daggers stepped aside as he walked out of the room with his scye hovering at his shoulder. He opened the door to the next room and motioned toward the four Wrynd, keeping the huddled, terrified townsfolk inside from leaping out the window.

"You'd better leave," Hatcher said to his Wrynd. He pressed the vial of ink to a vein in his right arm. A needle in the vial struck him like a viper, and the vein turned black.

As the ink rushed into his system, Hatcher relished the thought that the Greywalker believed they couldn't win with teeth, claw, fist, and strength. The Greywalker knew nothing of his fury. In time he would.

Hatcher roared and closed the door. The screaming started.

CHAPTER EIGHTEEN

EYE OF THE STORM

I

Knowing there was so much interest in his death might be a surprise to Harley, but not much of one. Once people got to know him, they usually wanted him dead.

He sat on the hood of Victor's pickup twenty klicks outside of Price, waiting for any sign of the old man and not entirely sure what he would do once he saw him. Twice he'd watched the apple peddler do the impossible. He hadn't intended to kill his wife. The blast to the NG tank was meant to give the couple a chance to escape. He still wasn't sure why he tried to save them. He acted on impulse. It was on impulse he sat on the truck waiting for the old man when he should be far away.

Impulse and curiosity.

The apple peddler could have killed him. Harley was good with a slayer, but whatever forces the old man held in his hands would have proven better. He spared him, and Harley wondered why. He supposed he was just stupid enough to sit around and find out.

As he waited, his thoughts were on his mother somewhere in the deserts of the Navajo Nation. He couldn't reach her by Link but knew danger was coming for her. The world was unraveling faster than he imagined. If she was to survive, he needed to get to her. First, he would see what the old man had to show him.

Harley had lived in this speck of the world for more than ten years, roaming here and there, but eventually ending up back at the farmhouse on the outskirts of Orangeville. He didn't know why. It just felt like home.

While he sat and waited for the old man, he considered how in all the time he lived in the town he saw the apple peddlers a handful of times and never paused to give them a moment's thought. He remembered the old woman trying to give him one of her apples and being denied by the old man. Why would he do that? He was just a boy. Perhaps everything was by the apple peddler's design.

The Marshal told him to keep an eye out for the Greywalker. Other than the legionnaire's story of him taking away her link-tag, few stories attributed supernatural powers to the man with the grey eyes, but Harley saw the powers in the old man. What would Marshal Tempest think if she knew such a man was alive and walked the Wilderness?

Harley lit a cigarette and smoked it slowly while the morning sun stretched higher into the sky. It was another warm July day with hardly a hint of cloud. It was looking to be a dry summer once again, and by August what was green would be kindling. Most of it already was.

He connected to his scye and sent it scouting toward Price. The day before, after making good his escape from the Wrynd-infested city, he sent the scye into Huntington to see Quinlan turn toward Fairview Canyon. He wished them luck.

His scye found the old man stumbling south two klicks from where he sat with a cigarette dangling from his mouth. He looked rough, ragged, and badly dehydrated. There was no way he would make it another thirty kilometers to Orangeville on his own. When he lowered the scye within the old man's reach, he batted at it as if it were a fly, his eyes glazed and delirious. Harley frowned. He watched him kill more than twenty Wrynd with a flick of his wrist, but now he was dying of exposure walking the highway.

He sent the scye soaring again, and before he brought it back, he turned it north. There was dust on the highway, and Harley's scye raced toward it.

"Son-of-a-bitch!"

Two semi-trucks headed south on the highway. They pulled cattle trailers behind them and inside were scores of people clinging to the slotted walls. Through the scye, he could hear them screaming. At the steering wheel of the trucks were Wrynd, and Harley looked twice to be sure. Sitting on the roof of the cab of the first truck was Hatcher. He was grinning madly and slung around his waist was a holster and sidearm. A red scye floated by his right ear. They would be on the old man in minutes.

In the past few days he started to worry his instincts were off kilter and would, in the end, get him killed. As the Wrynd bore down on the old man on the road, Harley tossed his cigarette away, climbed into his truck, and raced to meet them.

"Things are about to get intrestin."

II

Hatcher slept among the carnage he wrought and woke covered in blood. He felt magnificent. The ink coursed through him, and he felt alive, more powerful than he had in weeks. It was a good day to rip, tear, kill, and eat.

When he walked into the hotel lobby, Reflex sat askew in a chair, snoring softly, and Solar lay curled up on the floor by the hotel desk.

He didn't wake them but went outside to find the semi-trucks Reflex gathered. The boy had painted Hatcher's name in blood on the doors.

He stretched, cracked his neck, and examined the old trucks

with interest. They would serve nicely.

He took his first dose of ink years before and walked away from the life he knew and loved. In all that time, he hadn't driven a vehicle, used a weapon, or taken advantage of technology except to order more ink. He found himself relishing the return of a life he held so dearly. He drew his sidearm, and the slayer felt like an extension of his hand. He looked forward to using it soon.

He let Reflex and Solar sleep for another hour then kicked them awake and ordered them to make things ready. They gathered the prisoners out of the reception hall and herded them into the cattle trailers, enjoying the sounds of their screams in the morning air.

Dagger Ash strolled through the hotel lobby, smiling smugly, his scye floating beside him. Hatcher nodded to the former Marshal. Ash had been his most trusted dagger for years, and the role suited him much more than the role of Marshal ever had.

"You survived the Hub, I see."

Ash shrugged. "Had me a time or two. Would have had the Marshal if not for the Emissary and the Legion."

Hatcher slapped him on the shoulder. "We are betrayed, and vengeance is ours."

"Vengeance against?"

"The Lord Judge himself," Hatcher replied. Reflex brought him a case of ink, and he opened it to examine the vials inside. Ash nodded toward it.

"We'll be biting the hand that feeds us."

"We'll do more than bite," Hatcher said, and Ash pursed his lips and looked away. Hatcher turned to Reflex and Solar. "Bring four not so enthralled in the flare. I need them to be able to think and be useful. You two come with me. Dagger Ash organize the others and be prepared. We go south until we find the old man. When we do, we stop the trucks and unleash our cargo." Hatcher stepped outside and strode to the cattle cars, slapping the side, and Neands screamed and climbed over each other to get beyond his reach. "We let them out one at a time. We squeeze them through the chute like cattle and, when we do, you inject each one of them, twice."

Reflex grinned. "They'll be uncontrollable."

"Yes, they will."

"We should attack as one force, one shield," Dagger Ash said softly.

"We fight more than one enemy, Dagger Ash. The old man is but one. We also seek the Greywalker and Harley Nearwater."

"A mist of legend and a lone Indian. Are these enemies worthy of the Wrynd?"

Hatcher climbed on top of the first truck and stared down at Ash. "Their deaths will bring the Lord Judge from his Wheel, and we'll feast upon his dreams!"

The semis wove through the wreckage in the city until they reached the highway, and then picked up speed. Hatcher rode sitting on the roof of the cab of the leading semi, enjoying the sensation of the air whipping past him, of the dryness of the blood on his chest and legs, of the feeling of the slayer at his side.

The air was shimmering off the old asphalt as they made their way out of the city. At first, Hatcher thought it might be a mirage, the tiny dot on the horizon, but as they drew closer, his eyes focused, and he knew it was the old man, stumbling south. He leaned forward with anticipation. A flash of light beyond the apple peddler caught his attention, and when he looked up, he saw Marshal Walker's pickup flying toward them.

Hatcher roared with approval. With rage. With hunger.

III

Harley's truck screeched to a stop twenty meters from Edward. The semis were running side by side down the highway with Hatcher standing on the hood of one, waving his arms. Just short of where Edward stumbled along, oblivious to everything around him, the trucks stopped on the four-lane highway and turned with one truck's nose facing west and the other facing east. Six Wrynd scrambled out of the cab and raced to the trailers. One of them used a cattle prod to force the screaming hostages in the trailers, and they crowded toward the back, where the other Wrynd funneled them out, injecting them in both arms as they passed through.

Those infected stood dazed then screeched a blood-curdling scream. Their mad eyes flashed with a storm of raw energy, desire, compulsion, and hunger. The first thing they saw when overcome was Edward Toll.

They roared and raced toward him in ones and twos, and then there were dozens. Harley scrambled out of his truck with his slayer in one hand and a water bottle in the other.

He cut down the closest and the Wrynd at the trucks fired back. The pulse blast whizzed a meter over Harley's head. They weren't good, but they weren't bad.

"Wrynd with slayers. It just keeps getting better." Harley ran to the old man, grabbed him by the arm, and when he did, the last of the apple peddler's energy exhausted itself. He sank to his knees on the hot asphalt. Harley brought the bottle to his cracked lips, and the apple peddler drank greedily. Another pulse blast ripped away the road only centimeters from Harley's left knee.

He fired off eight quick bursts and eight more Wrynd dropped to the ground. When they did, more than a dozen of the other flaring Wrynd ripped into them. One thing to count on was Wrynd not being particular about what was on the menu when they flared.

A roar made everyone stop in their tracks; even the Wrynd eating their recently fallen comrades lifted their heads and looked back when Hatcher stomped on the hood of the truck.

"Harley Nearwater!"

Harley sighed. "When did my name become a curse?"

He should have moved on. Hatcher's scye raced toward him, and Harley flicked down his eyeset and sent his scye racing to meet it. The scyes met, clashing together in a blast of light and sparks. Harley's knees buckled, and he fell on his ass from the impact. He tried to slip the scye around Hatcher's, but every move he made, the Wrynd countered, and with every strike of one scye to the other the two men flinched and grunted from the effort.

At his feet, the old man still drank from the water bottle but made no effort to stand. Harley fought scye to scye against the Scimitar, and the other Wrynd raced toward them. There were too many of them and not enough of the fallen to distract them anymore.

"Scuttle this." Harley pulled his sidearm and fired. The blast tore through Hatcher's left shoulder, and the Wrynd tumbled from the truck. He aimed at the closest Wrynd, who were dangerously close by now, and ducked as two more blasts from the armed Wrynd went wild.

"Old man," he screamed. "I don't know if you have a Jedi mind trick up your sleeve or can make lightning come out of your fingertips, or your arse or any other orifice in your crackin' body, but I'd appreciate any help you could give about now." A male Wrynd dove toward him, and he kicked him hard between the legs. "Flare that!"

Harley went to pull the old man to his feet, and the apple peddler stared up. His eyes were far away and full of sorrow and dark anger. "The end is coming," he whispered.

"No shit!"

Thunder rolled around him, and Harley felt the earth tremble. When he cast his eyes to the east and west, there was a cloud of dust racing toward them.

"Oh, shit."

Hatcher heard it as well. He clambered back on top of the truck and fired. Harley shot back wildly, then the Rages hit, and he dove under his truck.

A herd of elk came first, fifty or more of them, and he counted ten great bulls among them. They ran over the attacking Wrynd. Behind the elk came cattle, coyote, and antelope. There were groundhogs, field mice, lizards, and creatures Harley couldn't even recognize.

Crows swirled in the sky like black rain, and a dozen or more horses trampled down the Wrynd in their path. Harley watched six Wrynd tackle a great bull elk, biting, scratching, and clawing. These new Wrynd had no teeth filed into daggers or nails filed into claws, but the ink gave them strength and the bull fell dying.

It was of little consequence. In a matter of minutes, it was over, and the Wrynd army Hatcher unleashed lay dead or dying on the road. Hatcher stood on the hood of his truck, staring in disbelief. He aimed his slayer at the head of the old man. A murder of crows enveloped him, and his scye went to work trying to cut them down. Reflex and Solar clambered on top of the semi and helped the Scimitar clear them away. Harley could see no other Wrynd standing.

During the Rages, the old man only knelt on the ground beside him, and he knelt there still. The empty water bottle lay on the ground in front of him. He was unharmed. It was as if the Rages made a wide berth around him, purposely avoided putting him in harm's way.

When the last of the attacking Wrynd died a grisly death, the animals turned their attention to Hatcher and his daggers. Harley lay still under his truck, and even the groundhogs and field mice didn't look his way.

As they surrounded the three surviving Wrynd, the old man finally lifted his head, as if awakened from a dream. He looked at the death around him, and then slowly climbed to his feet. All the mass of wildlife turned his way.

"Stay down!" Harley whispered, but the old man paid him no

mind.

The animals came to encircle him. A great elk, possibly the largest elk Harley had ever seen, stepped toward the apple peddler. The bull looked like a king, like a king of all nature. The old man caressed its muzzle with one of his gnarled hands, and the bull bowed his head.

A painted horse weaved her way through the other animals. Astride the horse, hugging its neck, was the little girl Harley sent into the Wilderness. She looked to be sleeping. The horse stopped in front of the old man and nuzzled him, then knelt. The apple peddler draped his arms over the horse's mane and fell forward. The little girl roused and gripped his skinny shoulders. The paint stood, with the old man astride. Edward Toll sat up and glanced at Harley.

The look they exchanged was one stretching back through time, to when Harley was but a small boy holding out his hand as a kindly old woman tried to give him an apple from an orchard that couldn't possibly be real. It was a look of denial. A look of deep and everlasting hatred.

The old man turned his head, sparing Harley his vengeful gaze.

The animals turned as one and ran to the north in a thundering mass of nature, except for the horse carrying the apple peddler and little girl. She turned and trotted south. Harley twisted his body to watch as she picked up speed and galloped away with the two clinging to her back. He stayed staring for several minutes, just staring, and then remembered Hatcher and his two Wrynd, and scrambled to his feet.

The Scimitar sat on the hood of his truck, and the other two Wrynd sat beside him. When Hatcher looked toward Harley, there was blood pouring into his right eye from a deep gash in his forehead. Harley holstered his weapon and rushed for his truck. It was most definitely time to go.

A Wrynd screamed, scrambled from the bed of his truck, and

ran at him so fast Harley couldn't react. He fell, and the Wrynd pounced on top. Something black and cold flashed before Harley's eyes and hit the Wrynd in the chest.

Harley scrambled away. There was a shadow, or what looked like a shadow. As it attacked the only sound was the screeching screams of the Wrynd. The shadow reminded Harley of a dog or a wolf tearing at its prey, but not a dog or wolf he ever hoped to meet.

When it was over, the Wrynd was a horror Harley couldn't gaze upon, and the shadow turned to him. From the blackness there he saw eyes, pink, glowing eyes. Then it was gone, dashing to the east. Harley climbed inside the truck and closed the door.

He started the vehicle and turned toward home and stopped when he saw a flash of light. A wall of black clouds was rushing from the south, and within them, lightning crackled. Another Rage was building. He turned his head west, and over the horizon could see the dot of a Federation battlewagon in the distance, growing larger.

"The end is coming."

Harley turned around and headed north. He nodded at Hatcher as he passed, then picked up speed and drove away from the storm.

"It never rains," he said.

IV

The old mare carried the shepherd easily as she galloped south. Once, long ago, before the Rages, she was a young filly on a ranch. She was born there, and a man cared for her, and she felt loved by him, but then the Rages came, and she knew she must hunt humanity. She must hunt, and she must kill, even though it was not of her nature.

The little girl and the old man riding on her back, especially the old man, were outside of the Rages, and as she carried them, she felt the sorrow inside them but didn't know how to lift it. She rushed them toward the apple peddler's orchard and felt the girl caress her side. The mare hoped she might help ease their pain.

As the storm rushed toward them, full of lightning and thunder and vengeance, it parted for the mare, and she took the old man home.

V

The man with the grey eyes stood on a hill overlooking the highway. He wore a faded duster that kissed the ground as he bent low. He let fine grains of sand rush from his left hand to his right, from his right hand to his left, as he watched the Wrynd attack the Castaway and old man. When the animals came, he smiled, and when the apple peddler rode away with a girl child on a beautiful painted horse, he found himself grinning happily. Harley Nearwater was right. It was an intrestin world.

Harley drove north, racing away from the storm. The surviving Wrynd chased him, and the man with the grey eyes watched them flee and let the sand fall from his hands. A shadow slinked forward, looking at him with its pink eyes. He nodded approval and opened his coat. It faded inside, its eyes lost in a sea of eyes staring out from the grey man's duster, like stars on a cloudless night.

VI

The Rages wrapped dark and deadly arms around the deserts of Castle Valley, blotting out the midday sun, swirling dust into the heavens faster and faster until it cut like glass everything it touched. Harley drove north, pushing the pickup as fast as it would go, but the storm already encircled him, trapping him in its baleful eye.

When constructed, State Route 10 cut through hills that looked like colonies for monstrous ants. Driving through these cuts on a blustery day, which was an everyday kind of day in the spring and early summer, crosswinds would pummel vehicles and try to rip the steering wheel from a driver's hand. Trying to drive through these same cuts at 150 klicks an hour while fleeing hurricane strength winds was another matter altogether. He cursed as the wind tossed the truck right and left and it ended up off the road, its nose buried in the soft embankment of a hill.

He threw the truck into reverse and started to back onto the road, but when he looked out on the valley and saw one and then two, then three tornadoes touch down he thought better of it. He put the truck in park, hunkered down, and decided to wait it out. If there was a safer place to be while the storm raged, it was beyond his reach.

Before the Rages, when the world didn't seem so intent on humanity's destruction, tornadoes were almost unheard of here. They were an oddity and seldom had any real strength. Of course, so were swarms of locust, rivers of blood, disease, pestilence, and any of the other highlights of the apocalypse, but they were all commonplace now. The world was ending, and humanity thought they were living in a utopia. Harley reclined his seat and pulled a beer out of the center console refrigerator.

"Welcome to the future."

He caught a glimpse of Hatcher passing in the big truck. They had unhooked the cattle trailer and were crawling back toward the city. They didn't see Harley half buried in the side of the hill, and he raised his beer in a silent toast.

The storm continued to rage; the wind still howled, and the rains came down in horizontal sheets that blurred his vision. Thunder rumbled across the desert like some angry beast. The Wrynd would be hard pressed to make it through, and he counted himself lucky the wind pushed him off the road within the cut of the hillside. It offered more protection than he would find anywhere else. Sometimes, even the damned had a good day.

He fell asleep to the sound of thunder, wind, and rain hitting the windshield and dreamed of his mother. In his dream, he was a little boy again. They lived in a single-wide trailer in Kayenta, Arizona, and his mother worked at the Conoco convenience store in town, where they still sold gasoline, but mostly natural gas. They had a dog; a yellow lab he named Spot for some ridiculous reason only a small boy could understand.

The dog loved everyone except Harley. Spot would snarl whenever he tried to pet him, and he wondered now, some 32 years later while sleeping in a dead man's pickup, if the dog hated him because he named him Spot. He didn't think so. Harley's mother told him he had a way of bringing out the worst in people, and he guessed the talent extended to dogs as well.

Harley's father was a roughneck in North Dakota. He would come home only rarely, but when he did, his mother would smile and be happy, and he would be happy as well because his father was kind to them and would bring them presents.

He remembered a baseball he brought him and a glove to go with it, and even though he couldn't catch or throw very well, his father took him outside and tried to teach him and laughed because he said Harley threw like a little girl. Come to think of it; he guessed he did.

Then came fusion, and there was no need to go to North Dakota, but his father left anyway. He knelt on the ground outside of their trailer and said goodbye for the last time. He remembered there was no lawn in the yard, just dirt, everywhere was dirt, rock, and little else. His mother planted an apple tree, but it died, and it stood like a skeleton in front of the porch.

"I've gotta go Har," he said, holding onto his skinny arms. He called him Har all the time and would laugh and say, "Har Har Har," and Harley would laugh back. Wade was his name. His father's name was Wade. Sometimes he forgot, but he remembered in his dream. He had the most unusual eyes, Harley remembered. They would change colors, sometimes green, sometimes brown, sometimes grey, depending on whether he was happy or sad, angry, or glad.

"Why do you have to go?" Harley asked, and he wasn't crying because even then he didn't cry, even when the dog bit him, even when the bigger boys beat him at school, he didn't cry.

"For work. I need to go for work."

"But Mom says there's not any work anymore 'cause of the fusion."

"I've still gotta go. Gotta find something," his father said.

"Will you come back?"

"I will. Will you watch after your mom for me?"

"I will."

They both lied.

Before Harley's father left (whose name was Wade), he reached behind him and pulled a pistol. It was a 9mm. He held it to Harley as an offering. "To protect your mom. Do you remember how to use it?"

Harley nodded, took the gun, and his father left and never came back. The first thing Harley did with the gun was kill the dog. He was nine.

Then began the Energy Wars, and even though the war never came to America, they heard about it often enough, and he remembered his mom watching the news on an old-fashioned television in the front room.

He was thirteen when the United States passed the Right to Income law, and he remembered the awe and wonder he felt when he learned that RTI extended to anyone fourteen and older. He would be old enough in a year. He would have an income. He would be free. The day after he received his first RTI funds, he packed his bags and told his mother goodbye.

She was getting ready to go to work when he came into the front room; the pack strapped to his skinny back and his father's pistol tucked in the back of his jeans. She was going to work even though she received her RTI funds every week. A week's RTI was more than a month's worth of pay from the country store she started working at when the Conoco closed, but she was going to work anyway. He remembered thinking she was a crazy woman, his mother.

"Will you come back?" she asked him. She didn't look surprised he was leaving; he thought she almost looked grateful.

"I'll come back."

He did come back, but not for some time. He made his way to Denver, which was in a construction boom, transforming into a Hub, and rode his first White Dragon east, hopping from one rail line to the next until he ended up in Minnesota.

Minnesota was as close as he could get. All of North Dakota was Wilderness. The Exodus had begun, and everyone was moving to a Hub. He walked the rest of the way, catching rides when he could, and spent the next year crisscrossing the state, looking for any sign of his father. He never found him.

When he saw his mother again, he was seventeen, and his mother looked like she had aged twenty years in the three he was gone. A man lived with her, and when Harley saw the bruises on her arms, he pointed the gun at the man's head. He left without argument. He saw her twice more since; the last time was four years earlier.

She'll be dead soon enough. The voice was a harsh slap in his dream, and he opened his eyes. They were bloodshot and weary. The voice sounded like the rasp of Hatcher, and even though it was only a voice in a dream, he knew it was telling the truth. If his mother still lived in her trailer in Kayenta, she would be dead soon. The Wrynd would either push her to a Hub or devour her. And you couldn't push his mother.

The storm still raged outside, and Harley popped his last beer and drank slowly. He was hungry, but there was no food. He smoked a cigarette instead, cracking the window just enough to let the smoke out and a bit of the wind and rain inside.

His thoughts turned to the old man and the wildthings who rushed to his rescue, and he puzzled for answers. The world was a marvelous place, he knew. Humanity could do so much. They could replace one body part for another with a simple visit to a Medprint. Bad heart? No problem, print another one and a quick surgery later they would be on their way home, good as new. If they didn't like the world the way it was, they could slip into the Vale and create their own MyRealm. They could request to live at any Hub in the world or even the Wheel circling the planet, and they at least had a chance of getting a relocate permit. Even if they didn't, what did it matter? In the Vale, they could live there without being there.

Humanity had solved most of its ills, and if the world turned against them, it was a problem, but not an insurmountable one. Despite all of that, despite all the wonder and glory at humanity's fingertips, there was nothing Harley saw nor heard to describe what the old man kneeling on the pavement had done.

He flicked his cigarette butt out the crack in the window. It would be nice to have some answers, and since he wasn't going anywhere any time soon, he could at least see if he could find some. He slipped on his eyeset and entered the Vale.

VII

The battlewagon hovered on the outskirts of the valley, bobbing like a buoy as the wind howled and the storm raged. Thousands of lightning bolts pummeled the desert floor and tornadoes twirled their destruction. Cirroco watched from the bridge of the airship, smiling softly, her tail writhing slowly. Captain Moroni came to stand by her side, hands clasped behind him.

"We dare not take the ship into the Rage, Emissary."

"Dare not? Who dares not, Captain? You or I?"

"Venturing into that storm is not bravery; it is simply foolhardy.

Our sensors would be blind. It would accomplish nothing."

"Don't fret, Captain. I wasn't asking you to risk your ship. Stay right here. We'll wait and watch."

"Wait and watch for what?"

"Something interesting to occur, Captain. Something interesting." Cirroco turned back to the window.

Two significant Rages in as many days. While it wasn't unheard of, Rages of such ferocity were rare in this part of the world. To her, it signified Gaia's awareness of the events transpiring here.

"I may yet find myself a ChristGaian," Cirroco mused.

"What?" Captain Moroni raised an eyebrow.

"I'm having a conversation with myself, Captain. Please don't interrupt."

She pressed her hands against the window of the bridge and stared down at the valley below. Somewhere down there was the Leap the Lord Judge foretold, and they weren't the only ones aware of its existence. The Earth itself seemed to have an interest in this new creature walking among them. The only question was whether the Leap would be humanity's savior or Gaia's.

"Don't be coy," Cirroco said with a purr, her lips almost touching the window as her tail drew circles on the glass. "Come out from the shadows and show yourself. We're excited to glimpse your power."

Thunder rumbled, and she trembled. It was all so glorious to imagine, the power waiting out there, somewhere.

VIII

Harley linked to the Vale version of the Provo City Park he visited while at the Hub and sent an invitation for Marshal Tempest to join him. He didn't expect she would. He sat on a park bench and listened to classical music softly playing in the background.

There was no one there, and he watched as a gentle breeze

swung the swings and whispered through the trees. He liked it here, even though it wasn't real; it was a wonderful place to visit. He gave himself a book to read, an old-fashioned paperback novel, a Louis L'Amour western, and he enjoyed the feel of the paper in his hands. His mother used to read him his novels before putting him to bed. He was thinking too much of his mother and shook the memory away.

He read the first chapter before anyone disturbed him, and when he looked up, Jodi was walking toward him from the playground. She wasn't wearing her uniform. Instead, she wore a simple pair of shorts and a sleeveless shirt, and he admired her strong legs and trim body. Her hair was down and flowed over her shoulders. He wondered two things at once; the first was why she chose to appear to him in such a manner, and the second, why had he chosen to live alone? The first he hadn't a clue. The second was because people, in general, annoyed him, even beautiful people.

Jodi sat on the bench beside him and smiled as she surveyed the empty park.

"All alone, Harley?"

"You're here."

She nodded. "But why sit in a park without any people? You could have Fillers at least. It wouldn't be so depressing."

"I can't abide Fillers."

"Can you abide anyone?" she asked. Harley was silent for a moment, and she laughed. "I'll take that as a no."

"Thinkin' on it."

"Why did you call me here, Harley?"

Harley leaned forward and let the Louis L'Amour novel dissolve. "I was thinking about balance."

Jodi leaned forward as well. "Balance?"

"Balance can be a tricky thing to restore, once it's lost." He clasped his fingers and let them touch his dry lips.

"Agreed," Jodi said softly.

"I was just wondering when you have Wrynd using linktags, using scyes, pulse weapons, and driving vehicles, how that might upset the balance in your Seven Realms."

"I was wondering the same thing."

Harley turned, and their legs touched. He felt a charge like electricity course through his body. "It's your territory, isn't it, Marshal?"

"It is."

"Well, the lunatic army that attacked your Hub is still out there in the Wilderness. They're quite intent on killing me actually, which may be of no concern to you, but is a mild one to me."

"I understand."

"But that isn't the biggest problem with balance you're facing."

"What is?" Jodi asked.

"You have Gandalf out there as well."

"Gandalf?" Jodi raised a perfect eyebrow.

Harley stared at her blankly. His right eye twitched. "Never mind." He paused for a moment and then told Jodi an edited version of the Wrynd's encounter with the apple peddler, leaving out any mention of Quinlan Bowden and his family. He wasn't sure why he didn't include them, but it felt like the right thing to do.

When he finished, Jodi sat quietly, staring into the distance. When she turned, her brow knotted, and her eyes danced with questions.

"Is he the Greywalker?"

"No. He's something else."

"How can you be sure?"

"Just am. I think I saw something of the Greywalker's out there, at the end. If it was, I don't have much interest in meeting up with him."

"What do you think they are? The Greywalker and this old man?"

"Something beyond the Federation's Legion and even their

mighty Marshals. What I saw of them is beyond anything in any version of reality you claim to control. They twist reality like your Shifts twist it in their MyRealms."

"Perhaps what we think is reality isn't it at all."

Harley tilted his head. "May be, but it's the only one we've got."

"The Lord Judge believes there will be a leap in evolution. A being who has evolved abilities beyond any human. A superhuman who will usher in a new era of humanity."

"I don't think they're any evolutionary leap. I know this old man. I just never knew he could do what he can do."

"If they're not the Leap, are they a threat?"

Harley shrugged. "May be they're an answer."

"To what?"

He traced the curve of her arm next to his with his eyes. "To us."

"Us?"

"I met a young man on the trail who told me we were rotting."

"We?"

"Humanity. We're rotting, and Gaia knows it and is cleansing herself. That's what the ChristGaians believe. It's the reason for the Rages. Maybe the Greywalker and the old man are the answer to us. Something of humanity that hasn't spoiled."

Jodi pursed her lips. "Do you think you're spoiled, Harley?"

Harley thought back to the day on the swing when he watched the old couple hand out the most beautiful apples to the people of Orangeville. He'd reached for one, and the old man snatched it away.

"I know I'm spoiled."

Jodi studied him quietly, and he found her gaze pleasing. "What do your people believe, Harley Nearwater?"

"My people?" Harley's sat back and grunted. "My people." His mother sometimes told him stories when he was small, before his father left, before she grew to hate him. He remembered something of a Changing Woman, but nothing more. The last time he saw her, she wore a ChristGaian cross. He didn't know if she was a Christian when he was young or if she followed the beliefs of the Navajo. It didn't seem to matter. Whatever the beliefs of his parents or his people, those beliefs had done little to shape the man he was. "I think whatever my people are, whatever they believe, they'd rather I not speak for them."

Jodi smiled softly. "What do you suggest I do about it, this imbalance in the Wilderness?"

"I know what I'd do."

"And what's that?"

Harley stood. "I'd strap on a sidearm and take care of what needs to be taken care of."

"Such as?"

"You have a Wrynd Marshal in your territory using his scye. He's killed how many thousands in your cities already?"

"Emissary Storm and the Legion are on their trail. They'll be dead soon enough."

"You don't believe that any more than I do."

"How do you know he was a Marshal?"

"His scye is red, just like yours. Tell me he isn't."

"Killing Hatcher would serve your purpose rather nicely."

Harley winked. "Wouldn't hurt."

"And the Greywalker and this old man who commands the Rages?"

"I'd steer clear of them, but that's just me."

Jodi stood and they looked into each other's eyes. Beethoven's *Piano Sonata No. 14* played in the park. "Do you know where this old man went after the Rage saved him?"

Harley narrowed his gaze into a squint and shook his head. "I don't." The lie came easy to his lips. "Good day, Marshal Tempest." He left the Vale in a blink, leaving her standing in an empty city park.

Outside, the storm began to wane, and he slept for a time. When he woke, he opened the door and climbed out, and his boots sank into the sand. He made his way to the highway. Harley walked to where the slope of the hill ended and could see the entire valley. Lightning and thunder played a symphony to the north, and the black clouds still roiled. He caught the first whiff of smoke and looked west. The mountains were burning. With the wind, a firestorm would soon be racing north, south, east, and west.

Above the mountains, the massive battlewagon slowly dropped into the valley. It was heading toward Price.

It was time to move. He could go home and rest up for a bit. After a good night's sleep or two he could pack the truck and go through the San Rafael Swell until he hit old Interstate 70. There was still a service road following the high-speed rail.

He could drive until he hit US-191 toward the ruins of Moab, where a small hamlet of Neands and Pilgrims still lived and were preyed upon by Wrynd, who came down the Colorado River to terrorize the natives and eat lunch. From there it was an easy route south to Kayenta.

He could save his mother and forget about Wrynd, Greywalkers, and old men with powers they shouldn't have. He could forget about Marshal Tempest and how it felt to sit beside her, even in the Vale, and he could try to find a bit of peace in his world while there was still a world to find it.

He turned and headed back to his truck, already starting to smile because he missed his house, sitting on his porch and looking down on the sleepy small town and not worrying about people and how uncomfortable they always made him feel.

He took two more steps, and from the heavens something swooped and seized him in a powerful grip. Before he could do anything at all, something swept him off his feet and he soared north, toward Price, toward the battlewagon.

All he could think as the earth fell beneath him was every weap-

on he owned was in the cab of his truck.
So was his hat.

Chapter Nineteen

Oath of Fealty

I

Jodi stood in the empty Vale park after Harley Nearwater faded away. The Castaway troubled her greatly, but she couldn't deny any of what he told her. That troubled her even more.

She had made mistakes, and they were coming home to roost. She'd been too ambitious, and it had always been so.

Growing up in the Washington Hub, she only wanted to go west, to be in the great outdoors. She wanted to see as far as she could see and feel the age in the dry mountain dust. She wanted to hunt the great beasts of the Wilderness, to prove she was their equal. Mostly, she wanted the power that came from shining brightly, and there were too many stars to shine brightly here. They were less stars and more maggots infesting a carcass, squirming, and bloated, impossible to tell apart. She would never be all she knew she could be.

So, she pushed herself. She was the top of her class in school, in college, in history graduate studies. She was the best at her physical conditioning, the best at her weapons training, the most adept with the scye. She was a Marshal at twenty and selected as Chief Marshal of the Rocky Mountain Hub at twenty-five, a star she won because of her success in the Vegas Uprising.

The Neands of Las Vegas thought to start a civilization outside of the Seven Realms. They were building a fusion plant of their own, and she was one of those sent to convince them the Federation wasn't their enemy, that they should come in out of the Wilderness.

Things turned ugly and had it not been for the wandering castaway who stood with them when surrounded and out gunned; they would have died. She never asked Harley why he chose to help, and he never gave her a chance. When the battle ended, when the Neands of Vegas were either dead or subdued, he disappeared into the desert. Until now. She wondered why after three years he came strolling back into her life.

In days her entire world, everything she thought was real, true, and honorable, was suspect. Her Hub attacked by Wrynd and leading them a former Marshal who answered to the Lord Judge himself. They attacked the Hub with enough ink to infect thousands, and now more than 4,300 people were dead. Dead and their deaths lay at the feet of the Lord Judge of the Seven Realms. The same Lord Judge who sought the power of the Leap. What might he do with such power? How could she best serve justice?

She slipped from the Vale and returned to her apartment. She changed into her uniform, holstered her slayer and scye, and turned to the door. There was a knock. Before she could answer, the door opened, and High Judge Trevok slid inside, flanked by two of his advocates.

Trevok clapped his hands when he saw the surprise on her face. "Marshal Tempest! Did we catch you waking from a nap? I find it odd you could sleep after allowing so many of your charges to die at the hands of the Wrynd."

Jodi backed away. "I allowed nothing, High Judge. I think you know very well who holds the leash of the Wrynd."

Trevok only smiled. She tried to keep a piece of furniture between them. If they truly meant her harm, she could fight, but to do so would mean throwing away everything she ever thought she was. She wasn't sure she was ready for that. Not without more answers.

"When the Emissary said the Lord Judge had many tools at his disposal, that he had ways to test whether Harley Nearwater was the Leap, you knew he controlled the Wrynd and that he would unleash them on the Hub. You allowed him to kill thousands of your people. The very people you claim he means to lead toward godhood."

"Oh, Marshal, how naïve you are," Trevok tittered.

"I'm getting tired of being told that."

"Don't worry. You won't be much longer." Trevok continued to advance, and the advocates separated and went to block her escape. "We're all tools of our maker, Marshal Tempest. We each have a purpose under his design. And the Lord Judge is our maker. We're clay in his hands, and our purpose is whatever he chooses. The Leap is in the Wilderness, and even now we close around it. In time we'll harness its power and achieve our glory as a species. We'll subdue this petulant planet, and we'll reach for the stars. The Lord Judge will lead us to our destiny."

"And if Gaia and this Leap you seek turn against you, can you defeat a sentient planet? Can you destroy something beyond us in ways we can't even imagine?"

"We can," Trevok said. "And we will. It's a pity you won't be here to see it, but I believe your role as Marshal has come to an abrupt end. Justice for my people demands it." Trevok nodded, and his advocates unslung their scyes.

"You know nothing of justice," Jodi snarled, unslinging her scye. She leapt into the air and landed a kick to the side of the head of the first advocate as her scye clashed against the others. Her hand went to her slayer, and she pointed it at the High Judge. The second advocate threw herself in front of the judge, and the pulse blast meant for him pierced her heart. Jodi howled and spun to run from the room. "You know nothing of justice!" she repeated. "But you will."

She dashed for the doorway, and four other advocates rushed toward her. Behind them came a squad of legionnaires, and she turned and ran back into the room, blasting out the balcony doorway with her slayer. She jumped onto the railing and threw herself into space, and her wings swooped in and snatched her away. It carried her west, into the Wilderness.

She traced the Link signal of her conversation with Harley and sent her wings toward it as she slipped into her office in the Vale.

She sat behind her desk, breathing heavily, at a loss for what was best. She always thought only to serve justice, and in the end, she was only a weapon of a dictator. She looked out the window at the sleeping city in the Vale. Hatcher told her the true monsters were the people locked away here, hungry, savage and without compassion. She wondered if perhaps he was right about that as well.

Humanity in the Seven Realms was feral. They had lost compassion, empathy, and hope. They were more ferocious than the Wrynd could ever dare to be. They waited in the Vale, sedated but hungry to feast. To what purpose? Jodi looked up at the Wheel, staring down on the world, and shuddered.

She called out for Bon and Montana, the only people on earth whom she thought might consider her a friend. They answered her call within seconds and strolled through the door of her Vale office. She had to fight back a sob seeing their smiling faces.

"It's good to see you," Jodi said.

"Good to be seen, Marshal," Montana replied, grinning broadly. "You should come to MyRealm someday and glimpse me in my element. I'm truly magnificent."

"Only if you've a mind for perversion, Marshal," Bon said, slapping her large friend on the chest. "What do you require?"

"Your friendship," Jodi offered, and this time her voice did crack. "I've led you astray. The Federation isn't what we thought. There's no justice here. I mean to find it, and when I do, I ask for your support in defending it."

Bon arched an eyebrow, resting her hands on her slayers. "I serve you, Marshal Tempest. You've never led us astray."

"I'm no longer your Marshal."

Montana folded his arms solemnly. "Where are you going? We'll dance with you."

Jodi shook her head. "The Lord Judge means to make himself a god. I mean to stop him. But what I need from you is to be the Marshals you are. If I survive this, I'll need friends in the Seven Realms."

"What do you mean to do?" Bon asked.

Jodi gritted her teeth and stole the words of a monster. "I mean to tear the Lord Judge from the sky."

II

Edward hobbled across the wooden bridge separating his orchard from the rest of the world. The storm had come and gone, and other than a gentle rain, none of it disturbed his apple orchard. In the distance, the dark clouds still broiled, and he could smell a hint of smoke in the summer breeze. For weeks to come the mountains would burn.

He stared north and sensed the Castaway was in harm's way. He was now without weapon and surrounded by his enemies. Edward found no matter how hard he tried he couldn't bring himself to care.

He remembered the man Harley Nearwater when he was but a boy. He remembered him swinging at the park and that his Sara noticed him and took him an apple from the orchard. When he glanced toward the young boy, Edward's eyes glimpsed the future, and he saw that this boy would bring death to his Sara.

It would come at the hand of the boy swinging on a swing, reaching for an apple. Edward knew even at that moment it wouldn't be an act done in malice. The boy on the swing would be trying to help, in his way. It didn't matter. Sara would be dead. He denied the boy the apple. When the boy looked up at him, he hoped he knew, even as a small boy, that there was an old man who hated him. He hated him very much.

Edward also sensed Quinlan Bowden and his children were almost safely home. They hurt, and they grieved, but they were safe. For now.

Standing on the edge of his bridge leading to his orchard, he knew a visitor had been here, a creature of power, possibility, cunning, and hatred. In time, he would have to parlay with the Greywalker.

In the little house he called home, the little girl cast aside by everyone she ever dared to love sipped apple cider and refused to cry. He wasn't sure what to do with her, or even how to possibly heal her wounds.

He looked down the canyon road and knew in the days and years to come there were those in the tiny town of Orangeville and the great big world beyond who would suffer. There would come a time when he would have to do something about that. It wouldn't be today. Today, he would sit and remember Sara.

He turned his back and walked across the timber bridge, which was old, but not quite as old as he. He wrapped the orchard around him like a cloak and let the world slip away.

III

Pinnacle Peak stood defiantly, majestically among the bluffs. It was a tower of dirt and shale of the desert like an exposed and fractured rib of the Earth itself. Jodi dropped Harley at its base as she released her wings and flipped to the ground beside him.

He spun, stooping low, his right-hand rushing for a sidearm that wasn't there. Jodi stood in front of him, her right hand resting casually on her slayer and her scye hovering beside her.

Smoke swallowed the sun as the fires in the mountains raged. She didn't seem particularly concerned, but since she had wings, there was little reason for concern. Harley, on the other hand, felt a bit anxious.

Weaponless, he stood and clasped his hands in front of him, smiling softly.

"I liked you better in the shorts," he said.

She nodded. "I'm on duty now."

"And what is your duty?"

"Justice."

"Whose justice?"

Jodi paused, scowled. "Perhaps the worlds."

"And what part do I play in your justice?"

"There are mysteries at work in the Wilderness, Harley Nearwater, and you're somehow caught up in them. It's time to find out why."

Harley sighed. "I kinda thought that might be on the agenda when you scooped me up like that. Never had a beautiful woman sweep me off my feet before, Marshal."

"Stow it, Harley."

"Don't suppose you'd give me a weapon; make this an honorable fight?"

"Don't suppose." She pulled a pair of binders from her belt loop and tossed them at his feet. "Put those on."

Harley considered saying no and forcing her hand but knew from the ice in her gaze if he forced her hand, she would play it, and the dance would end. It was better to wait and see what other opportunities might present themselves than to rule them all out. He slipped on the binders and smiled a smile that looked like a grimace.

"Who are you, Harley Nearwater?"

Harley squinted into the distance. Smoke was starting to waft into the valley. "Just a no-account, Marshal. All I've ever been."

"You're not the Greywalker?"

"You know I'm not. So, what's your plan?"

Jodi checked the binders. She smelled like wildflowers. "There's several Wrynd down there who are interested in your whereabouts."

"The same Wrynd who slaughtered your Marshals and killed the citizens of your Hub. I'd rather not be on the Wrynd menu if it's all the same."

"I don't think it will come to that."

"Why's that?"

Jodi shrugged, and Harley grinned. "You think the Greywalker, or the apple peddler is going to come storming into town and save ol' Harley Nearwater, don't you? Save me and kill the Wrynd for you."

"It crossed my mind."

"Not going to happen. They have no interest in me."

"So, you say. But every time there's been anything out of the ordinary in the Wilderness in the past few days, you've been at the center of it. Bit of a coincidence."

"I have a talent for being in the wrong place at the wrong time, Marshal."

Jodi called her wings, and it swooped down and attached. She picked up Harley, and they flew toward Price. "We'll just see if your talent can present itself one last time."

The flight into Price took less than two minutes, and Harley tried to enjoy the ride. It looked like it would be the last flight he ever experienced. He glanced up at the early evening sky and could see nothing of the Wheel. Dangling from wings over the desert might be the closest he ever got to it. It was a shame, really.

IV

Dusk was rushing toward them, and Price was ghostly quiet when Hatcher, Reflex, and Solar returned in defeat and pain, bleeding from countless little wounds and several larger ones. The crows pecked and tore their flesh, and the shiftless wanderer shot him. Hatcher stared forward, a storm on his bloody forehead, his eyes distant. His scye sat inactive in his lap. The shot that crippled him was a marvel. How did the Castaway manage such a thing?

Hatcher knew Solar worried he might lose too much blood but didn't dare ask if she could tend his wounds. She was afraid he might kill her for even suggesting such a thing. She was right.

She looked at Reflex, who had deep gashes in his face and hands, and he nodded at her, smiling weakly. Hatcher knew when she linked to order three medkits. He considered ripping out her throat but didn't.

Other than Dagger Ash, she was one of the few Wrynd in the shield a Shift before turned. Hatcher knew she took it as a source of fierce pride he trusted her enough to allow her to live when she could access the Link. She was a fool.

Hatcher sat in the jump seat of the old semi, his mind wandering the past as his arm bled down his side, pooling in the seat and soaking his tattered pants. There was little in the way of pain, but Hatcher seldom felt physical pain. It was the mental pain that wracked his body. Pain, loss, and thoughts of revenge.

He was aware of Solar and Reflex beside him, aware of their concern and Solar's desire to feed. He again considered ripping out her throat to see if it might quell the storm of his thoughts, a storm broiling with failure, hatred, and longing for a life no longer his. He let the storm wash over him. It was a long time coming.

He knew when she ordered the medkits because he had a tracker implanted on every Wrynd with a linktag. He knew he was losing too much blood and took a mental note to reward Solar for her foresight when this was over. If he didn't kill her first.

Reflex turned the rattling semi off the highway and maneuvered the truck around the fallen Wrynd slaughtered by the apple peddler. Hatcher sighed and stared ahead. His tattered tongue ran along his fanged teeth. He used to have beautiful teeth. His teeth used to be white and straight, and they were his without enhancement. He looked at his bloody arms and the gruesome tattoos beneath the blood. He used to have so many things.

Reflex took the off-ramp, and the truck coasted down Main Street to the hotel, its lights flicking on as the smoke of the forest fires swallowed the sun. Fires scorched the mountains, and within the city smoke and flame engulfed the shuttered remains of the university. The entire city might burn before the night was through, but Hatcher couldn't bring himself to care.

There were close to a thousand Wrynd surrounding the hotel, milling about aimlessly, some sleeping, some eating actual stork-ordered food, while they waited for the return of their Scimitar. Hatcher didn't recognize most of them.

They were the recently turned and had flared through their first dose of ink and were now waiting for the moment when they could flare again. He was running out of time.

He had a few days keeping his Wrynd horde together and organized, then they would start to submit to ink withdrawal, and the madness would come, the self-mutilation, the death. He had enough ink to keep his most capable skean alive. But to what end? If he were to exhaust it all so everyone could flare, then few days remained. There would be no more ink coming by stork. He had a weapon in his hands that would quickly fade away. If he was to use it, he must use it now, even if the weapons had thus far proven useless against what he hunted.

Harley Nearwater was a man, just a simple man. He might not be able to kill the demon in the shape of an old man and the apparition known as the Greywalker, but surely his Wrynd could kill a simple man. After that, it no longer mattered. He would welcome death. He had forsaken everything for duty to the Lord Judge only to face betrayal. The only thing left now was the sweetness of vengeance, then the relief of a cold death.

When Reflex parked the semi, Hatcher opened the door and climbed out, more unsteady on his feet than he believed possible. His scye hovered at his side, and even it seemed unsteady, glowing not so brightly as before.

Solar went to the waiting stork and accepted the three medkits. She handed one to Reflex, who took it with a worried glance his way. She brought the second one to him, and he wobbled on his feet, latched onto the truck door with his right hand and shook his head to clear his vision. He planted his feet and took the pack with a nod at Solar. She smiled shyly.

"Reflex," his voice was barely a croak. He cleared it. "Tend to your wounds, and then organize the others. Find Dagger Ash. I want to know who among us has experience with a weapon. Any weapon, pulse, sword, dagger, it doesn't matter to me. Gather every weapon you can find in this hellish city and test them. If they have skill, separate them from the rest of the shield and give them ink. Let them flare. I want them back after, ready to move."

"Move where, Scimitar?"

Hatcher looked at him, his face bloody and torn, his eyes red. "Toward vengeance." He took the medkit and walked toward the hotel, growing steadier on his feet as he went. The scye floated behind him.

In his room, he dropped the medkit on the bed. He stripped out of his clothing, opened the medkit, and the medical unit floated in front of him and made a quick scan of his body. It focused on the blast torn, gaping hole in his left shoulder first, using a half dozen slender metal arms to clean and suture the wound while administering a shot of medical nanites to help with the healing process.

It informed him sweetly that the muscles of his left shoulder and arm were too severely damaged to repair without a visit to a medprint. Hatcher nodded and told it later as he went to sit on a bar stool and let the drone finish its work.

With the severe wound sutured and the minor ones cleaned and repaired, the drone returned to its case and shut down. Hatcher went to the bathroom to shower. Blood flowed between his arm and the powerband, and he linked and unlocked it long enough to clean it away. His arm beneath the band was already growing pale and pasty. Like death. He left the powerband off, and after showering, tossed it on the bed beside the medkit.

He ordered new clothes and food. While he waited for them to arrive, he went behind the bar and pulled out his old pack; the pack where he had hidden his scye and sidearm. The pack holding his betrayal to the Lord Judge.

He fished inside and brought out another item of betrayal to his lord. The memory cube was an antique the size of his fist. He pushed a circle imprinted on one of its sides, and a light band flashed from another. It was a simple hologram, and it showed him in painstaking detail the memories and treasures of a life forsaken for duty.

He watched the moving and still images there, and the moments trapped in time seemed to be so long ago. It was more than twelve years since called before the Lord Judge.

It was an honor few could ever help to obtain, the Lord Judge told him. Hatcher, who was Marshal Balanger then, wished Vania could be with him. He wished Vania could see him reach the glory a lifetime of dedication and service earned him.

The Lord Judge, sitting upon his throne in a chamber so opulent, so glorious to behold Hatcher fought tears as he knelt at his feet.

"I am a Marshal of the Federation, knight of the Seven Realms; I am the sword of justice. I do your bidding, my Lord Judge." Hatcher's voice cracked with emotion and pride as he pledged himself to his lord, and when he looked up, the beautiful Lord Judge was smiling down.

His reward for service was to give up everything he held dear. His title, his star, his scye and his sidearm. He was to give up his only child. His life as he knew it was to be forfeit, and he was to become a Wrynd. Not only a Wrynd, but a Wrynd Scimitar, a monster of the Wilderness, and he was to destroy with teeth, claw, fist, and strength the enemies of the Federation. He was to push the Federation's people to a Hub or devour them.

They must protect humanity, endow their rights. It was the duty, the glory, and the privilege of the Seven Realms. It was the reason for its existence. The Federation Senate forbade the forceful relocation of citizens from the Wilderness, and the Exodus had ended. Those who would come to the Hubs had already arrived. The rest would remain in the Wilderness unless properly motivated. The Senate must abide by the people's wishes, but the Lord Judge must answer to a higher authority. He must guide his people to their destiny, a destiny of which they were oblivious.

Humanity had all but ruined its calling, but the Seven Realms saved them, redeemed them, and gave them purpose. The Federation gave them dominion over the Earth and the Vale, with the potential to dominate the universe itself, in the proper time. The Marshals were his servants of destiny, as were the Wrynd. To lead the Wrynd required men and women of great strength, great character, and determination, men and women who could control their emotions even as ink consumed them with hunger, swallowed them in chaos.

Marshal Trenton Balanger bowed his knee and swore his new oath of fealty to Lord Judge Syiada, and Marshal Balanger died where he knelt, and Wrynd Scimitar Hatcher was born. His only weapons were to be teeth, claw, fist, and strength until the Lord Judge called him forth into battle. He would terrorize the Wilderness and drive those living there to the Hubs or slay them. He would forget Vania and anyone he knew in any realm. He would become an outcast, an addict, a cannibal. The Federation would care for Vania as the royalty she was. Hatcher swore his oath.

Shortly after, he made his betrayal, before the carefully planned death of Marshal Balanger, he ordered his memory cube and stored the images of a life forsaken. He purchased his pack and hid away the cube, his scye, and sidearm. While he felt guilty for disobedience to the will of his lord, he thought he deserved this much for what he gave. He deserved some small trinkets of a life once his.

Before he left the Wheel, a medprint transformed his straight, beautiful teeth into daggers; lengthened, strengthened, and filed into claws the nails of his hands and feet, tattooed the grotesque images of death and mutilation on his body.

Two shuttles left the Wheel that morning, the one he flew on and the one the Histories reported he flew on. The second one exploded over Panama. There were no survivors. The other flew toward North America. As the transport hovered over the red rock of the Utah desert, Syiada's servants injected him with ink and tossed him out the cargo hold. St. George and the Rocky Mountain Hub twinkled in the distance.

He killed seventeen people that night on the outskirts of the Hub. He ate some of those he killed, delighting in the discovery of what parts were sweet, what parts were bitter, relishing in the joy of the flare. The next day, with the flare subsiding, but the memory and hunger of it still in his mind, a stork arrived with a case of fifty vials of ink. He started his shield that day, careful to keep their numbers small so as to not raise the alarm of the Federation Senate. They were a pestilence, like the Rages, but they were of no great concern.

He crossed paths with Harley Nearwater in the years since becoming Scimitar. He was someone the Neands and Pilgrims in the Wilderness feared almost as much as the Wrynd, so he served his purpose. Not killing him when he could was a mistake.

Hatcher couldn't say he was happy in this new life because there was no happiness among the Wrynd, only hunger and lust. He was all but insatiable in his hunger and lust and understood that was why Lord Judge Syiada chose him.

Then came the day he saw Vania. His daughter. The memories of the life he used to live flooded back.

Seeing Vania after so many years shook Hatcher to his core, and he found himself on his knees. She was young and powerful, beautiful beyond measure. Everything he hoped she might become. He watched her, and her pathetic husband and children play in the park, and he knew he must reach out to her, despite his vow. He deserved his daughter back. He sent his daggers to gather her up. He abandoned her as a teenager, and the reunion was not as he hoped. She ranted and wailed against him, but when he pierced her arm with ink, she was ferocious beyond measure.

She cried and begged for her life, prayed for her husband and her children, but when the ink stained her veins, she was voracious and killed all five Pilgrims he set aside for her. The next day, with the flare soothed within her, he arranged for a mobile medprint to meet them in a clearing on top of the mountain and she received claws and fangs. She was finally the greatest champion the world ever saw, just as he knew she would be. Back when his duty didn't forbid his dreams.

Two weeks later she died by Harley Nearwater's sword, struck down by a coward just as she was to devour her husband and reclaim her children. Together, as mother and grandfather, they would have raised them to be the prince and princess of the world. Looking at his memory cube of the daughter he once knew, doubt danced on his brow. Vania said her husband's name before Harley killed her. He cried at her, and she said his name, and Harley used that moment to strike her down.

Hatcher turned off the cube and tossed it back into the pack. She would have killed her husband. She would have killed him and stayed if the Castaway hadn't intervened.

Harley Nearwater killed his daughter, and he was present when the apple peddler slayed his Wrynd. He didn't know who the old man was, but the Castaway did. The old man held power beyond anything Hatcher had ever seen, but he would find a way to kill him.

The clothes and food arrived, and Hatcher dressed and ate and thought of vengeance and Lord Judge Syiada, who betrayed him.

There was a knock at his door, and Reflex opened it slowly. "Scimitar?"

Hatcher stood and stretched. His arm still ached, but the medkit had done an excellent job. He felt much stronger. "What is it?" His voice felt like his own again. He had regained his purpose, and his purpose was revenge.

"The Marshal is here."

Hatcher gritted his teeth, strapped on his sidearm, and put on his powerband. If the only way to vengeance was through the Marshal, then so be it.

"Are there others with her?"

"No. She brings the Castaway. Harley Nearwater is with her. He's wearing binders."

A slow, joyful, terrifying grin washed over his face. He roared with hatred, with anger, with triumph. He spun up his scye and raced out the door.

V

They landed in the parking lot of the Castle Valley Inn and were immediately surrounded by Wrynd. Jodi sent her wings to hover over the city and calmly smoothed her uniform as if she was preparing for a meeting. She glanced around as the Wrynd gathered. For the first time since becoming Marshal, she was truly alone. Bon and Montana might answer her call, but if they did, it would be treason. The badge on her chest was meaningless now.

A skinny young female Wrynd aimed a slayer and fired. Jodi's scye deflected the blast, and she sent it to strike the woman in the side of the head. She fell dead on the pavement.

Dagger Ash walked out of the darkness and into the streetlight, smiling. His scye hovered beside him. He tapped his sidearm softly with his right forefinger and nodded to Jodi. "Where's your friend? We have a dance to finish."

"A dance for another day, I'm afraid."

"Pity," Ash said.

The night was settling fast, and with it came the smoke from the mountains. In the distance, the fires advanced, burning, roaring, consuming. Jodi didn't give it long before breathing in Price became something of a chore. The fire wasn't likely to stop until it took the city. She didn't think it would be much of a loss.

Another slim Wrynd rushed into the hotel, and a short, attractive woman with a sadistic smile sidled up to Harley. "Looks like I might get me some man jerky after all," she whispered.

Harley narrowed a gaze. "Not sure you could digest me, girly." The young woman snarled and stepped away.

A roar erupted from the upper floors of the hotel, and Harley sighed. He didn't look as worried as Jodi thought he should. But Harley never appeared to be what he should.

"He sounds excited to see me," he muttered to Jodi.

Jodi nodded. "If you have help coming your way, you might want to ask it to hurry."

The big Wrynd Scimitar stormed out of the hotel and cast a murderous glance toward Harley. The lights of the parking lot were shining brightly, but not bright enough for her to see a way out of this if those she thought might be watching Harley didn't come to save him.

"Harley Nearwater!" Hatcher cursed and raced toward him; his clawed hands raised above his head. The Wrynd parted.

The instant before he laid hands on him, Jodi stepped between the two, and her scye hummed menacingly. Hatcher batted her scye away with his, but before he could take another step, Jodi pulled her slayer and pointed it at his forehead.

"Hold." She said it softly, but with authority. Out of the corner of her eye, she saw Harley grin. She was pleased even as her nerves made her shiver in the dark.

Hatcher took a deep breath and lowered his hands. "You bring him to me, Marshal, and then won't let me have him?"

"You'll have your chance." She lowered her slayer but didn't holster it. The Wrynd Scimitar was clean and freshly showered. Jodi thought Harley looked considerably worse for wear than a maniacal cannibal.

"What are we waiting for?"

"I was hoping to see something of this old man and the Greywalker."

"The Greywalker won't help him!"

"How can you be so sure?"

"He told me so!" Hatcher roared.

Jodi bit the inside of her lip to hide her surprise. "You've met the Greywalker?"

"We've met. He has no interest in Harley Nearwater."

Harley smiled and whispered. "Told you." His breath tickled her ear.

"But the old man might."

Hatcher paced, his claws clenching and unclenching. "You think this one has friends out there who will come to his rescue?"

"They did before."

"Ahh! He was just in a fortuitous location. Looking at him now, I realize what a fool I was to think anyone of power would befriend a man like Harley Nearwater." Hatcher stepped toward the smaller man and hovered over him. "What say you, Castaway? Do you have any friends, any friends at all in this great big world?"

"Well, I used to count you as a friend, until I put a blade through your whore's heart."

Harley smiled up at the Wrynd, and Jodi shook her head as she watched Hatcher's neck pulse. A vein in his forehead was now on prominent display. It looked like a lightning bolt. She tried to get between the two of them, and Hatcher lashed out, throwing her aside. He grabbed Harley by his shirt collar and lifted him into the air. He tried to raise his left fist and grimaced in pain. Harley grinned, and Jodi thought perhaps he wanted to die, after all.

"She was my daughter!" Hatcher used his forehead like a hammer to strike Harley's, and he fell to the ground, rolling to a stop beside an ancient semi.

Jodi climbed to her feet as Harley scrambled under the truck. Hatcher reached for him, and a scream of panic and fear pierced the night air.

"Rages!" A high-pitched voice shrieked.

The Wrynd scrambled for cover as wave after wave of animals exploded through the parking lot. It wasn't a Rage, not truly, Jodi realized. It was a stampede of every animal calling the mountains home as they fled from the fury of the firestorm.

Jodi crawled under the truck beside Harley as a herd of elk numbering in the hundreds dashed through the parking lot. Even a larger herd of deer, then cattle, sheep, coyote, bear, and hundreds of other animals followed.

Together, the animals made a giant, writhing ribbon of nature with a common destination, away from the fire. At the sight of the Wrynd, some of the animals attacked. As Jodi watched, dozens of Wrynd fell, and the rest scrambled for the hotel. Hatcher had disappeared.

"Are those moose?" Jodi asked, incredulous. There were three trampling through the parking lot.

"Yep. Moose. Wouldn't surprise me to see a couple of giraffes, an elephant or two, and some trained monkeys next," Harley said.

Jodi looked at him, and he was grinning like a fool. She fought the sudden urge to kiss the ugly cowboy. He had a way about him, that was for sure.

The screams of the Wrynd and animals combined into a furious roar through the parking lot and smoke billowed down from the approaching fires. Jodi stared at Harley, fighting a smile of her own.

Harley held out his bound hands and winked.

"They're not coming for you, are they?" Jodi asked.

"Would you?"

Jodi released the binders with a thought, and Harley handed them back. He looked at her sidearm, and she shook her head.

"No chance."

He shrugged and cast her one last glance, then scrambled out from under the truck and into the cab. When the last of the animals raced through the parking lot and down Main Street, she climbed from beneath the truck, and he started it and drove out of town.

As the Wrynd streamed out of the hotel, Jodi stood in the parking lot and watched Harley drive away. This time, she didn't try to hide her smile.

VI

The man with the grey eyes learned over the years to not be surprised by anything. He'd seen too much, been witness to too many miracles, not to know they were true and all too often completely without direction. They simply happened from time to time, and those caught in their path could be pleasantly surprised or destroyed.

He watched Harley Nearwater escape death several times during the past few days. The first time was because whether he saw anything of value in the man or not, he couldn't deny Harley had skill and a certain animal instinct keeping him one step ahead of his bad luck. The other two times had been because of his association with Quinlan Bowden and his children. The young father had been a concern to the man with the grey eyes, but no longer was because he returned to the Hub. Quinlan Bowden and his children were back where they belonged. For now.

Harley showed a change in character of late that was disturbing. He showed a change in character when he let Quinlan and his children live after their first encounter with the Wrynd. He even gave the young man his sword!

He showed a change in character when he stopped to help the old man and his wife. The fact his actions resulted in the death of the old woman was the only thing of value the man with the grey eyes could see coming out of the whole ordeal. He waited to help the apple peddler, to try and save him even though he knew the Wrynd were coming. Why would Harley Nearwater do something like that?

The Greywalker sat and stared in amazement from the roof of a collapsing discount store as animals rampaged through town, a mass of nature fleeing the forces of nature. That they were all running in the same direction gave him a moment of pause to test the air and see if the Apple Peddler might not be playing a part. He was surprised when he could feel nothing of his presence. Surprised, but not terribly so. It was simply a miracle, and Harley just happened to be one of the benefactors. The surviving non-Wrynd residents of Price were also benefactors. They used the opportunity to head south as well and escape the dead city by whatever means they could. Most of them would become a victim of the animals they now followed, but that didn't in the least diminish the glory of the miracle taking place.

He was also not surprised when the Marshal released Harley. He knew she had the mettle to kill him but lacked any real desire. Like Harley, she was a wildcard worth watching. When Harley drove into the night, the man with the grey eyes followed him with senses he developed over countless years. The truck turned and headed toward the canyon, toward mountains that would burn. The Greywalker dropped from the roof of the two-story building and landed lightly on his feet.

He walked south, humming softly to himself, as he sometimes did.

CHAPTER TWENTY

ALLIANCES

I

As Harley disappeared, the wind shifted directions, and smoke billowed behind her, clearing Jodi's line of sight. She caught movement out of the corner of her eye, a shadow dancing in the night.

Something sat on top of the building across the street. Something watched. It dropped off the two-story building and landed easily enough, as if the drop of more than twenty meters was of little consequence. It walked south down the middle of the street, more clearly into Jodi's field of vision. It was a man of average height, wearing a long coat in the middle of summer. In the darkness, she could make out none of his features, but she knew who he was.

"The Greywalker." Her voice was a hush in the night. The Wrynd coming out of the hotel were making a racket, but above their din, she thought she might hear humming, the pleasant humming of someone quite pleased. The figure in shadows walking just out of reach of the streetlights might have turned to her when she whispered, might have flicked her a wave as he walked out of sight. She couldn't be sure. What she was sure of was he wanted her to see him.

II

Hatcher pushed through his Wrynd as he made his way outside. He was once again bleeding from the forehead, and a had new gash across his abdomen. The herd of elk trampled him to the ground, and he managed to roll out of the way and crawl into the lobby.

Harley and the semi were gone and standing in the parking lot with her hands on her hips, and a smile on her face was Marshal Tempest. She let him escape.

"Where is he?" Hatcher spoke softly, coolly, but there was no mistaking the menace in his voice. Jodi didn't seem to notice.

"Not here." She was still smiling.

Hatcher drew his sidearm and fired. The pulse blast should have cut a hole through her chest, but her scye deflected it, and the blast went wide. Hatcher's scye dove at her head and Jodi did a somersault while her scye countered, coming up on her feet and drawing her slayer. She didn't fire. Hatcher fired repeatedly; each blast countered by Jodi's scye. The other Wrynd watched in silence as their Scimitar attacked and the Marshal parried. With each attack, Hatcher realized the young woman was faster than he, faster than he'd ever been.

"You can keep trying to kill me," Jodi said as she deflected another attack. "Or we can go and get them."

Hatcher stopped firing. "Them?"

Jodi strode toward him. "Harley and the Greywalker. He was watching from across the street."

Hatcher stood puzzled and then smiled. "So, Harley does have a friend."

"Who'd a thunk it?" Jodi drawled.

He stared into the dancing smoke, his eyes far away and his face blank. Jodi snapped her fingers impatiently. "Let's go."

Hatcher gave Jodi a sidelong glance, but let it be. "Dagger Ash!" he called.

The gunslinger pushed through the crowd. Among them all, he looked as if he had just awakened from a siesta. He was smiling, and Hatcher marveled. He would be Scimitar one day, if he survived.

"We need transportation for the Wrynd," Hatcher said softly.

"How many of us?"

"All of us."

Ash shrugged and summoned Reflex. The young dagger puzzled for a moment, then grinned, slapped his hands together, and pointed at Hatcher. "School buses."

Hatcher nodded. "Go get them."

"We're going to school, Solar!" The young Wrynd screamed, and they both dashed into the night.

Some of his Wrynd looked like they had seen better days. There were middle-aged, overweight men and women in the group and youth who looked no older than twelve or thirteen. The only reason they were there was because they knew this was the only place to get another dose of ink. He wondered if they would be of any significant help in their quest.

"Do you really mean to take everyone?"

Hatcher grinned, showing his fanged teeth and Jodi scowled.

"I want them all. A little old man defeated us. What if this Greywalker's power exceeds his? We attack as a shield."

The young woman shrugged, and Hatcher considered the wisdom of this uneasy alliance with the Marshal. She was good with slayer and scye, better than him, perhaps better than Dagger Ash. She would be of more use in killing Harley and the Greywalker than his Wrynd.

"Harley is yours, but the Greywalker, when we take him, is mine." Jodi strolled through the hotel doors. Her scye trailed after.

III

Once outside of Price the animals scattered, most running west into the desert, some turning and going south, even more simply stopping in the fields outside of the city. Harley continued down the old highway, a sense of urgency building. Hunted and with no weapons while driving a truck groaning with every klick, he was running out of options.

West of him was his pickup and weapons. Southwest of him was home and a life he once took for granted, but no longer did. He could continue going southeast and eventually reach Kayenta, perhaps even find his mother, but the road was long and fraught with danger. He had no way to protect either of them. If he did find his way there, the Wrynd would be right behind him. He had to find another place to hide and wait for them to lose interest. All he needed was an opportunity to double back and reach his weapons. Then he could make a stand.

He stopped the old semi in the middle of the highway outside of the ghost town of Wellington. If he kept going southeast, he might be able to find weapons in Green River or Moab but doubted it. Green River had nothing left worth taking. Moab was a better choice, but it was almost barren as well. He could find himself trapped between two hordes of Wrynd. To the southwest was the desert. He could double back and try to reach his truck but ruled it out. Hatcher would expect as much.

Sitting in the middle of the road in a dying semi, Harley turned his eyes to the mountains of the north and a smile curled his lips. Now that, they wouldn't expect.

He turned and headed toward a burning mountain.

IV

Harley drove toward the burning canyon with the headlights off. Twice he almost drove off the road and down a ravine into a dry wash. He slowed the semi to a crawl and squinted into the moonlight to make his way. The fires were behind him now, and the wind had shifted, pointing south rather than east, and buying him time. The inferno pointed toward Price, and he grunted in satisfaction.

"Let them burn."

After two hours of crawling toward the canyon, he stopped the truck and climbed out to stretch his legs and relieve himself. He had driven a little over twenty klicks. It was slow going, but the truck would be a clue he dared not leave behind. If they found him it would be a means of escape faster than boots on pavement. The road now offered two choices. He could continue up the canyon or turn right and drive into a trap of cliffs. He aimed for the box canyon.

He scanned the skies. To the north, the sky was black, and the fires in the mountains glowed. To the south, the sky dazzled in starlight and the Milky Way was an endless ocean of beckoning calm. He sighed and leaned against the truck grill to smoke a cigarette. He had six cigarettes left and no means to get anymore. He tried to enjoy the smoke.

The moon was a half circle in the west and played peek-a-boo in the burning sky. The Wheel glowed, and he frowned, staring up at it from so far below. There were 10,000 people living in a giant wheel in the sky, floating in the vast and endless ocean of Outland. He wanted to be one of them. In all his life, that was the one thing he could remember he wanted. He wanted to live in the Wheel and look out and see the Earth floating below and know he wasn't a part of it; he was somehow separate from all the cares and turmoil.

When he was a boy and learned of the Wheel, learned people

lived in space, he grasped the idea tightly and wouldn't let go. Dad left, and his mother was sad and angry and didn't seem to like him very much, so he held onto the thought that someday he might live in space.

He knew of the Vale and all the things to experience there; he could fly or swim underwater or be anything he wanted to be. He knew it was pretend, and even though the kids at school taunted him because he was a stupid Neand, he knew the Vale wasn't real. The blinkers might think in the Link they were doing amazing things, but they were really sitting on a chair blinking their eyes and tricking their mind. That's all the Vale was, a clever trick, like when Dad told him he was coming back but knew he wasn't. Just a trick, so they didn't think about what was real.

The Wheel was real, though. He could look up into the night sky and see it shining there. It was a real thing. People were living in space. They weren't on this planet at all, only floating above it.

Harley took another drag on his cigarette and remembered going to Mom as she got ready for work to tell her about the Wheel.

"Did you know people are living in space, Mom? They live on a giant wheel in space. It's a wheel so that it can spin, and they won't just float around, but be able to walk around. I would rather float around, but they spin it because the people there want to walk."

"I know about the Wheel, Harley." His Mom said in the same voice she always used after Dad left. It was a robot voice. It was a dead voice. It had been a year since Dad left, and Harley didn't think he saw her smile once in all that time. He wasn't doing a respectable job taking care of her, he knew. Dad wouldn't be happy at all.

"I want to live on the Wheel someday. I could live on the Wheel, and you could visit."

"I don't think there are any Navajo on the Wheel, Harley." She was buttoning her blouse, and it was a little tight. Mom was eating a lot more since Dad left. She would sit on the couch and watch movies on the old-fashioned television, and she would eat Cheetos and hardly ever say a word to him, but that was okay because sometimes she would let him watch the movies and sometimes she shared the Cheetos. "I don't think you would find one Navajo on the Wheel in space," his mom said.

Harley sat on the edge of her bed, considering. "Maybe I could learn to be an astronaut, then they would need me in space, and I could live on the Wheel."

His Mom looked at him, and her eyes looked as dead as her voice sounded. "You have to be good at something to be an astronaut, Harley. The only thing you're good at is killing. Remember the dog?"

Harley remembered, and he looked at the floor, ashamed that he killed the dog, but not sorry. "I remember."

His Mom brushed past him. "You're a no-account, Harley. That's all you'll ever be." The screen door slammed as she left him sitting on her bed.

Harley blinked away the memories and finished his cigarette, tossing the butt into the ravine. The smoke from the fires curled like tendrils across the sky and blotted out the shining ring of the Wheel.

"Sure would have been something." Harley climbed back into the truck and moved on.

He pointed the semi up Dugout Canyon Road and let it crawl, barely a hiccupping shadow creeping in the night. It was twelve klicks until the road ended, and Harley fought nodding off as he drove. The truck groaned, and something in the engine began to whine, but it trudged on. As dawn approached and he still saw no sign of pursuit, he held onto a glimmer of hope he might slip away unnoticed.

He could smell the smoke from the wildfire as the canyon narrowed and the cliffs on either side became rocky and barren. He knew the fire was traveling faster than he was.

Dawn greeted him by the time he pulled to a stop before a barricaded gate. The gate was three meters tall, made of chain link, with concertina wire on top. It was old and sagging, but still intact. Harley peered at it through the windshield. There was a large, faded sign standing on leaning posts on the other side of the fence that read Dugout Canyon Mine. A no trespassing sign hung beneath it. Both signs had been the object of target practice over the years.

The big truck's engine rattled, and Harley frowned. It wasn't going to be taking him back out of the mountains. He backed the semi up and turned the wheels, pointing it toward the jagged tree line and the rocky slope below. The river trickled at the bottom, and Harley put the truck into gear and hopped out as it crawled to the edge and slid down the cliff. Trees cracked and groaned as it crashed its way to the bottom. He went back to the fence and followed it as it stretched down to the river. A section bowed between posts, leaving a large gap. He wasn't the first person to crawl under the fence over the years, but he hoped to be the last.

His boots echoed in the box canyon as he made his way to the mine. Many of the old mine structures were still in the canyon, including the tipple and many of the conveyors, and as Harley walked deeper into the canyon, he felt he might be walking among ghosts; not the ghosts of those who died here, but the ghosts of dreams and hopes and a way of life. Once men and women worked here, sweated, and strained to follow a coal seam under a mountain and bring it to the surface.

As his boots followed the path they too must have walked, he wondered what kind of people would do such a thing? Were there any people like that left in the world? He looked up into the sky, where he knew the Wheel must spin. Perhaps there were some like that up there, but he didn't know if there were any down here anymore. Humanity had moved on, and whether they had lost something or gained something, he had no idea.

He had explored the old mine years earlier while hiding out

after a little theft and more than a little killing. The mine was decades closed, far before he was born, but it still held treasures. He was gambling some of the treasures he found while exploring still worked. He had bet his life on it.

There was no vegetation as he went farther into the canyon. Any soil that might allow it to grow stripped away or concreted over. The faint wind swirled up and out of the top of the canyon, so he hoped the fires might dash along the cliff face and sweep over them and the smoke might funnel out. In case it didn't, he hoped another miracle might be within reach.

While the ancient relics of the mine lay scattered across the site, there was little sign of coal. A reclamation process started but never completed carried away the coal but left everything else. The Rages came, the Exodus began, and the reclamation abandoned. A coal mine in a remote area of eastern Utah was of little concern with civilization trying to return entire cities to the Wilderness. Fences went up, the mine became forgotten along with the people who had toiled there.

He made his way to the mine portal and stood with his hands on his hips. Someone with time and explosives on their hands had blasted open the capped portal. Now a jagged hole large enough for men to walk through two abreast led into the darkness of the abandoned mine. Harley stepped closer and looked inside. The breath of the mine whispered. He didn't want to go into that darkness but knew he had to be ready to do just that.

He walked back toward the mine offices and went inside what had once been mine rescue. There were boxes of self-rescuers, and while the code date had come and gone decades before, they gave him some sense of comfort.

They might be protection should carbon monoxide contaminate the mine. He knew that might be the least of his worries but grabbed six of them and took them to the portal. He walked a dozen meters into the mine and deposited them, feeling in the dark for a likely place. Once inside, he was blind, and a trickle of fear danced up his spine as he wondered what in the hell he was thinking.

With the self-rescuers stowed, he rummaged through the offices until he found several metal garbage cans, and he carried them to the stream, washed and filled them with water he sloshed into the darkness. He scoured the mine but could find nothing that ran off a powerband. The only light he would have would be from his lighter. He sat on the rubble outside the portal and smoked another cigarette. That left him with four. Four cigarettes, dirty water in a trash can, and a hole in a mountain he dearly hoped didn't have dead air waiting to snuff him out.

Maybe it wouldn't come to that.

He heard a crackle from the canyon and looked down to see fire licking the trees.

"May be it would," he said.

V

Jodi watched through her scye while Harley calmly smoked a cigarette outside of an abandoned coal mine with wildfire creeping ever closer. She found herself smiling.

His ploy to hide from them almost worked. Jodi sent her scye down the highway as far as Green River and then doubled back, searching for where Harley left the main road.

The fact that there were few arterial roads didn't help the Castaway, but even so, there was an awful lot of territory to cover. Hatcher and Ash searched with their scyes, and she was close to giving up on finding him. The risk of using the Link and satellites was too great to take. She traced the road leading toward the burning mountain because it occurred to her if it was anyone else, they would never seek shelter there. Harley wasn't anyone else. Zipping above the treetops, she caught a twinkle of light on the ground. It was the sun reflecting off one of the mirrors on the semi Harley dropped over the side of the cliff. It signaled her like a beacon.

The fires were drawing closer, and she was going to call up her wings and go after him, but Hatcher wouldn't hear of it. There was an issue of trust between them that was growing tiresome.

"He might die in the fires."

"Then he'll die in the fires."

"Hmmm. Smoked castaway. Sounds tasty." Jodi learned the grinning girl's name was Solar. She fought the urge to kill her.

Instead, she just stared. "I hope you die soon."

They stood outside of the buses at the mouth of the canyon, waiting for the wildfire to burn what it was going to burn and move on. It looked like it might burn everything. While they waited, Jodi sent her scye to Price and found the city all but consumed, but there was no one left to care. The mountains above the city smoldered, and there was little in the way of vegetation left. Above the city the battlewagon Sidon floated, and legionnaires descended on wings. They were running out of time. Emissary Storm would be upon them soon enough.

Hatcher's little helper came back to the hotel with six school buses, and the Wrynd piled inside and headed south. Hundreds of others followed in every odd assortment of vehicle they found. The dust alone would be a beacon for Cirroco and the Legion, if not for the fires and smoke.

"So, we just wait for the fires to do our work?" Jodi asked.

Hatcher spat. "Do you think the fire will consume him?"

In fact, she didn't. "It could take a couple of days before we can get through. The Legion will be here before we can strike."

Hatcher nodded. "We'll flare, and then we'll strike, is that enough for you, Marshal Tempest?"

"You have nothing to feed on, Scimitar. The animals have fled, and the city is burning."

"Oh, I'm sure we'll find something."

In the end, they did. They found each other.

Hatcher pulled a dozen metal cases from the first school bus, and as each Wrynd convulsed with ecstasy, they turned and injected themselves with the drug as one. Hatcher stared at her, smiling, as the ink entered his bloodstream, and then the flare had him, and he attacked. She climbed onto the roof of the closest bus as the massacre began. The screams of the dying and the killing echoed through the night.

Jodi considered calling her wings and leaving until it was over, but she couldn't stop watching as the Wrynd attacked and killed one another, ripped, tore, and ate. Three times Wrynd tried to climb onto the bus and get to her, and she cut them down with her scye. They fell on the ground, consumed by the others.

When dawn came, it was over, and of the 1,220 Wrynd who left Price, only 706 remained. They did her work for her. They gathered their weapons, clapped each other on the shoulders, and licked the blood from each other's bodies.

The fires shifted and raced east and south, and while the mountain still smoldered, it looked like they might be able to reach the canyon where Harley hid. The Wrynd piled into the buses, cars, and trucks, and left. Jodi stood in the doorway of the lead bus and watched as Reflex aimed for the canyon. He was grinning and licking the blood off his lips.

She looked behind her and could see no sign of the battlewagon, but it was there and the might of the Federation with it. If the Greywalker were the Leap, she would have little time to snatch him away from the Lord Judge before the Emissary was upon them.

The Wrynd were going to be of little use but perhaps they would be enough of a distraction so she could do what she must.

VI

Harley made it through the night better than he expected. The fire encircled the canyon, and for a time, the smoke was thick, and he stepped inside the mine. He could look out from within and not feel quite so blind.

The wind scooped the smoke from the canyon, and he was soon able to step back outside. The fire passed him by, and he lit a cigarette to celebrate. He had two left, but if he was lucky, he could start walking out in a day or so. If he went cross country, he could make his way to his truck and go home.

He fell asleep under the stars, warm from a burning mountain.

He woke to the sound of vehicles coming up the canyon, and his hope of the evening before washed away. They found him, after all. He had no weapons, no food, and no way out of the canyon.

"That's just the way of it," he said with a sigh.

The portal stood above the rest of the mine and, standing at its entrance, Harley could see everything below, the tipple, the old conveyors, the load-out, and the mine offices. He could hide among the old buildings, but it wouldn't do him any good. It would be only a matter of time before they found him. The only place to go was inside the mine, and there was nothing in there but darkness and death. The mine served its purpose to save him from the fire but wasn't his salvation at all. It was his tomb.

He stood at the mouth of the portal when the first bus slammed through the gate, ripping it down as it pushed through. The other buses followed, and dozens of other vehicles poured into the narrow canyon. There were hundreds of Wrynd, all enraged.

Jodi was among the Wrynd, and when she saw Harley, she nodded in not an unfriendly way, but he knew there was no hope there. He was the bait, and whether she caught what she was looking for or not, his life was forfeit.

Hatcher stood beside her and noticed him standing above. He raised his arms in triumph.

"Harley!"

All hell broke loose. One of the Wrynd fired a pulse blast that hit the portal behind him, and then everyone was firing at once. There was pulse fire, rifle fire, shotgun fire, and even an arrow whizzed past his head. Harley dove to the ground.

Hatcher was roaring for them to stop, but no one could hear him, or perhaps they were just so hungry to kill they didn't care. He crawled to the portal and ducked inside, peeking back at the Wrynd. From one of the buses, someone ran with a decidedly larger weapon in his hands.

"Oh, shit," Harley said.

He stooped and ran into the mine as the Wrynd fired a grenade launcher. He tripped over something in the dark and sprawled on the rough floor. The blast threw shrapnel down the mouth of the mine. The mountain rumbled, and he looked back as the portal collapsed and the last of the light from the world winked out.

He sat up coughing, and darkness pressed.

He was buried alive.

CHAPTER TWENTY-ONE

ADDRESSING PRAYERS

I

Harley stood and cracked his head on the roof of the mine, cursed, and sat down hard, seeing stars. But at least he saw something. He crawled toward the portal, hands and knees stumbling over sharp shards of rock until he eventually came to a rough, uneven wall. He could hear nothing on the other side of the cave-in and wondered if they would dig him out or leave him to die alone in the dark.

He found no joy with either option.

He fished in his shirt pocket for his last two cigarettes and felt a moment of panic when he thought he lost his lighter. It was there, and he thanked whatever gods might be listening for that one bit of luck. He lit his cigarette, and the flame cast a wavering light that only pushed at the darkness but didn't penetrate. He sat back, smoked, and tried to remain calm. Caged in the dark, he knew death was coming. It was just a matter of time.

Darkness took on a physical form eventually, and for Harley it was all-enveloping. It was cold, it was harsh, and it was hungry, of that he was sure. It was hungry, and he was the only thing on the menu. When it came time to feast, he wondered if he might scream. He thought he would.

As he sat in the darkness of the mine and his mind raced backward. He remembered why he didn't like darkness, not complete darkness anyway. He enjoyed the night, but the night wasn't darkness, because even in the dark of night there was some light, shadows among the dark. He feared complete darkness, and his mind opened the door to a memory he locked away a lifetime before.

He shot the dog. He took the pistol Dad gave him, shot the dog, and watched the life bleed out of it. If he felt anything, anything at all, he couldn't remember what it was. His mother discovered him and the dead dog, and she was upset.

She struck him across the face, over and over. He felt as she struck him that she was striking him for something other than the dog, because he didn't think she cared for the dog all that much.

She took his gun, grabbed him by the arm, and pulled him into the house. She shoved him onto the couch and ordered him to stay. He sat because his face hurt, and his mother was upset. He didn't like seeing her like that, didn't like thinking she was upset because he shot Spot.

There was a closet in the hallway of the house. It was a small closet, and his mother kept the vacuum and the broom there and winter coats. As he sat on the couch with his face stinging from her slaps, she opened the closet door and threw everything out; the vacuum, broom, the coats, and even a toy soldier Harley looked for everywhere but was unable to find. It was right there in the closet all the time, and he reached for it, but his mother took him by the scruff of the neck, tossed him into the closet, and closed the door.

Harley sat on the floor and waited to see what might happen next. There was light leaking from beneath the door and along the edges, and he could see the shadow of his mother as she paced back and forth. Then she stomped into the kitchen. When she came back, he heard a sound, a *skrrrppp* he recognized but couldn't place. Then part of the light leaking from the doorway disappeared, and it became darker.

Tape! It was tape! She was using duct tape to steal away the light, and he was proud of himself for figuring it out. The light left him little by little, and when the last *skrrrppp* sounded and the last piece of tape was stuck to the bottom of the door, Harley found himself in darkness. Complete and utter darkness.

The screen door opened and slammed shut, and there only silence remained in the house. He stood and tried to open the door, but it wouldn't budge, and he realized she used a kitchen chair to block the door. He pounded and yelled for his mother, but she didn't answer, because she wasn't there. Eventually, he sat back down. Even then, he didn't cry.

Not yet anyway.

He didn't know how long it was before he sensed he wasn't alone in the closet, but eventually, he understood the darkness was not just darkness, it was something cold and something hungry. He soiled himself then.

It wouldn't be the last time.

He searched with his fingers along the floor, and at the back of the closet, he found a hole. It was a small hole he could fit two fingers through, and he wondered what made the hole in the back of the closet when he wasn't screaming, crying, and wetting himself.

When he grew tired of screaming, crying, and wetting himself, he heard mice behind the wall, scurrying. He thought he might have felt one crawling across his arm, and he screamed some more. He wasn't sure if it was a mouse at all, or something else, something dark and evil and feeding on him, one nibble at a time.

He didn't know how long he was in the closet. It was more than a day and less than a week, but other than that he wasn't sure. What he was sure of was the darkness was with him, and while it didn't consume him, it enveloped him, every part of him, and he found another reason to scream. He found another reason to cry, and he couldn't stop.

When his mother opened the closet door, food and water waited for him on the kitchen table. Ravioli, his favorite, and he ate and thanked his mother for the food. After he ate, she sent him to the bathroom to clean the mess he made of himself. While he scrubbed away the urine and feces, he thought that he loved his mother and should do a better job taking care of her, as his father asked. He should do a better job.

But when he had the chance, he ran away and left her all alone.

The memory washed over him as he sat in the mine, and the only sound he could hear was his breathing. It was jagged and rough, and it was scared. He felt the darkness pressing into him and gritted his teeth and tried not to be afraid. He was no longer a boy, and this was no longer a closet.

"I'm going to die down here." His voice was calm and collected, and it was hollow and without emotion. From down the shaft, he thought he heard the darkness reply yes; he was going to die down here.

After a time, he started to laugh. Laugh because what else could he do? Cry? Eventually, Harley Nearwater did that as well. He cried, laughed, and cried some more as the darkness sank into his lungs. When his bladder released and he soiled himself, he laughed even louder and cried even harder. Eventually, he fell asleep, holding his lighter in his hands.

When he woke, he was calmer, and sat up. There was still no sound outside the mine. He thought he might hear water dripping somewhere but couldn't be sure. He flicked his lighter and lit his last cigarette, and while he smoked, he thought back to the days before and what led him to the end of his life in the darkness of a dead coal mine.

It started with a death. It would end with a death.

He tried to remember why he killed the legionnaire in the hotel. Her name was Kara. Terrified and alone, he killed her because she pointed a pulse rifle at him. Was that the real reason? Did he really kill her because she pointed a gun at him? A lot of people pointed guns at him over the years, and he hadn't killed them all.

"That wasn't the reason," he said in the dark. His voice sounded giddy, almost childlike. He killed her because she said things that couldn't be true. She said things that mocked the world he accepted as reality. In the days that followed, every piece of that reality was torn asunder.

The end is coming. She said with a dying breath.

Since he pointed his sidearm and ended her life, he had done things the Harley Nearwater before that day would have never done. He saved a young man and his children when it gave him no benefit. If they died, the Wrynd might not have come looking for him, but he saved them. In Price, he did what he could to save them again, and later he tried to save the old man, not once, but twice.

He had done things contrary to his disposition, and he realized the man he always was, the man who grew from the boy released from the darkness of a broom closet, was no longer the man he wanted to be. He wanted to be something else.

"I'll change," he whispered to the darkness. "I'll change. I want to change." His whisper became a prayer, and he wondered when he last went to church? Had he ever gone to church? He remembered once being with his parents and going inside a beautiful building, and he thought that it might be Christmastime. Dressed in their best clothes, he sat between them and was happy.

They were quiet, but that was all he could remember. They were quiet, and he was happy. Was that church? He didn't know, but he found he couldn't stop praying. "Help me get out of here, and I'll change. I'll be better. I'll do better." He didn't know who he was praying to, perhaps only his mother. She let him out of the darkness once; perhaps she could again. It felt good to pray.

Something moved in the mine. He couldn't hear it, but he could feel it, a shift in the ocean of blackness. Somewhere in the darkness, something heard his prayer.

"Why would you want to change, Harley?" said a voice like sandpaper on metal, and Harley Nearwater's screams became so much more than ever before.

He didn't know how long he screamed, long enough that it hurt not only his throat but down into his chest. He screamed until he could scream no more, then he stopped.

"There now," the sandpaper voice scratched again, sounding pleased, sounding amused. "Got that out of your system?"

Harley reached for a slayer that wasn't there. "Who's there?" He didn't like the sound of terror in his voice, but it was there. Yes, indeed, it was there.

Laughter filled the shaft, the giddy laughter of a school child, and rather than muffled, absorbed by the darkness; it floated and echoed. "I'm a friend, Harley. Just a friend. You could use a friend, I think. You've soiled yourself, I see, sitting there in the dark. It's the broom closet all over again, isn't it?"

Harley could feel the cold urine on his jeans. Although he didn't know how whatever it was in the tunnel could see he soiled himself, the truth was the truth; he wet his pants like a scared little boy. Harley flicked his lighter, and the small flame cast what light it could. Something right beside him blew it out, and he screamed again.

"What do you want?" He struck out in the darkness and found only darkness.

"Want?" Harley could hear the smile on the gritty voice. "I was just in the area, just passing by, you might say, because I'm a wanderer on the path, just like you, Harley. I travel here and I travel there, helping where I can, hurting where I can't. I was passing by when I heard your little prayer."

"You heard my prayer?"

"Why, yes, I heard your prayer. You didn't address it, you know."

"Address what?" He flicked his lighter again, and this time it stayed on. Just out of reach of the tepid flame, he thought he might see something, greyness in the black, a shape that might be a mouth and two holes above it that might be eyes. "Address what?" he asked again.

"Why your prayer, of course. You didn't address it. Just 'please help me, oh please oh please' but you didn't address it. So exactly to whom were you praying? God, the Almighty Himself, or Satan, ol' Mr. Scratch, as I like to call him. He hates that name, by the way, which is why I like it so. So, which is it, the Shepherd or the Jackal?"

Harley peered into the darkness and could see nothing that could tell him who he shared the mine with, but he thought he knew. "God, I guess."

"Good enough. I rather thought so, what with the all the 'I'll be better, I'll do better' nonsense. You must be careful when you pray, Harley; you've got to be careful indeed. If not properly addressed, anyone could answer your prayer. Anyone at all."

"Like the Greywalker?" Harley shifted in his seat. The floor beneath his buttocks was becoming painful.

The voice in the darkness chuckled. "Bah. Greywalker. He's but a myth, isn't he? The boogeyman in the Age of Renewal?"

"So, you say."

"Yes, so I say."

Harley cupped his chin in his hands and tried not to be afraid, tried not to scream. It was so difficult. Here before him, in the dark, was the person who changed his life forever. "Why did you leave her for me to find? The legionnaire. Why did you leave her there?"

There was a shuffle of stone, and Harley imagined the Greywalker sat across from him. "I left her in hopes you might alter your course, Harley Nearwater. That you might find happiness. That you might find peace." The voice in the darkness sighed. "If you chose otherwise, I thought your choice might reveal the plots

391

of man and gods alike. Their plan for us as the great unraveling of our creation ends. But I underestimated your ability to survive. To create chaos. You are quite a talented man, Harley. The lives you touched, the lives you altered while I was distracted elsewhere will take time to discover."

Harley swallowed hard. His throat was dry, and his voice shook as he tried to use it. "Who are you, Greywalker?"

"Just a castaway. Same as you." More rock rubbed rock, and when the voice came from the darkness again, it whispered in Harley's ear. "Aren't you going to ask if I'm an angel of God? Perhaps God the Great Shepherd Himself, come to answer your prayers?"

"Are you?" Harley sobbed.

The Greywalker laughed, deliriously happy. "No. I'm afraid not. God doesn't make house calls, you see; you must go to him. Climb the mountain and all that nonsense. And before you ask, I'm not the Jackal either. Scratch and I don't see eye-to-eye on things, I'm afraid. I'm just another happy traveler on the path, who happened to hear your prayer."

"Are you here to answer it?"

There was silence in the mine, and when the voice answered, all the humor drained away. "Well, that is the question, isn't it, Harley? Truthfully, I've been watching you. I've peered into your soul and found no redeeming qualities whatsoever. Normally, I find that an attractive trait in a person, but with you, it gives me pause. Both the Shepherd and the Jackal would struggle to find a use for you, and while I value you, I still wonder if you may not be one who would create more mischief than you're worth. You have talents; there's no denying that, and if someone could only find a way to harness them, they could be of immense value. But for now, you're like a pulse rifle waiting for someone to pull the trigger. A scye, waiting for a mind to wield it. It might be better if I put you away, out of sight, out of mind, do you know what I mean? Until your talents might best be used."

"Talents?"

"Oh yes, talents. You have many talents, Harley, some you may not even realize. You're quite talented at making people hate you, for instance. You're quite the catalyst. You've shaped the course of things for years to come, put pieces into play in the great and final act of this grand charade I hadn't even been aware of, I'm ashamed to say. You've awakened shepherds I wished would stay sleeping, put people on paths that may lead to ruin. Putting the genie back into the bottle is no easy thing, Harley. I can't have you mucking about freeing genies before their time."

Harley shook his head. Whatever was in the dark with him was completely mad. "Who are you?" he shouted.

"I'm a little black rain cloud, of course." The voice said.

"What?"

The Greywalker sighed. "Those out there." There was a tap on the stone, close to Harley's head. "They think I might be an evolutionary leap they can harness to make them more than they are. They're fools, of course. I'm older than they imagine, and evolution passed me by long ago. My powers, however slight, are beyond them, so they think they must be mystical when they're nothing more than a whisper between intelligences that recognize one another."

"What?"

"Am I rambling again? I have a habit of doing so. Know this then, Harley Nearwater. I hope to be an atheist someday, that's who I am. I hope to not believe in Heaven or Hell. But I've seen the face of God, and I've seen the claws of Satan. I know something of them, and they know something of me, and while I don't presume to match their glory, their power, and their delusion, I hope to match their persistence, and that one day they might grow weary of this game and leave us be."

"Us?"

"Us. Humanity. The grand comedy we are and yet may be. The

realms of man are to come crashing down. Unless we find a savior. The Lord Judge thinks himself that savior, but he's a fool facing a war he cannot win. I, on the other hand, have decided to be that savior. I'm just as foolish but far more determined. Presumptuous? Probably so, but there it is. I face heaven and hell and deny them both."

"I've lost my mind," Harley sobbed.

"Quite so. But I've found it, and now I must determine what to do with it. Should I put you on the shelf for a later day; a day when your talents might better be utilized, or should I let the sad people outside this mine dig you out and make a snack of you? Decisions are such difficult things."

"All things considered, I'll take the shelf," Harley whispered.

The Greywalker gasped. "Will you? Will you truly? It will come with its challenges, I'm afraid, considering the desires of your prayer."

Harley shifted his legs, prepared to stand, although there was no place to go. "Challenges?"

"Yes. Challenges. If I were to help you from this place, I would have but one demand."

"Which is?"

"Don't change a thing, Harley. Go back to being who you are. Go back to being the boy who stepped out of the dark closet. Don't change a thing. You've displayed quite a few deviations from your true character of late, and the chaos in your veins has made a mess of things difficult to remedy. But I still see value in you and will save you from your fate if you promise you won't be anything other than what you were before."

"And if I can't?"

"Then I'll visit you, I'm afraid." Harley felt movement in the mine. He struck his lighter, and a face was terribly close to his own, a dark face with grey eyes and a gaping mouth with razor teeth. "It won't be a pleasant visit, Harley. Not pleasant at all."

Harley scrambled down the mine shaft, and his lighter clicked off.

"Are we agreed?" The voice sounded pleasant again, pleasant, friendly, and tinged with good humor.

Harley opened his mouth and sealed his fate. "Agreed."

"Excellent." Something scratched in the darkness, like boots against rock, and the shaft suddenly glowed. He shielded his eyes with his arm. The Greywalker was holding lightning in his right hand, and it pulsed and danced with a life all its own.

The man holding the lightning looked like just an ordinary man in a long duster and jeans. He wore cowboy boots, and his chiseled face, shaded with stubble, was handsome. His hair was dark like Harley's. He looked like someone Harley might once have known. The Greywalker grinned, and his teeth were white and straight, not fanged at all.

His eyes were grey, and swimming within them was humor, compassion, darkness, anger, pain and suffering, and everything Harley ever imagined and many things he hoped he never would. The Greywalker nodded at the lightning in his hand and laughed. "It's a neat trick, don't you think?" He turned to face the collapsed portal and threw the ball of lightning.

The lightning struck and exploded outward. Not a pebble, not a speck of dust flew toward Harley and the grey man. It all went outward, like a bullet from a gun, and the mouth of the mine blew open. Harley and the Greywalker emerged from the dust and the coal into the midday sun.

A dozen Wrynd had been trying to dig Harley out when the portal exploded. What remained of them was now on the other side of the canyon. The rest of the Wrynd stood beside the buses, and among them were Hatcher and Jodi. They ducked behind the nearest bus as the rock rained down.

On the horizon and approaching fast was a great battlewagon of the Federation and dropping from it like flies were hundreds of wings streaking toward them.

As the Wrynd raised their weapons, the man with the grey eyes looked at Harley, standing on the edge of the mine in soiled clothing, and winked happily.

"I hate Wrynd. Don't you hate Wrynd?"

He unbuttoned his duster, and within it looked like nightfall. There were stars blinking inside the grey man's coat, pink stars. The shadows began to pour out like a flood, taking shape into something that might be a dog, or a wolf, or a nightmare. They turned their pink eyes to the grey man, and when he nodded, they dashed toward the Wrynd. The killing started.

II

Jodi shook her head to clear her vision as the mine portal erupted. She ducked behind the bus, and when the downpour of destruction ended, she looked up to see Harley and the Greywalker stroll out. The Wrynd raised their weapons, and she found herself fighting a smile. Then the man with the grey eyes opened his duster, and the nightmares poured out.

The shadows fell upon the Wrynd, and blood flowed. They opened fire, but the Greywalker and Harley beside him seemed oblivious. Every shot went wide. The shadows continued to pour down the hillside, leaping into the air to envelop the Wrynd in their path, and the screams of the dying was a piercing echo in the canyon. She watched as Wrynd tried to fight back, but found nothing to bite, nothing to claw, and nothing to rip. As a shadow rushed toward her, she sent her scye into it, and the weapon passed through, and the shadow kept coming. She flung herself back and sprinted to the bus, scrambling up the open door and flipping herself on top.

Below her, Hatcher fired his slayer and sent his scye flying toward Harley and the Greywalker. He dashed up the hill, screaming like the possessed.

It was a slaughter. She aimed her sidearm at the Greywalker's head and fired off five quick blasts. Each shot seemed to veer away from him at the last moment and strike harmlessly to either side. He looked at her, and she saw him shake his head. A dozen shadows suddenly turned her way, their pink eyes glaring.

"Shit." She called for her wings and knew it would arrive too late.

III

The Battlewagon Sidon skimmed 165 meters above the ground as it hugged the canyon. Its great triple decks almost scraped the surface of the jagged cliffs. Captain Moroni stood rigid, looking out the bridge, giving orders to his helmsman, in short, concise barks. Ahead of the airship, arcs of pulse blasts flew into the sky from the canyon floor.

Cirroco stared at a control screen, zooming in on the carnage ahead, and Captain Moroni followed her gaze, giving a satisfied grunt. "We've found your Wrynd, Emissary."

Cirroco watched, enchanted as the shadows ripped and tore at those below. "The Wrynd and something more. Something much more."

"What are your orders, Emissary?"

"Destroy them all. But this one." She pointed at the dark figure standing at the shattered mine portal. "I want this one alive. If he is to die, it will be at my hands."

"And the other?"

Cirroco shrugged. "He's of no consequence. Send him to hell with the Wrynd."

Captain Moroni nodded and turned to his lieutenant. "Hold your cannon fire. Focus pulse blasts on the Wrynd and dispatch the Legion wings. Clear out the Wrynd." The lieutenant nodded, and the battle began.

IV

Harley was numb as he watched the chaos around him. Hundreds fired pulse blasts toward him and the creature standing beside him, but every blast fell short. He felt his knees buckling and almost fell, but the Greywalker reached out a hand to steady him.

"No time for napping, Harley." The man with the grey eyes beamed. "Isn't this fun? This is so much fun!" A pulse blast sent rock shrapnel erupting into the sky. None of it came near them.

The battlewagon loomed, and the Greywalker cast a glance its way and smiled. "Do you want to see a neat trick?"

The man with the grey eyes raised his arms outstretched, and Harley felt static electricity swirling, raising the hair on his head. Purple sparks of energy danced across the ground with manic glee, and from the sky, thunder rumbled. The Greywalker stood transfixed, and when he finally turned his head, his face was beatific, and his eyes were no longer grey but danced with a myriad of colors swirling in a storm. "Watch this," he said and pointed a long finger at the battlewagon.

Purple lightning reached up from the canyon floor and danced across the bottom of the battlewagon as green lightning flashed across the airship's decks. Something exploded, and fire licked the sky as the airship groaned and listed to the side.

"I love fireworks!" the Greywalker said with a giggle.

V

The Sidon bucked violently, and an explosion ripped open a large section of the lower deck of the ship. Legionnaires fell, screaming over the side, and Cirroco shouted in glee.

An emerald bolt of lightning burst across the canyon and erupted, skipping across the horizon, and fifty wings dropped like rain.

Beneath the airship, a Wrynd with a scye stood on a mound of earth and stone, striking down every legionnaire who dared approach, and Cirroco watched him with appreciation. The Wrynd, all but destroyed, the shadows who hunted them gathered to pounce upon the one still madly fighting. It was a pity one so determined should die so needlessly.

"This is madness!" Captain Moroni screamed, holding the side of his command chair, and struggling to stay upright.

"Isn't it, though?" Cirroco agreed.

"It is impossible. All of this!" He waved his arms out the bridge windows. "We have slipped from reality to fantasy, from science to wizardry. Our world is not as it was."

Cirroco grinned and gripped the captain by the neck. She kissed him fiercely and laughed. "Our world was never our world to begin with, Captain! Don't you see that?"

Another explosion shook the airship, and Cirroco noticed the first bead of sweat forming on Captain Moroni's brow.

"Run away, Captain!" Cirroco said.

Captain Moroni gaped, and she could see the panic building. He nodded and turned to his lieutenant. "Run away!"

"Sir?" the lieutenant asked.

"Retreat! Get us the hell out of here before it is too late."

Cirroco dashed out of the bridge, and as the great airship banked right and rose out of the canyon, she jumped from the deck. Icarus gathered her up.

She aimed toward the Wrynd facing the shadows, and as they prepared to strike, she reached out and caught him in the talons of her wings. Dagger Ash thrashed madly, and his scye rushed toward Icarus. Cirroco whispered into his ear.

"Another day, my sweet. Live to fight another day."

Ash looked up and smiled with ferocity.

"Another day!" he roared.

Lightning caressed the canyon cliffs, and Cirroco flew away from the maelstrom. "Delightful!" she screamed. "So delightful."

VI

Jodi ducked as lightning erupted above her head and explosions from the battlewagon sent debris raining down into the valley. A dozen shadows poured on top of the bus, and pink eyes danced as they slid toward her.

She didn't bother trying to fight them; they already proved they were above any attack by a mere mortal. The shadows advanced, and Jodi somersaulted away.

She was back on her feet and running the length of the bus when her wings swooped low, and she jumped out to catch it. The shadows chased after. One of them latched onto her leg, and she screamed in agony as long gashes appeared wherever it touched. The shadow slipped away as her wings soared. Drops of blood rained as she flew higher and rose above the canyon.

She strapped into her wings and the pain from the wounds of the shadow tore at her soul. She felt consciousness slipping away. Her wings carried her east, toward the battlewagon.

VII

Hatcher, the Scimitar of the Wrynd, dashed up the hillside, dancing out of the way as shadows pounced toward him. They were silent as they killed, but someone was screaming. It was him. He was screaming, and soon he would be dying.

Behind him, he knew his Wrynd were falling, knew the Federation had arrived and its betrayal was complete. He didn't care. The Greywalker was within his grasp, and so was Harley Nearwater. Before he died, he would wring the life from them. Beside him, Reflex and Solar ran, firing their slayers, and every shot missed the target.

Two shadows fell upon Solar, and her body turned to a mass of gore. Reflex stopped as she fell dying, about to yell in horror and more shadows fell upon him, and he was gone, his throat ripped away before his cry left his parted lips.

Hatcher made it to the portal, and his scye flew true toward the grey man. He howled in triumph. The Greywalker reached up and caught the scye in his right hand. It glowed and crackled, and he squeezed. The scye crumpled like paper, and Hatcher cried out in anguish as the connection disintegrated.

He stumbled toward the man with the grey eyes and snarled at Harley cowering beside him. His time would come. As soon as he finished with this monster, he would deal with Harley Nearwater. He raised his arms, and the Greywalker stepped forward as if to embrace. Hatcher looked into his eyes. There was sadness there as the Greywalker reached up and touched him on the temple, softly, compassionately.

At the Greywalker's touch, for just a moment before he died, he remembered everything he once was, everything he might have been, and everything he sacrificed for his sense of duty. He remembered abandoning his sweet daughter when she needed him most. He remembered tearing her from her family and turning her, like him, into a monster. He remembered everything he did in the name of the Federation, and tears cascaded down his bloody cheeks.

"Oh," Hatcher said, and his eyes were blue once more, and his vision was clear. He died where he stood, at the Greywalker's feet.

Chapter Twenty-Two

Aftermath

I

The Rage passed her by, and Brinna Wilde continued her long walk across the mountains.

The horror of the days behind her still stalked her every step, and she spent far too much time looking back rather than looking forward, she knew. Mamal would chastise her if she only could. Since her escape from the Hub and the attack of the Wrynd, she made her way south, catching another White Dragon, intent on leaving these mountains far behind.

In the end, she sat in her seat in the all but empty train and looked to the east at the mountains touching the sky. A voice from her dream called to her, and she sprang to her feet and slipped on her eyeset to beg the Dragon to stop at the next station. The dream that brought her here was out there, waiting for her in those mountains.

The deserted station looked as if it hadn't seen a passenger in years. Brinna disembarked, slinging her pack across her slim back, and adjusting her slayer in its holster. She stared up at the mountains and knew her future waited for her somewhere, up there. She determined to find it, her hand gently caressing the ChristGaian cross that no longer seemed such a burden.

For three days she walked, forever fearful a Rage might take shape, forever fearful the beasts of the Wilderness might surround her and snatch her life away. They never came, and she spent the evenings curled on the ground, shivering in a fireless night.

At the end of the third day, she stood at the summit of the mountains, stared down at the forests below, and knew her destination was somewhere down there. She summoned food by stork, and as she ate, she wondered if the dream was real or just fantasy. Then she fell asleep with the sun caressing her smooth skin.

When she awoke, a horse gazed at her. She screamed and scrambled away, pulling her slayer. It was a painted horse, and as she pointed her sidearm at it, the horse pawed the ground impatiently, turned, and walked away, down the canyon.

"Wait!" Brinna called and gathered her pack to give chase.

All the long day and into the evening she followed, and when she thought surely she had lost it, she would top a hill or cross a stream, and the horse would be there, waiting for her. She stumbled on, and the horse nodded encouragement as it led the way.

Brinna came out of the mountains and into the foothills of the valley where the trees were sparse and the river more meandering and knew she was close to the haunting dream. The painted horse was still ahead, and as the mountain gave way to the valley, the horse picked up its pace and began to trot. Brinna ran to keep up.

"I ain't got four legs, you peckerwood!" She cried, but the horse paid her no mind.

The old road they followed narrowed and hugged the river. Cottonwoods leaned toward her, great arms of limbs casting shadows in the afternoon, and even though the horse kept its gait, Brinna slowed until she was barely walking. On the other side of the river, beyond the cottonwoods standing like sentinels, she could see other trees huddled together. They were apple trees, and she stood transfixed.

She was standing in her dream.

The horse whinnied, standing meters ahead, stomping its right hoof impatiently. Brinna smiled despite herself and ran to catch up. The horse stayed where it stood, and when she reached it, the mare nodded and stomped the ground once more.

Brinna looked to her right and saw the bridge. It was a small, wooden bridge stretching to reach the other side of the river. Cottonwoods shrouded the slim roadway on the other side. Her knees felt weak.

"This is it, idn't it?" she whispered, and the horse nodded.

Brinna turned to face the painted horse and dared to reach out. The mare lowered her nose, and she touched it lightly, her fingers dancing and afraid.

"Thank you," Brinna said. "Thank you for bringing me here."

The horse flicked its ears and trotted into the dusk.

Brinna turned and faced the bridge. She adjusted the straps on her pack, caressed the butt of her slayer, then gripped the Christ-Gaian cross as she stepped onto the old bridge and walked across to her future.

II

Quinlan Bowden sat on a straight chair in a dark house and listened for the chitter of despair. It was there in the back of his mind, and he did his best to ignore it.

Despair won in the end. It crushed his dreams and consumed the only life he ever hoped to live. But it hadn't destroyed him. It simply changed everything he was and ever hoped to be. Now he had to find something else.

They made the long trek across the desert and over the mountains to the Hub once more. They ventured into the Wilderness in search of the one they loved, and in so doing, they found and lost her. There was nothing else to do but go home.

Still, Quinlan wondered if perhaps there was. Sitting on the chair, grinding his teeth, and trying not to pull his hair, he wondered and worried perhaps the best thing for him to have done was to follow an old man who peddled apples and brought lightning from the sky.

"When the time comes that you need shelter from the storm, come find an old man and his apple orchard," Edward Toll said, and the words gave Quinlan comfort.

He walked to his kitchen table, where three weapons lay hidden beneath an old blanket. He pulled the blanket aside and stared at them with a storm on his brow. He picked up the pulse rifle first and held it awkwardly in his hands. No longer how long he held it, he wasn't sure it would ever find its target in his hands. He put it aside. The next weapon he picked up was the cutlass Harley Nearwater tossed at his feet after slaying his wife.

Quinlan used it to kill as well, and as he held the black blade came a steely confirmation of violence yet to come. He slid it back into its scabbard and picked up the third weapon. It was the scye that belonged to the only Marshal who ever cared to try and help them in their quest. He died so doing. Quinlan held it in his hand like a promise. He knew the scye was useless to him but kept it anyway. Perhaps, someday, he would find a way to use it to right a few wrongs.

He went to the window and stared down at the courtyard, where his family once gathered to be a family. Noah and Raizor were swinging on the swing set, legs kicking as they reached for the sky. It was still the place where his family gathered.

He opened the blinds and smiled at his children. They looked up and waved, and he waved back. Over the mountains a storm brewed.

He slipped on his boots, stepped outside, and went down to be with them. There was always despair to chitter in his ear, but for today he would cast it aside. For today he would be happy, enjoy the family he had, and remember the love he lost.

III

High Judge Trevok's shuttle touched down on the upper deck of the Battlewagon Sidon, and two of his advocates descended the gangplank, scyes glowing and hands clenching slayers. Cirroco strolled toward them, bemused, and touched them lightly on the arm.

"Quite the flourish. Impressive, but the battle has come and gone." She took a step up the gangplank and called into the shuttle, "Yoo-hoo! High Judge! It's safe to come out. All the monsters are gone."

Trevok exited the shuttle with a scowl and brushed past her. Behind him came two hulking Marshals, mirror images one of the other. "You've failed to capture the Leap, as the Lord Judge commanded, Emissary Storm."

Cirroco laughed. "If the one we faced is the Leap, we're in deep waters, Trevok."

"If not the Leap, then what is this Greywalker?"

"Something more, I suspect. The universe is a marvelous place, High Judge, and we've only dipped our toes into the pool. The Lord Judge seeks to know the depth of it, and he's learned much this day."

Trevok frowned. "If the Lord Judge accepts your failures, it's of no consequence to me, Emissary. I've come for the traitor. It's time to restore order to my Hub."

Cirroco smiled and bowed. "Your Marshal awaits your audience, High Judge," she mocked.

High Judge Trevok and the Marshals followed Cirroco as she led them across the deck of the airship toward the medical clinic. They wove through the bowels of the ship, and when Cirroco turned and waved an arm through a wide doorway, the three strode inside and gathered around the woman who once was a Marshal of the Federation.

She writhed in pain, and Cirroco thought it a pity.

IV

Jodi clutched her right leg, a torn and bleeding mass of flesh. The medprints to either side of her hovered but granted no reprieve from the shadow's attacks.

High Judge Trevok smiled as she writhed. His finger dipped into the gore of her leg, and she screeched in agony. He brought his bloody finger to his lips and licked them clean.

"You cared so much for justice, Jodi Tempest, but failed it in the end." He nodded toward Elijah Apgar, who stared down at her with joy in his eyes. "There's a new Marshal in town," Trevok tittered.

Elijah ripped the Marshal star from her chest. He flipped away the fabric of her tunic and pinned the star to his chest.

Cirroco stood passively at the back of the room, and Jodi thought she might see compassion in her eyes but knew there would be no one to help her now.

Trevok turned Jodi's face toward him. "You think yourself so much beyond me, but in the end, you see you're nothing. You failed in every way. Elijah has taken your place as Marshal, and in the Wilderness, there will be a new blade." The High Judge turned to Ephraim, who raised a vial of black death between his fingers. "A new Scimitar will be born this day."

Jodi's eyes opened wide with terror and the High Judge cackled. "Oh, no need to fear, Tempest. We would not trust you as Scimitar. You have proven your uselessness as a leader. Ephraim will be Scimitar, his brother Marshal. A family of leaders for the Federation." He pinched her chin harshly between his thin fingers. "But you will be a monster. Our new Marshal has requested a pet of his

own. A chained one. To flare, rip, and eat whoever he chooses."
He held a black vial of ink before her horrified face. "For you, Jodi
Tempest, the justice you desire will forever be beyond your reach."

Jodi screamed and tried to escape into the Vale. She reached out
to her father a world away, prayed for some small glimmer of hope,
and the Vale was denied her as well. There was a presence in her
mind, and she realized it had always been there, watching her, waiting, and plotting. *"Your fate awaits you,"* the Lord Judge's thoughts
boomed, and Jodi sobbed.

Jodi's panicked eyes found Cirroco Storm and the Emissary
bowed her head.

The High Judge gripped her ruined leg, and she screamed in
horror and hopelessness.

The flare rushed to consume her.

V

The battlewagon and legionnaires fled, and there was nothing
left living in the canyon except for Harley and the man with the
grey eyes. He looked at him and tried to catch his breath but found
it difficult. The Greywalker regarded him softly as the shadows
returned.

Harley felt their pink eyes upon him as one by one they slipped
within the darkness of the Greywalker's duster.

"Don't lose your hat, Harley." The man with the grey eyes held
out his right hand, holding Harley's Stetson. The man who was
more than a man smiled a pleasant smile. "Har Har Har!"

Harley just stared, his mind in turmoil, his memories ravaging,
and the grey man nodded softly. "Remember our bargain, Harley
Nearwater." The two exchanged a glance, and Harley thought of
the face in the mine, a face unlike the one looking at him now. A
face he never wanted to see again. "Remember it well."

A dust devil swirled around the Greywalker. As it swirled, the man slowly dissolved until Harley was alone on the side of the hill with death all around.

"It's a neat trick. If you know it." The voice whispered behind his head. When he turned around, there was no one there.

CHAPTER TWENTY-THREE

FIVE DAYS DEAD

I

Sunday morning slipped into Sunday afternoon on a hot and cloudless day, and Harley Nearwater should have been five days dead. He wasn't, and that was the problem. At least he thought it might be a problem, feared it might be a problem, tossed and turned all night worrying his not being dead might be the biggest problem of his life.

But he was alive when he should be dead, so he decided the best thing to do on this too damn bright Sunday afternoon was sit back and get good and drunk. A waste of a perfectly wonderful day some might say, and Harley surely wouldn't disagree. Since he should have been five days dead, he hadn't made any plans.

No plans at all.

Of course, that wasn't entirely true, and a nagging voice in his head screamed the lie for what it was. He was doing his best to drown that little voice with cheap beer and cigarettes. Because admitting he had plans, admitting he had those plans five days after he should have been dead was completely out of character for the man who used to be Harley Nearwater and must be again.

Being out of character was dangerous. Now, wasting an entire

410

Sunday drinking alone was in good character. Well, not good character, but certainly his character, something he had done all too often before the day that should have snuffed the dull and meaningless light that was his life from the world.

Remaining in character was something, perhaps the one thing he paused to consider in the past five days. He chewed on that thought constantly since death came searching and was unable to find him. He chewed on it still, and just because he hadn't completely digested the idea, didn't mean he couldn't or wouldn't.

Remaining in character was the most vitally important thing in his life. If he wanted to have a life, that is. He remembered smiles in the dark, sandpaper laughs and whispered promises, but mostly he remembered the eyes staring at him, through him in the dark, dissecting him. He nodded as he took another sip of beer. Yes, it was best to remain in character.

He stood with his cowboy boots all but buried in the fine dust of the San Rafael Swell. Before him was the Wedge, and he alternated between standing and sitting all morning, but always looking at the jagged valley below, where the San Rafael River meandered listlessly through the canyon.

He watched the sun creep higher in the sky, squinting as it brought tears to his bloodshot eyes. When the sun sneaked behind him, he continued to squint as the day brought a slight breeze, picked up dust, and settled it down.

All the morning and into the afternoon he looked down on the canyon, never once admiring its beauty, only using it as something to focus his eyes upon as he drank and thought, thought and drank over the one subject he knew would haunt him for the rest of his life, remaining in character.

When the Greywalker disappeared inside the dust devil, Harley picked his way down the hill, trying not to look at the carnage of what remained of the Wrynd. He stopped to pick up a slayer but couldn't bring himself to remove the holster from the gruesome remains of the person who once held it. He climbed into the nearest bus, started the engine, and turned it around. There was blood dripping down the window, and he thought it might belong to Marshal Tempest. He turned on the wipers and washed it away.

He drove out of the still smoldering mountain in silence, and when he reached the highway, he turned back toward Price. The city had burned, but not completely, and he passed a family walking down the middle of the road. The father was holding a hunting rifle, the mother held a pitchfork, and the boy held a machete. He looked at them as he went by and recognized the boy. He had pointed him to a car lot and refused his offer for lunch.

"You might be a boy lover."

Harley flicked them a wave as he passed and realized it was out of character.

He found his truck where he left it, half buried in the sand along the side of the highway. His sidearm, scye, and eyeset were inside, and so was the baseball bat he exchanged for his sword. His hat had been there, too, but the Greywalker had magically plucked it from the seat. "Har Har Har." He found himself smiling and then had to fight to keep from crying.

He was able to get the truck back on the road and drove it home. He linked, ordered food, cigarettes, beer, tequila, and rum along the way. The stork was waiting for him when he pulled into his driveway. He drank and then ate, and then he drank some more until he could finally sleep.

It was fitful.

He stayed drunk all the next day, and in the morning of the third day, he climbed into his truck and drove toward Straight Canyon. The apple orchard was there, and it looked peaceful, calm, and deserted. He stood on the edge of the timber bridge, smoking cigarettes. He wondered what he might find if he were to cross the bridge. Would Edward Toll be waiting for him somewhere on the other side? Would he let him pass? Would he protect him from the

Greywalker and his dark promises? He didn't know and was afraid to ask.

He went home and sat on the porch, and as the afternoon began to wane, he slipped on his eyeset and sent his scye south. It skirted across the desert like a firefly through the San Rafael, and then chased a White Dragon, then through the ruins of Moab and Monticello and into Arizona.

Soon the scye was hovering over a dilapidated single-wide trailer, where he had grown, dreamed, and cried. A home where he said goodbye to his father and become hated by his mother. The dead apple tree was gone, but little else had changed. He let the scye hover by the front window as he peered inside. There was no one home, but he could look down the hallway and see the closet was open; the closet where he learned in the dark everything wasn't the same as it was when the lights were on.

He sent the scye downtown, but, of course, there was no longer a downtown in Kayenta, if there ever had been. In the entire town, he only saw a half dozen people milling about.

He was about to bring the scye home, but something made him make one last pass over the trailer, and he saw movement from the window. His mother opened the door, and it looked like she had been sleeping. Her hair was mostly grey now, and she was thin, very thin, like she was wasting away. Her mouth showed no sign it ever held a smile, and neither did her eyes. It made Harley sad just looking at her.

Startled when she saw the scye floating outside her front door, she looked frightened at first, but then her brow furrowed and her eyebrows rose, and she held up a finger and rushed inside. She came out with a notebook and pen in her hand. She scribbled on the notebook and turned it to face the scye.

"Harley?"

The note said, and Harley felt a sob slip from his lips.

"Just talk. I can hear you if you talk," he said. He had no idea how he could respond, then he choked back his tears and let the scye dance across the dirt in front of his boyhood home.

"Yes," he scribbled on the ground.

She smiled. His mother smiled at him. She wrote on the notebook again and held it up. "Wheel?"

She pointed to the sky, and Harley whispered, "No." He hadn't made it to the Wheel. She was right, after all. He was a no-account. He scribbled "no" in the dirt.

She nodded and wrote again, and Harley cried at what she wrote. "Love you. Miss you. I'm sorry."

He responded with the scye scratching on the ground. "Love you. Don't be sorry."

His mother nodded, and tears streamed down her face as she took pen to paper and held up her last note. "Come home," the note said.

"Yes," Harley whispered on his porch overlooking Orangeville. Yes, he would go home, and he would gather her up, and bring her back to Orangeville, and keep her safe just as he promised his father. He would keep her safe from the Rages. Then he remembered the Greywalker and the promise he made and wondered if keeping her safe would be out of character. Would it be contrary to the man he was and must be again?

He fell asleep on the porch, crying. He slept all the next day. And he didn't dream. On the fifth day, he took his beer, cigarettes, and fears and went to the desert.

He was five days dead.

Harley chased his beer with a cigarette and dropped the butt into the empty can. He carefully placed the beer can on top of a beer wall he was building beside his battered blue cooler. The beer wall was now four stories wide by four stories tall and waived precariously in the soft breeze. He fished in the cooler until he snagged another beer and hauled it out, slammed the lid and popped the top. The vibration of the cooler's closure rattled the beer wall, and it tumbled down, fifteen of the sixteen empty cans clattered beside him, but the sixteenth rolled toward the cliff's edge. He stuck out his foot and caught it before it could fall over the side.

He started to bring the fresh beer to his mouth, looking at the empty can he saved from tumbling over the side. Five days ago, he wouldn't have stopped the can. Five days ago, he wouldn't have built a beer can wall.

Five days ago, he would have tossed the empty cans over the side of the cliff and flicked the cigarette butts over as well, vaguely wondering if the cigarettes would start a wildfire in the valley below, but not caring one way or the other. Did that matter? Was that a change in character? Was that enough to bring back the man with the grey eyes? He moved his boot blocking the empty can and let it roll off the side, then swept the rest of the cans over the side with his leg, spilling beer down his chest in the process.

He stood and paced back and forth along the cliff edge, suddenly worried and afraid staying in character was going to be more complicated than he'd ever imagined.

The wind was picking up, and a dust devil careened blindly into his truck, spewing sand through the truck's open windows. Harley held his breath and waited for the Greywalker to appear. The dust devil spun itself out. He sat back down, placed his beer between his legs, and dug another cigarette out of his shirt pocket.

The wind coiled around him, and he put his hand over the beer as dust turned his dark hair something closer to grey. Before long he wouldn't need the dust to help turn it grey, no sir. Before long, he was quite sure he would grey without any help at all. He once heard stress and worry could make a person go grey, and he had plenty of stress, plenty of worries.

His eyes burned, a little from the dust, a little from the sun, but mostly from exhaustion. With the cigarette still dangling between his fingers, his eyes closed and he felt sleep rushing to embrace. As he slipped away, his dreams turned to his mother, and he remembered her through his clouded vision as a woman who loved him and who he loved back, then he remembered the promise he made to his father to take care of her.

He lied.

When he woke, he thought of the Wrynd. Scimitar Hatcher and his shield were gone, but others would take their place. If his mother stood a chance against them, he needed to go to her. Her only hope was if her son lived up to the promise he made to his father.

Come home, she had written, and before that, *Love You. Miss you. I'm Sorry.*

Harley tossed his last beer over the side of the Wedge and kicked his now empty cooler after it, listening as it clanked its way to the bottom. He flicked away his cigarette and stumbled toward his truck. It was time to go.

He drove slowly away from the Wedge, back toward the world he knew. The gravel road came to a fork, and he stopped and put the truck in park to smoke again. To his left was the road home, to Orangeville. To the right, he could cut through the desert, cross the Swinging Bridge, and keep going until he was in Kayenta. If his mother was to live, he needed to turn right.

Between the forks, in the distance, he saw a cloud of dust against the mountainside, and he watched as it drew closer. As it did, he could see beneath it a swarm of activity. He climbed out of his truck but could still not see what was coming. He climbed onto the hood and cupped his hands over his eyes.

It was a herd of horses running toward him from the desert, and he marveled at their number. There were hundreds, and leading the way was a painted horse he recognized.

The horses drew closer, and before he quite knew what was happening, they encircled his truck. Still, they galloped around him, growing closer with every revolution. He couldn't quite keep the crazy grin from his face as the horses slowed to a trot, then a full stop. He could see the wildness within them, but for the first time in five days, he wasn't afraid.

The painted horse came to him, nodding, and pawing the ground. Harley sat on the hood of his truck, grinning like a fool, not even caring if the horses raged and stomped him to death.

The painted horse nuzzled his arm, and Harley reached out a tentative hand and touched the side of her face, then caressed her softly. He wasn't in the least surprised when he started to cry and hugged her.

"I'm sorry. I'm sorry. I'm sorry. I'm sorry," he said repeatedly, and the horse seemed impatient and nodded some more. Harley finally understood and hopped off the truck.

The other horses backed away, and he stood in front of the paint. She pawed, and he threw himself upon her back. She carried him away, into the desert. She trotted at first and then galloped, and before he could quite believe what was happening, she was sprinting. The other horses were running with her, and Harley sat straight on her back, held out his arms, and laughed like he hadn't laughed in his life.

After a time, the painted horse brought him back to his truck, and he slid off her back. She let him caress her face, and he thanked her for everything she gave. Then the horses turned and disappeared into the desert.

Harley was alone once again.

He looked up where he knew the Wheel must spin, and even though he couldn't see it, knowing it was there gave him comfort. As he climbed into his truck, he knew from deep within an apple orchard a sad and lonely old man reached out and told him he was sorry for denying him the simple gift of an apple, that might have made all the difference.

He sent the horses to make amends, and Harley understood they were not only meant to make amends but to guide him back to a path he must walk alone for a while longer.

He'd been put on the shelf. He didn't know what the grey man meant, but he agreed to the bargain. What he did know was what the Greywalker meant when he told him he needed to stay in character. Turning right would be out of character for the man he was and must be again.

He remembered the voice in the darkness, the mouth full of razors and the grey, grey eyes making promises. He never wanted to see those eyes again. He'd do anything to avoid seeing them again. Anything at all.

He turned left and headed for home.

He would remain on the shelf.

He would remain in character.

II

The Greywalker stood on a hill looking down at a little house where a sad man sat on a sad porch, lost in despair and loneliness. He knelt and cupped his chin in his hands and pitied Harley, as much as he was able.

In a few short weeks the Castaway had spiraled into a dark depression that may yet claim him. He was disheveled, filthy, and drunk, sinking quickly into madness. It was probably for the best.

The man with the grey eyes sighed, and the wind toyed with his hair as he watched the man he'd put on the shelf. He considered the future. Things had almost come unraveled, and the chaos of Harley Nearwater had been at the heart of it.

He would bear watching. He might seem beaten, but the Greywalker didn't dare underestimate him. Perhaps he made a mistake in letting him live. Could he keep Harley from mischief in the weeks, months, and years to come? The Greywalker knew many things, but that he didn't know.

Balance was a delicate thing, and the Greywalker hoped he had restored it, for a time. He cast an eye toward the heavens, where the Lord Judge of the Seven Realms perched in his mighty Wheel, dreaming dreams of the stars and godhood. Meanwhile, somewhere out there in the deep, true gods plotted the end of everything.

Syiada's search for the Leap would continue. It was madness, but it would continue. The Leap was still out there, in the future, and when it arrived, the end would be nigh.

In the distance, thunder rumbled. Gaia's wrath awaited. Humanity may yet have a season to prepare. A respite before the final storm, when the Seven Realms would come crashing down.

The Greywalker stood and nodded toward the sad man on the sad porch.

"Intrestin days ahead," he said.

END OF VOLUME I

Made in United States
North Haven, CT
12 April 2022